By JAIME SAMMS

NOVELS
Better
Not As Easy As It Looks
Off Stage: Right
Stained Glass

NOVELLAS
Angel Elegy
Renegade
Still Life

Published by DREAMSPINNER PRESS
http://www.dreamspinnerpress.com

NOT AS EASY AS IT LOOKS

JAIME SAMMS

Dreamspinner Press

Published by
Dreamspinner Press
5032 Capital Circle SW
Suite 2, PMB# 279
Tallahassee, FL 32305-7886
USA
http://www.dreamspinnerpress.com/

Not As Easy As It Looks
© 2013 Jaime Samms.

Cover Art
© 2013 Paul Richmond.
http://www.paulrichmondstudio.com
Cover content is for illustrative purposes only and any person depicted on the cover is a model.

ISBN: 978-1-62798-217-7
Digital ISBN: 978-1-62798-216-0

Printed in the United States of America
First Edition
November 2013

For my family, as always, for their unwavering support, and especially my dad, who taught me the family values that are at the heart of this book.

ACKNOWLEDGMENTS

I have to say thanks to my big sister, Kay, for introducing me to the Canadian band High Valley. It was their song "On the Combine" that inspired the story and a conversation with Kay and her daughters about where I found my stories that convinced me I had to write this one. They might not remember the conversation—it wasn't a very long one and probably didn't seem that important at the time—but it meant a lot to me to talk about what I do and what I love, so thanks. Love you gals lots.

Special thanks to Ariel, too, for being on the other side of the chat window. I hope you know how much you help just being there. You're a true inspiration, hon.

PART ONE—DON

FARMERS AND POETS

Present day, age twenty-eight

UNDER the sounds of the grain shushing into the hopper behind Don, the chunking rumble of the combine's engine complaining alerted him to its imminent meltdown. Again.

"Fucking hell!" He disengaged the thresher and slowed the machine to a stop. Not that he could do anything about it out here on his own. For a few minutes, he sat in the cabin and stared out over the expanse of golden fields, less than one quarter shorn and covered in straw.

"Fucking hell," he muttered again, removing his ball cap to swipe his arm across his brow. It was goddamn hot out. But that was good, he reminded himself, eyeing the hazy horizon. Not a cloud darkened the sky at the moment, but the oppressive heat and humidity hinted at an oncoming storm. Rain was the last thing they needed.

Now if they could figure out why the cabin's air-conditioning didn't work, other than that the entire machine was fucking older than God, he'd be happy.

He could sit here all day, or he could get off his ass and find a solution. He could check some belts, blow away some of the grain dust, and if he was lucky, whatever was knocking around in there would be obvious. Then he'd have something intelligent to say to his mechanic when he called. He'd worry about how he'd pay him later.

Shoving an upturned pail out of his way with one foot, he slapped his cap back in place and got up to open the door. The only difference in temperature was the increased airflow over his face. Like a hot blast from a furnace, the breeze dried the sweat on his temples to a stiff crust, and he tried to remember what it felt like to love his job.

Not his job, he reminded himself for probably the eightieth time that morning as he lifted the cap off his head and swiped the back of his wrist across his sweaty forehead. This was his life. His home, and his family, all of it was wrapped up in making this harvest profitable. Even as he had the thought, his breast pocket rang and he sighed. Now what? He fished his cell out and hit the answer button.

"'Lo?" He didn't even look at the call display as he put the phone to his ear.

"Hey, babe, do you know where the extra set of keys for the Jeep is?"

Don frowned into the hazy distance and wondered why Griff needed to know that. He shook his head, realized his partner wouldn't get that answer, and grunted a no. "Why?"

"Thought I'd bring it over to Howe's this afternoon. See if he can—"

"No."

There was a pause. "I'm sorry?" Griffith's voice went flat. "No?"

Don had to stifle a sigh, and he sank onto the bucket next to the driver's chair. "We can't afford it. I have to get him to come all the way out here and look at the combine."

"Again?" There was definite annoyance in Griff's voice.

Don wanted to haul off on a tirade about how they couldn't last another year if he didn't get this harvest in, how they couldn't afford a new machine, how yes, the combine was a piece of shit clunker too old to do its job anymore, but that was too fucking bad, it was more important than Griffith's piece-of-shit clunker Jeep from 1970-fucking-something. And all this just so the man could have his own wheels. All Don let out was a clipped "Yes, again." And hung up.

The call to Howard's garage was quick and required only a small amount of begging. A sob story about being stuck out in the middle of the field got the busy mechanic's assistant agreeing to ask Howard to drive out so he could take a look. Don's offer to pay extra for making the field call was flatly refused, with the young man on the other end of the phone all but coming out and saying he knew that kind of premium was beyond the reach of Don's bank balance.

Did the entire county know they were going bust? How perfect.

Sweat trickled down between Don's shoulder blades, and he let his gaze drift over the fields again. How often had he admired that view? Since he could remember. He'd grown up on this farm, already third generation when his father had put it in his hands, and he was going to be the one to ruin it. Not that it mattered. It wasn't like he and Griff had anyone to take over from them when they were too old to keep it going. He was already older than his own father had been when he'd begun teaching Don how to do this exact job, on this exact machine.

September, age twelve

CREEPING carefully down the steps, Don placed a hand on the rail and leaned hard so his weight wouldn't make the third step from the bottom creak. He could hear his parents in the living room discussing things he wasn't supposed to hear them discuss.

"Andrew can drive the combine, Donald. Just like he has for the past seven years."

"Andrew is not coming home just to harvest, Mary. Leave it."

"Little Donald is just too small—"

"You need to stop calling him that. He's perfectly capable of learning the ropes. He's already older than Andrew was. You don't give that boy enough credit."

A smile crept over Don's face. Finally.

"What about school? You know how he loves—"

Don's gut tightened to knots as his father spoke over his mother again.

"Open your eyes, woman. You coddle him too much and ignore what you don't want to see. Pack his lunch, but he's coming out to the fields with me tomorrow and for however long it takes to get all the hay in. Someone has got to run this place when I'm gone. Time he learned." There was a rustle of paper and Don could imagine his father straightening his newspaper and holding it up in front of himself, effectively ending the conversation.

His mother made an unhappy sound but didn't argue further.

Touching two fingers to the green and purple bruise over his collarbone, Don drew in a breath and let it out carefully. No one had asked him where it came from. His mother had tutted. His father had eyed the mark, eyed him, and in his steady gray eyes, some curtain had drawn away and Don had seen the moment of decision. As he backed up the steps and returned to his room, he wondered how much of what Don hadn't told them about being cornered in school hallways his father suspected.

A lot more than a traditional-minded farmer was willing to talk to his twelve-year-old son about, it had turned out. He didn't find that out until very much later in life.

But then, one thing Don had always loved about his father was that they didn't need to talk about every little thing. Some things remained understood between them from the moment they were acknowledged with a silent nod or a smile that reached deep into the old man's eyes. Understood, rarely said out loud.

Which was fine, because his mother made up for that lack of verbiage and then some.

"Now make sure you eat everything, and drink. There's plenty of water in the jug."

"Mom, I know!" Don pushed her hand away from fussing with his bangs and plopped his ball cap on his head. It was the only feasible way to control the heavy growth of black waves, short of a buzz cut, and he looked even skinnier and paler with no hair. The curls, at least, gave him substance.

Annoyingly, she turned the cap around so the brim shadowed his face. "Use sunscreen"—she stuck the bottle into the pocket of his shirt—"and reapply, or you'll be crispy by noon." She clucked her tongue and touched his cheek. "So pale."

"Mom!"

"Here." She handed her husband a tall thermos and kissed his cheek. "Don't be too much of a bear, dear. You know how you are before you've had enough coffee."

"Shut it." Don watched his father grin happily and give his mother a much more solid kiss. It made him smile to watch her eyes close and her hand run down his chest. The kissing might be gross, but he liked that they could argue and kiss practically in the same breath.

"Alright, kid." Donald Sr. patted his wife's ass and turned to his son. "You ready?"

"God, Dad." Don made a face. "Really?" After all, a kiss was one thing, but that was his *mother*, for crying out loud. He pulled his cap down to hide his blush and grabbed the cooler she had packed. There was a lot more lunch in there than she normally made for him when he went to school. He wasn't sure how sitting on the combine was going to take more energy than sitting in a chair at school, but whatever.

His father laughed and clapped a hand onto his shoulder. "You won't think it's so bad soon enough, son. In fact, you'll be the one kissing the girls."

Don flushed deeper. "I doubt that very much." Now was probably not the time to tell them there was zero to no chance he'd ever kiss a girl. *Ev-er*.

Turned out his mother was onto something with the lunch thing, though. Despite the air-conditioning in the combine's cab, the sun beat in through the surrounding windows and his shirt stuck to his ribs inside of an hour. Between that and the constant noise and vibration, and the need to perpetually rebalance himself on the upside-down bucket his father had placed on the floor next to the driver's seat, he was famished by the time they stopped for a midmorning snack.

"Takes it out of you," Donald Sr. said, his tone matter-of-fact.

Don grunted and stuffed another chunk of muffin in his mouth.

"Slow down!" His father chuckled. "No one's going to take it."

Don just about froze, mouth full, fingers digging into the remains of the muffin.

"Don?"

Shit. He glanced up to see his father's eyes narrowed slightly and his head tilted to one side. "Nothing," he mumbled, with the faint hope the old man would drop it.

"Hmm." He took another bite of his own muffin and a sip of coffee, then took a tin mug down off a hook on the back wall of the cab. A quick blow inside rid it of most of the grain dust, and he poured a second cup of the dark liquid, which he handed to Don. "I doubt it's nothing." He let Don take the mug, then reached and peeled back the collar of his shirt to get a look at the bruises.

Don sniffed at the contents of his drink and managed not to squirm away from the scrutiny. He took a tentative sip and made a face.

His dad laughed. "Put some hair on your chest, kid." But he patted Don's arm gently and his smile was just as soft. "Don't worry about it. By the time you've tossed a few bales, they'll think twice about messing with you, son. Guys like that aren't interested in bothering a fellow who looks like he might hit back and hurt them."

Pulling in a breath, Don gulped a swig of hot coffee and swallowed it down. "Sure," he said. "Maybe."

"Trust me. You don't actually have to hit them back. Just look like you could do some damage if you do."

"Right." He glanced up from his mug with a cracked, halfhearted smile. "Because I'm not at all scrawny or anything."

"You'll fill out. Give it time. It was the same for your brothers. Same for me when I was your age." He studied Don, his gaze speculative. "I do remember that far back, you know."

Don almost laughed at that.

His father smiled. "First date with your mother was right here." He patted the wall of the cab. "Sittin' up in Daddy's combine, golden September afternoon. Her head on my shoulder." His smile was soft and full of memories. "Bouncin' all over the damn place, and she just smiled and petted my arm. Nothin' sexy about being a farmer, son, but she saw somethin', I suppose."

He let out a happy sigh and finished off his own coffee before wiping the mug out with a napkin to hang back on its hook. "Let's get this cleaned up and get back at 'er. This hay is not going to fall over and sort itself out for us."

Don smiled crookedly as he packed up. His father was half farmer, half poet. Wasn't that hard to see what his teenage mother must have.

Don's smile drifted away once they were back in their seats, though. Trying as hard as he could, he could not imagine a version of that fairy tale that ended the same way for him as it had for his parents.

SUMMER SKY BLUE

THE phone ringing again snapped Don away from that far-off memory.

"Yeah?" He slapped it to his ear and Howard Campbell's voice, low and grating, dropped him squarely back into his partially harvested field.

"You rang, sexy?"

"Don't." Don fought off the rush of goose bumps up his arms. "I need you out here."

Fuck. That was a poor choice of words.

"It was only a matter of time," Howard crooned in his ear. "Been waitin' to hear those words—"

"Don't be an ass. The combine's down."

This time Howard sighed dramatically and made a small whimpering sound. "You only want me for my tool."

"I'll call Chuck, then, if you're going to fuck around." Again, with the poor wording.

Howard laughed.

Don wouldn't really hang up on him, and likely, Howard knew that. Chuck Townsend's garage was in the next county, and he wouldn't hesitate to charge Don through the nose for a field servicing.

"Fine, fine." Howard's tone lost the sultry lilt. "What should I bring?"

Don hesitated. He hadn't even opened up the housing. One thing he was not, and that was a mechanic of any stripe. Hell, even as a kid, he'd been hapless, needing one of his brothers—or sisters—to help reset the chain on his bike when it kept falling off. He was a jinx when it came to machines. That bike had never had issues until it became his.

"So gay," Howard muttered under his breath. "Just pack a little of everything, then, shall I?"

"Sorry," Don muttered. "This is why I call you."

"Mmmm-hmmm. Be there in twenty, sugar."

"Fuck. Off." Don hung up and stuffed the phone back into his pocket. He didn't mind the blatant flirting. Griff, on the other hand....

But then, Griff wasn't here. Griff was back at the house, moping because his toy was broken and Don refused to pay for getting it fixed.

"Stop it," he told himself fiercely. It wasn't Griff's fault he was stuck in the house. It was the broken foot, and that was down to the fuck-ugly, nasty horse. And the horse was only ugly and nasty because he'd been mistreated. And there, that was the thing about Griffith McAllister that Don loved. The fact he could see the sweet side of that animal through all the teeth and hooves and attitude, and that he was determined to find a way to get to it no matter how mean the horse was to him.

That was the side of Griff only Don ever got to see, even from the start.

October, age twelve

GOING back to school after nearly a month in the fields with his father was like entering an alien world for Don. He knew he should recognize it. He'd spent the better portion of his childhood there, after all.

On the combine, he'd been his father's partner. A man doing his job. Here, he was the skinny kid again. Skinny, weak, and clumsy. It took all of a half hour through those doors to be reminded of that fact.

"Farmer Brown!"

Terrance Hawthorn. His father was a cop. His mother worked at the bank. He was taller than every other kid in the elementary school, and half the ninth graders at the high school. He never wore boots or got his hands dirty. It was only Nike high-tops for him, and he had flunkies more than willing to do his dirty work in exchange for a cut of the spoils: that being immunity—mostly—from his tyranny.

Don shrugged his backpack more securely onto his shoulders and tried to decide how hard he'd fight for it.

One of Terrance's sidekicks batted the ball cap off his head and he glanced after it, but didn't try to pick it up. They'd only knock him over if he bent for it, or worse. The last time, one of them had humped him and set the others laughing hysterically at his embarrassment.

"Don't give them the satisfaction," his dad had said during one of those lunch breaks on the combine. "It's no fun for them if you don't react."

How was he supposed to not react when someone's hand flew out and slapped across his cheek, leaving, no doubt, a red streak across his pale skin?

He blinked, but clamped his lips tight shut.

There was a pause at his silence, and then Terrance stepped forward.

"So what's old Farmer Brown brought for lunch today, I wonder? What's he got in his precious pack?" He winked at Don and grinned an ugly grin. "That where you keep your glittery unicorns, fag?"

That hurt more than the slap. Don blinked again, desperately wishing his eyes would not water like that. He took a step back.

A body insinuated itself between him and Terrance's advance.

He didn't see the motion the interloper made, exactly, but he heard the crunch and saw Terrance's head snap back just before his whole body leaned and tilted, then crashed to the floor. He landed on his ass with a howl.

Before he could properly register what had happened, a rough jerk on his pack hauled him backward onto his own ass and another body straddled him, fists flying. He got his arms up just in time to protect his face, and then the weight left him, there was yelling, and he was being pulled to his feet.

"Office!" someone shouted. "Now!" Mr. Wright, his eighth-grade homeroom teacher and the school's guidance counselor, pointed the way down the hall.

In all, six of them remained to be trouped off to the office. Himself, Terrance, three of his buddies, and the strange kid who'd intervened.

Don had never seen the other boy in his life. He was nearly as tall as Terrance, but he was thin, almost skinny, and he wore a leather jacket, like Terrance, but pointed boots and jeans that looked like they'd seen the inside of a barn once or twice, and possibly even the back of a horse. He was a farm boy, right down to those boot tips. Blue eyes, blond hair—he was a summer day in the middle of the gray school hallways. His tanned face with freckles sprinkled lightly over a strong nose and cheekbones turned to Don, curious.

Don felt his jaw drop and hurriedly looked away just as the kid shot him a wide grin. That grin dragged his attention back and held it that fraction too long that always made other boys glower at him. This kid was no exception. He frowned and tossed his hair as he turned his back.

Shit.

"Sit, all of you," Mr. Wright instructed, pointing to the five chairs lined up along the wall beside the office door.

Terrance was the first to flop down in one of them, tipping his head back against the wall and tenderly poking at his nose. It wasn't even bleeding, but he made noises like he'd been shot anyway. His cronies followed his lead and slumped into the other chairs.

Don eyed the last chair. The stranger motioned to it, offering him the seat, and leaned on the wall next to it. Separating himself from the rest of them, Don leaned on the wall on the other side of the hallway.

Eventually, the principal, Ms. Thornloe, stalked out and crossed her arms in front of herself.

"Just what are we going to do about this?" she asked.

The boys all stared up at her. Terrance had a half sneer on his face, but he didn't say anything. His friends glanced to him, followed his example, and clamped their mouths shut.

"Fighting in the hallways. Honestly." She shook her head. "We will have to call your parents."

"My dad's on a stakeout." Terrance smirked. "Probably," he added when Thornloe fixed him with a stern glare. "You should call my mom."

Mama's boy, Don thought, but didn't say anything. Most likely it would be his own mother who came as well, since there was no way his father was going to drop work to come and sort out a school fight.

The strange boy pushed himself away from the wall and pointed at Don. "He didn't do anything."

Oh fuck. Perfect. Make me out to be the victim. Thanks for nothing, asshole.

"All of your parents will be called," Ms. Thornloe said, casting one of those looks at Don. "I don't care who started it or why."

Of course you don't. Because you can't piss off the big bad cop daddy, and the farmer doesn't rate.

Don kept those thoughts to himself too, and glared down at his scuffed and dusty boots, wishing he was back on that bone-jarring, noisy combine breathing crop dust and drinking cold, bitter coffee.

"Also, a week's detention for each of you. Perhaps spending a little bit of time together in a healthy, controlled environment will help you all to get along."

Not fucking likely.

Don couldn't help glancing at the strange boy, though, and finding the kid looking back at him. Instantly, they grinned at each other, as if sharing the exact same thought.

Then Don flushed, because *everything* made him flush, he was so pale, and he had to look away. Not before he saw the slight frown that marred the other boy's expression, though.

OF COURSE, Terrance's mother was the first to show up. She promptly berated everyone within earshot and scuttled her precious son out of the building to have his face X-rayed. Anyone could look at him and know nothing was broken. It was only the fuss he was making and his mother's instant reaction to it that prompted the school to defer his detention until he was "back on his feet."

Don knew there was no chance Terrance would spend one second in detention. He never did. His friends scowled at him as his mother propelled him away down the hall, and he glanced back at them. His expression read *suckers* in every line.

Don could not figure out how they didn't hate him, but they always came back for more. And even as he thought it, they all turned their attention to him and the scowls deepened. There was his answer. By doing nothing at all, Terrance had just deepened these boys' dislike of Don, and all he'd done was walk through the school doors and mind his own business. Somehow, though, all this had just become his fault.

He sighed and sank to the hall floor as, one by one, parents showed up and dragged boys into the office. The other three weren't removed from school. They slunk back to class after their respective parents left, and one of them even managed to land a painful kick to Don's thigh as he passed where he was sitting. Another bruise to try and explain or hide.

The last two awaiting parental rescue, Don and the strange boy, sat at opposite ends of the row of chairs and waited in silence. Nearly half an hour ticked by before the kid politely asked the secretary if he could go to the washroom. He came back promptly and took the seat next to Don.

"Hey," he said as he sat.

Don made a noise that might have been a "hey" in return, or might have been "leave me alone." He wasn't sure yet.

"I'm Griff." The boy held out a hand. "Griffith McAllister."

It would be rude to ignore him, so Don took the offer. "Don Jenkins." He left off the part about being the fifth Jenkins with that name, because declaring himself Donald Jenkins the Fifth was just… ridiculous.

Griff's hand was calloused and strong, his grip dry and sure. Don felt like a runt with his skinny hand engulfed in that big mitt.

The handshake trailed off and Don's fingers twitched, as though reluctant to remove themselves from that warm clasp.

"You, uh…." He swallowed "You're new?"

Griff nodded. "My dad just bought a place down Grey Road 12."

Don thought about that for a few minutes, going over what he knew of the area in his head.

"The old Pauls's place," he said finally.

Griff nodded. "I guess, yeah. Close to some miniscule place called Waudby?"

"We're practically neighbors, then," Don offered. "We own lots of land down Townsend Lake Road and on the far side of Waudby."

"Cool." He nodded slightly and offered a small expression close to a smile, and they fell silent again for a few minutes.

When the quiet stretched to the point Don was counting the ticktocking of the hallway clock, he reached for something safe to talk about.

"Thought that farm was sort of…." He hesitated, unsure how to put it without offending. "Old," he said at last.

Griff laughed. "It is. Barn's full of holes. House is run-down. Have to keep a bucket by my bed to catch the rain." He flashed a grin. "But you know." He shrugged one thin shoulder. "It's home."

More silence.

"You have a lot of animals?" Griff asked after a while.

Don shook his head. "Some dogs. A donkey. Mom keeps a couple of sheep and goats for the wool. Dad shears them for her and she spins it, knits it. She sells sweaters for more than I can believe anyone pays for them, but tourists." He rolled his eyes. "Crazy."

Griff chuckled.

The sound rolled over Don in a wave of shivers.

"What's the donkey for?" Griff asked.

Don thought about that a minute, then shrugged. "No idea."

That earned him another soft laugh, and he grinned. "Stupid thing eats more than the goats, kicks the fences down about once a week, and bites. Katie named it Barney. I think it might be on its third or fourth name. I used to call it Steven."

"Steven." Griff looked at him from the corner of his eye.

Again, Don shrugged. "I—don't know. He looks like a Steven to me."

"We have horses," Griff informed him after a few more minutes of silence. "Dad breeds them. He knows horses."

Don nodded and silence fell again.

"So, who's Katie?" Griff tossed his head to get the long bangs out of his eyes, and followed the motion with a sweep of his hand. His fingers moved almost delicately over his face, but he seemed unaware of the motion.

Don blinked and found Griff watching him through his distraction, blue eyes bright with curiosity.

"Here it comes," Don said.

"Here what comes?"

"Wait for it. Katie is my little sister. She's almost three. Talia is five and Megan is eight. I'm twelve, Peter is fifteen, and Andrew is eighteen, and Jennifer is twenty. She's got a job in Markdale and lives with my aunt. Sometimes she comes home weekends. Andrew just went to Wilfrid Laurier this fall. He's taking agricultural studies, but between you and me, he won't last one semester. He'll switch to something with more math. I think he'll talk them into letting him go to U of T next year for architecture. You should see my room. Well, it was his before he moved out, and it's awesome."

"Seven kids?" Griff whistled.

"Almost eight. Mom's pregnant again. She hasn't said anything, but I can tell."

"How?"

"She eats saltines for breakfast, stopped drinking coffee, and takes a nap with Katie every afternoon." He nodded. "She's going to have another girl."

"How do you know that?"

Don lifted a shoulder. "Just a hunch." After another short stretch of silence, he looked at Griff again. "You?"

"Me what?"

"Have any sisters? Or brothers?"

Griff shook his head. "Just me and Dad. Mom was a seamstress, but she left last year to go to school in Toronto to become a designer." He made a face. "Or so she says. I think she just followed the guy she was sleeping with. I'm not much of a city kid, so I came out here with Dad and the horses."

"You like it?"

"Other than the assholes, yeah. But every school has assholes."

"Yeah." Don pursed his lips. "I guess." He didn't really want to be reminded of needing his ass saved earlier.

"What they said." Griff shifted in his seat, squirming and pushing at his jeans as though they were tight or his hands were sweaty. "Is it true?"

Don whipped his head around to look at the other boy, panic seeping into his gut. Before he could quite process what Griff was really asking, or formulate an answer, his mother's voice careened down the hallway ahead of the clop-thump of her wooden-soled clogs.

"Donald Jenkins. What is going on? They called to say you are fighting? In the hallways?"

Don groaned, but the interruption was welcome.

"Mom—"

"Do not *mom* me, young man. On your feet."

"Mrs. Jenkins." Griff sprang up, but the look Don's mother turned on him shut him up.

"And this is the boy you were fighting with, I presume?" she said, her voice hard.

"No! Mom, God. Would you stop?" Don glanced up and down the hall, expecting doors to open and teachers' heads to poke out to see what all the noise was about. "This is Griff. He's...." He didn't want to say *he's the kid who kept me from getting a broken nose*, so he improvised. "He's my friend." He shot a look at Griff, who looked startled for just a second, but covered it quickly with a wide grin and held out his hand.

"Ma'am. Griffith McAllister. I just moved onto the Pauls's farm with my father this summer. Nice to meet you."

"Oh." Don's mother didn't hide her surprise nearly as well as Griff had. After a moment's pause, she took the offered hand and shook delicately. "Well. Yes. Nice to meet you too, Griffith." She shot a look at the office door. "He has manners, at least, Donald. Now"—she pointed—"inside." Her voice went hard and high-pitched again. "March."

Don rolled his eyes as she turned her back, and he waved thanks to Griff for accepting the pseudolie.

Griff grinned, and the expression gave Don a peculiar thrill.

"You know, it doesn't matter," Griff whispered quickly as Don passed, and Don slowed to glance at him, confused.

"If it's true, I mean." Griff's grin faltered, but stuck. "It wouldn't bother me, I mean." He gave a little shrug. "I'll see you later?"

"Uh." Don stared at him for what might have been a heartbeat, if his heart hadn't actually stopped in shock. The moment was filled only with those earnest blue eyes and shock of blond hair and freckles. "Yeah," he said finally. "See ya."

"Donald!" His mother's shrill command startled him out of the moment and he jolted.

"Coming," he muttered and followed his mother into the office.

HE'S MY FRIEND

IN AN odd way, sitting on the combine platform in the open door to the cab felt a lot like sitting in that far-off school room serving detention with three boys who hated him and one who seemed always to be studying him, waiting for him to do something. Only he didn't know what he was supposed to do, exactly.

And that was how he felt now.

Unsure and off balance. Griff wanted his Jeep fixed, and Don wanted to fix it for him. Like he wanted to fix everything for Griff. Like he wanted to spend money they didn't have on a horse no one could ride and who was useless as a stud because he'd damage any other horse that got near enough for him to kick. But Griff had a way of getting under his fences, and before he knew what he was doing, there was the horse, taking up space and fodder in their barn, and here was Don, wondering how he was going to fix the combine with the two grand he no longer had because he'd sunk it into that ungrateful animal.

Griff, he knew, never manipulated him on purpose. That was not his way. He was about as honest and straightforward as it was possible to be. And he knew their situation as well as Don did. The difference was, he had an unfailing belief that everything always worked out because they were good people and that was all it took.

Don wished he could have that kind of enthusiasm and faith.

Some things, though, were outside his power to do anything about. He didn't control the downward spiral of the market, the weather, the slow and steady march of progress that wanted to put his relatively modest family farm on the market as suburban wasteland.

Like the combine being too old to run predictably, their relationship seemed to be running on slipping gears and frayed wiring.

Still, he could think back to when both seemed new, shiny, exciting.

October, age twelve

GRIFF looked at Don with open skepticism. "It's… a big tractor."

Don laughed. "No, it's not. It's a combine, and look at it. It's gorgeous."

This time, Griff's expression slid right into open amazement. "This really turns you on!"

"Fuck off!" Don shoved him, mortified and red to the tips of his ears.

"It's okay, you know." Griff shoulder bumped him and they resumed walking down the street, past the farm equipment sale lot toward the diner where Don's mother worked three shifts a week. "I think it's cute you get all excited about shit like that." He didn't move away, but walked just that much closer so their shoulders occasionally brushed, and once, Griff's fingers knocked against the knuckles of Don's hand.

"Cute?" Something sticky lodged in Don's throat, and he had to swallow hard to dislodge it. "What the fuck is that supposed to mean?"

"You swear an awful lot, don't you?" Griff said, turning his attention to something on the other side of the street and stuffing his hands into his pockets.

"No I don't. Shit!" Don tripped over a raised sidewalk crack and pitched forward. He'd been trying to see what was so interesting across the road. All he saw was Howard's Garage and the youngest of Howard Sr.'s sons, Howe Jr., rolling a tractor tire across the parking lot. He had his overalls stripped to his waist and his arms bulged with the effort of moving the big wheel. Sweat made the thin white material of his muscle shirt almost transparent, offering a peek at a chest just starting to fill out.

Griff laughed and grabbed his arm before he made a complete fool of himself and pitched onto his face. "Of course you don't."

"Shut up."

Draping a companionable arm over Don's shoulders, Griff yanked Don's head in and ruffled his hair before shoving him through the open diner door.

Don stumbled over the threshold and caught his balance on Griff's arm.

"Really, Donald." Standing in the center of the diner, arms full of steaming plates of food, his mother frowned at him.

Guilt jarred Don and he snatched his hand away from Griff to comb his fingers through his unruly black hair. "Hey, Ma."

She jerked her head to the staff booth in the corner of the room closest to the hinged portion of the counter and the kitchen. "Go sit down."

Leading Griff to the booth, Don attempted to calm the race of his heart. He had no idea why he was so nervous, but he forced the feeling away and slid into the booth. One of the other waitresses was already there and Griff slid in beside him, so they were both across from her.

"Hey, Macy."

"Hi, kiddo."

"Hi." Griff smiled thinly, a flash of expression that vanished so fast Don wondered if he'd actually seen it at all.

"Griff, this is Macy Campbell. She's Howard's older sister." He bobbed his head toward the garage across the road. "Howard works with his old man at the garage."

"So I hear you got in shit again today, huh, kiddo?" Macy said, chawing her gum as she spoke, and then blowing a huge bubble that she managed to suck in just before it snapped all over her face.

Don shrugged and proceeded to line up the utensils on the table in front of him. "Whatever."

"Wasn't his fault," Griff added. "Some asshole—"

"Leave it," Don snapped, sounding harsher than he'd intended.

Griff didn't quite manage to hide the hurt expression by turning to gaze out over the busy diner.

"Some people are just assholes, huh?" Macy said. "Don't sweat it. Got some lunch specials left over. You boys want?"

"Sure." Don nodded.

"I'll sneak ya some soda, yeah?"

"That'd be great, Macy. Thanks." He glanced at Griff. "Cola or ginger ale?"

"You got coffee?"

Macy lifted one eyebrow but shrugged. "Sure. Stunt your growth, though."

Griff looked up at her and a half grin twisted his face. "You seen me? I could use a little stunting."

Don didn't think so. He liked the way Griff towered over him. He'd noticed over the past few days that with the tall boy at his back, people gave him a wider berth, and he could get used to that.

"Be back in a jiff." She got up and smiled over at Don's mother. "I got this, Mary. Then I'll bring coffee 'round?"

"That'd be a help, Macy, thanks." Don's mom blew a thick black curl off her forehead and spared a glance and a tired smile for Don before turning back to clearing dirty dishes from an empty table.

"So what's the lunch special?" Griff asked.

"Free food." Don straightened his fork again and watched his mother work. After a few minutes, he said, "Wednesday, so it's free fish and chips, I think."

"Oh."

"You allergic or something?" Don knew some people couldn't eat fish.

Griff shook his head. "Nah. Free's good." He grinned and pushed his fork and knife across the table so he could lean both elbows on the plastic cloth. "Think your mom will mind—"

"Mind?" Don's mother set glasses of water down for all three of them and slipped into the seat Macy had vacated. "Mind what?"

Griff straightened and dropped his hands under the table, into his lap.

"Griff needs a ride home," Don said. "There's no late bus on Wednesdays." He shrugged. "No practices, so no buses, so detention left him stranded. We have to pass right by his place. I told him we'd give him a ride."

She studied Griff for a long few minutes, then sighed. "Of course. Your parents work, Griff?"

"No ma'am. Well. Yes, I suppose. Dad's got the vet over right now looking at a pregnant mare and"—he shrugged—"Mom lives in Toronto."

"Oh." She studied him again, as though his new information shed some sort of illumination on him. "I see," she said finally. "Well, we'd be happy to bring you home."

"Mary!" A gruff voice from the kitchen rang through the diner. "Soup's up for table five!"

"Yeah, okay, Jake," she called back. "Thank you," she muttered under her breath as she slid from the booth and scooped up her water. "I'll have Macy pack your dinners to go, okay?"

"Jake in a pissy mood again?" Don asked.

"Just best he doesn't see you eating here."

"That's bullshit," Don complained. "He'd throw that shit out anyway. What difference does it make if we eat it?"

"I know. It's just easier, sweetie. You can take it to the park. It's nice out. And don't tell your father."

"I know, I know."

She smiled again, more tired than before, and trooped off to collect the soup for table five.

Macy brought them two heavy paper sacks and to-go cups for their drinks, and they hustled the smuggled food out to the park, where they found a bench and dug in.

"Your mom going to get in trouble for this?" Griff asked as he picked the breading off his fish.

Don shrugged. "Jake's a bear, but he likes her. Has since high school, so I'm told. Which is just creepy, but whatever. He'll let us get away with it because we're hers. He gets pissy about it because he doesn't like my dad. I suppose that's how it goes when you didn't get the girl."

"Sure." Griff stuffed a few fries in his mouth and closed his eyes. "God, those are good. I'm starved."

"No doubt. You should staple your lunch to your forehead or something so you don't keep forgetting it."

Griff smiled around his food but didn't reply. He was too busy inhaling it to talk.

They finished long before Don's mother's shift ended and wandered the park, the streets, and the corner store until the guy behind the counter told them to buy something or get out. They left and strolled back to the diner. Howard Jr. was just waving over his shoulder to his father and older brother. He had a wad of money clutched in one hand and jogged across the street to the diner as Griff and Don walked up.

"You're the new kid," he said, holding the door open for them, but addressing Griff.

Griff frowned slightly. "Yeah."

"Hey, Don." Howard grinned wide. "You got detention for getting harassed. Nice work."

"You're an asshole," Griff growled, putting himself between Don and Howard and blocking Don's access to the diner in the process.

"Griff, don't. Howard's just teasing. He's all right." Don didn't want Griff getting into more trouble over him, and he didn't want a brawl here. Pilfered food that would have been trashed otherwise was one thing. A fight on the premises would get his mother fired. Besides, he liked Howard well enough. At least his teasing was more good-natured than malicious.

"He shouldn't talk to you like that."

"All right." Howard lifted both hands and took a step back. "Chill out. It was just an observation."

"Keep it to yourself," Griff warned.

"Griff." Don braced himself and reached over to touch the other boy's arm. "My mom works here, man."

That at least got his attention, and he broke his hard glare at Howard to look at Don. "Yeah. Sorry."

"Sure," Don mumbled as he squeezed past his friends, unsure why any of it had to be such a big deal.

The ride home was a torturous inquisition. Don's mother asked what he thought were incredibly prying questions about Griff's family, and yet his friend answered them all politely.

"He seems like a nice boy," she said as they pulled out of his drive after dropping him off.

Don shrugged.

"I take it he's not one of the ones who accosted you."

"Mom."

"You don't have to put up with that, you know, son."

A snort of laughter escaped before Don could stop it. "Look at me." He pushed at his tangled curls and held out both thin hands in front of himself.

"What about you?" She glanced over and smiled indulgently. "You're a perfectly good-looking young man."

"I'm *pretty*." He sighed. "I look like you, and if I was a girl, that'd be awesome. But I'm not."

"You can't help the genes you were born with, Donald."

"I know that." He twitched, sorry to have made her tone change from that indulgent, if annoying mother voice to this: clipped and hurt. "And Griff doesn't care what I look like."

She made a sound he couldn't possibly interpret.

"Or how I act," he added, to see if she would expand on the noise and make it coherent.

After a few moments of silence during which she navigated the short expanse of road left between Griff's ranch and their farm, she spoke. "I'm sure Griff is a perfectly nice boy, Don."

Silence. Don waited, but she clamped her lips tight.

"But?" he prompted as she turned off the road into their long drive.

"He's new, that's all. You don't know much about him."

"I know he punched a kid in the face for me. What else is there?"

There came that sound again.

"Mom?"

"Donald, I worry, that's all."

"Well, you don't have to worry about Griff. He's a good guy." That didn't seem enough of an endorsement in Don's own mind. "I like him," he added, and glanced at her to see how she would take that.

He didn't add *he's the only friend I have and I want to keep him as long as I can before he figures out what a loser I am.* That didn't seem to be the argument that would put her at ease.

The topic of conversation changed as they pulled to a stop, though; his father and brothers approached and shanghaied Don to help with the hay bales that needed unloading and storing in the loft. He was glad for the diversion.

The next day, there were no questions when Griff came out of detention, bypassed the waiting school bus, and hopped up into the truck next to Don and his father. With his help that afternoon, the end of the hay was safely stored, and conversation around the table miraculously didn't linger on Don, his school delinquency, or prying any further into Griff's family life.

Don's younger sisters all took an immediate liking to the exotic blond, and he indulged them far longer than Don thought he should.

"You keep that up," he said as he walked down the drive with Griff, their way lighted faintly by the porch light and a few fireflies, "and they'll conspire to keep you."

"I can think of worse things." He smiled, and in the semidark, he looked less hardened than he did in the light. "They're cute."

"Much cuter than me, it's true," Don agreed with a laugh.

There was a distinct pause. A car approached around the bend and stopped in front of them. "I wouldn't say that," Griff said as he opened the door. "Hey, Dad!" He got in, closed the door, and hung out the window to look up at Don, who was standing with his mouth open, trying to figure out what the comment had meant, exactly.

"See you tomorrow, Don!"

"Yeah." Don waved absently. "Sure."

Griff's father said something Don didn't hear, and Griff laughed, a happy, joy-filled sound and said "Whatever," to his father as they drove away.

KISS AND TELL

HOWARD'S red pickup threw up a trail of dust along the road, a visible gray cloud against the harvest gold, smelling exactly the same as it had when he was a kid watching the taillights of his new best friend's father's car.

Bracing himself for the never-ending stream of flirting and innuendo Howard would throw at him, he raised a hand to wave as the mechanic pulled off the dirt road into the laneway leading into the field.

A thick mahogany thatch of shaggy hair flopped in a damp mass into Howard's face as he got out of the truck. He swept it all up and back into the confines of a ball cap as Don hopped to the ground and hurried over to help with the tools.

"Any idea at all what's up with the beast this time?" Howard asked as Don opened the truck's tailgate.

"It's making that clunking sound again," Don offered, knowing the nonspecific answer was going to get him, at the very least, a look.

True to form, Howard rolled his eyes. "You're sure it's not the harvesting or threshing—"

"I'm sure."

Andrew had actually inspected all of the combine's parts at the beginning of the season. He might not have wanted to be a farmer, but he never hesitated to offer his expertise and help to maintain the equipment. Peter had footed the bill for replacement belts and servicing in exchange for Don's promise to harvest his small acreage when the time came.

Peter's field was barely big enough for a machine this size to maneuver in, but the amount of time it would save him in harvesting the fodder for his alpacas and llamas was worth the monetary outlay to help keep it running.

"Your brothers are sure, you mean," Howard pointed out.

"Whatever." Don slammed the tailgate up. "Can we just get this done so I can get back to work?"

Howard snorted. "If I didn't know better, I'd complain that you don't like my company." He winked and knocked shoulders with Don, running a hand down the front of his shirt. "All this, though. How can you resist?"

Don snorted. "I'll give it my best shot."

That got Howard laughing for real, but he did meander over to the combine and open the housing for the engine, releasing a waft of heat and oil stink.

August, age sixteen

HEAT rose off the pavement in waves as Don pushed the bike along the side of the road. The shimmering clouds of it shook the long yellow line into a squiggle of indeterminate length, and he watched as a truck dipped into the hollow between the hill he was climbing and the one beyond.

Crickets in the tall grass to his right drowned out the sound of the engine until the truck was once again visible, topping the hill.

Don sighed. He'd hoped it might be Peter or Jennifer driving out to see where he was. He should have been home half an hour ago, and if the chain hadn't fallen off his bike—again—he would have been. Now, he was still a good twenty-minute walk from the laneway to the closest fields. At least once there, he could turn off and leave the stifling heat of the tarmac behind.

He plucked at his T-shirt and lifted it away from his body. There wasn't enough air movement to allow for even a breath of it to cool his sweat-slick skin, though, and he didn't dare take it off. It might look hazy out, but he knew he'd have painful blisters on his shoulders inside of ten minutes if he dared bare them to the elements.

The truck slowed and stopped at the crest of the hill, and as he drew alongside, he recognized the yellow-on-red lettering proclaiming "Howard and Son's Garage" to be the finest in farm equipment servicing in the county.

"Hey." It was the "Son" portion of "Howard and Son" peering out of the air-conditioned cab now. "That thing works better if you ride it, cowboy." Howard grinned, showing off a row of flashing, perfect white teeth. At seventeen, he knew just exactly how gorgeous he was and didn't hesitate to flaunt it one bit.

"Chain fell off," Don said, sending a quick, twitching smile in response. The older boy, older by just a year but already graduated from the local high school, always managed to say just the thing to make Don hope the ground would swallow him up.

He wasn't mean. He just… was, and Don felt *less than* around him.

Howe—everyone called him Howe to differentiate him from his father, but Don didn't, *couldn't* think of him as a Howe—flicked his head toward the back of the truck.

"Toss it in. I'll give you a lift. You're going to have a fucking stroke walkin' all the way home."

"Thanks." Don's smile this time was more genuine.

"Hotter than a hustler's backside out here," Howard muttered as Don hurried past.

Dammit, he'd almost made it without blushing, too, until he heard that comment, and the following chuckle, no doubt elicited by the pink in his cheeks.

He said nothing as he heaved his bike into the back of the truck and went around to the passenger side to climb into the cab beside Howard.

"You're a shy one, still?" Howard observed as he pulled back onto the highway.

Don shrugged.

He could feel Howard watching him, casting quick glances over at him as he drove.

"You would think with all the shit going around, what with Griff coming out and all, you'd be a little tougher."

Don shrugged.

Griff and he had remained friends since that very first week in detention, and he hadn't needed to hear his best friend say the words to know the guy was gay. As far as they were concerned, that fact didn't matter. They were friends, end of. Who Griff kissed under the bleachers was nothing to Don. He didn't care.

"Griff didn't exactly come out," Don said, when Howard continued to watch him. "Hawthorn outed him. Not the same thing."

It hadn't been a pleasant scene, either. Hawthorn, increasingly frustrated over his inability to rattle Griff, had finally set him up, paying off some guy to lure Griff under the bleachers at homecoming and then cry rape.

Nobody really believed Griff would do such a thing, but any speculation he might have hidden his sexuality behind flew out the window, and he'd made the decision not to deny at least that aspect of the encounter.

Don had never doubted him, but the idea of Griff kissing anyone, anywhere, made him grumble and he wasn't sure he was ready to confront the why of that head-on. Not yet.

"Still, must have been a bit of a shock for you?"

"We've been friends since we were twelve, Howard."

"Mmm." Howard nodded. "Lots of sleepovers."

"Fuck off."

"Just sayin'."

"Just sayin' what, exactly?"

Howard shrugged. "Why do you call me Howard? No one else does."

"Does it bother you?"

"No." Howard glanced at him, and there was an odd expression on his face. "You're not gonna make this easy on me, are you?"

"What are you talking about?"

Rather than answer right away, Howard pulled the truck off the road into a narrow laneway that would, eventually, lead back to Don's family farm. It was surrounded on both sides by a thick hedgerow and had multiple places for one tractor or truck to pull over and let another pass. Howard pulled into one of these that offered a particularly opaque screen of brush on three sides. With quick motions, he put the truck in park and turned off the ignition.

"What are you doing?"

"Everyone's been dying to know, Don. You and Griff *have* been friends for almost five years. Neither of you have ever gone out with a girl." He tipped his head to one side. "Or another boy, for that matter. You don't think people wonder?"

"Take me home."

"I will."

"Howard."

"One kiss."

That shocked Don to silence and he snapped his head around to look at the mechanic. "What?"

"I'm not going to blab it to the whole world or anything. This is just for my own edification. One kiss."

"No!"

"So you're not, then." He let out a small huff of a sigh and made to turn the key in the ignition.

"I didn't say that," Don said, very quietly, in case he really didn't want to say it out loud at all. But wasn't this his chance? For nearly a month now, he'd been sitting on this fence, wondering. Had Griff kissed the other boy? Had they done anything? Had Griff ever done anything with someone else? If he did, why didn't he ever do it with Don? Or did Don even want him to?

Fuck, it was too complicated. Griff was his best friend.

He examined Howard's profile now. He was gorgeous in a gruff, rugged sort of way, though not with the same refined, sharp features that Griff had. With his dark, nearly black hair and deep brown eyes, he was almost the polar opposite of Griff. Snapping his head back around front, Don fixed his gaze on the horizon. Should the fact Don thought of Howard as gorgeous mean something? But then Kerrie-Anne Claymore was gorgeous, too, all sunny blonde and blue-eyed, and forever smiling. She had legs like no one Don had ever seen before, and her laugh was infectious. She sat next to him in political science class, and he couldn't count the number of lectures he'd tuned out talking to her. She was fun and flirty and pretty, and blonde, like Griff.

Fuck. How could he be sixteen and not know this basic shit?

Realizing he'd been staring out the windshield in silence, Don worked up just enough nerve to look over at the older boy sitting, just as silent, next to him.

"You are, though," he said, finally cluing in to the other side of the equation.

Howard shrugged.

"Why do you want to kiss me?"

That got him a laugh, and he wasn't entirely sure it wasn't at his expense. But it was short and Howard choked it off. "Forget it." He cranked the key in the ignition and the truck sputtered at him. "Fuck off!" he snarled at it, smashing a hand on the steering wheel.

"No, Howard." Don turned in his seat and grabbed Howard's wrist. "Did you mean it?"

"No. I go around asking guys to kiss me all the time, because that's not going to get my ass kicked or anything."

"So kiss me, then."

"Don, leave it. The moment's kind of over, dude."

"Fuck that." Don pulled at his arm and slid across the seat, pressing his knee against Howard's thigh. His heart thumped, slamming too quick a pulse against his throat, and the leftover conditioned air in the truck wasn't enough to keep a bead of sweat from trickling down his back. "Do it."

"You're an idiot." Howard shot him a glare that softened almost instantly. "I'm going to hate us both for this."

He threaded his fingers through Don's hair and didn't kiss him so much as he crushed Don's lips with his and twisted their bodies until he'd flattened Don against the back of the seat. Don's head impacted the back window. His breath stopped, his blood rushed—all of it straight south—and his heart hammered emptily against his ribs.

Thought vanished, and when Howard's hands fumbled at his belt, he only moaned and spread his legs, bucking his hips out to make more room for those big hands to paw at him.

He didn't need to breathe or think. Instinct guided his own hands, and before he knew it, he was touching hot, sticky flesh. His fingers fumbled over sparse hair and tripped over nubs of flesh, returning, when Howard moaned into his mouth, to worry nipples into hard points.

"Fuck, Don." Howard's words mashed against his neck, and he allowed the bigger man to shove him over, back to the passenger side where they had more room.

Belt buckles clanked, curses cracked open and fell into groans, and frantic hands groped and fought against tight jeans and clinging boxers. Then there was flesh, glorious and hard under sweet, velvety smoothness. Howard's grunts turned short, soft, messy. His kisses trickled into patters of lips and tongue and teeth over Don's neck and chest, and his hand jerked spasmodically on Don's dick.

The buildup was fast enough to be painful. The release intense enough to black out Don's vision and lose a few seconds of time in the void.

"Oh, shit."

Howard's curse brought him back, and there was no heady afterglow. Just a mess.

"Shit," he echoed. Then he laughed and wagged his sticky fingers in Howard's face. "Who taught you the definition of kiss?"

Howard's look of horror turned to a grin. "You did. I think. Just now."

"I'm… not sure I got that one right."

"And here I thought you were the smart one." Howard flopped back onto the seat beside Don, turned his head and grinned at him. "We'll have to give it another go sometime."

Don studied the drying jizz on his hands. "Yeah."

"Well, I guess I have my answer, anyway," Howard said as he found a rag to wipe his fingers. He handed it to Don before straightening and tucking himself back into his pants.

"Yeah." Don smiled at him. "Me too." Howard was gorgeous. He couldn't deny that fact. But he wasn't Griff. Dropping the greasy rag to the floor, he looked around for something more useful to clean himself with.

"What was your question?" Howard had his hands on the keys, but he hesitated. "You had a question?"

"I was wondering if Griff and that asshole actually did anything under the bleachers."

"He never told you?"

"I never asked."

Howard nodded and started the engine. "Why not?"

Don quickly straightened his clothes and, for lack of anything else to do about the mess on his fingers, began to lick it off. "Guess I didn't want to know."

"Dude, that's just… nasty." But there was a smoky glow in Howard's eyes as he watched Don finish cleaning off his fingers, and Don couldn't resist the urge to leave one in his mouth just a bit longer than necessary.

"Fuck," Howard turned his attention back to driving and pulled out of the bypass. "You going to tell him?" He wagged a hand in the air between them. "About this?"

Don shrugged. "If he asks. Maybe." He glanced at Howard and caught the tail end of a fierce scowl. "Or…?"

"Nah, dude, it's all good. Us fags gotta stick together, right?"

"Whatever."

"You might want to stretch the truth a little bit, though. I mean, what? Thirty seconds, and you're off? Dude, that's just embarrassing."

"Like you can talk there, speedy." Don punched Howard, hard enough to make him wince, and they both continued the ride in grinning silence.

IS IT WORTH IT

"I THINK that's got it," Howard said as he emerged, grease smudged across his cheek, from the vicinity of the engine. The dark smear made Don think of that afternoon, years ago, when Howard had used a grease-smudged rag to try and wipe away the evidence of their first encounter.

"That's what you said last time too," he blurted, snatching his attention back from that thought.

Howard shrugged and swiped a wrist across his forehead, leaving behind another smudge. "I'm pretty sure this beast has parts older than either one of us," he pointed out. "I'm good. Not a miracle worker."

"Modest too, so that's awesome." Unable to resist, Don scrubbed a thumb over one of the grease smudges. He succeeded in making it a larger, fainter smudge.

Howard grinned at him and sauntered toward his tool cases.

"What do I owe you?" Don asked as he followed, carrying handfuls of the mechanic's paraphernalia to lay out over the tailgate.

For a few minutes, Howard wiped down his equipment in silence and snapped the wrenches and screwdrivers into their cases, meticulous about getting them back in their housings.

"Call it a favor?" he said, tone lifting as if he was voicing a hope he didn't expect answered.

"I'm not a charity case," Don said, dropping the tools with a clang on the truck bed. "Send a bill. I have to get back to work."

"Don!"

"You don't make a living giving shit away for free, Howard."

"Excuse the fuck out of me for trying to do my part, asshole!"

"Fuck you!" Don turned and stalked back to the combine.

Behind him, Howard's tools clattered and slammed.

Don didn't look back.

"Field service costs extra, you know!" Howard shouted as Don clambered up the ladder to the cab of the machine.

Don froze on the top rung of the ladder.

"I don't put out for just anyone," Howard said, voice softening.

"Fuck off," Don growled, releasing the words into the familiar sphere of banter. He glanced down to where Howard was standing near the foot of the ladder.

"Let me do this, Don. You don't need another bill. You need a break."

Don hopped off the ladder and landed next to Howard. "I need about a dozen," he admitted, glancing to the horizon and the ominous darkness gathering there. He leaned on the bottom rung. "Every year it gets worse."

Howard leaned next to him, close enough their shoulders touched. "You think you're the only one?"

"Of course not. Economy's shit. Prices are in the toilet. I know all that. And the deed's sitting out on the table every night, mocking me."

"You're not seriously thinking about selling."

Don said nothing.

"Dude, this farm." Howard glanced out, gaze sweeping over the long view of the land Don had yet to harvest. "It's your life," he said quietly.

It took a massive surge of willpower to look at the other man. "But it's not Griff's," he pointed out, even while he refrained from saying a whole lot of other things.

"Does he know you're considering this? Does anyone? Because this is the first I'm hearing about it. I mean, what would you do? Where would you go?"

"We can keep the house. Sell the rest."

"And watch the city creep out and swallow a hundred years of Jenkins history whole? Are you out of your mind?"

"I'd be out of my mind to stay. There's no money in this business anymore."

"So find a new business." Howard turned and slapped a hand on either side of Don, gripping the ladder's sides and penning him in. "Peter did."

Don lifted his head to look into Howard's face. "Peter got out while he could. He's got a pocket-sized strip of land and a herd he can manage on his own." He shook his head. "You don't need this much land to raise wool factories."

Howard grinned. "Then raise something else." He shifted, leaned a little closer and leered.

"You are a fucking pig!"

Grinning wider, Howard agreed.

And just for the barest breath, Don saw something elusive flicker through Howard's eyes. The brown got a fraction darker. The grin faltered. "How—"

And then it was gone.

"You"—Howard punched Don's shoulder, hard—"have to get back to work. I"—he turned and resumed carefully stowing his tools—"have done my good deed for the day." He tossed a flirting grin at Don over his shoulder. "But just to prove what a great guy I am, I'm going to do my bit. I'll put out some feelers. If the guts of that thing are as sound as you say they are, then the next thing to do is replace the engine. I'll see what I can do to find a used one that'll fit it and your budget."

"You are a great guy, Howard."

Without turning, Howard nodded. "I know."

"And you know Griff always makes supper enough for three."

Howard shook his head. "Don't, Don."

"Howard." That million and one things he needed to say crowded to the tip of his tongue, tripped over one another to get out, and fell in a silent jumble, unsaid. Again. He closed his eyes because looking at the man's back was too familiar a view, and nothing he had tried had ever worked to change the fact Howard always left at the end of the day.

"Get back to work," Howard said softly. "That grain is not going to lie down and sort itself out for you."

Don smiled. Just what his father would say.

September, age sixteen

THERE was no way Don's father could not realize they weren't alone in the barn. He didn't know why his old man didn't say anything, but he had to know Howard was in the loft. How could he not?

"Bright and early tomorrow, son. That grain isn't going to—"

"Lie down, yeah, Dad, I know!"

"You tell your teachers you'd be away for a few days?"

Don grinned. "Told 'em I'd be out for the rest of the month."

"Ted Mannings can't do his harvest this year. His back."

"I heard."

"Easy enough to get from our place to his." Donald Sr. eyed Don, all of five foot eight and still skinny, even at almost seventeen years old. The "filling-out" stage had just never happened for him. "You reckon you can handle our old Betsy on your own this year?"

Finally! Don grinned eagerly. "'Course I can!"

His father nodded, apparently satisfied. "Good. Six a.m. Peter brought her out to the field today, so we'll ride out together and I'll drop you off."

"Yes, sir!"

With one more nod, Donald Sr. headed for the barn door. He stopped on the threshold. "Your father know where you are, Howe?" he asked, loudly enough to be heard over the snuffling of the sheep outside.

"Yes, sir!" Howard called, for once sounding like the kid he was, and not the mock adult he wished he was.

"Good. I expect you'll be headed home soon."

"Yes, sir!"

Donald studied his son for a moment longer. "Six a.m. comes early."

"Dad! I know."

"Condoms aren't just to keep girls from getting pregnant, son."

"Oh my God!" Don blinked, too shocked to even blush right away. "Really, Dad? Really?"

His father's eyes flashed, a bright glint of humor threading through his features and crinkling his eyes. "I was sixteen once." He grinned outright. "Say hello to your father for me, Howard."

Don was still sputtering long after they were alone in the barn.

It took a bit to work himself up to facing Howard, but finally he turned to ascend the ladder into the loft.

Howard was hanging through the hole in the floor above. "Do you think your dad and my dad—"

"Fuck no!" Don spat. "God damn fuck, no! That's just gross."

He flopped into the hay beside his friend.

Howard leaned on one elbow beside him and traced a line down the row of buttons of Don's shirt. "You think it's gross?"

"What? Our dads?" Don made a face. "Don't you?"

Howard shrugged and rolled onto his back. "Imagine it, though. Young lovers, all hot and—"

"Eww! No, I'm not going to imagine it, no!" To shut him up, Don rolled on top of him and clamped his lips over Howard's mouth.

That seemed to do the trick, because for the next while, the only sounds in the barn were their heavy breathing and the occasional giggle and, eventually, a lot of panting and soft moans.

When it was over, Howard watched him quietly.

"What?" Don fidgeted under the scrutiny.

"Your dad knows why I come over."

"So?" Don flushed now, thinking about his father's earlier words. "He must be cool with it, or he would have kicked you out."

"Yeah."

Don frowned and looked up from buttoning his shirt. "What?"

"My dad…."

"Wouldn't be cool with it, I guess."

Howard shrugged. "Who knows with him? He's perfectly happy with the whole fucking world when he's sober."

Don studied the other young man for a few minutes. "That's not so often these days, huh?"

Another shrug lifted Howard's shoulders, but he kept his head down. "Guess not."

"You know, that bruise on your shoulder—"

"Don't, okay?" Howard asked, looking up and meeting Don's gaze. "I don't wanna be that guy."

"What guy?"

"The one everybody feels sorry for 'cause his old man knocks him around. It ain't like that."

"Then what is it like?" Settling cross-legged in the straw, Don managed to use the motion to shuffle a bit closer to Howard. "You know you can tell me… whatever. I won't say anything if you don't want—"

"It's not like anything."

"I know what it's like—"

"No, you don't." Howard shifted, flexing the shoulder in question. "It isn't the same as some schmuck at school stealing your lunch money."

For a moment, Don stared at him. He didn't know what to say to that. He wanted to be the kind of boyfriend who knew how to help make it better for Howard, but he wasn't. Griff was the guy who always knew how to do this kind of thing. But Griff wasn't here; he hadn't been around much all summer, in fact. Not since Howard had begun escaping his home in Don's barn.

"Shit, that was a crappy thing to say," Howard whispered. "You put up with shit at school, I—"

"Never mind." Don brushed it off.

It took a while for Howard to let it go, and they sat in that awkward space for a long time. Finally, Howard sighed. "So what about us?" he asked. "Does anyone else know?"

"How do I know? It's not like I go around telling everyone."

"Do you think it's gross?"

"Oh God, we're not talking about our fathers again, are we?"

Howard shook his head and his dark shag flopped into his eyes. "I'm talking about us. Why don't you tell anyone? Do you think it's gross?"

Don snorted. "You know why. People find out I actually am a faggot, Griff won't be enough to keep my head on my shoulders. Why would I make myself a target?"

"You're scared of getting beat up?"

Standing and shooting Howard a look, Don headed for the ladder. "You've never been the skinny little shit, Howard. No one ever wonders if you're gay even though you hang out with me, so you don't know." He slipped down the ladder as quickly as he could.

"You think I'd let anyone hurt you?" Howard asked, following on his heels.

"You think you could stop it? Having someone else fight my battles would only make it worse. Trust me, I've been avoiding getting my ass kicked for sixteen years. I'm not giving them any more ammunition."

"So I'm not worth it."

"Griff's not even worth it."

As soon as he said it, he knew it was wrong. Howard's face closed. His eyes shot acid sparks and he turned on his heel.

"Howard!"

"I gotta get home!" Howard threw a leg over the seat of his dirt bike, not even bothering with his helmet, though Don knew if he got caught riding it without the thing, the bike would be confiscated, and that was only if his father was sober.

"Howard!" Don's second shout was lost in the roar of the bike's engine.

"How—" His third cut off in a spray of gravel that bit into his shins and thighs and raised a cloud of dust that left him coughing. By the time he got his breath back, Howard was gone.

WORTH A RISK

EVEN the trail of dust from the truck was blown away on the hot breeze by the time Don had made one round of the field. Whatever Howard had done, it held, because he was well into the second field when his phone rang. He was loath to stop and answer it, but there was no way he'd hear anything with the engine running, and if it was Griff, he didn't want to ignore him.

He pulled it out, hit Answer, and told the caller to hang on as he shut the machine off.

"Yeah?"

"Hey."

"Griff?"

There was a thick silence for a few heartbeats.

Don's chest tightened. Panic set in. "Griff? What's wrong?" The last time this had happened, he'd listened to silence for four heart-stopping minutes that had felt more like days, called back to get Griff's voice mail on the first ring, and rushed home to find Griff unconscious on the barn floor and his nasty horse grazing in the front yard.

"Why didn't you want me to call Howe this morning?" Griff said after a moment, making Don's heart speed from stopped to well past its normal rhythm and rushing headlong up into his throat.

"What?"

"Howe, Don. Why didn't you want me to call him?"

"I told you—"

"He was with you, wasn't he?"

"The combine was down. I told you."

"So that's why I saw his truck coming out of the laneway." He said the words, but it wasn't a question. It fell just short of an accusation, in fact.

"Yes."

Panic receded. Don's tension didn't ease. His heart remained where it was, twisting and turning like Griff had noosed and hung it there. Now he wished he'd ignored the phone. But no, then Griff would have stewed in his suspicions all day until Don got home.

More silence filled the conversation with unpleasant innuendo.

"Griff," Don said, trying to make his voice calm. "I have to get back to work."

"Yeah. Of course."

"Look, I'll come home for supper, okay?"

"What, so he gets the field call and I get to cook for you?"

"No! That isn't...." But why did he have to explain, over and over, that Howard had come out to do his job? Nothing more. Why wouldn't Griff believe that? "That isn't what I meant," he said. "I'll just work till dark, then. You don't have to do anything."

"Fine."

"Griff—"

"You have to get back to work, right?"

He couldn't stop the sigh. "Yes. I do."

"Okay, then. I'll see you when I see you."

Snip. There went his heart, plummeting and landing somewhere under his work boots.

Don nodded, but didn't get a chance to reply before the phone went dead.

Why was it he felt like he was disappointing everyone he spoke to lately? He closed the phone and slipped it into his breast pocket where he would feel it vibrate if Griff called back. The combine drowned out all other noises as it roared back to life.

September, age sixteen

"IS IT always this loud?"

Don squirmed at the feel of Griff's breath on his neck as his friend shouted into his ear. He nodded affirmative and pushed the earmuffs back in place. "Use the radio, jerk," he said into the microphone with a laugh.

"So this is cool." Griff fidgeted on the upturned bucket set beside Don's seat. No doubt he was trying to center the small cushion on the bucket to save his ass from going numb. "Where did you get the headsets?"

"You see how my pansy theater obsession pays off? They got a new set in the drama department for backstage. They were tossing these out, so I asked Mr. Jefferies if I could have them. Howard fixed them for us, and there you go."

"Howard."

Don glanced at his friend and smiled. "Yes, Howard." He hoped his words hid the unpleasant contortions in his gut. He hadn't actually heard from or seen Howard since he'd driven off in a huff on Monday night. Now, Saturday afternoon was waxing, and he was getting the message loud and clear.

Beside him, Griff fidgeted again and his knee brushed, or, rather, slid with a fair amount of pressure, along Don's thigh. "Well, that was nice of him, I guess."

It was unsubtle in the extreme, and Don jerked so violently the combine responded and he had to focus on getting it back in a straight line. That was the key, his father always said. Keep the thing in a straight line, and he'd be okay.

He glanced over at Griff once he was back in control. Now his friend was very deliberately not touching him. Straw-colored hair fell at such an angle Don couldn't see his eyes, and he stared straight ahead, his gaze fixed on the horizon, his jaw tense.

Should he say something? Part of him wanted to comment on Griff's attitude toward Howard. Most of him wished the tension that pulled at their friendship would go away, but he feared the only way that would happen was if Howard went away too. He didn't want that. But then, he didn't get a choice about that. Maybe it was already fact.

"Are you... mad or something?" he ventured at last.

"No." The word sank into the silence.

"You're fucking full of shit," Don said at last. Because Griff was the only person he could talk to like that. Because he never wanted that to change, so he pushed the issue. "You don't like Howard."

"He likes you too much."

"What the hell would you know about it?" Don said. He'd reached the end of the row farthest from the house, the one part of the field hidden from the road by thick hedgerows and from the house and barn by the gentle swell of land in between. He turned the combine off and ripped off the headset. "You never come around while he's here, so you don't know anything about him."

Griff's headset hit the floor with a thunk and he swiveled in his seat, eyes blazing, jaw jutting. "I know his motorbike roars down the lane and past my house in the middle of the goddamn night, sometimes."

It had never occurred to Don Griff would have any idea Howard had spent time at Don's house, let alone that he'd been monitoring the other guy's comings and goings. "What the hell does it matter when he's here?"

Griff stared at him for a long moment. "What is he doing here in the middle of the night?"

"What the hell does it matter to you!"

"Are you that dense?" Griff asked, a growl in his voice Don had never heard before.

"I'm not dense. You don't talk to me."

"Don't talk to you?" Griff stared at him. "I always talk to you!"

"About baseball and horses and my little sisters and my mother's cooking, yeah. Not about Howard."

Griff scowled and leaned against the back wall of the cab. "Why would I want to talk to you about your fucking boyfriend?"

Boyfriend. Don's jaw hit the floor. The word almost eclipsed the fact that Griff had just sworn at him, which he never did. "Is that what you think he is?"

"Isn't that what you call the guy you're fucking?"

"*Fucking*? Who the hell told you that?"

"You have absolutely nothing in common with him. Why else would he be here?"

"You're mental."

"So you're not...?"

Don felt the thin layer of truth begin to crack under him. "Not what?"

"Fucking, dimwit."

"No," Don said, able to be definitively honest about that point, at least. One stable step toward the safety of honesty.

"So then why's he here all the time?"

"What?" Don asked, trying to tease. "I can't have other friends?"

"That's all he is?"

So much for sure footing. "Does it matter?" Don asked. "He's not you."

Griff turned a look on him and it held so many things Don didn't quite understand. Or were they things he wasn't sure he wanted to understand? "So. He's just the guy you have sex with, and I'm just the guy who… what?" His blue eyes darkened and his lips turned down. "What am I, Don?"

"You're my best friend," Don replied. No hesitation there. That fact was the rock, the foundation, and anything else was built around it. There was no chance of losing his footing there.

Griff nodded and to Don's horror, he was reaching for the door handle.

"What are you doing?"

"Going home."

"Why?"

As he watched, Griff's broad shoulders slumped. When had they gotten so wide? His head dipped and the line of his spine curved. Had his waist always been so narrow?

"You make everything impossible, you know that?" Griff asked.

"What everything?" Don was losing ground here, and realizing his rock was crumbling away beneath him. Nothing was as stable as it had been that morning when Griff had shown up at his door, grin on his face and bounce in his step. It had been like the past month of clandestine meetings with Howard and the unease he felt over not telling Griff about it had never happened. The tension that had been developing between him and Griff because of it vanished in that one sunny, blue-eyed grin.

Griff's smile, just his presence, had washed away the sick unhappiness of Howard's departure and replaced that feeling with one of relief. Griff was back. Or maybe Griff had never left and it was only his preoccupation with Howard that had made it seem that way.

Now, the sick rushed back tenfold, because Howard was just Howard. Sex was fun, but Griff was his. And Griff was the one about to leave.

A low growl issued from Griff's chest and he turned. "You've got to be the densest person on the fucking planet."

Don blinked at him. Griff never swore.

"I don't understand."

"Obviously." He shook his head, tossing strands of gold and sunlight over his face and past the clear blue of his eyes, like wheat on the horizon. And that look went on forever.

Until Griff was too close to focus on and of much more immediate importance was the taste of the coffee they'd been drinking and the mint gum Griff always chewed. Eclipsing whatever was behind his eyelids—closed now because there was nothing to look at—was the feel of calloused fingers on his cheek, then his neck, and the slither of wet tongue into his mouth, past lips still parted in shock.

Griff was kissing him.

It was clumsy and wet and more real than any kiss Howard had presented him with. It was as strange as a boy stepping between him and threat and punching it in the face. And it was as ordinary as a boy climbing into the cab of his father's truck like he belonged there.

He hadn't even gotten his head around the fact of it before it was gone.

Griff watched him, eyes wide, fingers still lightly connected to his face.

"You… smell like horses," Don said.

Blond brows collapsed in confusion and the blue clouded over.

"Howard never kissed me like that."

"Holy *fuck*!" Griff spun and reached for the door.

"Howard's gone!" Don shouted. "He's gone, Griff."

"What do you mean? Gone?"

"We had a fight. He took off and I haven't even spoken to him since."

Griff's head bobbed once, slowly. "That's why you've been so…."

Don waited, but his friend didn't say anything else. "So what?" he asked finally.

"Sad."

"I'm not sad over Howard."

"Bullshit."

Another swear.

"I'm not." And he wasn't, exactly. At least, he didn't think he was. "He asked me if I thought what we did was… gross."

"I don't think I want to—"

"Just listen." Don knew Griff probably didn't want to know what they'd been doing. But it was part of the thing that mattered. Part of the foundation, now. "I guess… he thought I was ashamed of it."

"Are you?"

Don shrugged. It didn't matter that Griff couldn't see the gesture. "Doesn't matter what I think of it. Doesn't change anything."

"What do you mean?"

"We did it once… I don't even know. It was sort of by accident."

Griff snorted. "Oops. I fell and kissed a boy." He shook his head. "You're so full of shit."

More swearing. He'd never heard Griff swear before, and here he'd dropped them all in the space of five minutes.

"I don't know. It wasn't planned. It just happened. I wouldn't have done it, or done it again if I didn't like it. I kissed Kerrie-Lynn once, too, and that was gross."

Griff chuckled. "Yeah. Wendy Scofield. Course, I was, like, ten, so what did I know, right?"

"You know when it isn't what you want."

"So you wanted Howard?"

"Listen." Don held his breath. He wanted to explain. To make Griff understand, but he didn't want to make Howard the bad guy. He hadn't actually done anything wrong. If anyone had been in the wrong, it had been Don, not Howard.

"Okay," Griff said slowly. "I'm listening. So talk."

Don let out a breath and nodded. "So I told him I didn't tell anyone about him and me because I didn't want to get the shit kicked out of me when people found out."

"I wouldn't let anyone hurt you," Griff said, his voice fierce and quiet and full of all those things in him that made him stick up for small, skinny boys he didn't know.

"I know you wouldn't."

And there. That was not the same answer he'd given Howard at all, was it?

"I know you wouldn't, Griff. That's what Howard said, too. I told him, basically, he couldn't protect me, and he wasn't worth taking the chance. Well." Don drew in a breath and let it out, because the next bit was him taking a hammer to his own foundation in hopes he was just knocking away the loose flakes and not smashing it to smithereens. "What I told him was that not even you were worth it."

Griff gasped.

"Wait. Let me explain."

"There's more? Christ!"

"I said that, and it was cruel, Griff. Don't you see? It pretty much told him he was less to me than you are."

"And yet I'm not worth taking a risk for."

Don blinked hard and swallowed. How to explain he'd been wrong about that?

Finally, Griff turned just enough to look at him, and there were tears on his cheeks.

"Shit. I'm sorry." He was dense. He had no idea what he was apologizing for. But Griff was crying and there wasn't anyone else around who could have caused it. He was lousy at this shit.

"For what?" Griff asked, sniffing and wiping the back of his hand across his cheek.

Don shrugged.

"This is stupid," Griff muttered, turning back to face the front of the cab.

"I guess." Don smiled weakly and reached to turn the engine back on. It roared to life and when he glanced over at Griff, his friend's proximity made his heart jump.

This kiss was less wet and a little longer. Griff leaned over to put his mouth next to Don's ear after and shouted, "Don't kiss Howard anymore."

Howard had left.

Don grinned like an idiot as he got the behemoth machine moving again.

Griff had kissed him. Griff was his. His what? He grinned wider. Just his. That was good enough.

JUMPING IN, BOTH FEET

THE vibrations of the combine nearly eclipsed the vibration of his cell, and when Don finally registered that it was ringing, he decided not to answer it. Lost in the memory of that first kiss, he wanted to stay a little longer in a place where life had been infinitely less complicated. Now, his back ached, his ass was numb, and the line between what he'd harvested and what he hadn't was blurring into the dusk. He just wanted to get the field done and get home.

But home to what, exactly?

To Griff, his broken foot and his suspicions and his boredom, when all Don really wanted was a hot bath, a good meal, and a long night's sleep.

The phone rang again.

He dug it out of his pocket, glanced at the caller ID, and dropped it back with a sigh. Griff.

When had he stopped looking forward to a chat with Griff?

The vibrations stopped then started again, repeating the sequence twice more before Griff finally gave up.

Don rode the combine over the last few passes, parked the machine near the hedgerow, walked to his truck, and headed for home. He had debated knocking off early to clean the machine before calling it a day, but decided against it. He was worn-out, and it wasn't the kind of job he could afford to skimp on, or miss something because he was tired. He'd ask Abe to come out with the air compressor in the morning. The last thing he needed was to miss something in the near dark and end up with a combine fire to sink the farm for good.

He was barely paying attention to the ride back to the barn when something flashed, pale and out of place in the dusk, and startled him out of his fugue.

"What the hell?"

September, age sixteen

DON squinted into the dusk as he walked. There was something on the dark road ahead. Occasionally, a dim beam of light bobbed and a small patch of gravel was briefly exposed to the wavering light, then it would disappear again. The vagueness of it sent a ripple of unease through him. The light was too high to be a person with a flashlight or a car headlight. No engine sounds meant it wasn't Howard's bike or a tractor.

What the hell was it?

The light flared again, sweeping down the road almost to where he walked, and then blinked out again.

He stopped.

He wasn't afraid. Just… what the hell flashed a light seven feet in the air and made no sound as it moved?

"Jesus." He actually took a few steps back before stopping again.

"Don?"

The light-wielding creature knew his name? The beam flared again and struck him in the face. He nearly jumped back.

Griff laughed. The familiar, vibrant sound washed every other emotion away, and under it Don recognized the clop of horse hooves.

"Jesus fucking Christ!" He lifted a hand to ward off the beam of light. "You trying to scare the crap out of me?"

More laughter and Griff lowered his flashlight, then clicked it off.

"Sorry, dude. Usually I let Maggie"—he patted the horse's neck—"find her own way. She can probably see better in the dark than I can, but I like to know where I am every now and then."

He drew up alongside Don and the horse nuzzled at his hair.

"God, she's huge."

"A little taller than average, yes. A veritable giant for her breed." He patted the horse's neck once more. "But a gentle giant, so Dad breeds her for riding ranches. You have no idea how many… big people who've never set foot in a barn in their lives want to ride a horse. The ranches need calm horses that can bear a bit of weight. So I'm training her. Want a ride?"

Don slid his hand down the horse's soft nose. She blew out a loud huff and bobbed her head, and he jumped back. "Shit, she's huge."

"Stop swearing," Griff said amiably as he reached over and took Don's hand. "Come here. Put your foot in the stirrup and swing up behind me."

"I'm not sure—"

"Stop being such a farm boy." Griff was already hauling on his arm. "Grab the back of the saddle and pull yourself up. Come on."

With his friend's help, Don managed to lift himself off the ground high enough to actually reach the stirrup, and then he could swing his other leg over the horse's rump. "Shit, this is fucking high off the ground."

Griff laughed at him again and tucked Don's hand against his abdomen. "Hang on tight, then, scaredy-cat."

"Not scared," Don muttered. "Just." He glanced down and couldn't decide if the darkness was a blessing or a curse. It wasn't quite dark enough to completely hide how far off the gravel was from his soft body. But it was dark enough that he felt like they were floating through the night, only the two of them and not another soul around to know about it.

"The combine is a lot higher than this," Griff pointed out as he clucked to the animal and she started moving.

Don jerked and gripped, flinging his other arm around Griff's waist.

"It has fucking walls!"

That got him another chuckle, but Griff also flattened one hand over Don's and squeezed. "I won't let you fall, Donny. Promise."

"Why are we going for a ride in the dark anyway?" Don asked, shimmying forward a bit and trying not to imagine sliding off the horse's backside.

"Because you were working, I was working, and now we're finished, and if we go back to your place, your sisters will try and cute me to death. If we go back to mine, my dad will hand you a drill and make you help drywall the kitchen."

Don smiled into the darkness. "Shouldn't we be helping your dad drywall the kitchen?"

Griff shrugged. "Maybe." He sighed and pulled Don's hand further around his waist. "But then, if we don't, he'll get tired and just go to bed for a change."

Don felt a slight sag in Griff's body.

"He works too hard," his friend said. "He won't take a break. Just keeps sayin' he needs to get the place finished for me. Like he's got a deadline or something. Like I care what the house looks like."

They rode for a while in silence. "Soon as the harvest is over, we'll all come over and help get it done, okay?"

"You guys don't have to come over to fix my house."

"'Course we don't." Don leaned a little closer. "And you don't have to come over and look after my sisters so we can harvest, but you do."

Griff shrugged.

Don felt the movement in the ripple of muscles across Griff's back.

"Your sisters are cute."

"You know we take advantage of anyone who thinks that for as long as they still think it," Don warned. "People are beginning to think you're a bit delusional. Their spell usually wears off in a few weeks. You've been falling for them for years now."

"I don't mind helping out. Besides, Megan is teaching me to cook."

"Megan can cook?"

A sharp bark of laughter greeted that. "You are such a guy. Long as there's a meal on the table when you come in, right? No idea how it got there."

Don straightened a bit. "I just thought—"

"Your mom is awesome, but how do you figure she was cooking you supper while she's at the diner? Of course Megan can cook. So can Talia, some of the easy stuff, anyway, and"—he twisted in the saddle to punch Don in the arm—"so can I, I'll have you know. That stew you ate last night was all me, butch."

"That was good stew."

"You're a jerk. And very lucky your sisters are cute, or I might quit."

Don settled into a comfortable lean against Griff's back. "Don't quit. I like it when you're there for supper."

Griff snorted softly. "Hang on."

He made a clicking noise at the horse and shifted his weight. She tossed her head and turned off the road. The world was suddenly uneven and swaying, and Don hugged Griff tight as the horse descended off the side of the road along a steep path. Griff took out the flashlight to brighten the way, letting the horse pick out her own footing. The rocking and extreme angle of the descent made Don tighten both arms and press himself against Griff's back as he swore under his breath.

Once off the road and under the trees, the trail leveled out to a smooth track, and Griff adjusted his light to the lantern feature and rested it on the pommel in front of him. "Any chance of letting me breathe again, there, tough guy?" he asked, patting the back of Don's hand.

"Jesus!" Don grumbled, trying to relax. Griff was warm, though, and solidly comfortable.

Griff only snorted and guided the horse to the deeper darkness under the trees overhanging the path before reining her to a halt.

"Good enough."

Don was still clinging to him, eyes squeezed tightly closed and cheek pressed to Griff's back.

"You can let go now."

Don had to force his arms to unwind and his spine to straighten.

"Get your foot in the stirrup and swing down, same as you got up."

"We're there?"

Griff laughed. "Much as I love the way you hang on, yeah, we're here."

"Where?"

"Swimming hole I found. Almost off the property, but still ours. Hop down."

Don did, nearly falling on his ass when he missed the stirrup and the ground was a lot farther away than he remembered. There was enough light filtering down from the bright full moon that he could watch Griff swing easily out of the saddle. He made it look easy and beautiful, and the sight stole Don's breath, dried his mouth. He had to swallow hard and work up enough spit to speak.

"What are we doing at a swimming hole in the middle of the night?"

"Swimming, dummy." Griff led the horse to a largish clearing and picketed her to a stake already in the ground near the center. His actions were spare and efficient, like he'd done this a million times. It took him only moments to tend to her buckles and straps before he returned to Don's side, looking into the inky-dark water. "I come out here every night when it's this hot. Don't have to pay for the water, and it's cool." He punched Don's arm. "Come on."

He hurried to the water's edge, peeling off his shirt as he went. Don watched him kick off his shoes and shuck his jeans. No socks, no underwear. He should have blisters everywhere, but all Don noticed was long, lean limbs glowing in the moonlight a few seconds before Griff ran and cannonballed into the middle of the pond.

"Come on!" he shouted as he surfaced. "It's just water!"

Just water and naked Griffith.

"Fuck," Don whispered. "Jesus fuck."

A lot more slowly than Griff, Don shed his clothes, waiting until Griff dove to kick off his shorts and jump into the water. He did not need his best friend noticing his raging boner. The shivering cold took care of his discomfort immediately, at least, and he swam out but left more than an arm's length of space between them.

"Nice, uh?" Griff said, spraying a fan of water in Don's face.

"Yeah." Don dunked his hair and came up again, shaking cascades of water out of his waves. It was nice and beautifully cool on his bare skin after a long, sticky day guiding the combine through the fields. Air-conditioned or not, the cab was stuffy and loud and it was goddamn bright in the sunshine all day. It was nice to swim in the dark. Pond water washed away the itchiness of straw dust stuck in every crease by sweat, and the darkness was soothing now that he was off the horse.

"Your teeth are chattering," Griff pointed out as he swam closer.

Big hands gripped Don's arms under the water then ran up and down in quick, firm strokes over his skin.

"Not that cold, are ya?" Griff asked.

"Nu-uh." Don shook his head and treaded water, knees knocking against Griff's.

"Good." Griff drifted even closer, keeping his hold on Don, preventing him from backing off.

"Griff—"

"Okay, so it's not very original, but I kissed you a week ago and nothing. I got tired of whacking off to that kiss and imagining—"

Crickets filled in the rest of Griff's thought.

"Imagining what?" Don asked.

"Uh… nothing. Forget it." Griff let him go and swam for shore.

"Griff! Hey!" Don paddled after him and hauled himself out of the water, reaching his friend as Griff snatched his jeans off the grass. "Hey!"

Don lunged for the jeans and tore them from Griff's hands. "Imagined what?"

Griff turned his back and for the first time since the day Don had met him, he realized Griff wasn't being the brave one.

"I—I imagine it too, you know." Don said, fumbling over the words and crumpling the denim in his hands. "With you, I mean."

"You better not be standing there in the buff and telling me you imagine it with another guy," Griff warned, trying to sound tough and glib and failing pretty miserably.

Don shook his head.

Griff didn't move.

Don would have to be brave. This once, he'd have to be the one to make the first move, and if it terrified him, it wasn't as bad as the way he'd missed Griff when he'd stayed away over the summer because of Howard.

Taking the few steps between them got easier the closer he got because Griff didn't move. He tilted his head, as though listening, and gulped when Don touched his back with his fingertips.

They were going to have sex, Don realized. It wasn't like falling into some pseudo thing with Howard. Griff was his best friend. His rock. He took the last step and wrapped his arms around Griff's waist again, laid his head on Griff's shoulder. His cock had definitely renewed its interest and pressed hard against Griff's buttcheek.

"Jesus," Griff whispered.

"Yeah."

Griff's feet shifted slightly, and Don instinctively tightened his hold. "This is happening?" Griff's soft whisper of a question clicked inside Don's head, and he pressed a cheek to his broad back.

"If you want—"

"I do. God, Don, I do. Did, have since… forever." He turned then and wrapped his own arms around Don's shoulders. His thick cock pressed next to Don's, and Don had to cling as his knees wobbled.

"You never said."

"I thought you were straight. Then you were with Howe." He pressed lips to Don's temple. "Why Howe?"

Don looked up at him, but couldn't see more than a silvery-gray image of the other young man. He didn't know how to answer the question. He didn't know if there was an answer to the question. There hadn't been a reason for being with Howard other than opportunity and comfort. Howard instantly accepted everything about Don, no need to question or wonder or try to defend all the small things that made him feel inadequate. Howard didn't feel the need to protect him or care for him; he just assumed Don could look after himself.

"He's not you," was all Don could come up with. Each of them had something the other did not. Each of them offered something the other couldn't. He rested his head against Griff's chest. "And he's not here, Griff." Lifting his head, he sought out his friend's gaze.

"No, he's not." His fingers tipped Don's head back further, resting under his chin and holding him still as he bent for a kiss.

THEY spent a lot of time that fall at their water hole, even long after it was too cold to swim anymore or make love in the open air. Wrapped in scarves and sweaters, it was still nice to sit among the fallen leaves, hold hands and find new ways to pleasure that didn't include freezing their asses off if they could help it.

Don learned to ride passably well. Griff's house was finished, finally, after five years of living in a construction zone. They bought skates and took winter rides to their pond. They taught Don's sisters to skate as the girls took over cooking and cleaning for both households. They settled into their senior year with the confidence that nothing else mattered.

Eventually Don remade his friendship with Howard. Griff didn't question it and eventually admitted he liked the older boy, despite frequently reminding the mechanic he might have been Don's first, but Griff had him now.

"You deserve him," Howard would tell him. "You can deal with that way he has to make everything perfect for everyone. I want no part of it." He'd grin and mock punch Don's shoulder. "I was just in it for the sex."

If he ever regretted peeling out of Don's life and leaving room for Griff to slip in, he never said so.

The school year passed. Another summer came and went. Don and Griff turned eighteen, graduated, and no one around them questioned their togetherness.

Childhood sweethearts, Don's sisters teased, but what was there to be offended by? That the bond had tightened so much was good. Life didn't let them stay inside that sweet new lovers' cocoon nearly long enough, and they were both glad of the support when the world crashed back in on them.

COMPLICATIONS

THE flash of white startled Don and he jolted, bringing the pickup to a crooked stop. In the headlights, the flash resolved into a horse and rider and he cursed. *Griff.*

"What the hell are you doing out here?" he muttered to himself. "Riding with a broken foot, have you lost it?"

Griff's face was sheeted in sweat and his shirttails danced in the lifting breeze. His furry chest gleamed almost as pale as the horse, unnatural and frail-looking in the closing darkness. There was no saddle on the horse, even, and Don's heart leapt at the danger of his lover trying to ride with one useless foot.

"I tried to call!" Griff shouted over the truck's engine and his horse's hooves clattering over the hard earth. He held his hand up like a phone beside his face as he galloped up.

Don shut off the engine. "What the hell are you doing out here?" he asked again.

"I tried to call," Griff repeated. He reined in beside the vehicle. "Why didn't you answer?"

"I—" Don huffed out a breath. "Sorry. I was on my way back."

Griff's cast dangled against the horse's side, useless to help him guide the animal. The horse shifted away from the bulky limb nervously.

"Would you get off the horse before you hurt yourself? What the hell is so important it couldn't wait fifteen minutes until I got home?"

A look of frustration passed over Griff's features, but he pushed it aside, swiping his hand over his face. "Don, there's been an accident."

A chill swept through Don. He'd heard that phrase too many times in his life. An accident had taken his mother when he was twenty-five. *Accident* had been the word used when Howard's brother died. It had even been bandied about over the deaths of Howard's parents, though everyone knew the ugly, unspeakable truth. *Accident* had been the word Griff used to exonerate the horrible horse that had broken his foot and nearly kicked his head in. *Accident* was a stupid, ugly, irrelevant word used when people didn't want to talk about unthinkable things.

"Who?" He wedged the word up his throat and past his lips.

"Howe, Don. Coming over the rise on Traverston Road. Asshole who hit him didn't even slow down."

"Is he—" Breath came only in short, sharp bursts that didn't do enough to keep his head from swimming.

In three heartbeats, Griff had somehow got off his horse and inside the truck next to Don. "No, babe, he isn't. Breathe, Don." Griff's hand stroked over Don's head and down his back. "Come on. Just breathe."

Don nodded, accepting the offered anchor to get his breathing under control.

"How bad?" he asked as the panic finally began to recede.

Griff pulled in a breath and settled awkwardly, sideways in the seat. "He's banged up pretty bad. Broken bones all over the place. The hospital called about an hour ago, but he was in surgery. That's all I could find out over the phone, even though we're his emergency contact."

Don nodded. Who else? Howard's parents were gone. His sister had moved to the other side of the globe to escape the confines of their small town and the gossip. His brother had taken a more permanent escape, driving the car his father had left him over the bluff the day before their funeral.

"Okay." Griff tugged on Don's hands. Don gripped the wheel with force he couldn't break by himself. Griff had to pry his fingers loose. "Here's what we're going to do. First, get out of the truck." He laced his fingers through Don's one loose hand. "Come on."

"Can't leave it here."

"Yes, you can. It's just the truck. Howe needs you—us—right now. Come on. You can ride with me. We'll go back to the house. Peter is there. We can take his car and he'll worry about the rest, okay? Come on."

Don continued to stare at the center of the steering wheel. "Griff...."

"Babe, it's going to be okay. Let me take care of this." He stroked his fingers along Don's, urging him in a soft voice to let go. "Howe needs us."

June, age nineteen

HOWARD rocked, arms wrapped around his waist, staring. What was Don supposed to say? He looked over Howard to Griff, who shrugged and ran a hand over their friend's back.

"He was drunk," Howard said quietly. "When I got home, he was pissed drunk. I told Ma to go to Aunt Jenny's. She never listens—" He swallowed hard. A fresh wave of shaking took him over and both Griff and Don moved closer, pressing against him, because what else could they do?

"The first shot woke me up." For long moments, Howard stared into the distance. "She would have screamed. If she was hurt or scared, she would have screamed." He shook his head. "She didn't scream, so I knew. I wasn't supposed to be home. None of us were, so I just stayed there up in the attic. He never looked for us there. Narrow staircase freaked him out." He lowered his head onto his knees and keened for a few minutes. "Would have shot me too," he whispered. "If he knew I was there. So I pretended…."

Silence wrapped around all three boys and eventually Howard leaned on Griff's shoulder. "After the second shot, I snuck out the window. Went to the garage and slept there."

There was more rocking as Howard rested his chin on his knees and stared ahead. "I should have done something. Called an ambulance. Not left them… like that… just…."

"No," Griff told him and, to Don's surprise, wrapped a comforting arm around the mechanic. "You couldn't have done anything but got yourself shot."

Don said nothing.

"That how you'd want to remember them, huh?"

A small, pathetic sound leaked from Howard and Griff held him tighter.

"It isn't, Howe, I promise you that." He pressed his mouth to the side of Howard's head and gazed over at Don, at a loss.

"Macy'll need you now," Don added, sliding his arm around Howard's waist as well.

Howard nodded. "Jeff wrecked the car. He didn't even wait until their funeral."

Once again, Griff and Don locked gazes over their friend's head. Howard's older brother, Jeff, had indeed wrecked the hotrod their father had left him.

"Did you notice Aunt Jenny looks so old now?" Howard asked. "She was always prettier than Ma."

Long silence.

"That was a lot of funerals for her to arrange," Howard said.

The three of them leaned closer, Don and Griff closing in around Howard as he began to sob. He slept between them that night, all three piled on Griff's bed, exchanging the kind of comfort none of them had to talk about.

IN THE morning, Griff's father sat them down at the table without a word, filled plates and, gradually, bellies with good food. He put them to work in the horse stalls mucking and spreading new hay. The work was simple, time-consuming, and hard. Lunch came and went, suppertime arrived, and Griff's kitchen was filled with Don's family, his sisters loading the table with good food and his parents keeping everyone focused.

Nineteen years old and Howard buried most of his family. Whatever residual jealousy Griff might have had over him seemed to disappear over that one night together.

The summer progressed and Howard kept his livelihood going, proving to the locals he was a far better mechanic than his father had ever been: reliable, talented, and above all, sober. Macy's boyfriend accepted a job in New Zealand, and she gladly packed up her life to follow him there, eager to leave the gossip and losses behind. Gradually, the town began to forget the tragedy that had ripped Howard's life open.

By harvest time, things had slipped into a new rhythm. Peter's small herd of alpaca began to thrive alongside their mother's sheep. His new girlfriend, Sophie, taught him everything she knew from a lifetime raising llamas on a farm three lines over.

Andrew graduated and took his first internship in a small firm in the city that specialized in green building. Don took his father's place on the combine, accepting the huge thermos of coffee and the lunch cooler from his mother with a small smile.

"It'll be fine, you know," he assured her. "I can take care of this, and Dad can rest."

She returned his smile, but the sadness underlying the expression twisted up a few strands of worry around his heart. "He'll be fine," she agreed. "He just needs some rest."

"You make sure he takes things easy. I know he wanted to overhaul the old tractor for Pete, but Howard will be by this weekend to look at it, so don't let him go too crazy."

"Donald." She smoothed her palm over her apron. "You know your father. When has he ever taken things easy? Not this time of year."

"Mom, everything is under control. You tell him I will drive the damn combine home and kick his ass if he gets up to too much. He needs to shake this thing that's making him sick."

She sighed. "Yes, dear."

Don chuckled and kissed her cheek. "All right. I have to get a move on. That hay is not going to lie down for me."

"So much like him," she said.

Not really. Don was very much not like his father. But she wanted to see the similarities, and it was easier not to argue. "Okay. I'll be back for supper."

"Be careful, sweetie, and make sure Abe has cleaned that machine thoroughly. You know how your father worries when he doesn't get a chance to inspect it himself."

"I'll make sure. He doesn't have to worry. He's the one who taught me, remember? And you can remind him of that fact too, if he gives you grief."

He left the kitchen, headed for the yard, only to find his father not resting on the porch where he'd gone after breakfast, but standing next to the combine talking to Abe, the farm's hired hand.

"Dad, what are you doing?" Don asked, swinging his lunch and coffee up onto the platform outside the cabin. "I thought we talked about this. I'll be doing all the harvesting this year."

"Just checking, son."

Don glanced at Abe, who rolled his eyes and grinned. "That's your dad, Donny." He pounded a bit of good-natured affection into Don's shoulder with his open hand and cocked his head. "I pass inspection, Mr. Jenkins?"

The man was nearly as old as Don's father and had worked for him since Don could remember. Why he never called Don Sr. by his given name and never got miffed at Don's father for rechecking his work, Don never understood.

"Always do, Abe," Don's father said. "You always do." He patted a hand on the combine's metal skin and sighed. "First harvest I'm going to miss since the year your brother Peter was born, Don, you know that?"

"You aren't missing anything, Dad. You're just not riding the combine this year. Nothing else is changing. And it's about time too. You've done it every year for twenty years. Time to pass the torch, yeah?"

He met his father's gaze and saw all kinds of thoughts pass through the gray depths. "You're a good boy, Don," was all he said as he turned and made his slow, methodical way back toward the house.

For a few minutes, Don and Abe watched him.

"He ain't movin' so good," Abe observed.

"It's his back," Don admitted. "Been giving him a lot of trouble lately. Last thing he needs is to rattle around on top of this beast eighteen hours a day for the next two weeks."

"You teach that boyfriend of yours how to run it, Donny," Abe advised. "Good idea to have backup, kiddo."

Don glanced at Abe, who was watching him speculatively. "Griff's not too keen on the whole giant tractor thing," Don reminded him. "He's got a thing about the noise and the dust and the, well, unenvironmental"— he waved his hands in the air, encompassing the combine and gas-powered air compressor Abe had been using to clean it—"thing."

"Mighty particular, ain't he?"

Abe's confused frown made Don smile. "He's got a big heart. I like that about him."

"Well, then Howard could stand to get out of that garage of his for a day or two."

Don shook his head. "That garage is saving his sanity. I wouldn't ask him to. Not yet."

"You don't think it's part of the problem?"

Don shook his head. "His father took everything from him. Most of which no one can ever replace. The garage is the one thing he's been able to take back and call his own since it happened. He needs it and I respect that."

Abe's smile grew soft. "You take good care of those boys, Don. Don't know how you do it."

It was Don's turn to frown. "We all look out for each other," he replied.

"Looks complicated from where I'm sittin', son."

"It isn't." Swinging up the ladder, Don dismissed his old friend's worries. "Howard needs us. Me and Griff, we got his back, because everyone who was supposed to love him let him down. We won't."

"Don!" The clatter of hooves on gravel stopped Don halfway up the ladder, and he looked down the drive to see Griff cantering toward them on his latest project.

This new horse was a skinny bay mare that looked too small to bear his lanky frame. What did Don know about horses, though? Griff had told him he'd found her at an auction, way underweight and looking like no one was going to buy her. He'd made an offer and the seller, glad to get her off his hands, accepted. She was a nervous sort, unable to abide anyone touching her but Griff when he'd bought her at the beginning of the season. Now, she was still too thin, but her coat was glossy and her eyes bright, and she cantered up and nuzzled at Don's shirt, nosing for a treat.

"Sorry, girl," he told her, patting her head. "You got to give me more warning if you want a treat. Now you'll have to wait. I'll come by tonight if I have time, yeah?" He scratched at her jowls, and she tossed her head gently.

Griff eased her around to get closer to Don, leaned over, and kissed him, the gesture made easy with Don on the ladder and Griff on the horse. "Just came to see you off," he said. "I can't come out today. Howard has some field calls to make. He asked if I could do a few lube jobs and oil changes for him."

"I still can't believe he talked you into this," Don said. "Mr. Green-is-better fixing cars."

Griff grinned. "Well, if they're running properly, they're better for the environment, right?"

"If you say so."

"I do. Come over for supper tonight?"

Don nodded. "Probably. Once I've checked in with Dad."

"I'm cooking. Around four? You can always go back out after if you have to."

Don smiled and reached for another kiss before agreeing, then watched Griff canter off back down the drive.

"Phone's so much faster," Abe observed.

Don grinned. "It was the kiss he was after," Don replied. "The rest was just incidental." He winked at Abe. "Though if you ask him, he'll tell you he does it for the horse."

Abe shook his head. "Complicated," he muttered as he wandered away.

DON never had a chance to meet Griff at his house. His father came rumbling through the field in his old truck around noon, joining him in the cab despite all of Don's protests.

"I'm not here to check up on your work, son," Donald Sr. said as he settled on the thicker cushion he'd brought. "This is my privilege, after all. Come to see all my lessons pay off."

Don grinned at him and started up again once his father was settled.

It was too loud to talk, and it didn't seem like his father had much to say anyway. Don worked for a few hours before breaking. He wouldn't normally stop in the middle of the day, but he could see the discomfort on his dad's face, watched his restless fidgeting, and decided to shut down for a few minutes and a cup of coffee.

"Why are you really out here, Dad?"

Don Sr. smiled into the tin cup Don had handed him, sipped, and then glanced up to return the calculating look he must have noticed in Don's expression. "You know I'm proud of you, son."

Narrowing his eyes, Don nodded. "I know."

"Not as young as I used to be."

"Dad?"

"Your brothers, Don, they have their paths set out. Andrew's job at that architectural firm in the city makes him happy. That girl of his, and her son." His father's face crumpled into a soft smile. "He dotes on the boy like he was his own flesh and blood."

Don nodded. "Mark's a good kid." He clasped his father's shoulder briefly. "And Andrew takes after you, doesn't he? Just accepting things the way they are and making it right for folks. He loves Alicia, you know. They're a good couple."

Don Sr. nodded. "He does. They are. And Pete hasn't said anything, but I'm sure he's going to accept Sophie's father's offer to manage his place. She loves those camels—"

"Llamas, Dad."

His father sipped and waved a hand. "Fur factories." But an indulgent smile played about his lips. "Overgrown goats. And he's had some success with the alpacas. 'Bout time they merged those herds."

Don chuckled at his father's euphemism. "You're probably right, though he'll say yes because she wants to keep her parents' business going."

"And it's a good business, and he should say yes. That's what a man does. He sticks by his partner."

So effortlessly, he had been led out onto the shaky ground of his less-than-conventional love life. "Sure," he said, attempting to keep the conversation neutral and safe.

"If I'm going to, Don, I have to start thinking of selling up."

"Selling?" Shock zinged through Don and his coffee sloshed. "Why would you sell?"

"I'm old, boy. Rickety. Three hours on this beast and I think I've jostled a few bones loose already. I can't do this anymore."

"Well, I can!" *And you're not old*! he wanted to say, but bit his lip to keep the protest against time silent.

"But do you want to? For the rest of your life, is this really what you want? What Griff wants? Or Howard?"

"I don't… know what they want." He frowned and licked drips of cooling coffee off his fingers. "But it's what I want, and it's who I am." He braced himself and met his father's steady, waiting gaze. "I'm not a very complicated man. I'm a farmer. This is my home."

"And family?"

He shrugged. "Don't sell my farm," was all he said.

It elicited a heavy sigh from his father, and for a few more minutes, they sat silently, watching the cloud shadows drift across shorn fields.

"Don, you only just graduated from high school. There is a whole world of colleges and experiences out there for you. You might meet someone. You might want kids…."

"Dad." Don set his now-empty cup down and picked up the thermos, turning it over in his hands, searching for the right words. "I'm not ever going to get married. You know this, right?"

His father chucked Don's chin and snorted. "Have you told Griff this? That boy might have something to say about that."

Their gazes met and Don broke into a grin. "Okay. So we're clear. I don't need college or experiences out there." He waved an arm at the windshield. "I have everything I need right here. The best teacher I could ever ask for, a home, family, friends." Heat crept softly into his cheeks and his smile warmed. "Love. I don't need anything else. Remember what you told me about you and Mom getting together? That's all I've ever wanted, and I have that."

"Things are so different now, Don. The world is complicated."

"I'm a pretty simple guy, Dad," he said again.

His father's expression grew serious. "And have you mentioned that fact to Howard?"

Don dropped his gaze. "Dad, I know it looks weird from the outside, but it isn't complicated at all, okay?"

"Don, I'm not about to judge. Believe me. I just don't want to see any one of you boys get hurt. It's a small town. People talk, and you all need to be able to do business."

That was a fact Don was well aware of.

"Howard's already doing better business than he did when his father ran that place. You know that as well as I do, and not one of us has tried to pretend we are anything other than what we are. If people were going to find another mechanic, they would have by now."

His father nodded minutely. "You didn't think any of this through."

"Dad—"

"I don't remember being this young, Donny." He smiled. "Or this brave." He patted Don's knee and used it to leverage himself to his feet. "Okay. You win. I'll be meeting with a lawyer later this week, and I'll fix up my will."

"Dad!" Don shot to his feet.

"Oh, relax. I'm not on my way out yet, son." He let out a slight, deflated sigh. "This past month, though... I don't shake things off like I used to. Anything can happen. I want things in place. You've got a lot to learn before I leave this place to you. And know right now that I'll be looking after every one of your siblings, and this place is all I have to leave anyone. You'll have to share."

Don nodded dumbly, processing the sudden fear, the spike of adrenaline, and the watery-around-the-edges relief before he found enough saliva to actually speak. "Of course."

"Good." Don Sr. turned to back down the ladder, but he stopped at the top and smiled once more at his youngest son. "You're a good boy, Don. I told you, didn't I? You'd fill out one day."

Don couldn't help glancing down at his thin, wiry frame and snorting. "Sure, Dad. Still waitin' on that one."

His father just grinned and climbed off the machine. "Back to work, boy!" he called up. "This hay isn't going to lie down all on its own!"

Don laughed and waved him off, cleaned up their coffee break, and settled back into his pilot's chair. He'd just been handed a torch of some sort. He wasn't sure if he was proud or terrified. The thought kept his mind busy long after his four o'clock dinner date, though.

Maybe that conversation with his father, the newfound sense of responsibility, the realization that he *did* want what his father had, was what kept him preoccupied so much he forgot about it. He wanted that fairy-tale life, the one he'd grown up in. He wanted it for Griff. For Howard. God knew Howard deserved the fairy tale, more now than ever.

When Griff's Jeep kicked up a cloud of dust down the laneway a few hours later and he noticed the rapidly descending dusk, Don parked the combine and climbed down to meet the vehicle.

"Hey!" He waved as Griff pulled up next to his truck. "Griff, I'm sorry—"

Griff grinned at him. "It's fine. I saw your dad coming back around three-thirty. I was dropping Howard off. He wanted to stay out here for the weekend, and not at his apartment." He shrugged as he hopped out of the Jeep. "Guess he's not used to all the quiet, yet. He's helping Pete feed alpacas."

Don nodded, watching as Griff swung around and pulled a cooler from the back of his vehicle. "Brought supper to you."

"I'm done now," Don said. "We can go back."

Griff gave him a huge smile. "No, I brought supper to you." He set the cooler down and went back for a blanket and his portable cassette player. "Spread this out somewhere, will you?" He retrieved the cooler and began to walk toward the shaded area near the field's edge. "It's quiet out here. No sisters, no parents." He glanced over his shoulder. "No Howe. I mean I love the guy, but sometimes just you and me is nice."

Don nodded and followed, found a relatively flat area free of sharpened wheat stubble, and spread out the blanket.

Supper was thick sandwiches—roast beef still warm from the oven and spiked with just the right amount of horseradish—and beers, nicely chilled from the ice, with sliced-up fruit to finish it all off. Simple. Perfect. And quickly devoured by two very hungry young men. Not a lot of conversation passed between them. Not a lot had to be said.

The quiet continued when the beer and sandwiches were finished and Griff pressed play on the tape he'd brought. Country music love songs floated on the evening air, barely heard over the sounds of kissing, then moaning, and eventually, soft, needful cussing as both young men fought with too many clothes.

Don barely felt the occasional itch of a mosquito bite over the throbbing of his pulse just under his skin. He didn't care about the hard ground or the scratch of the wool blanket when Griff's bigger, weightier body crushed him into the earth. All he knew was hot need, hard cock, and calloused hands sweeping over every inch of skin, abrading sensitive areas, not nearly strong enough on his own toughened, work- and weatherworn arms and legs.

"Griff." He bucked, shoving hips and cock hard against Griff's. He didn't have enough leverage with his legs pinned together under Griff's straddle. He couldn't get enough friction or pressure.

"Got a plan," Griff assured him, fumbling for his discarded jeans. "Brought something." He pulled out a small tube Don couldn't read in the dim light.

"What?"

"Lube." There was a grin in Griff's voice.

Don didn't have even the slightest chance to protest. The cap hit his chest and bounced away and Griff shimmied down his legs. A second later, his lover's wet, cold hand engulfed his cock and he cursed, sharp and shocked.

"Fucking hell! That's cold!"

Griff only snorted back laughter and slathered on more lube. "Need lots," he informed Don.

The tube made a wheezing splat as he pinched the last drops out and reached behind himself. Fascinated by the gesture, and his imagined image of what was going on back there, Don forgot about the breeze cooling his erection, the bugs, and the bumpy ground. His mind filled with images of Griff's thick fingers up his ass, and he dropped his head onto the blanket.

"Fucking hell," he groaned.

Griff huffed out a few breaths. His hips gyrated. The muscles in his forearm bunched and released, and Don had to cup his balls and bite his lip to keep himself from demanding to see, touch, feel, anything.

"You ready?" Griff asked, voice breathless with excitement.

Don nodded. "Yeah. Shit, Griff."

Griff shuffled on his knees back up Don's legs until he was positioned and his cheeks closed around Don's cock.

They both let out soft gasps—half surprise, half pleasure—as the tip of Don's prick put pressure on Griff's opening.

"Wait." Don almost pushed Griff off him, suddenly unsure. "Shouldn't we have… protection?"

Griff grinned down at him. "Never done this, Donny. Not with anyone." His eyebrows slammed down over his eyes. "You?"

Don shook his head. "Not this. Not anything more than you and I have done." He felt heat flood his cheeks. "Howard," he said, clipping the name off when Griff's scowl deepened.

Then his lover's face cleared and his smile was back, softer than before. "Yeah. Howe." He leaned down and kissed Don hard and full, delving his tongue deep into Don's mouth before sitting back up. "But not this."

The reminder that the last few months had changed a great deal of things for all three of them washed through Don, and he cupped Griff's face in his hands. "You sure you want to? With me?"

Griff lifted a shoulder and pulled in a deep breath. "Wanna try."

Don nodded and placed both hands on Griff's hips. "'Kay, then. Me too."

However this was supposed to go, it was quickly evident Griff hadn't anticipated the reality.

"Oh Jesus! How do people do this?" He gasped and fought against Don's hold, lifting himself before more than the barest tip of Don's cock had entered him.

"Forget it." Don scrambled up to sitting, pulling his legs free of Griff as he pushed the other man back. "Babe, we don't have to."

"It was my idea," Griff muttered, head down, the flush in his cheeks visible even in the darkening evening.

"It's okay," Don insisted, running a hand along Griff's tense shoulder.

Griff straightened and pulled up straight, away from Don's touch. "No, it's not. I want to be—" He flushed even deeper, but held Don's gaze. "I want to be that guy, Don."

Don almost laughed but managed to hold it back. "That guy?"

"Fuck you." Griff pushed himself away from Don, flopped onto his ass, and pulled his feet up tight to his body, hiding his flaccid cock, and wrapping his arms around his knees.

"What guy, Griff? The one who punches out bullies for me? Teaches me to ride and swim and skate and brings me supper in the field and offers—" Don held out both hands toward Griff's naked form—"this? Jesus, Griff, you already *are* that guy."

"I wasn't your first," he whispered, turning his head so Don couldn't see his face.

"We're gonna have a whole fucking lifetime of firsts, Griff, I swear. You and me."

"And Howard?"

Howard. This was about Howard.

Don crawled across the blanket, closing the space between them. He wrapped his legs around Griff, getting as close as possible, Griff's toes under his ass cheeks. "Remember the night? The first time on your bed?" Don asked softly.

Griff nodded, lips clamped tight shut.

"You held him all night, Griff. You kissed him first. Did I get mad? Did I say no?"

Griff shook his head.

"None of us did."

"I know," Griff whispered.

"If we're having a conversation about Howard, we should be having it *with* Howard."

"Soon as we talk about it, it gets too complicated."

"It doesn't have to be." Don smiled and tried to tug Griff's arms loose and wiggle into his lap.

"Don." Griff hugged him, kissed his neck, and buried his face under the fringes of his dark hair. "Only you could think what we're doing is not complicated."

"It isn't."

"Stubborn," Griff whispered. "It's complicated. Messy. He loves you."

Don straightened. "That bugs you."

"Shouldn't it?"

Don shook his head, but studying Griff's face, he saw doubt and it shook him. "I love you, Griff."

"And Howard?"

Don watched Griff's face. "What do you want me to say?"

Griff pulled back, insulating himself with acres of space on the corner of the blanket, even though only a foot separated them. "The truth, Don. I want you to tell me the truth."

"The truth." Don slumped, cross-legged in front of Griff. "No, you want me to tell you I don't love him."

"Wish I'd never kissed him," Griff lamented, dropping his forehead to his knees.

Don shook his head, scooted closer, and touched his lover's cheek. "Don't say that, Griff. You don't really wish that."

"How would you know?"

"Baby, because I know you. You kiss people for the same reasons you punch them."

"What?" Griff lifted his face, and to Don's horror, tears stained cheeks splotched with color under his stubble.

Don cupped his cheek, kissed him, tender as he could. Griff's fingers were warm as he smoothed them down over Don's cheek. Don let his eyes drift closed and there, behind his lids, was the image he'd carried with him for months. The memory of Griff's fingers tracing through Howard's tears, Griff's lips on Howard's, Howard's desperate gaze, and Griff's soothing, gentle touch, calming him, claiming him, keeping him.

He'd always thought seeing Griff kiss someone else would kill something inside him. It hadn't in the least. Everything he'd wanted to give Howard, Griff had given the man first, and Don hadn't been able to find a word of protest for any of it. But seeing Griff struggle with it cut deep.

"Babe," Don said, pulling back just enough to free his lips for speaking, "I love that you saved him. I love that you did that for him." He caressed Griff's cheek. "I love you."

"I didn't save—"

"Yes, Griff, you did. You do. Every time you cover at the shop for him. Every time you smile at him. You think he's around because of me, but you're wrong. He loves you too. I see it when he looks at you. You could have kept the wall up that night, but you didn't. Babe, you folded him into your world and let him know he could count on you, and of course that means something to him. He doesn't know what to do about it anymore than we do, but we'll figure it out."

"How can you…?"

Don smiled. "You punched out a kid for me. Why?"

Griff shrugged. "Didn't like the look of him. Any guy who pushes a kid over just because he can deserves to know what it feels like. He hurt you."

"You didn't know me."

Griff grinned. It wavered, fell, and came back, this time held long enough to make it to his eyes. "I *did* like the look of you." He shrugged. "Even on your ass on the floor I knew you would never hit him back. You don't hit back. Someone had to do it for you." Another shrug. "I elected me."

Don smiled at him. "And you punched out Howard's terror of being alone." Don smiled. "One punch, one kiss—"

"Lot more than one kiss, Donny."

"Whatever."

"You honestly think we can do this."

"We are doing it."

"People are going to think we're crazy."

Don shrugged and reached for his pants. "People can think whatever the fuck they want. It's not complicated and it's not confusing and it's not crazy. It just is."

Griff remained quiet and naked, watching Don sort out his boxers from his jeans.

"I know what you want me to say, you know," Don said, focusing on his busy work.

"I only want you to say you don't love him if it's true that you really don't," Griff insisted.

When Don did look up, he saw Griff's terror of the truth. He crumpled his jeans into his lap. "Actually, you want me to say *you* don't love him. Because it's scary knowing you love two people. Thinking one of them might leave you over it. Sharing." He swallowed hard and dared to meet Griff's gaze. "It's terrifying," he whispered.

Griff nodded.

Silence between them, filled with crickets and breezes and uncertainty.

Finally, Griff moved, crawling forward and pushing Don to his back on the blanket. "Nothin' wrong with being scared," Griff said, plastering the words to Don's skin with kisses.

"You love him," Don said, blending his voice with the hum of insects.

Griff nodded against his neck. "Tried to hate him for a while," he confessed. "Didn't take."

Don smiled up at the emerging stars. "See how uncomplicated that is?" he asked.

"I will never understand you."

"That's okay." Don threaded fingers through Griff's blond locks and squirmed under him as kisses grew adamant and words lost importance. There was nothing on earth less complicated than making love and they did, long after it got dark and the day's warmth dissipated.

ALWAYS GETTING HURT

"REMEMBER when Howe's folks died, Don, and you looked after him?" Griff asked, nuzzling close, stubble rubbing against Don's neck. "We took care of him. We kept him with us." Wet heat trickled against Don's skin.

"Griff?"

Griff sniffled and straightened, wiping his hand across his face. "Come on. Get on the damn horse." He shuffled across the seat and pushed the door open, hopping down on his good foot before Don could stop him.

"Griff!" Scrambling to catch up, Don shoved his own door open and jumped out. "Hey!"

"Help me get on the horse!" Sharp anger sliced the words at Don and he flinched. The horse stepped away from the biting tone, hooves skittering on gravel.

"What's going on?" Don asked, reaching to steady the animal, confused by Griff's abrupt change in demeanor.

The horse danced to the side, stomping and snorting at them, and Griff cuffed it gently on the neck. "Stop," he admonished, though the animal ignored him and kept prancing sideways, swinging its hind end around toward the sheer ditch edge.

"Enough!" Griff shouted, drawing his hand back again.

"Griffith!" Don intercepted another cuff. It wasn't hard, not meant to do more than get the horse's attention, but there was something wild, off-kilter in Griff's eyes, and it scared Don.

Griff's arm strained against his hold. His eyes blazed. His throat worked.

"Talk to me, babe," Don said softly, ruthlessly boxing away his worry over Howard and redirecting his concern to Griff. "Come on. You can't punch this one out. Talk."

"He keeps getting hurt, Don."

"Okay." Don nodded. Gently, he pried Griff's fist from the horse's reins and used the truck's running board to get onto the animal's back. He held out a hand and braced to give Griff the needed support to mount behind him. "We'll look after him, just like you said, right? Like we always have."

August, age twenty-seven

HOWARD'S shop was a shambles. Tool trays had been overturned, shelves thrown down, car parts scattered across the stained concrete.

"Jesus, is that blood?" Griff asked, staring at the dark splatters. "Howe!" He pushed through the mess toward the back of the bays, shoving shelving units aside and kicking wrenches and sockets from underfoot as he went. "Howe, goddammit!"

Don followed silently. It wasn't blood. It was grease, or used oil. *Howard*! He screamed the name in his head, afraid if he even tried to use his voice, nothing would come out past the fear.

A muffled thump reached them through the sound-insulated floor above.

"Howe!" Griff shouted louder, hurried his steps, catapulting a rolling tool chest halfway across the garage bay to get it out of his path to the stairs.

The apartment door was closed and locked. Griff pounded on it, both fists turned battering ram and leaving definite dents in the security steel.

"You're going to break something," Don said quietly, slithering and shoving to put himself between the door and his boyfriend. He got his keys out and the door opened before Griff could do any more damage to it, or himself.

The apartment, at least, didn't look like it had been disturbed.

A few dark spatters trailed across the living room hardwood, through the kitchen, and disappeared under the bathroom door.

"Howard?" Don called, deliberately keeping his voice low and a hand on Griff's heaving chest to hold the big man in check. He'd charge through the apartment, clumsy, bullish, to get to Howard, and Don sensed the closed bathroom door was a sign Howard was not prepared for that blunt an approach. "Howard, you here?"

The knob to the bathroom door wiggled, turned, and the door swung partway open.

"Griff, you gotta not freak out," Howard said. His voice was simultaneously thick and nasal. Like he was speaking through swollen lips and a broken nose, Don guessed, without having to see their lover.

"What the hell happened?" Griff demanded, pushing the door all the way open with one hand and dragging Don out of his way with the other. "Let me in there."

"Griff." Don tried to keep him back, but Griff was bigger and far more determined and almost slipped by before Don managed to plant himself in the bathroom doorway.

"Howard, what happened?"

"Crossed signals," Howard said.

Don fought against anger as he turned to face Griff and hold him back as well. "Go get ice, Griff."

His lover growled and pushed against Don's restraining hands on his chest. "Get out of the way."

"Griff, go in the fucking kitchen and get some fucking ice." He kept his voice low, neutral, though the fury battering his insides came out in curses and intensity. "Please."

With a snarl and a raised finger at the open door behind which Howard hid, Griff spun and stomped back to the kitchen.

Don entered the bathroom and closed and locked the door behind him. He turned, braced himself, and took a look at Howard's bloodied face. "Jesus," he whispered.

"Not as bad as it looks," Howard assured him.

Don shook his head. "What did you do, Howard?"

His friend tried to grin, winced instead, and slumped onto the edge of the bathtub. "Doesn't matter."

"Shit, asshole, someone trashed your shop and your face. It matters."

This time, Howard managed a smile on half of his face. "I swear he was checking me out," he said. "Coming onto me, even. All I did was suggest—"

Don shook his head, held up a hand. "I suggest, Howard, you don't tell Griff you propositioned some random customer." He seethed a moment in silence. "Fucking *asshole*," he muttered under his breath.

Howard's shoulders slumped. "Why does he get any say in who I sleep with anymore? Why do either of you?"

Don turned on the taps, wet a cloth, and crouched in front of Howard. "Because clearly, you can't pick them yourself," he replied, acidly sarcastic as he pressed the cloth to an open cut above Howard's left eyebrow. "And because we love you."

"We love you," Howard mocked.

Don had a momentarily overwhelming urge to hit the man. He pressed the cloth to the cut and glared at the seeping blood and forced the impulse back.

Howard winced, pulled away, and Don spread a hand over the back of his head to hold him in place.

"That hurts!"

"Yes, it fucking hurts," Don spat at him, loosing just a fraction of his anger, but keeping his gaze fixed on the cut. He didn't dare look into Howard's eyes. He didn't dare. What would he see there that he didn't want to acknowledge? What would he see that continually drove Howard from him and Griff to strangers and one-night stands and months on end of distance and silences broken only by professional contact?

The door handle rattled. The latch clanked, and they heard the sigh of material against wood, the thump of a body softly impacting solid barrier, and Griff's even softer exhalation. "I'll pack some clothes, Howe," he said a moment later. "You're coming home. Ice is on the table out here."

"I live here," Howard muttered and dropped his gaze when Don glared at him.

"Who was it?" Don asked after Griff's footsteps died away across the apartment.

Howard shook his head.

"You're not going to the cops?"

"And say what? I hit on a guy."

"Oh fuck, Howard, that is not a fucking crime." Though it made Don furious to hear Howard's injuries blamed on bigotry, showing attraction to another man was not a beating offense. "Trashing your shop and beating you up is a crime, though, and you need to press charges."

Still he shook his head. "I can't tell you, Don."

"Why?"

"Because it doesn't matter. And if I tell you, you'll tell him"—he pointed to the closed door and, presumably, Griff on the other side of it—"and he'll go all batshit on the guy, and then Griff's the one going to jail. I won't—"

"You fucking—" Don clamped his lips shut, head shaking, hands shaking, body quivering with the effort of holding back a string of vitriol. "Of course he'd defend you."

"He shouldn't."

Don clenched his teeth and felt the muscle in his jaw popping as he ground his molars. Silence reigned as he continued to bathe away the blood on Howard's face. "Eight years," Don said finally, pushing his voice just to a stage whisper so Howard could hear. "Eight years they've been dead, Howard. When the hell are you going to get it through your thick skull it wasn't your fault?"

"What are you talking about?" Howard yanked his head free of Don's touch, gripped his own nose, and straightened it with a vicious twist of his fingers. For a few seconds, he swayed, then reached out an arm, blindly searching for something to hold onto as his eyes watered and spilled over.

"Oh God." He slumped forward and Don caught him, easing him onto the floor and wrapping his arms around him. "That hurt."

Don stroked fingers through Howard's hair, delicately picking through the tangles matted by blood and pressing his lips to his friend's crown, waiting out the shaking and moaning. He swallowed a few times, forcing anger, fear, helplessness down, down, down into his gut where it wouldn't impede his speech.

"Stop doing this to yourself," Don whispered, unsure if Howard would be able to hear him this time. "Stop trying to punish yourself for what you couldn't control. What your father did, what Jeff did, none of it had anything to do with you. Whatever they were thinking, I mean we'll never, ever know what they were thinking. And Macy left because she couldn't handle it, and that's okay too. But that's about her."

"It didn't happen to you. You can't understand."

"It didn't happen to you, either, Howard," Don said, pushing him to see into his eyes. "You're still here. With us. Let us make this right."

"You think you can fix things," Howard said. "You can't. You can't make this easy or even better. You can't build a perfect life for everyone and just expect them to agree you know best."

Don furrowed his brow. "I'm not trying to build anything perfect. I'm just trying to love you. Help you. You had a crappy family. Doesn't mean that all you deserve is crap."

Howard shoved Don away, knocking him on his ass and into flimsy vanity doors, and pushed himself up. He grappled until his hands gripped the edge of the tub, and he pulled himself up onto it. "I *loved* my family, asshole! I *loved* them! They weren't perfect, but they were mine." He pounded a hand on his chest. "I just want that back. I want something that's *mine!*"

Don stared up at him, unable to breathe through his shock and the pain radiating up his arm from his elbow where it had gone through the pressboard door.

Behind him, there was a cracking sound, a breeze, and then Griff's forbidding presence. The door handle landed on the floor next to him as Griff reached down and pulled him up, putting his wide frame between Don and Howard. "I'll fix the damn door later." He tossed the bag he'd packed at Howard's feet and waved an arm around, indicating the blood in the sink, on the floor, even, somehow, the garage below. "You have what's *yours*, Howe. Congratulations. Much joy." He turned and bundled Don out of the room. "Let's go."

"Griff...." Don tried to protest, but he didn't know what he was protesting, exactly.

"I didn't mean—" Howard began, but Griff spun and pointed a thick finger at him.

"We have tried, Howard. We've tried, over and over, to give you something better than this. You keep taking off, sleeping around, fucking over everything we wanted for us. So screw you. Next time you get your head beat in for trying it on with the wrong guy, call your dead fucking mother to come clean you up."

"Griff!" Don tried to turn, demand he apologize, but Griff clamped a hand over his bicep and forced him through the kitchen, the living room, and out the door.

"Enough," he growled. "I've had enough. Ungrateful son of a bitch can have his trashed shop and his broken nose and his ruined life." He slammed the apartment door behind them and hurried down the stairs, propelling Don before him. "He can't break your heart again. Enough is enough."

Silence drowned any thought of conversation on the drive home. They went in the house and up to bed without speaking. Once darkness closed around them, though, they reached, touched, and clung.

They tried to make love, but neither of them came anywhere near erect and it quickly degenerated into kisses pecked out in the quiet, caresses fumbled with trembling fingers over skin clammy with the sweat of fear and failure, until restless sleep finally crowded in.

It didn't last.

The bed shifted for the umpteenth time and Don rolled onto his back. "Griff?"

He heard only shuffling beside him and reached over to find his lover's pillow indented, warm, but empty. He sat up. "Griff?"

Griff sat on the edge of the bed, fully clothed, hands clasped between his knees, elbows on his thighs. He reached down and picked up a boot.

"It's"—Don picked up the clock and peered at the glowing numbers—"three-thirty in the morning. What are you doing?"

Griff stuffed his foot into his boot and stomped it lightly into place. Still silent, he bent to tie the laces.

"Let me get my jeans," Don said quietly. "And leave a note for Dad. He can call the boys to come and look after the animals until we get back." Don's nephews would make sure everything that needed to get done got done.

Griff nodded and started on his other boot.

They didn't have to talk as they left the house and got in the truck. Griff drove back to Howard's, and they weren't surprised to see all the lights on, in the shop and apartment alike.

"Never could abide the dark after…." Griff trailed off.

"Come on." Don opened his door and fished out his keys. He'd only inserted them into the office door lock when it opened and Howard stared out at them.

For what seemed like forever, they all three stood staring at each other. Finally, Howard moved aside and waved them in, then closed and locked the door behind them.

Without a word, Howard returned to what he'd been doing—sorting through a messy pile of oil filters. Some he placed back on the righted shelf, some he tossed into a box, and others into a pile on the floor beside him.

Griff joined him and began sorting, setting the good filters on the shelf and the ruined ones in the box. Howard reached past him, removed the first ripped filter Griff had tossed in the box, and chucked it into the pile. Griff reached into the box and pulled out a filter.

"Tractor," he muttered, and put it back.

It was the only word any of them spoke all night.

By the time the sun crested the rooftops across the street, the shop was back in some semblance of order, the ruined parts and broken tools inventoried and marked for replacement. The whole night passed in silence, and Don reflected that it spoke volumes as to how well they knew each other after eight years of patchwork love and trials, how well they could communicate when they wanted to, that they could have done it all without a word spoken between them.

Don let out an exhausted sigh and faced the others.

"Thanks," Howard said softly, studying the scuffed toes of his boots.

Don smiled and cupped his face, trying to get him to look up. "Home?" he asked.

But Howard shook his head and shuffled out of his reach. "I live here, Donny." He lifted his face. "Okay?"

No. Not okay, even remotely, but what could he do?

"Howe—" Griff tried to impose his own will, but Don touched his arm.

"Griff." Howard shook his head and moved even farther from them. "I live here, like you said. This is my life."

"Bullshit," Griff whispered, stricken.

Howard shook his head. "No it isn't. You're right. Not about me being ungrateful, because I can never be grateful enough for what you've done for me. But about me creating something here apart from you guys. Something that's mine."

"Jesus, Howard." Don closed the space widening between them and reached. "No."

"Yes, Donny." He twisted his lips until he found something like a smile, but it was as sad and fucked up as the life he claimed he wanted.

"Don't do this."

"I'm closing shop today," Howard said, moving back to the bottom of the steps to his apartment. "I need to get some sleep. Thanks for helping me clean up. I'll call you about the old tilling tractor Pete wants, and we'll set something up later in the week if you can wait that long. I think I found a source for parts."

"The tractor? Really?"

"It's what I do, Don. That's my job."

"I don't give a shit about your damn job!"

"It's all I have!"

Don turned on his heel and hurried for the garage door, but he could hear Griff's angry voice behind him.

"And here I promised him I wouldn't let you break his heart anymore."

"Well, then you should be happy about this."

"You don't get it," Griff almost shouted.

Howard snorted. "Actually, I think I'm the only one of us who does. Go home with him, Griff. Be happy you punched out another demon for him. He needs that. I don't."

Don shook his head. Stupid Howard. He needed that more than anyone Don knew. But he was a stubborn jerk. And despite everything, what his father had done to him had never healed. Well. Everyone Howard had loved had hurt him, left him in the most horrible way possible. How could he be expected to trust anyone after that?

Don flung open the truck door and slammed it closed once he was in. A few moments later, Griff joined him, quietly closing his door and starting the engine.

"Griff—"

"Give him time, Don."

"For what? To hang himself?"

Griff shuddered. "We won't let that happen. He can push us out of his garage. He can't make us stop caring." His chin jutted and he spread his arm over the back of the seat to see behind the truck and back away from the garage. "I decide who I love and who I don't, and he'll just have to deal with it."

Don found a smile at the bottom of the pit he seemed to be floundering in, and he glanced at Griff. "I love you."

Griff kissed him, long and fierce, and then pulled the truck around and out of the lot.

EMPTY TABLE SETTINGS

"ARE you next of kin?" a nurse asked.

"Do we look like next of kin?" Don retorted. "We're his family. What room is he in?"

"Don." Griff took his hand and clamped down tight, squeezing his fingers uncomfortably. "His sister has been notified," he informed the nurse. "She's his only living relative and she's in New Zealand. We are his emergency contact." He pulled a folded sheaf of papers out of his pocket. "We also have power of attorney for personal care."

Breath whooshed out of Don's lungs. "What? Why did you bring the papers here?" He grabbed Griff's arm and yanked him around to face him, squeezing back the oozing fear to get words up his throat and past the constriction. "I thought you said he was okay."

"Shh." Griff squeezed tighter. "Trust me."

The nurse didn't insist on seeing the documents once she'd taken in Don's reaction. "Okay, honey. Come on." She patted his shoulder and gently turned him around. "We have enough trouble with this sort of situation. People coming in, demanding to see loved ones they haven't had contact with in years, trying to keep partners out. They think the middle of a crisis is the time to undermine loving relationships they don't approve of." She shook her head, a fierce scowl on her face. "Makes me want to kick a few asses, and you'd think, these days, it would be different." She rubbed a soothing hand over Don's back and offered a small, understanding smile. "My mistake. You do look a lot like him. You understand. I had to make sure you have his best interests at heart."

Don glanced between her and Griff. "Can I see him now?"

"Of course. Come on."

She led them down the bright hallways, into an elevator, and up two floors. "This is the nurses' station for this floor," she told them when they arrived at the station on the third floor. "These boys are here to see Mr. Campbell." She smiled at the nurse on duty. "Everything is in order."

The duty nurse nodded curtly. "Thanks. You know you don't always have to walk everyone up."

"I know." Their guide smiled at them, tilted her head at her co-worker, and gave her uniform a little tug. "You do your job your way, and I'll do it mine, sweetheart." She turned to Don and Griff. "He's in room 315. He might be sleeping, so let him rest. He's had a hard day."

Griff snorted. "You think?"

Her smile was still kind and patient. "Your friend is a lucky man, escaping with some broken bones and bruises. But he has a long recovery ahead of him. So be kind to him."

"Always," Griff promised.

December, age twenty-seven

DON sniggered as his sisters jostled for position around the Christmas table. It was Katie's first Christmas back home from university in Waterloo. The first year after their mother's death, she hadn't been able to bear coming home for the holidays, and her sisters had gone to her. It had been more a sad occasion than a happy one, and they were determined not to repeat the experience.

This year, it was traditional Christmas Eve dinner, just as their mother would have done, and with a flair that would have made her proud. Everyone was present, including Mark, Andrew's adopted stepson who had at last, at eighteen years old, given up on his birth father making any real time for him, even over the holidays. All five women argued happily over place settings.

Griff plopped down on the couch next to Don and handed him a beer. "He should be here."

So almost everyone had come.

Don leaned and kissed Griff's cheek in reply. What could he say?

"It's Christmas." Griff plucked at the label on his bottle. "We're really going to just sit and wait for him to call? Hope he's not sitting alone in his apartment getting plastered?"

"I invited him." Don settled against the couch cushions at his back and let out a breath. "There's only so much I can do, Griff. I asked him to come. If you want me to, I'll call again. I'll beg." He'd do whatever he could to get this look of loneliness off his lover's face. Even ignore the way it ate into his heart to know he wasn't enough.

"I should go drag his sorry ass over is what I should do. Enough is enough already. It's been what? Four months? He proved his point. He doesn't need us. I get it. Now he should just accept what's real."

Don smiled, but shook his head and wrapped himself in steel to not feel the hurt of failing them both. "He'd fight you tooth and nail and you know it." And it would be another nail in the coffin of the relationship between the two most important people in Don's life. He was out of ideas. Nothing he'd thought of had fixed the fight they'd had over Howard's wrecked garage and indiscriminate behavior.

"I am so sick of pandering to this idea of his," Griff muttered. "He's our family. He should be here."

Don shook his head and rubbed a hand over Griff's back. All the strength in those broad muscles and his lover could not hold on to Howard and keep him from slipping further away. "You can't fight this for him, Griff." Neither of them could, but Griff didn't believe in anything he couldn't punch out.

"You don't know that. Maybe I could. If he would just talk to us and tell us what's really going on."

Don smiled sadly at his partner's back. Griff was so convinced there was a way to just fight off every bad thing that ever happened to anyone he loved. No one but Howard could fight off whatever was going on inside his own head, though, and Griff hated to admit that there was nothing he could do. Through the months that had passed since the fight, they'd had such little contact with Howard it was impossible to tell if he was getting any better at all. Frightening to think he might be getting worse.

He let his gaze wander through the room, taking in his family: sisters, brothers, nieces, nephews, and even the strays Griff had collected. A slinky, beautiful border collie that knew horses almost as well as Griff did curled by the front door. Abe, who both Griff and Don's father insisted should be a part of the family meal after all these years, sat in the most comfortable chair in the room. And sweet, shy young Albert Hawthorn, of all people, whose presence was down to his new job working on Griff's horse farm as well as apprenticing with Abe, sat quietly in one corner, taking in the chaos. Soon after Howard's beating, the younger man had appeared on the doorstep, and Griff, unable to turn away anyone who needed help, not even the younger brother of Don's childhood tormentor, had brought him into the fold as he would any stray, human or animal, who had nowhere else to go.

It was obvious to anyone who looked at him or spoke to him that Albert was gay. Don shuddered to think how his bigoted father and brother would react to that knowledge. A decade and more later, time had not tempered either of them. The McAllister/Jenkins farms were his safe haven, and Don thought it fitting to share his sanctuary with the young man. It was the best revenge he could think of to visit on the older Hawthorn brother.

Don watched as Megan yielded her fight to sit next to their father and instead, placed her nametag between Sophie and her youngest, Alex. She smiled sweetly at her sister-in-law. "For tonight, you don't have to wear Alex's supper, Soph."

Peter hugged first his sister, then his wife, then scooped up said son and spun him toward the kitchen. Alex giggled hysterically as he was twirled away to find a snack.

"You don't have to, Megan. He is my kid."

"Maybe I want to sneak my peas onto his plate," Megan replied.

Sophie laughed. "Make sure he doesn't have a straw handy. You can thank your brothers for showing him peas fit in his sippy cup straw. I'm still finding them under my couch." She mock-glared over at Don, who held up his hands in innocence.

Admittedly, he had taught his nieces and nephews a fair number of underhanded and hilarious ways to rid their plates of unwanted food, but the pea shooter trick, he actually was innocent of.

"Nice!" Mark nodded approval to Andrew, the only possible culprit left. "Way to go, Dad!"

They high-fived and Sophie snorted. "Bad influences all round," she muttered good-naturedly.

Almost lost amid the hubbub of Sophie relating the pea-shooting incident in more detail, Don caught Megan folding a tag with Howard's name and placing it on the plate between Griff and Don. He shook his head at her minutely, but she only smiled back and went about her business.

Don let out a long sigh.

Griff smoothed a hand down his thigh and left it lying on his knee. They both sipped beer and watched the table setting in silence.

Ten minutes later, Megan and Katie announced they were out of Clamato juice for the caesar and clattered out into the snow.

"Where the hell are they going to get Clamato juice on Christmas Eve?" Don's dad muttered, shaking his head.

"Convenience store in town, Dad," Don said.

"Everything's closed on Christmas Eve," his father insisted. "It's tradition."

Don and Griff exchanged glances. "Our tradition, sure. Lots of other traditions in the world than the ones you grew up with." Don lifted Griff's hand and kissed his knuckles for emphasis. "I think the couple who bought the store are Hindu or something."

His father nodded and shrugged. "Still, it's a free day off. I'd take it."

Don grinned. "You've never taken a day off in your life and you know it."

Again, his father shrugged. "It's only work if you don't enjoy it, Donny."

"Well, he does have a point there," Griff said.

"And speaking of work," Pete piped up, "we still have three barns full of animals to feed before we eat. Who's going where?"

"Horses!" Alex called, gleefully running for the kitchen, the back door beyond, and his rubber boots that had been left in the heap of outerwear in the mudroom.

"No, buddy, sorry, but we're going to look after our own animals. Uncle Griff and Uncle Don will go feed the horses."

"Alpacas stink!" Alex mourned, little pixie face squishing up into a frown.

"He can come, Pete," Griff offered. "If it's okay with you. Plus, I had planned to use some of these kids as weapons of cute overload to convince Dad to come over for supper."

Pete shook his head. "Spoken like a man who has none. Send a horde of mischief-makers over there and he'll run for cover!"

"Pete, you stay with Andrew and visit with your dad," Sophie offered. "The girls and I will go feed the stinkers."

"Mom!" A harmonic whine went up from Pete and Sophie's daughters, but they did get up and trudge toward the back door and their outerwear.

"I'll come." That from sunny Bernadette, Andrew's daughter. "I think they're cute."

The two girls who lived with the alpacas and llamas proceeded to tell her all the animals' finer points of disgustingness as all three disappeared into the kitchen in a noisy bunch.

"Hey, Dad?" Mark sauntered up to Andrew, hands stuffed into his jeans pockets. "You mind if I—?"

Andrew tossed up his hands. "Pick a barn, kiddo. No one's going to turn down an extra set of hands. Borrow a pair of boots, though. Yours cost a flaming fortune and shit stink don't come out."

Mark grinned. "My father. So eloquent." He glanced around at the others, hopeful.

Robbie, Pete's oldest, jumped to his rescue. "Come on." At eleven, he was nearly as tall as Mark, already eighteen and looking like he might finally stop growing. "You and I can take care of Grandpa's donkey and the horses Uncle Griff keeps here." He led Mark toward the kitchen with a wave.

"I'll join you," Albert said quietly, getting to his feet and offering Mark a shy smile.

Mark blushed to the roots of his bright red hair and nodded, stuffing his hands in his pockets and ducking out the door.

The din quieted and Don glanced around. Pete, Andrew, his wife Alicia, Jennifer, his father, and Griff glanced at one another, almost shell-shocked at the sudden quiet. The silence itself was loud after the chaos.

"Oh! Heaven! Quick, lock the doors!" Jennifer crowed gleefully.

Don laughed out loud.

Griff shoved his hands into his pockets with a sigh. "He should be here," he said again, and turned toward the kitchen and the door.

Don couldn't stifle the sigh that finally loosed the storm of misery roiling in his gut. He hung his head and was following Griff when his father spoke. "Boy's right, Donny. Howard is family. It's Christmas. He should be here."

Don nodded. "I know, Dad. And I wish I could do something about it. But I can't." And wasn't that the absolute crushing truth. He had a vision of what his family should be, and he couldn't make it happen. Everyone saw how it should be. He'd failed to make it reality. Silent, he went after Griff.

Thankfully, Alex was a chatterbox. His almost-five-year-old observations of the snow banks—they were taller than he was—the very ugly upholstery in Don's truck—baby-puke brown, apparently—the fact his radio seemed stuck on country music—by design, in fact, Griff assured the kid. Don had programmed all the buttons to tune to the same station to prevent his father from tuning to the chatterboxes on the CBC. He hadn't even finished the explanation when Alex was rattling on about the excitement of being allowed to ride in the front seat where he could even reach the radio buttons.

"Well, I guess I have to, huh, because you don't have a backseat—" He twisted his little body around as far as his seatbelt would allow and peered up at the edge of the seat. "Nope. Unless it's teensy. Is it teensy, Uncle Griff? Hey, is Uncle Howard coming? Because he should. He could fix your truck, Uncle Don, and put a backseat in. Then you can drive your kids places when you have some. Are you having kids? You should. We're fun." He spun back to face front and thumped his mittened hands into his lap. "Grandpa says so. Hey, how do two boys have kids, huh? Or is that why you have three of you?"

Don couldn't decide if he should laugh, be mortified, or chuck the child into the snow bank.

"I thought three-year-olds couldn't talk," Griff muttered.

"I'm practically five," Alex informed him, eyeing him critically. "Maybe you need to take a kid course first. You don't know much. I've been talking for *ages*."

"No sh—"

"Don!"

Alex pointed at Don. "You were going to say shit." He collapsed into a ball of giggles.

"New plan," Don muttered. "Do not show this kid to your dad. He will lock us out until the holidays are over."

Griff barked out a laugh, which sent Alex into new paroxysms and even got Don smiling.

"You want I should ask your dad to come to Grandpa's, Uncle Griff?" Alex asked, turning his deeply serious brown eyes on Griff. "I can get people to do stuff. I just look cute—" He demonstrated. "—and ask real nice and say *pleeeeaase? Please, please, please, please* like that."

"And that works," Griff said, his expression dubious.

"Every time. Well. Except for my sisters, but nothing works on them. On Robbie, though. Actually, Robbie's awesome. He does anything I ask. Before I ask, even. He's like, the best big brother on the whole planet. I'll share him if you want." He looked up at Griff. "Everyone should have a big brother."

Griff nodded. "I have big brothers," he assured the boy.

"You do? Where? How come I never met them? I want to meet them. Can they come for supper?" He batted long, dark lashes. "*Pleeeease*?"

Griff laughed and held up a hand. "Calm down! Don't turn that on me!" He looked over the boy at Don. "I'd hire big brothers if he does that again!"

"Told you it works," Alex crowed. "So can I meet them? Are they at your dad's place? What do I call him? He's old, but he's not my grandpa. Is he? Do I call him Uncle Grandpa?"

Griff smiled and ruffled Alex's hair. "Call him Uncle Jim, I guess."

"Griff's dad would be more like your great uncle," Don said.

Griff snorted. "I dare you to call him that."

"I'll call him Grandpa Jim," Alex decided. "Because everybody that old should have grandkids. I can be his honorable grandson."

Griff's snort became a laugh and Don chuckled.

"Honorary," Griff corrected him. "Honorary grandson. I think he'd like to have one of those."

"What about your brothers?" Alex asked. "Are they there? Can I meet them?"

"You know them. They're at Grandpa's. Your Uncle Andrew and your dad are my big brothers."

Alex studied him a moment, glanced at Don for confirmation, but Don kept his eyes on the bumpy laneway between his farm and Griff's and waited to see what came next. He had no doubt this child could talk Griff into a corner before they drove the last three hundred yards to Griff's barn.

"Those are Uncle Don's brothers. Not yours. They're your in-law brothers. You get those when you get married. Like Mom did." He grinned. "Mom says she got so many in-law people when she got married, it's like she has her own whole town."

Don couldn't stop a wide smile. "She's right. Your dad and I have a pretty big family."

"So, since you married Uncle Griff, now he has a town of in-law people too, huh?"

Don nodded as he pulled up in front of the barn. "Something like that, kiddo. But if you ask me, Griff was sort of a part of the family before he and I—"

"Eeew! That's like marrying your brother. Gross."

Don and Griff met gazes, startled.

"Um," Griff ventured.

Don shook his head slightly. The kid had talked them both into that corner.

"Horses," Griff said gruffly, and opened his door. He got out and turned to help their nephew.

Alex slithered deftly after him, landing on all fours on the ground, popping up and shouting "I'm all right!" before either of them had a chance to ask.

"So," he asked, batting his lashes and going from triumphant to serious in that space of time. He took Griff's hand and Don's, as soon as he'd come around the front of the truck. "When are you guys going to marry Uncle Howard? Hey, Mom says maybe I shouldn't call him that. Should I? I mean, he's yours, so I think I should, because that makes him mine too. My uncle, I mean, right? But maybe she meant I should wait until you marry him too. Can you do that? Three people, I mean. Swing me." He waggled at both their arms and leaned as far forward as he could.

"Alex," Don began, but Griff stopped them, swung around, and crouched in front of the little boy.

"You should call him Uncle Howard, because he's family."

Alex nodded, round little face sober.

"As far as getting married, well, technically, Uncle Don and I aren't."

"Why not?"

Don cocked his head. "Yeah, Griff, why not?"

Griff smiled up at him. "Because the law says only two people. I'd marry you, but then there's Uncle Howard."

Don nodded.

"Dumb law," Alex proclaimed. He took Griff's hand again. "Swing me."

Griff sighed, stood, and they obliged the little boy, swinging him between them until they were close enough to the snow bank to let go and send him sailing into the soft embankment to land with a shower of hysterical laughter and a puff of snow.

Griff fished him out, since he was laughing so hard he couldn't work his short arms and legs well enough to navigate the depths, and set him back on his feet. He dashed immediately for the barn.

"My God," Don breathed, watching him go.

"What everyone actually needs," Griff decided, accepting Don's hand as they followed after the snow-suited whirlwind, "is a precocious four-year-old to set the bare essentials out and keep them honest."

Don made a face. "I think the world would implode." He shook his head, laced his gloved fingers with Griff's, and strolled toward the barn and waiting horses. "As it is, I can only imagine what kinds of questions Pete and Sophie will get when we get back."

"They might never leave us alone with him again."

"That might not be a bad thing." Don kissed Griff's knuckles and stopped outside the door.

"How's that leather taste?" Griff asked, playfully wiggling his fingers under Don's nose.

"Mmmm." Don leaned in and stuck out his tongue. "Good enough to kiss."

Griff was good at power and Don was sure he needed to display some now. Griff needed to control something to get over not having any control with Howard.

Taking the cue, Griff did kiss him, hand at the back of his head, cold snow dribbling down under his collar, hot lips claiming all Don's attention for a few minutes. When he finally moved away, Don held his gaze steady.

"When we're done, we'll bring your dad and Alex back to the house, make our excuses, and ride into town. If he doesn't want to come to us, we'll go to him."

Griff's smile glowed in the afternoon sunshine. "I love you." He kissed Don, another breathtaking, commanding kiss that curled his toes.

"Gross!" Alex called from the far end of the barn. "Hey! Where's your kid-sized hayfork? You guys need to get kids so you have the stuff you need!"

"No shit," Griff muttered.

Feeding the horses proved as entertaining, with Alex's commentary, as the ride over had been. They exchanged Don's truck for Griff's father's car for the short jaunt back. Alex was thoroughly disgusted at being relegated to the backseat, though he took a bucketful of glee in announcing to Griff's father that he was now Grandpa Jim.

"I don't get a say in this?" he'd asked.

Griff shrugged. "The kid has spoken, Dad. You have an objection, take it up with him."

"And good luck," Don added.

"You Jenkins clan seem to swallow families whole," Jim observed.

Don's cheer vanished. "Everyone has a choice, Mr. McAllister."

"And some of us need a better understanding of what that choice is, son," Jim replied softly. "That old saying about leading a horse to water only counts if you take the lid off the barrel." He leaned forward and his strong fingers dug into Don's shoulder. "Never met a horse yet who wouldn't drink once he smelled how sweet the water is."

"What are you *talking* about?" Alex asked. "We already watered the horses." He peered out the window as Don pulled into the driveway. "Can I play with my cousins?" He was already fumbling with his seatbelt as he asked.

"Sure," Don told him. "I'll just tell your dad we left you in the barn—"

"'K, thanks!" And he was gone.

"Pete!" Don called into the house as he entered the kitchen. "We left your son with the horses. He was telling them some story about a black stallion?"

"Smart move," Pete agreed. "Captive audience. Come get in here. You're letting in winter."

They stomped into the mudroom and peeled out of their coats and boots, and followed Pete through to the living room so they could make their official excuses before riding into town to Howard.

PART TWO—GRIFF

HOW TO UNBREAK A HEART

GRIFF didn't have to look at Howard lying in that hospital bed. He knew he was hurt. He knew he would get better. He was more concerned about Don, who hadn't stepped foot in the hospital since his mother had died. Her accident had been far worse than this, and he'd seen her once and been unable to visit again.

"Don," Griff said softly, leaning his crutch against his ribs and touching Don's back, smoothing a hand over his sweat-soaked shirt. "Babe—"

He shook his head, spun abruptly, and buried his face against Griff's chest. The force nearly knocked him off his one good foot. "Oh Jesus, Griff, I can't." One shuddering breath, then another. "Can't do this again."

The sound of footsteps clomped down the hall, the door opened, and someone entered the room behind them. Griff looked over his shoulder as the door swung shut with a whoosh. "Dad." He smiled, grateful, and gently handed Don to him.

"Pete and Albert have got everything at home under control," he informed them. Griff had a sudden flash of guilt for not even giving a second thought about such mundane things as fetching the abandoned truck or feeding the animals.

His father must have seen the thought in Griff's face, because he patted his shoulder and gave a small sad but knowing nod.

"You worry about your men, Griff. Let us take care of the rest." He patted Don's shoulder and led him toward the door. "I'll take him out in the hall."

Griff nodded. "Thanks."

Watching them go, Griff couldn't blame Don, really. His mother's car had been struck by a skidding snowplow and crumpled like tinfoil. That she'd survived at all had been a miracle. That she'd succumbed to her injuries not a surprise. The doctors hadn't really begun to talk to the family about the necessary amputations; her body hadn't fared much better than her car. Everyone knew there wasn't much point. All they could do was attempt to keep her comfortable and give her a chance to say good-bye to her family.

Sighing, Griff turned back to the bed and studied Howe. His left leg was lifted, held in place with slings, a thick cast enclosing it toes to hip. His left arm looked much the same, and his right was thickly swathed in bandages, only his fingers free, the index finger clipped in a monitor sensor. There were bruises around both eyes, a neck brace. Who knew what hid under the blankets. Tubes snaked everywhere and Griff decided it was a good sign he wasn't wearing an oxygen mask. That meant his insides were most likely doing everything they should be doing.

"Hey." The soft greeting made him jump. Howe's face changed shape. It was an attempt at a smile through swollen lips.

"Howe." Griff breathed. It felt like he hadn't since that first phone call and the inrush of oxygen made his head spin.

"He's wrecked, isn't he?" Howe asked.

Griff barely made out his words but got the gist when Howe's eyes flicked to the door and back to Griff. He nodded and swallowed. "He's not the only one."

Howe's right arm shifted minutely. "Nope."

"God, you're alive," Griff blurted.

Howe gazed at him like Griff had just pronounced mountains tall and the ocean big.

Flaring his nostrils, Griff clamped his lips over so many things he wanted to say. He wanted to yell at him, cry all over him, hug him. "Fuck" was all he managed.

Another attempt at a smile crossed Howe's face, and he tipped his head, an indication Griff should move closer.

Lead weights, Griff's feet didn't want to move. His brain couldn't find the command to make his arms and hands work the crutches. His heart, straining to the breaking point, dragged the rest of him to Howe's bedside. He lifted a hand to cover Howe's bandaged one.

"Howe."

For a few heartbeats, they studied each other until Howe glanced at the nearby chair, and met Griff's gaze. "Stay here?"

Griff nodded. Don was with his dad. He'd come in when and if he could manage it. In the meantime, he wasn't alone. Howe needed to know someone would sit beside his bed and be there when he woke up. Griff could do that. There was nothing and no one to punch this time. All the tubes and casts and bandages prevented Griff from even holding him. What else was there for him to do?

August, age nineteen

IT WASN'T quite dark in the bedroom. It was hot and sticky, made worse by the proximity of three men crammed onto one small bed.

Griff hated the waiting thing. Sitting around and doing nothing when someone needed a serious ass kicking—he hated it. Always had, in fact, and that went right back to being six, seeing his mother standing over his father at the kitchen table, finger pointing, waving in his face, voice harsh from screaming at him, face red and ugly. He never yelled back. Never lifted either his voice or one little finger in anything that might be construed as self-defense. He just let her scream herself hoarse and calmly told her he'd do better.

Then he'd work his ass off to give her what she wanted only to have the goal moved to something newer and shinier at the last minute.

"Griff?" Don's voice drifted out of the semidark from Howe's other side.

Griff grunted.

Moonlight washed over the bed and the bodies tangled on it. Between them, Howe snored softly. His damp skin fused to Griff's thighs and chest. His dark flop of hair contrasted with Don's skin where his head was lying on his stomach.

Don had suggested trying to get him to sleep, which was why they'd moved to the bed in the first place. At first it had been Howe stretched out on the mattress, but he only stared at the ceiling, then at the two of them, and eventually, Don had climbed on with him, and in seconds, Howe had curled and laid his head on Don's lap.

That seemed to help for a while, but eventually his restless whimpering had led them both to lie down with him, same as they'd been sitting outside on the rooftop with him, and instinct had led to Griff kissing the sad sounds away.

There was no way to hurt any of the people who'd done this to him. They were all dead already. God knew, Griff wanted to hurt someone. But Howe had enough pain for a dozen someones, and so he'd tried to take some of it away. Maybe that had been the motivating factor. Who knew? He hadn't thought it through. He'd just—

"Griff." Don's hand found Griff's where it rested on Howe's hip. "You okay?"

"Yeah." He flattened his palm against Howe's lightly hairy skin. Don had so little body hair. Howe's vaguely furry body was a novelty. One Griff thought he shouldn't know about. But now he did. "No," he said.

Don laced his fingers through Griff's and squeezed.

"I don't know." Griff let out a sigh. Should he apologize? But Don didn't seem mad. And he hadn't left the room when it started. In fact it might have been him who'd decided to get Howe naked. Griff couldn't quite remember.

Don's fingers left Griff's, and Griff glanced at his face. A moment later, his fingertips coasted up Griff's arm, over his shoulder, and back down his chest until he couldn't reach any more.

"What did we do?" Griff whispered. In this light, Don was all darks and lights. Pale skin, dark hair, eyes nearly black and impossible to read.

He shrugged. "It'll be okay," he assured Griff. "Go to sleep. The funeral is going to be awful."

When were funerals ever good? And Griff didn't know how this mess they'd made with their best friend was ever going to be okay, but the way Don looked at him, like he was proud of him, had Griff willing to believe anything. At least for that moment in time....

Present day

"HEY." Something bulky and heavy patted Griff's hair, and a moment later, he realized he was resting his head on the side of Howe's mattress. The last few minutes were a hazy blur. The room was perceptibly darker and Griff grasped that the overhead lights had been turned off at some point. Had he fallen asleep?

Howe patted his head carefully with his bandaged hand.

"Hey." Griff blinked and smiled at him, bleary, brain-dead.

"Sleepy?"

He was. Griff shrugged and studied his lover's face. Was it less swollen? He pushed thick hair off Howe's forehead. "You want anything?"

Howe wagged his head from side to side. His gaze never leaving Griff's, like he was afraid if he even blinked, Griff might disappear.

"You okay?"

Howe's eyes widened a fraction and his lips quirked. But he nodded.

"You look like shit."

Howe contemplated that for a bit, but made no comment, verbal or otherwise.

"Where's Don?" Howe asked eventually.

Ashamed to admit he couldn't answer that question, and still trying to formulate a way to tell him that, Howe flopped his wrapped hand on the mattress and shook his head before he managed. "Forget it."

"You want him?"

He pursed his lips. "He doesn't do hospitals. He came. Good enough."

"I'll talk to him."

"'S okay."

Griff couldn't decide if he was looking sad or tired or mad or what. Too much of his face was malformed by swelling and discolored with bruises. It was hard to imagine Don coming to see him like this and not having a meltdown.

"You want me to tell him anything?"

Howe did that faint smile thing again and bumped Griff's hand with his. "Take care of him. I'm fine."

But Griff knew how he hated being alone. Knew how he hated admitting that fact, even to himself. Don had family all over the county to hold his hand. If he wouldn't come, Howe had Griff. He smiled back, nodded, and kissed Howe's forehead on a patch of skin that didn't look too badly damaged.

"You should sleep," Griff told him, noting how his lids drooped and every blink got a little bit longer, even though when he did open his eyes, they were fixed on him.

He nodded and let his eyes close.

When a nurse came through to check on him, he barely woke. She shooed Griff out of the room and told him to go home, but as soon as she'd rounded the corner and was out of sight, Griff went back in, stole a blanket from the neighboring bed, and settled into the poorly padded, high-backed chair beside his lover.

The last time he'd spent such a horrifically uncomfortable night, it had been in a horse stall, and the horse in question had been in nearly as bad a shape as Howe. Maybe not physically, but mentally and emotionally, that horse had been a mess.

September, age nineteen

SCRATCHY straw worked its way up under Griff's shirt, clawing at his back just above the waistband of his jeans. He had to admit the stiff horse blanket he had over him wasn't any better. He should have listened to his father and gone inside, but the animal seemed to wake every ten minutes, and about half an hour ago, instead of shying away from Griff when her big, sad eyes flickered his way and she realized he was there, her head lowered and reached, just a few inches, in his direction.

She was getting used to her human. She was beginning to understand he wasn't there to hurt her. She had to believe that before he could examine her properly. He was satisfied she wasn't in any immediate physical jeopardy, other than being underfed and overstressed, but he wanted to be sure. He wanted to get his hands on her, run them down every inch of every leg, examine her hooves and brush the dust and mud from her shaggy coat, comb out her tangled mane. She was a pretty little thing under all the neglect, and Griff knew he could prove it to her if she gave him the chance.

"Griff?" His father's voice whispered through the semidarkness.

The mare shuffled her feet, swung ponderously around to face the stall door, and Griff held still. Silent. With her rump toward him, he didn't dare make any sudden movement or noise that would cause her to lash out. Where he sat, his head was far too easy a target for those sharp hooves.

His father appeared across the aisle from her stall door, keeping a healthy distance. He knew horses better than Griff did. He'd taught Griff everything Griff knew, but not even close to everything he knew. Catching Griff's eye over the stall door, he nodded and gave a questioning thumbs up.

Griff nodded back.

"I'm coming in, son," he said, keeping his voice at that low, steady monotone. It was a conversational sort of soothing tone that made the horse prick her ears forward, but nothing more.

"I brought some supper. You haven't eaten all day."

He had had a few apples, and stolen a couple of carrots and peas from the garden, but essentially, his father was right. In his quest to earn this horse's trust, Griff had blown off everything else. His stomach growled as the smell of fried chicken and potatoes reached him.

A ten-minute eternity later, Griff's father had convinced the horse to let him past, and she once more stood where she could watch them both. His father settled on a hay bale beside Griff's nest of straw and blankets.

"Comfy?" he asked, handing over the plate.

"Not even a little bit. Did you make this?" Griff turned the chicken over, leery of the deceptively crispy-looking coating. He'd eaten enough of his father's cooking to know it wasn't always as benign as it looked.

He laughed. "I begged the neighbors. Megan brought leftovers."

Shaking his head, Griff picked up a leg. "One big happy family," he observed. "You and Don. Helpless farm boys."

That got him an indulgent smile. "Good thing we have you, then, son."

"Damn good thing," Griff agreed.

"How is she?" he asked after Griff had eaten about half the food. He nodded at the horse, and she swung her head around, like she knew he was talking about her.

"Slow and steady, like you always say. She'll come around. Doesn't like being in here alone, though."

"You think it's worth straw in your shorts?"

"Look at her, Dad. I bet everyone that's ever mattered has taught her humans are dangerous and mean."

"And you're going to change all that."

Griff nodded. "I am."

He dug back into the food his father had brought, but he could feel eyes on him. "What?" he asked between bites.

"You look so much like her, you know."

"The horse?" Griff asked, swallowing chicken and scooping potatoes in after it.

His father laughed softly. "Your mother, smartass."

Mashed potatoes turned to sawdust on Griff's tongue. "I'll dye my hair," he said flatly.

That comment received a chuckle, even softer than the last. "It's okay to look like her. She's beautiful."

Griff didn't remember anything of the sort. He remembered a red-faced, screaming bitch. Setting his fork down, he balanced the plate on his lap and glared at his father. "I don't want to talk about her."

"Griff, she's your mother."

"She's dead to me."

"Griff."

"She left!"

The horse shifted nervously, ears twitching back, nostrils flaring, and Griff dropped his voice.

"She left us, Dad." Why was he bringing her up now? They never talked about her. "She bitched at you for every little thing. You gave up your life to move into the city because that's what she wanted and look how she repaid you."

"Griff, you were very young."

"Not that young."

"Love is complicated."

Griff watched the horse for a few moments, studying the way she tossed her head, swung it a few times, located the human she trusted, and nickered softly. "Not that complicated," he said, lifting a hand toward her. After studying him for a moment, she took a step forward and pushed her nose into his palm. It was a brief touch, but a deliberate one.

His father watched, a soft expression on his face. There was no other way to describe that look. He used it only rarely—for foals, puppies, and occasionally, his son. "I was nineteen once too, you know, Griff," he said.

"Dad, it isn't about being nineteen. It's about how she treated you. I knew when I was six it wasn't right."

"You saw your parents fighting. I can see how that might have been upsetting."

"No, I saw my mother slowly turning into a monster. I saw you suck up every mean thing she ever said to you, I saw you break your heart over that stupid warehouse job, and I saw you leaf through the horse auction catalogs when you thought no one was watching."

"Griff."

"You remember we used to sit all weekend and watch the Calgary Stampede?"

He nodded.

The horse moved away, but not as far away as she'd been a moment ago.

"I'd ask about the cowboys, but all you ever talked about were the horses. Which ones would win, which ones were hurt, which ones would make good studs."

Griff watched the familiar smile, half sad, half proud, grow on his father's face. "Yeah."

"You were always right about the winners."

He shrugged and tilted his head as the horse shifted her weight and turned to watch him. "I know horses, son."

"You know horses."

"This one reminds me of Drake. You remember Drake?"

How could Griff not remember Drake? He'd been a lab/collie mix puppy his father had brought home on Griff's tenth birthday. There wasn't a combination Griff could think of that mixed as much brains and energy in a dog as Labrador Retriever and Border Collie. That dog had been a handful. His mom had hated him from the moment his dad had brought him home. Griff had trained him, taught him, and he would have been an amazing dog when he outgrew his puppy rambunctiousness. He never got the chance.

His mother had left him out in the backyard on a snowy December night. He jumped the fence to get to the front door and got hit by a car in the alley behind the house. They had found his body the next morning, frozen to the pavement with his blood. It had been obvious he hadn't died right away.

When silence had thickened so the sound of the horse's hooves in the straw was crisp counterpoint, Griff's father reached over and clapped a hand on Griff's shoulder.

"She would never have hurt him on purpose, Griff."

"She hated him."

"She wasn't cruel."

Griff looked over at him. "Dad, that woman is ten kinds of cruel. I'm glad she left."

"Don't say that. She's your mother."

"She was a lousy mother and a horrible wife. We did better without her."

"I won't deny that."

"Why did you marry her?" Griff asked after a while.

He shrugged. "I loved her. She was beautiful and exotic and she wanted me. A farm hand." He smiled, and this time it was all the way sad. "She wanted a mousy horse trainer with no pedigree."

"In other words, she was a rich bitch rebelling against her rich parents by marrying beneath her."

He winced.

"I think she missed the mark, Dad. She married way over her head. She never deserved you."

He shrugged at that, not agreeing or disagreeing. "The point is, son, the love, that part was easy. I felt it and I acted on it. Maybe it was a mistake, maybe it wasn't, but in the end, I had to deal with the consequences of that decision."

"Why do I get the feeling we aren't talking about Mom anymore?" Griff asked, picking up a piece of chicken and biting into it. If his mouth was full, he wouldn't have to answer awkward questions about his own love life.

"I know how you are with hurt creatures, Griff."

Swallowing, Griff focused hard on the crispy coating of his meal. "Howard is not a hurt creature."

"And if you truly believe that, then you should not be messing with him. He's very hurt."

Griff nodded. "Okay. So he's hurt. But people get hurt."

"He isn't a horse you can coddle and ply with treats and brush up till he shines. He's a human being, and you might not be able to fix him."

"All I'm doing is loving him. You said yourself, love is easy."

His father leaned back against the barn wall and watched Griff's horse as her head dropped and she began to drift. If she felt comfortable enough with this new human and their voices to fall asleep, Griff would take that as a good sign. "He was Don's first boyfriend. Are you accepting him because Don doesn't want to let him go? I can't say I see that ending well for any of you."

Griff set the half-eaten chicken down again with a sigh. "This conversation is going to go places you might not like, you realize that."

His father chuckled. A wide grin flashed over his face. "I've been around, kiddo. You'd be surprised."

Griff's eyes flew wide. "No." He held up a hand. "No, I think you should just… not… tell me that shit."

Broad shoulders shook with laughter his father struggled to keep quiet.

"God," Griff muttered.

After a few moments, he nudged Griff's leg with a foot. "You didn't actually answer my question."

"There was a question?"

"Why are you with him, Griff? Is it because Don—"

"No," Griff said quietly. "None of it was Don's idea."

"Doesn't have to be his idea for you to do it for him."

Griff poked at his potatoes. "I didn't."

There was a way to draw a horse out, get it to trust you. Mostly, it had to do with just spending time, being still and quiet and waiting. It could take hours. Days. Weeks, depending on the animal. Griff's father had gotten very, very good at the technique over the years. Griff only realized he'd used it on him when he started talking again.

"He was so hurt," Griff said, directing the words at his plate. "God. Who does that to their family?"

His father rubbed his back and cupped a warm hand at the back of his neck. It brought back a thousand times Griff had sat on his bed when he was little, crying his eyes out, and his father had sat beside him, just like this, waiting for Griff to talk and tell him what was wrong.

"His whole family left him," Griff said. "Or got ripped away."

"You can't replace them, Griff."

"I know that."

"So what are you trying to do?"

Griff shrugged. "Just love him. I don't know." Thinking back to that night, to Howard's desperate sobs, everything about him falling apart in their hands, Griff couldn't imagine hurting that much. He hadn't been able to imagine doing anything but trying to keep Howard together long enough to get through to morning, no matter what it took. That feeling had never gone away. He needed them.

"And what about Don?"

"He… I was the one who started it all, Dad, and Don didn't leave or say anything. He… if he didn't want…."

"Have you talked to him about it?"

Griff shook his head. How did you talk about something like that? The only person he had ever talked to about anything was his father, and he had no way to explain to him why he'd let Howard in, and why he couldn't shut him out now.

Like when Griff had bought his sad little horse the day before—he'd been so angry at the source of all that pain, but there had been no one to punish for it. The horse's owner had neglected her, then abandoned her. No one knew where he'd gone or why he'd left his animals behind to die. No one knew why Howard's father had gone off the deep end, and no one knew why his brother had gone off the cliff. Those things had happened, and now Griff had a broken horse and a broken boyfriend.

If he couldn't break any heads over what had happened to Howard, then he'd have to try and mend some hearts.

His father pulled him close and wrapped his arm around Griff's shoulders. "You never could stand by, could you?"

Griff realized, just like when he had been a kid, he was bawling. He kept his head down, sniffled, and wiped his face. "Guess not."

Something tugged at his hair and he lifted his face enough to see his new horse, lips flopping, like she'd been nibbling at his hair.

"You're a good girl," he told her.

"She has a good heart," his father agreed, because he could see things like that, right through the hide and bones of a beast to what it was made of.

Griff glanced at his father and received a smile. This expression was nothing like his earlier sad, unsettled one.

"You have a good heart too, Griff. Always have, ever since you were a boy."

Griff flashed a smile, wiping at his face again.

"You're a good man, son. I'm proud of you."

"Most fathers would be ashamed of the way I live."

"They'd be wrong. The only thing that has me worried, Griff, is that big heart of yours. Trust me, son, I know. The more you open it up, the easier it is to break apart."

"Like with Mom, you mean."

He nodded. "Like with your mother. She wasn't perfect. I knew that when I married her." He shrugged and gazed off into the dim depths of the barn. "Should I have stood up to her more?" He pulled in a deep breath and let it out in a soft sigh. "I can't go back and change that, and I regret how it affected you." He studied Griff a minute, then continued. "But then why should I regret it? I'm proud how you turned out. I am proud to call you my son, and I guess I'm just saying, if this is what you want, this thing with Howard and Don, if it's the right thing for you, you have my support."

And there, he had Griff crying again, but for different reasons now.

"Dad—" But what did he say to that? After he'd just trashed all the choices he'd made in love, here he was telling Griff he was proud of him for the wholly unconventional ones he'd made.

"It takes strength to take the chance you did. You could have lost Don over it, and yet you did what you felt. And you followed through. So yeah, I'm proud of you and Don both, for sticking with each other, and with Howard. Now. Eat up. This girl might seem passive enough right now, but once she's rested and fed, you'll have a lot of work to do with her. I'll see you inside."

He got up slowly, keeping a wary eye on the skittish mare. She had tolerated his presence, probably because Griff had, but now that he was up and moving again, all her wariness returned.

"I think I'll stay out here tonight," Griff said, observing the way his father moved and clucked and stilled, like a slow dance of heartbeats and hoof-strikes with the animal. "I think she can use the comfort of not being alone. She's been alone too long."

He nodded. "Figured you'd say that. I left a thermos of coffee and some more comfortable bedding just outside. You be careful. Treat her good."

"I will. And thanks, Dad."

He'd made it to the stall door and slipped out, glanced back and gave Griff a small nod. "Night, Griff."

"Night."

UNEXPECTED

GRIFF had fallen asleep in the chair. The thump of the hospital room door closing woke him up and he started to a sitting position. A shadow fell across Howard and a delicate hand landed on Griff's shoulder.

"Griff?" The soft, feminine whisper took a moment to place as he rubbed sleep from his eyes.

"Megan," he said finally. "What are you doing here?"

A cup of steaming coffee appeared in his periphery and he realized he was staring at Howe's still features, watching for the slightest sign of… well, of anything.

"Dragging your sorry ass home is what," she informed him. "You can't sit here indefinitely, babe."

"I'm not leaving him alone. Where's Don?"

"Having a nervous breakdown." She joggled the cup of coffee.

"Thanks." He took it, but didn't open it.

"Your dad's outside, Griff. He said he'd sit with Howe so I could take you home to get some proper rest."

"I'm fine."

"Griff." She took him by the shoulder and forcibly pulled him around. "Don's not fine. He's freaking out and he needs you."

Pulling away, Griff growled at her and rammed himself firmly into his chair. "He has all of you. Howe only has—"

"All of us, Griff—for God's sake, would you pay attention!"

Startled, he finally looked up at her. She'd been crying. Hard and long by the looks of it.

"What happened?"

"Howe got in a smashup, you idiot," she said, pointing to the bed. "My brother-in-law nearly died. And don't even start to argue with me about it because even if he's being a jerk about it, Howe *is* family, and my big brother is a complete shambles over him getting nearly killed, and he needs his lover, because I'm just his sister, and I'm not good enough for this. He needs *you*."

"Your dad—"

"Stop it."

"Stop what?"

She swallowed hard and clenched her fists, like she wanted to punch him and could barely hold herself back.

"Stop being thick," Howe supplied. "Stop avoiding the hard stuff and go check on Don."

"Hard stuff?" Griff turned on his lover. "Hard—"

He held up his bandaged arm as far as it would go and shook his head. "Don't shit me, babe. I know you two are having issues. I am not your excuse. Go see him and make it better."

"Howe—"

"I mean it, you stupid fuck."

Griff's eyes about bugged out at Howe, and a ghost of a smile crossed his lips.

"Go. Please. I know he won't come here. So go see him for me and tell him it's okay. I understand."

What was he supposed to do? Refuse to deliver his message?

"Tell him I love him, Griff, yeah?"

Griff nodded. "Yeah. Fine."

"Don't be mad at him. He does the best he can, and remember, he doesn't get pissed at you when you screw up, and you have. Plenty."

Griff stared at him, uncomprehending until Howe offered a crooked sort of half grin.

"You want to talk about the Hawthorns?"

Griff said nothing.

"Thought so. Go see Don. Take care of him."

September, age twenty-seven

GRIFF clamped his fingers tight around the square of leather on the seat beside him. It was all the incriminating evidence he needed. Howe might not have been willing to say who had beat him up, or what the real reason was, but this—he slammed the wallet onto the dashboard, disgusted at having to touch it—told him enough.

Terrance Hawthorn's driver's license slipped out. His thug-like face stared blankly into the night through the windshield.

Found under the spilled tools, splattered with blood, ID spilling out of it, the wallet had screamed "guilty" at Griff. He'd taken a few photos of it, exactly where and how he'd found it, then pocketed it without saying anything to Howe or Don. It wouldn't do either of them any good to know he knew who had hurt Howe. He didn't have any idea what Terrance had been doing in Howe's garage or why he had dared hurt Griff's lover, but he wasn't going to get away with it.

"Fucker!" He spat out the window and whipped a hand over his mouth as he pulled into the drive.

The house was small. Griff thought it should be bigger, but then a lot had happened to the Hawthorn family since sixth grade. Scandal, divorce, abuse of power, and karma had all taken their toll. Fifteen years later, though, Terrance was still the town bully, and his father still had enough influence to let him get away with shit no one else would ever dare try.

Griff parked and strode to the front door, knocking until the inner door swung open.

Terrance glared out at him, face obscured and vague behind the sagging screen. "What the fuck do you want?"

Griff held up the wallet without speaking, just to see his reaction.

His eyes went big, his flaccid cheeks nicely pale. "You steal that?" he snapped, jerking open the screen door and attempting to snatch it from Griff's hand. His movement was slow and clumsy, hindered by a beer or three too many.

"Why would I?" Griff held it up out of his reach.

"Why you got my wallet?"

"Who said it was yours?"

His face paled even more, realizing he'd given something away. "Isn't it? Why you here if it ain't mine?"

"You stay away from Howe, his garage, and you stay away from Don," Griff said.

"Why would I want to go anywhere near your faggot friends?"

"I'd say you tell me, but I don't give a crap why you were there. Just don't go back."

He sneered. "Or what? You threatenin' me? 'Cause my dad's a cop, you know."

Hadn't that been the threat he'd used in grade school? Griff was even less frightened of his washed-up cop father now than he had been when they were twelve.

"I know who your father is," Griff said.

"Then you know there's nothin' you can do about it." His sneer morphed to a slovenly version of superiority. "And 'sides, that fucker deserved a beating."

Griff spent the next few heartbeats congratulating himself on not punching Terrance's lights out. He'd been willing to admit Hawthorn's wallet could have been on the floor of the garage for a number of different reasons. Howe's was the only garage in town, and it was conceivable he'd actually been there on legitimate business and dropped it. Not likely, given the fact it was splashed with blood and the way the contents had been strewn across the floor, but conceivable. Now Griff knew for sure his suspicions had been right.

Still, much as he wanted to, he wasn't dumb enough to throw the first punch or threaten Hawthorn. He held out the wallet. "Stay away from my family."

"Little shit had it comin', way he was acting."

Griff studied the man squaring off in the sheet of yellow light spilling from the doorway. In joggers and a stained T-shirt over his stocky frame, bits of him bulged out from under the inadequate cover. Griff shook his head. Hawthorn was so not Howe's type. And what did he mean by "little shit?" Did he actually think of Howe as little? Because he wasn't. He wasn't as tall or broad as Griff, but he was in no way "little." They had all outstripped Hawthorn in height since school—only Don was leaner, his frame more delicate—and the once-bully didn't pose much of a real physical threat any more.

"I doubt it," was all he said.

A spark of motion deeper inside the house snatched his attention from Hawthorn, and he glanced past Terrance's shoulder to see Albert Hawthorn—his younger brother—dart down the steps and toward the kitchen. He stopped, saw Griff, and blanched.

Fuck.

Skinny, just-barely-out-of-high-school Albert, with his dark hair, darker eyes, and pale features, was exactly Howard's type. Please, *God*, let his bonehead friend not have hit on the kid.

Albert's eyes got big, he shook his head sharp and short, slipped though the kitchen and out the side door.

"Take your damn wallet," Griff snarled, thrusting it at Terrance, "and keep away from my people." Lord, how he wanted to bust the belligerent little man's chops.

"Your people." Hawthorn peeled his lips off his nicotine-stained teeth. "What the hell would I want with any of you pansy-ass faggots?" He snorted and grabbed the wallet.

"Better question, what would any of us want with a sloppy scrap of humanity like you? Just stay on your own side of the fence."

For the record, Griff did not throw the first sucker punch. Nor did he actually intend to break Hawthorn's nose this time. It was not his fault he put it in front of Griff's fist when he tried to block the second wild swing. He'd come by to return the wallet, but a man had a right to defend himself. He wasn't overly worried about repercussions. How would Hawthorn explain to his wonderfully protective father that he'd had his ass handed to him by a pansy-ass faggot?

Griff left him leaning on the doorframe, panting curses through the blood dripping over his top lip, and headed for his Jeep.

In the slash of light from the garage doorway and in clear view of the decidedly one-sided altercation stood Albert, watching Griff walk away. Griff stopped. He didn't know why, but he did.

"Well?" he asked finally, after the front door of the house had slammed and the porch light went dark.

Albert shrugged and crossed one arm over his stomach to grab at his elbow, as though he could make his already too-thin self smaller still. The other he stuck into his jeans pocket.

"You going to call someone?" Griff asked.

He shook his head.

"Do you know what happened at the garage yesterday?"

Nothing. No response at all. Unless you counted the way his face seemed to lose even more color.

"Howard didn't hit on your brother." It wasn't a question. Griff knew this. Howe would not give that jerkoff the time of day. *If* Terrance went to him for a car repair, Howe might fleece him, but would more likely refuse to serve him. His loyalty to Don would never allow him to take the man's business.

Albert's delicate brows angled down to shadow deep eyes.

"Did Howe hit on you?"

That earned Griff a vigorous shake of the kid's head that sent sandy brown hair flopping into his eyes.

Thank God for that.

"But Terrance was there."

Affirmative, if slightly reluctant head bobbing.

"He beat Howard."

He didn't phrase it as a question, and Albert's chin dropped, his face caved. A small sound came from him, and Griff wished to high heaven the kid wasn't so skinny and helpless or so obviously not heterosexual. How his bigoted brother and father had failed to notice this about him was beyond Griff. But then, maybe they hadn't missed it. Maybe they had simply decided to systematically break down every possible chance the kid had to express it, through intimidation, threats, and making examples of anyone he might aspire to be like.

"You want my advice, find a college on the other side of the country. Get on a bus and don't look back."

Albert lifted his head and peered at Griff through his lashes.

"Albert, it's only a matter of time until even your dimwitted brother puts it all together. You think just because you *are* his brother he won't treat you the same way he treats us? I wouldn't take the chance if I were you. Bigotry just gets uglier and more vicious the closer to home the target is. I promise you. And you can't hide forever. Go somewhere you can safely be who you are."

Griff had nothing else to say. Albert would run, or he'd stay. He'd come out, or he'd hide. It wasn't Griff's call, and he hadn't actually asked for any advice. Griff climbed into his Jeep and started the engine.

"Griff!"

And there it was. The fear that made his face so soft, his movements jerky and abrupt. Albert clutched the roll bars and looked into the vehicle, desperate.

"What?"

"I can't afford college!"

"Get a job. You don't have to leave this minute. Just—" He didn't believe that. Hell, *Griff* didn't believe it. If Terrance didn't turn around and blame this whole thing on him, whether it had anything to do with the kid or not—and Griff thought it probably did—he'd eat that damn wallet he'd found. He didn't like the kid's chances against his much bigger, much meaner brother.

The desperate look edged toward panic and Griff sighed. "Look, Albert—"

"Don's hiring, right?"

"Are you crazy? You can't work for us, Albert." He pointed to the sad little house. "They'll skin you alive the minute you get home from your first day."

He dropped his eyes, then—slowly—his hand. "You're right." He nodded. "I know."

"Fuck." Heaving a sigh, Griff tipped his head toward the passenger seat. "Get in. I hope there's nothing here you really need, because the minute they realize where you've gone, pretty sure you won't be getting any of it back."

Albert held up one finger, raced to the garage to grab a rucksack sitting just inside the door, and hurried back. He tossed the bag into the back of the Jeep and jumped up beside Griff. "Okay."

"Okay?" Griff glanced at his pack, at him, and shook his head.

This was about as far from okay as things got, but Griff threw the Jeep into reverse and got the hell out of there.

Once they were out of town and headed for the farm, Albert seemed to relax. He grinned across the front seat—a shy, worried expression, but it wasn't panic, at least.

"Tell me you're eighteen," Griff demanded. God, please let him be of age.

He nodded. "Be nineteen next week."

"Thank God."

His family might freak out, but legally he could do whatever he wanted and they didn't have a say.

"I've had that pack in the garage since I was sixteen, you know." Albert jerked a thumb over his shoulder at the bag he'd tossed in the back. "Just waitin'." Another glance shot Griff's way. "And I won't bring no trouble, I swear. If they get mean about it, I'll move on. Just...."

"It's fine," Griff lied. Don was going to kill him.

Don's father was out on the porch before Griff had parked. His own father wandered out after him and handed him a cup of coffee. Perfect. Double barrel.

"Where the hell have you been?" Griff's dad demanded. His gaze shifted to Albert. "Fucking hell, Griff, what did you do?"

"Nothing!" Albert practically shouted, too quick, too defensive. "I was walking. He picked me up—"

"Albert, shush." Griff turned to the men on the porch. "Can we go inside?"

The older men led the way and Albert followed, bag in hand, gaze on the walkway.

"Explanations, Griff," Donald Sr. said as they gathered around the kitchen table. He went to the coffee pot, poured two more cups, and set them down in front of Griff and Albert. Spread out over the surface of the table was a collection of photos Griff had taken with his phone at Howe's garage when neither he nor Don had been paying any attention. The photos showed Terrance's wallet exactly where he'd found it—half under a leaning tool chest—and how he'd found it—with its contents spilled across the floor and a spray of blood adorning Visa card, driver's license, and leather. Terrance's image was clear on the ID.

Albert fingered one of the photos, then drew his hand back to clasp it in his lap under the table.

"I was at the diner," Albert said quietly, "watching Howe change a tire." He stared into his coffee. "Terrance had gone next door to get something. I figured he'd be gone a while. I just went over to talk to Howe." He shrugged. "I don't know why. I just...." He shot a glance at Griff, around the table, then back at Griff. "You're right. About everything. I am... gay. And eventually, they'll find out." His face collapsed into a frown. "They'd never understand. I just wanted to talk, you know? I didn't mean for Terrance to see me over there. I only wanted to talk to him because he's... you know. Like me. I never thought Terrance'd—" His words ended in a choked-off sound.

"Albert," Griff's father said, when all four of them had sat in silence waiting for him to continue and it became clear he had nothing else to say. "Are you telling me your brother went back to the garage and beat Howe up just because you were talking to him?"

Albert shrugged, but nodded without looking up. "I guess."

"Nothing else happened between the two of you?" he asked. "You just talked."

Again Albert nodded, this time vigorously, as he met the older man's gaze, his eyes shining. "I swear, Mr. McAllister. Nothing happened. Howe was nice. He's the one who mentioned that Mr. Jenkins was looking for someone to help out around here." He blinked at each of us in turn. "He thought I should ask. That you might help."

Griff squirmed under his father's gaze. "You and your strays and projects, Griffith, I swear. Now you're even rubbing off on Howard." He turned to Albert. "We'll help. Of course we will. You get your bag and come home with me."

"Dad," Griff tried to protest. If Terrance came looking for his little brother, Griff didn't want him to find Albert and his father alone.

Of course, he shot Griff down with logic. "He can work here. Abe will show him around and teach him what he needs to know. He'll stay at the house with me and there will be no hint of impropriety. No chance for anyone to even suggest it."

"I'm of age, Mr. McAllister," Albert pointed out. "I can do what I want."

"Not the point, son. You know your father and brother better than any of us, and you left in secret." He speared Albert with a look. "You tell me what they'll do."

He had nothing but a shrug in answer to that.

"Did you tell them you were thinking of leaving?"

Albert shook his head.

"So they don't know where you are or why you're gone."

He paled. "I should go back. They'll only—"

But both older men shook their heads. "You'll do no such thing," Don's dad said. "You came to us for help, and we'll give it. You have to trust us. This is the best way to go about freeing yourself of a situation that could get very bad very quickly."

The poor kid looked absolutely miserable as he nodded agreement to the arrangements. What else could he do? Nothing. Not in the face of Griff's father gathering him and his things and herding him toward the door, or Don's father telling him to be back by seven a.m., since that's when Abe started and he wanted them to get the most out of the day. Not in the face of everyone being right. He was in a precarious situation. At least here, surrounded by friends, he had some protection if his family decided to blow a gasket.

Once Albert and his father had left, Don's father cornered Griff.

"You could have got yourself killed."

Griff shook his head. "Terrance is a bully, Mr. Jenkins. Not a murderer. He's too much of a coward for anything like that."

"Provoke him a little more, and that might change."

"You think I should have left Albert there?"

He expected him to say yes. He expected him to say there was no way he should have helped anyone associated with his son's childhood tormenter, but he shook his head. "I don't think that. It was an impossible situation with no good solution, and you did the exact thing my son would have predicted you to do. You picked a fight and landed on your feet. You looked after people who can't look after themselves. It's why Don loves you so much. Just don't go that step too far that ends up breaking his heart, Griff."

Shame heated Griff's cheeks for even thinking this man would have had him condemn Albert to his fate with his hateful family. "No, sir," Griff assured him. "I'll be more careful." For Don. Because he couldn't hurt his best friend and lover by getting hurt himself.

He nodded. "Good. I'm off to bed. Don's stayed in the house tonight." He pointed to the ceiling. "He's in his old room at the end of the hall. Try not to make too much noise. Seven a.m. comes damn early for an old man."

That should have been funny. Maybe it was. Griff was too tired to tell. They said good night. His father-in-law headed for bed. Griff gathered up the pictures, locked them in a file cabinet in the study, and trudged upstairs.

Don lay in wait. Light from the hallway bounced off his eyes as he watched Griff undress. Griff felt the weight of that gaze on his back and his movement slowed, prolonging the time before he had to face his lover.

"Who's voice was that?"

"Albert Hawthorn."

No response for a long time.

"Don—"

"I don't need you keeping secrets from me too, Griff." He sat up and wrapped his arms around his knees. "That isn't who we are. We've never—"

"I'm not." *Too?* Was he talking about Howard's affairs? Or something else?

"You found that wallet. You took pictures, printed them up, hid them. That's a whole lot of secret. You didn't breathe a word to me or Howard. You knew who did this to him, and you said nothing to either of us." He peered through the semidark, pinning Griff with a glare that made the space between his shoulder blades itch. "Where did you go in the middle of the night?"

"Nowhere, Don. Leave it." Griff winced as he climbed into bed beside Don and caught his knuckles on the bedside table.

Don flicked on the lamp and grabbed Griff's hand. The signs of a fight were perfectly clear on the pink, grazed knuckles, and they brought a frown to his face.

"What did you do?"

"Returned his wallet."

"And what? His face just fell in front of your fist?"

"Something like that, yes." Griff snapped out the light.

Don turned it back on. "Fucking tell me what is going on!"

Digging his shoulder into the mattress, Griff curled, his back to his angry lover. "It's dealt with, okay?"

"No."

His hand was so warm on Griff's chilled skin. Griff closed his eyes and focused on the calluses of Don's palm caressing his shoulder.

"Griff, this is not okay. You can't go fighting everyone who—"

"Beats up my family? I can so."

Don's lips touched where his hand had been. The hand he slid down Griff's arm and curled over his raw knuckles. Griff winced and sucked in a breath. He tightened his grip until Griff's eyes watered from the sting.

"Babe, that worked when we were twelve and all that was going to happen was a trip to the principal's office. This is my family too. You, Howard. Please don't mess with that."

Ranting and railing and even tears and teeth-gnashing Griff could withstand. Don's cool, calm logic always did him in.

Griff rolled onto his back and gazed up at Don. "Albert's gay."

Don nodded. "Yeah, and it snows in winter. So what?" He knew exactly how to get Griff to smile with those simple little statements of his.

"So yesterday, he was at the diner and he wandered over to talk to Howe. Nothing happened. They just talked. Howard suggested he come talk to you about the job."

Don's lashes fluttered as he rolled his eyes. A bit of hair flopped in front of his face, and Griff reached to push it back. "Does he even know one end of a horse from the other?"

Griff shifted his shoulders. "Doubt it. But then, I don't think that's why Howe suggested it. Anyway, Terrance saw him talking to Howe. My guess is, Terrance came back with a couple friends when Howe was closing and encouraged him to stay away from Albert. He dropped his wallet in the scuffle, I found it, recorded it, just in case, and brought it back."

"To 'encourage' him to stay away from Howe."

"I didn't go looking for a fight, Don, and I did not threaten him or throw the first punch, I swear. You can ask Albert. He saw the whole exchange. Terrance sucker punched me, and I defended myself. If his nose got broke, he should have been more careful where he put his face."

Don let out a sigh and flopped onto his back. "You should have told me, babe. What if something had happened? I wouldn't even have known where you were."

Rolling onto his side, propped on one elbow, Griff had a hand free and he ran it up Don's side, watching for the shiver when he reached the space between hipbone and ribs. "I'm here now," he whispered, transferring the motion from his palm to the backs of his knuckles, traveling up Don's chest to bump over his nipple. That won him a squirm and the view of Don's teeth coming out to bite into his bottom lip.

Griff leaned down to work his tongue under those teeth and pull the lip free.

Don moaned, opened his mouth, and Griff lay claim to every bit of that warm cavern he could reach.

As he walked his knuckles back down Don's body, he plucked bits of skin to pinch and twist. He'd never admit it out loud, but Griff could tell by the way Don squirmed, up into the touch and not away from it, and the sounds of delight he breathed into the kiss, that the sharp torture turned him on faster and harder than the sweetest, softest touch.

Griff swallowed every single sound, every breath, skimming over his near-hairless body, still a wonder this late in his twenties. He had only a neat trail of dark curls from navel to groin, which Griff followed, down and back up, over his chest to his other nipple.

Don's entire body tensed under Griff.

Wiggling his fingers, Griff lifted his lips from Don's to look into his eyes. They were dark with need, greedy but patient.

"Relax."

Don tried. He really did, but even relaxed his muscles quivered, small tremors beyond his control shimmering through his limbs.

Griff pinched and twisted lightly.

Don moaned, soft and low, and went beautifully, perfectly lax. "Griff…."

Griff took that sound too—his name, straight from Don's lips—and kissed him until his fingers tightened in the sheets and all his attention was on Griff's mouth and the breath he was stealing away. He'd stopped waiting for Griff to torture that nipple. Funny how he never asked for it, only took what was given. But Griff knew he wanted it.

This time he obliged, wondering if giving him as much of that pain as he thought he wanted would get his hand slapped away. Hard and fast, he pinched, twisted, and a gasp tore Don's mouth from Griff's, his spine arched, chest thrusting into the vicious touch. His eyes flew open, glazed over a glow of pure bliss.

"Jesus, Don, you're gorgeous."

Griff had no idea if his lover heard him, but he responded to the touch in ways that made Griff's blood boil, half afraid, half fascinated. What if he went too far? Hurt him?

"Don." Griff lowered some of his weight onto him. "Don."

He moaned—soft, breathy—and nuzzled his face against Griff's neck. His lips roved lazily over sweat-sticky skin. A leg wrapped around Griff's.

"Don, pay attention." Griff lifted himself up, braced for the near-heart-wrenching whimper he made as their bodies lost contact. He pried Don's fingers free of the bedspread and pulled both his hands over his head, leaning on his wrists. Past experience told Griff he would open his eyes once he was pinned, stare up, silently waiting for Griff to rock and grind them both to completion.

He did open his eyes. He was still slightly glazed, blinking and so vulnerable it made Griff nervous and giddy. "Talk to me, babe," Griff whispered.

He shook his head slowly, gaze never leaving Griff's.

"Did that hurt?" Griff asked, licking a finger of his free hand and sliding it over Don's nipple.

Don nodded, smiled slightly, and pushed his chest up into the slippery touch.

"You want more of that." Griff didn't really have to ask. He could tell by the way Don trembled and strained, arms pinned, hips pinned, that he wanted a lot more. Everything about him was so gentle and calm. Of the three of them, he was the most delicate, the most obviously gay and receptive, and Griff knew he'd always enjoyed the pinch of his skin between Griff's teeth. But real pain?

"How much more?" Griff asked.

He shrugged, frowned a bit, and tested the grip. "Just more." He paused, stilling under Griff, studying him. "Weird?"

Griff shook his head, thinking how deeply it affected him to see his lover enjoy it so much. He was achingly hard already. "But you'll tell me if it's too much."

Don nodded. "I would never let you hurt me." His smile was as gentle and calm as always. "I'd never do that to you, Griff. Trust me."

Griff kissed him at that, long and hard, until he was bucking and twisting his arms, digging his heels into the mattress, no doubt as eager to get off as Griff was.

"I'm in charge now," Griff informed him, wrapping Don's fingers around the bars of the iron headboard. "Hang on. Don't let go unless I say so."

Don's eyes got dark, deep, and still as he watched Griff. He didn't complain as Griff hauled him down the bed until he strained to retain his grip. His eyes widened, but his fingers tightened and his teeth came out again to bite his lip.

Instead of using his tongue, this time Griff nibbled Don's lip free, making him moan and squirm as Griff sucked it into his mouth to ease the teeth marks with soft licks. "Don't close your eyes now," Griff told him, and Don blinked up at him.

He couldn't always see what Griff was doing as he used fingers, nails, teeth, and lips to nip and pull at his skin. Griff abused the privilege a little, or thought he did, drawing yelps of pain from Don, but never a plea to stop. Teeth indented the soft skin of his belly, left marks that would bruise and leave tiny spots of color for days after. Griff took Don's cock in his mouth as he worked the backs of his thighs with his fingers, and listened to him gasping, panting for breath. The sweat on his skin made him slippery, and Griff had to hold Don's hips from bucking his cock too deep.

A long, desperate groan brought Griff's head up and they locked gazes.

Don's eyes were nearly black in the dim light. His hair stood in messy curls, tangled and damp, but he couldn't lift his head much and still retain his grip on the bars.

Don dropped his head and it hit the pillow with a thud as Griff slowly engulfed him one more time. The sound that came out of him was almost a sob. Griff sucked hard as he came off Don's dick and let it slap against his belly. That made him jump and whimper again, and Griff slid up to find his lips.

Taking them both in hand, Griff kissed deeply, hungrily. It seemed Don barely had the energy to kiss back, but his hips moved languidly, almost in time to Griff's hand, and in a few strokes, they both strained into release, breath held tight, bodies rigid, Griff's other hand pinning Don's head to the pillow by his hair as he sucked at his throat.

They came down together and Griff eased his fingers out of Don's curls. Don blinked, as though surfacing from some deep, hazy place. His lashes were spiked together, his cheeks were pink, and he had the biggest, most bewildered grin on his face Griff had ever seen.

"You're a mess," Griff whispered, spreading a hand through the come on Don's belly.

Don nodded, still grinning.

Careful of the tender red marks he'd left, Griff traced his fingers up Don's outstretched arm to his knuckles, still bent securely around the bars. "Let go."

He did, only to lace his fingers firmly with Griff's. If he had surrendered something during their lovemaking, it had not been his strength, because he held tight, firm, not desperate, and Griff found comfort in that reminder that his lover was strong and capable. He took pride in the fact Don put that aside for Griff, simply because he chose to.

"Ouch." The cuts on Griff's knuckles ached under his grip. "That hurts," he whispered.

"Sorry." Don kissed where he'd been squeezing and pulled himself to sitting.

"Guess I'm not like you," Griff said gently.

"Guess not." He cupped Griff's face, kissed him, and pulled back. "Are you freaked out?"

Griff took the time to think about that. He deserved a real answer, not one flushed with giddiness from one of the best orgasms of his life.

"Griff?"

He shook his head. "No." But was he? "Maybe." But not by Don. His own reaction to Don's enthusiasm for the pain had unnerved Griff.

Don scrambled back, pushing himself along the mattress until his back hit the headboard. "I don't—"

"Freaked out at myself, if anything," Griff assured him. "Not you. I wouldn't have thought…." He flared his nostrils, drawing in the scents of sex, sweat, semen, unexpected kink, and smiled. "This is new," he offered. "We'll figure it out. Like everything else."

Don eyed him from under a fringe of dark curls, but he nodded. "Okay." His eyes were dark, hidden, and he'd made himself small against the headboard, curled in on himself.

"What's freaky, if anything, is the thought causing you pain is okay. I don't know what to think about that. About me... liking it." Griff glanced at him, expecting to see some sort of disbelief or fear on his face. "You think that's weird?"

Don shrugged. "If I didn't like it, I guess it would be." He moved close enough to lean on Griff's shoulder and kiss his neck. "But I do," he whispered. "God, Griff, I fucking like it. Tell me I'm not a freak."

Cupping his head close, Griff buried his face in the dampness of dark curls. "You're not a freak, babe. I love you."

They were quiet for a while, listening to the house settle in the night, to each other breathe, to hearts beating and life twisting into this new, unexpected pattern. "I need you to promise me one thing, Don."

"Anything."

"Promise you'll tell me if it's too much. I need you to promise...."

"I already said, I'd never do that to you, Griff." He kissed Griff, soft, sure, and calm again. "I'll make sure."

Griff sighed as they parted. "Me too. I'll be careful. I'll listen."

Don nodded. His head was growing heavier on Griff's shoulder.

"Come on. Before you fall asleep and ruin the sheets with our mess. Shower." Griff prodded his lolling lover to his feet and they snuck down the hallway to the bathroom together.

FAMILY TIES, TANGLES AND KNOTS

DRIVING Pete's little car west along Grey Road 12 gave Griff a chance to stop, mentally at least, and regroup. Insects chirruped, loud over the hum of the vehicle. Morning sun glowed through the back window. The radio announcer piped her over-enthusiastic pre-coffee cheer between country pop songs and the entire world just felt… normal.

He'd run into Albert in the hospital corridors. That boy had been a mess, which had confused Griff. He knew he liked Howe but hadn't thought they were all that close. That was when he'd learned the drunk who'd spun Howe's truck off the road had been Terrance. He hadn't stopped or slowed to see the damage, if he'd even been aware he'd caused it. Apparently, his blood alcohol had been off the charts. A mile down the road, they'd found his truck folded, nose first, against an ancient oak tree. Streaks of the distinctive red and yellow paint from Howard's truck stained his bumper and the driver's side of the box. If his truck had won the clash with Howe's, it hadn't won against the tree. There hadn't been a mark on the gravel or grass at the side of the road to indicate he'd tried to slow down, turn aside, or stop.

Terrance Hawthorn wasn't going to beat anyone else up. Ever.

"I'm so sorry," Albert had told Griff in that hospital corridor, completely confusing him with the apology. It was his brother who was dead. Howe would heal.

"For what?" Griff had asked, gut clenching suddenly. After nearly a year of working with them, integrating into their family, was he thinking of leaving?

"For Howe getting hurt," he'd said, his tone leaning toward that of a patient teacher.

"Albert, you didn't do anything. It wasn't your fault."

"He was my brother."

"So?"

"You think I don't know how much he's hurt your family?"

"Not your fault. *You* are my family."

Griff had pulled him into a hug and, after a heartbeat of frozen silence, Albert had cried on his shoulder, clung, and Griff had done his best to absorb his pain and sobs. His father tried to take him off Griff's hands at one point, but Albert had turned his back on the old man.

"Give me my son!" Hawthorn had yanked at Albert's shoulder, shouting and turning red as Albert resisted him.

Griff had opened his arms, but Albert clung harder and shook his head.

"Get him the fuck away from me," he'd pleaded.

Both Don's father and Griff's had stepped up to intervene, but Albert's old man snorted, poked a finger into Albert's back, and snarled. "You're as dead as Terrance to me, boy. You deserve these faggot freaks." Then he'd turned on his heel and stalked away.

After a few hiccuping breaths, Albert straightened and glanced around. He smiled weakly and shrugged. "Maybe he's right," he'd said after a few moments of stunned silence. "Because I swear I never did anything to deserve *him*."

Griff's father had handed him a hankie, patted his shoulder, and led him toward the door. "Come on home, son. You need to get some sleep. And Griffith," he'd shot over his shoulder, "get your ass home, too, and see to Don. Howe's in good hands."

Home.

Griff pulled into the laneway that arrowed between the pastures of his father's place and the hay fields of Don's. Halfway down the long narrow track, he stopped the car. It was the one place on the lane both houses were in view, and he looked between them.

Home.

He'd lived with Don for ten years now. He glanced at his father's house. His truck was already in the drive, but the place was still and quiet. If he and Albert were both inside sleeping, who was with the horses? Who was supposed to take care of them, and Dad, and Howe and Don? How was he supposed to do all this?

A cloud of dust rose along the drive, outpaced slightly by Don's truck. It stopped at the barn and a tall figure hopped out. Robbie? No. A mop of red hair down the man's back flashed in the sunlight. Mark. When had he arrived from the city? An almost equally tall, dark-haired young man rounded the back of the truck and lifted something out. That had to be

Robbie. He was the only one in the family who approached Mark's towering height.

A sudden coughing rumble from the fields to his left startled Griff, and he looked over to see the combine lurch into motion. An arm swung up and waved from behind the cab's glass. He couldn't see who was driving, but he guessed it had to be Pete.

His eyes stung, and he blinked. If anyone had been around, he'd have blamed it on the dust blowing along the lane.

Home.

He put the car in gear and rolled toward the house.

Good God, he wanted home so bad.

November, age twenty-seven

WHOSE idea had it been to travel six hundred miles through the snowbelt to pick up a horse in mid-November? Sure, it wasn't guaranteed to snow this time of year. Not unless one was traveling with an ancient horse trailer that no one made snow tires for anymore, and an already high-strung horse inside.

"Take your time, son."

"Dad, really? You want to drive? Because I don't think I can actually drive any slower and still be moving." Griff shot a glare toward the passenger side of the cab.

"The horse can feel your nerves, son."

From twenty feet back, encased in its rickety steel contraption hurtling—well, crawling, really—down the highway, Griff was pretty sure his nerves were not the ones that had the damn beast shifting his weight around back there like he was in a rodeo.

"We have to find a place to stop," Griff said. "Anyone who's got an empty stall for the night will do. I can't drive in this anymore."

"You want to just randomly stop at a strange farm and beg?"

"If I have to. Don't you know anyone around here?"

He shook his head. "Closest place I know is still more than an hour away at this pace."

Griff sighed and flexed his stiff fingers, one hand at a time, before fastening them back around the wheel in a death grip. "Then keep your eyes open for a place that looks like it's been fenced for horses. Or a hotel with a really nice garage."

Five minutes later, his father spotted a place with Shetland ponies, heads together, tails to the wind, huddling in the blowing snow. Their coats were already shaggy and thick with winter growth, and they trotted happily along the fence as they pulled into the long drive toward the house.

Relief washed through Griff when the front door opened and a burly man came out wearing boots, a heavy barn coat, and work gloves. He didn't even stop the truck, but waved them past the house along a lane toward his barn, just like he'd been expecting them. Thank God. Horse people were horse people, no matter where they were.

Griff pulled up beside the barn while the stranger opened it up, and Dad hopped out and hurried to the trailer.

"No weather to be hauling in!" the Good Samaritan shouted over the wind.

His ponies looked on with curiosity through the fence rails.

"Didn't expect it to get this bad so early in the season," Griff admitted as he held out a hand. "I'm Griff McAllister, this is my father, Jim."

"Steve Case." They shook and Steve's hand was firm and reassuring. "It blew up fast. Does that a lot around here, but forecast says it isn't going to let up until late tomorrow. You're welcome to stay until it blows over. Let's get your load safe and warm."

"Thank you, so much."

He shook his head. "No thanks necessary." He grinned. "My girl saw you crawling along the drive. She was going to come out herself, if I didn't."

They rounded the trailer to help Griff's father get it open. The new horse snorted and stomped, lifting a back leg in warning. His tail swished and snow blew in around his legs. He was a beautiful animal but about as high-strung as they came. And he didn't know these particular humans from Adam. Griff wasn't sure how they were going to coax him out into the blowing cold and snow.

"Wait a minute. Let me get Bess," Steve said.

"Bess?"

He whistled and a small black-and-white dog came racing from the barn. She yipped at his feet once, ran a circle around everyone, smelling the strangers' pants' legs, then sat and looked up at Steve expectantly.

He patted her head. "Can you calm our boy down for us, Bessie?" He brought her to the trailer and motioned inside.

Griff had never seen anything like it. It took that dog less than five minutes to get inside past the horse's stomping, clattering hooves to sit, nose to drooping nose, and get him calmed down. After that, it took them a matter of minutes to lead him out and into the warm, sweet-smelling barn.

"I'll leave you boys to it," Steve said as he showed them to an empty stall. "Feed's there, hose"—he pointed—"and you can park off to the side, near the house. Come on in the back door once he's settled."

"I can't thank you enough for this," Griff's father told him, but Steve waved the thanks off.

"Least I can do. No kind of weather to be hauling a skittish animal around. You get him settled and come on inside. Wife has coffee on and she's heating up a bit of meat pie and gravy."

God, that sounded so good. Horse people were horse people. You had to love them.

As they worked to get the horse settled, the ponies wandered in and out of a small enclosure near the back of the barn. The opening they used was nothing more than a thick sheet of plastic, but it did the trick of keeping the winter winds on the outside and the warmth of shared body heat on the inside. It gave the hardy little beasts the freedom to come in when they needed to be warm, and go out if they needed to cool off under their heavy coats. It was reassuring to see the animals were friendly and well looked after.

Inside, the house was much like every farm kitchen Griff had ever been in. Rough around the edges, but clean and serviceable, and filled with generations of family mementos and items left behind over years of occupation.

Steve's wife, Regina, and his daughter, Beth, joined them with cups of coffee as they wolfed down the pie and gravy. They were both as friendly and outgoing as Steve. It was exactly the same atmosphere of Don's home, minus the endless parade of people.

"Yeah," Griff said in answer to Beth's question about the trip. "It was sunshine and clear roads when we left this morning. Snow started just after lunch and we thought we could press through to the other side before it got too bad. Guess it traveled with us, instead."

"No telling which way these beasts will go, once they get started," Regina said. "But no matter. You're safe and sound for now. We've got the room."

Griff held up his cell. "No service, though, I'm afraid. Do you mind if I use your phone? I'd like to call home and let them know we're held up."

She smiled. "Of course. I'm sure your wife must be worried."

Griff shared that immediate, half-paranoid glance with his father that had become habitual over the weeks since Howe had been attacked. He'd never hidden who he was. His father had never encouraged him to, but the reminder of how quickly and viciously people could react had been well learned.

"Oh." Regina's cheeks turned pink. "You're not married. I assumed."

"Not exactly," Griff admitted, hoping to leave it at that.

The poor woman looked so flustered, though, he couldn't refrain from saying something to alleviate her discomfort.

"It's a natural assumption. I've been with my partner for twelve years this past September, but we aren't actually married." Griff set his fork on his plate and sat back. "His name is Donald." He didn't want any misunderstanding. "And yes, he will worry."

"Donald." She looked surprised, then smoothed the expression from her face as she stood. "After sixteen years with Steve,"—she patted her husband's arm as she passed his seat—"I think we worry more now than we did when we were younger." She smiled at Griff. "We've come to appreciate what we have to lose, I think."

Griff nodded agreement. "I've known him most of my life. Can't imagine it without him."

Her smile was genuine. "Come with me. There's a phone in the study. You'll have privacy."

"Thank you." Breathing a sigh of relief, Griff glanced at his father to find him practically glowing with pride. They both stood, and his father began to gather up the dishes, but was quickly shooed from the kitchen for his efforts. Steve took him to the living room, and together they searched for a decent sport to watch on TV.

Once alone in the study, Griff heaved out a breath and sank into the office chair. As kind as this family had been, the drive and dealing with complete strangers was taking its toll on his nerves. He wanted to hear Don's voice and know he wasn't worrying about them.

"I accept the charges." Don's voice, as he spoke to the operator, sounded calm and quiet, just like always, and Griff closed his eyes and waited for the call to go through.

"Hey, babe," he said when they were connected.

"Griff. Where are you? I saw the weather channel." Worry twisted Don's words tighter than before, and Griff realized the calm had been a façade.

"We're okay. We found a place to hole up. Not sure the name of the farm, but the owner is Steve Case. He had a free stall and a couple of spare rooms. We'll wait out the storm and get on the road again tomorrow when it's safe."

"How's your dad? And the horse?"

Griff smiled. It was like him to worry about everything. "Fine. We're all fine."

"Good." He still sounded tight. Griff knew there was something he wanted to say but wouldn't.

"I was looking forward to being home in bed with you tonight," Griff said softly. He had to ignore the ache that brought on. It wasn't a lie.

"Miss you too."

"Tomorrow," he promised. "And I know exactly how to make it up to you."

Don actually groaned, and for the first time all day Griff smiled; it reached deep enough to melt a bit of the clawing cold.

"I'll hold you to that."

He allowed a grin and hoped his lover could hear it in his voice. "Only things you'll be holding, babe, are the bars of that headboard, I promise you that."

"Fuck, Griff." His curse was barely a whisper, and Griff imagined his lids fluttering closed, long lashes brushing his cheeks.

"You're palming your dick, aren't you?"

"So fucking unfair."

"Tell me about it," Griff muttered. He squashed his own dick inside his jeans. It wouldn't do to get off the phone with him sporting a boner that their new stallion would envy. At home, when it was just the two of them, Griff could walk around hard and wanting Don. It made his normally self-effacing lover preen to know all he had to do was suggest sex and Griff would get a stiffy. Griff loved watching Don's ego inflate knowing he could do that to him, and he loved even more the way he surrendered his ego when Griff tied him down and teased until he begged. But as a guest in the home of utter strangers, Griff was not about to insult them by acting like a horny teenager. There was no reason he couldn't give his lover a little taste of his own medicine, though.

"At least you can take care of yours," Griff reminded him. "And imagine all the marks I'd leave on you if I was there to look after it for you."

That got him another, deeper groan, followed by a soft gasp.

"Oh my God. You're jerking off."

"Fuck you. You started it."

"You're jerking off in the middle of the afternoon because I called and promised to leave bite marks all over you." The rush of knowing that left Griff breathless. It didn't help get rid of his own hard-on.

Don was quiet for a second. "I'm not jerking off. Yet?"

"You should be," Griff told him, responding to the question in his tone and pitching his voice a bit lower, a bit more demanding, and glancing at the study door. Heaven help him if it wasn't closed and his hosts overheard. It was securely latched, though, and Griff turned his attention back to the phone and the man on the other end of the line.

"Why should I?"

"Are you goading me?"

"I wouldn't dare." But his voice shook, in the same way his body trembled when they were just on the edge of that place where he gave up controlling everything and left Griff to take care of him.

"You actually would dare. You just did and if I was there, you'd pay for it in pain." Griff clicked his teeth together for emphasis. It was still Don's favorite way to receive that ultimate high.

There was no discernible reply to that. Only more guttural sounds and heavy breathing.

"I think I just fell a little more in love with you, Donald Jenkins. Beat faster. I want to hear you come."

"Griff...."

"Don't hold back. Make it good. I want to hear you."

He swore, a few whispered curses, whispered a garbled version of Griff's name, and more curses. "Jesus, I—"

"Louder."

"Gri—ungh!"

A warm glow spread through Griff at the sound of him hitting the wall of orgasm hard. "That's my boy," he whispered. Very, very rarely did their games enter the realm that required titles, but the catch in Don's breathing and Griff's inability to touch him or hold him as he came down made Griff want to reach out in some way to let his lover know he was there.

"Griff."

"I'm here."

"Gimme a sec."

"Take your time."

Griff listened to the shuffling as Don put himself back together. "Where are you?"

"In the kitchen."

That got Griff's attention. "At the house? Brave. Where's your dad?"

"Not sure. Hang on. I gotta put the phone down. I sorta missed the sink."

Griff laughed.

"Fucker." There was a clank and Griff heard the tap running, and then Don was back.

"Well," he said. "That was unexpected."

"Yeah. Imagine me driving home tomorrow trying to hide a perma-erection from my father while I'm thinking about you beating off in our kitchen. All that teenage angst revisited. Thanks. There will be payback."

He chuckled.

"God, I miss you, babe."

"It's only been a week," Don reminded him, though the reminder lacked much conviction.

"Ten days."

"I love you," he blurted. He rarely said the words. Not that Griff needed him to, but today, for some reason it was a relief to hear.

"Love you too."

For a few heartbeats, they communed in silence before Don brought them back around to the mundane. "That horse had better be worth an extra day."

"He's a beautiful creature. Wait until you see him. He really is worth every penny Dad paid."

"Good."

"You'll let the boys know to look after the herd another day?"

"Of course."

"How are they doing with that?"

"You'll see when you get home." There was definite familial pride in his voice, and Griff smiled. Family was everything to his man. Which inevitably led to thoughts of Howe, the fight, and how much Griff missed him.

"Good," he said, forcing his mind back to the conversation. "I should get off the phone, though. Long distance and all."

"Yeah." Don didn't hang up or say good-bye, though.

Griff wondered if they were thinking the same thing. Only one way to find out. "Don."

"Yeah?"

"I know we said we'd give Howe space."

"It's been two months," he said quickly. Was he agreeing that it had been too long?

"I don't want to rush him or demand anything. I just…."

"Dad already called him and told him he expected to see him here for Christmas Eve dinner. I don't think I was supposed to overhear it, though."

"*We* should invite him. I want him to come." God, how Griff wanted him back.

"Me too." He said it, but Griff had heard the hesitation.

"What is it, babe?"

"I haven't talked to him about Albert." Don sounded almost guilty about that lapse, and Griff, for the life of him, couldn't figure out why.

Much as he missed Howe, it irked him that his very absence could cause Don to doubt his own judgment like this. His voice tightened around that irritation. "If he was around at all, he'd know."

"And you're still mad at him, Griff."

Griff sighed and leaned his head on his hand. "Of course I'm still mad at him. He lied to us. There was nothing going on. All he did was talk to the kid. Why would he tell us there was more than that? Why would he want us to think he was screwing around if he's not?"

Don didn't answer right away. Did he know something Griff didn't?

"Don?"

"I don't really know anything, Griff. Except that I wouldn't skip using protection with him. None of us ever said he belonged to us and only us. What if he's right? Are we being fair? I mean, we live together. He's—"

"Been asked, Don. More than once."

Another long pause greeted that before he finally spoke again. "I love you."

It sounded like a precursor to something he thought Griff wouldn't want to hear. "I know that."

"So this isn't about that, okay?"

"What isn't?"

"Maybe he's right. Maybe it's time we just let him go. Let him get on with his life. If we can't give him what he needs, then—"

"Who says we can't?" Even to himself, Griff sounded harsh.

"He does, Griff."

"He's wrong." Two months later, and Howe was healed. At least physically. Obviously, Don was still skittish.

"You're like a bull in a china shop, babe. You can't pound love into him."

"He's got a thick skull."

Don chuckled and agreed, but his laughter died away quickly. "But a bruised heart. Don't you think beating him up over not being what we want him to be is only making it worse?"

"Wait a minute. Aren't you the one who said once that we shouldn't be having a conversation about our relationship with Howe unless Howe was there to have his say?"

"Yeah, but you and I need to be on the same page."

Griff shook his head. "No, babe, we don't." It had never occurred to him before this moment that he might love Howe more than Don did. "And if you're serious about cutting him loose, then we aren't on the same page at all, and this is not a conversation we should be having over the phone."

"God, Griff—"

"I'm not talking about this anymore right now."

Silence.

"Don, I love you."

"Yeah."

More silence.

Griff nodded. "Okay, then. I'll see you tomorrow sometime. We'll call before we get on the road."

"Okay."

"Babe—"

"See you tomorrow."

The line went dead.

Jesus shit, that hurt. Griff sat for quite a while staring at the phone until his father stuck his head in.

"Everything okay, Griff?"

Griff nodded, pushed to his feet, and mumbled something about checking on the horse. Before he had to face more questions, he fled for the barn.

THE second half of that ride home was significantly less eventful. Griff hadn't slept well, so his father did most of the driving, leaving him free to think.

Excellent.

What the hell had that conversation yesterday been about? After a sleepless night of thought, he saw Don's point that Howe could have an issue with Albert, but the kid had melded into farm life like he'd been born to it. Not only did he pick up the slack with the livestock on all three farms, but he'd learned everything Abe had to teach him about repairing farm equipment. He was even taking night classes at the college, paid for by Griff's father. A business investment, the old man maintained, though Griff saw through that to the soft heart he already knew beat hard beneath the weathered horse-rancher exterior. Albert had made himself indispensable, both to Griff's dad and to Donald Sr., and been a big help to Pete fixing fences llamas seemed to find inexplicable joy in kicking down. It was like he'd found a family, a place to belong that he'd never had before, and he'd jumped in with both feet. Griff wasn't about to turn him out now, and he knew Don wouldn't, either.

But then, he'd known Don would never shut Howe out of their lives too, hadn't he? Or maybe he didn't know anything at all.

Christmas Eve dinner was just around the corner, and he was glad Don's father had decided to include Albert in the family-wide event. Griff wanted Howe there too, but was that asking for trouble? Albert's brother and father never failed to take a verbal pot shot at any Jenkins they happened across in the street. So what if Terrance hadn't gone so far as to try beating anyone else up? His aggression worried Griff anyway.

He didn't understand how Don's family stood the harassment, but it rolled off their backs a lot better than it rolled off Albert's. He was blatantly ignored by his own flesh and blood. The rejection hurt him, but frankly, Griff was relieved. Had the Hawthorns tried to force him back home, he knew from experience Don's family would not have stood quietly by. They tended to close ranks around their own, and Griff could appreciate that protectiveness. It had encompassed him and his father, supported them through some very lean times. They wouldn't let Albert go quietly.

Griff had thought Howe was one of theirs, but now he wasn't so sure. None of them had tried to communicate with him since their fight, as far as he knew. He also knew his lover hadn't made any attempt to reconcile with Howe. Did it take Don's approval to be included in the clan? Maybe Griff's word wasn't good enough for them. Well, except for Don's father, who had been the one to call Howe about Christmas. But then, he was the patriarch. He didn't have to wait for Don's approval.

As for Albert, it made no difference how mean his family was or how violent they might get with him, they were still his family, and it was clear they wanted nothing more to do with him. He clung to the Jenkins's approval like a rodeo rider to a bucking bronco. Having been the beneficiary of their generosity himself, Griff didn't blame him one bit. He did suddenly wonder how far that generosity stretched. If Howard had worn out his welcome, what would happen if Griff resolved to keep him in his life?

It began to make sense to him why Albert poured himself so thoroughly into his work. If he made himself important to someone, his own family's betrayal might hurt less. Possibly, those someones would keep him when everyone else had abandoned him.

Howe had done much the same when he'd lost his family. He'd poured his heart and soul into his garage. He was doing it again now, to the exclusion of all else, including Don and Griff, this time. It was a constant ache neither of them talked about. It dragged at them, though. His absence was a presence in itself, and it hovered between them like a black shroud.

They both focused on Albert and his learning curve so they could ignore how much they missed Howe. It had been Griff's father's idea to leave him and Robbie in charge of the horse ranch, and Griff wondered about that. His father wasn't as young as he used to be. He might be looking for someone to take over. After all, Griff had lived with Don for almost ten years. He'd never really considered the future of either farm, and now he was beginning to see that he probably should. It was a clear and easy path to fall into Don's life and stay there as long as he wanted Griff. What if that wasn't going to pan out like he'd expected? What if his feelings for Howard ruined what Griff had with Don?

Cold sweat broke out over Griff's skin. Between one heartbeat and the next, the overwhelming need to puke rose.

"Dad, can you stop?"

"There's a rest stop in about ten minutes."

"Now, Dad. Stop now."

"Griff?"

It took him eternal minutes to safely pull truck and trailer to the soft shoulder, and Griff barreled out the door while he was still slowing down.

The delicious breakfast of sausage and eggs Regina had provided spewed into the ditch as he retched. It took a few moments to be sure he was done before he climbed back into the truck to lean on the door.

"Son?"

"Carsick, I guess," Griff lied. Not that he'd fall for it. His father always saw through him, and besides, he'd never been carsick a day in his life.

"Talk to me." He hadn't put the truck in gear, and now he rested both forearms on the steering wheel and studied Griff, who suspected he wouldn't budge from the side of the road until he knew what was wrong.

"It used to be so simple. I mean Don...." He shook his head and spent a few moments studying the calluses on his palms. "And Howard." Drawing in a breath, he pinched the bridge of his nose and rested an arm on the edge of the window so he could stare out at the rolling waves of white fields. "Don lets me take care of him. When he needs it. Howe. God, Dad, I could wring his neck. Why won't he let us help?"

"No one ever said this was going to be easy, son."

Griff snorted. "No shit." But it *had* been easy. Years ago, he'd made the decision to love them both. He hadn't stopped loving either of them. Turned out he was the only one in that position, though. After everything, Don was fed up and Howe was just too damaged to let them help him.

"You had a fight with Don yesterday." His father put the truck in gear now and watched out his mirror to make sure it was safe to get back on the highway. Griff supposed he was confident in his ability to keep the conversation going now that he'd got it started.

"Not even a fight. There was no yelling or accusations. It was just…." Griff shrugged. "I think we don't want the same things after all." He turned to look to his father, his constant, but the man was busy driving. "What am I going to do?"

"What you always do, Griff."

"Bull my way through Don's control issues and remind Howard how broken he is? Because that seems to be working."

His father smiled and it was so familiar an expression it made Griff wish for those lean days when it had been the two of them together, simple, fighting to keep their home and their horses and each other together. "Clumsy love is still love. They understand that about you. Have faith in them. Everyone doesn't trust and love the way you do."

"What if Don says it has to be him or Howe?"

His dad looked sad, but resolute. "If it comes to that, you'll know what decision to make."

"I can't choose between them."

"If it comes down to it, you won't have to."

"What does that even mean?"

"Look, Griff, I know your mother and I didn't exactly give you the best example of how love works, but that never stopped you giving yourself to not just one, but two very deserving men. Trust yourself. Let them trust you. And be patient. It's one thing to have this mutually unspoken agreement you all seem to have, but eventually, it was going to either dissolve or solidify. Neither one of those outcomes means you love them any less. It just means you finally stand your ground with both of them. You ask me, they both could use a bit of grounding."

"What does that mean?"

He shrugged. "Means they're opposite ends of a spectrum. Howe never knew what decent family could be and Don's never known anything but love and acceptance. You know both. Use what you know. Make your own family."

When he said it, everything made sense. It all sounded normal and perfect and practical. Griff wanted it to be that easy.

WHEN they got home, it was obvious his father had been right to leave the boys in charge. The barn practically glowed, it was so clean. The new horse's stall was pristine and the jumpy animal settled quickly in the spacious luxury the young men had readied for him. Getting him unloaded had been one of the easiest transfers they'd ever done, mostly thanks to Albert's gentle touch. He had the travel-weary beast of a horse calmed inside of ten minutes, and it let him go in the trailer, fasten the lead, and back him out without so much as an irritated snort.

"He has the touch," Dad murmured to Griff, practically glowing with pride. "Look at that."

"Kid knows what it feels like to be all nerves all the time. He's just doing what he wished someone would have done for him," Griff speculated. "Thanks for giving him this, Dad."

"Giving him what?" He looked at Griff, curious.

"A second chance at a family. At a home. A future."

He shook his head and chuckled. "I am very lucky you never volunteered at a pet shelter, I think."

He got a laugh out of Griff when he wasn't in the mood to laugh, and Griff loved him for it.

Once the horse was settled, the trailer cleaned and parked, and all the new tack stowed, Albert volunteered to drive Robbie home to Pete's.

"Andrew and Sophie and Mark are there," he'd explained. His brown eyes sparkled at mention of Andrew's stepson, and Griff had to wonder if that sparkle had anything to do with the frequency of Mark's recent visits to his uncle Pete's house. He'd always loved the farms, sure, but Griff had expected that to wane under the influence of his first year of university. All signs pointed to a city boy who yearned for the country. He'd already switched his major from some sort of environmental engineering to agricultural sciences. Something like the opposite of what Andrew had done at his age. Andrew had never been much of a farmer, but the son of his heart, whom he'd raised as his own since the boy was five years old, seemed to be the one who would take up the family business.

"Guess that's that, then," Griff said as they watched the boys drive off toward Pete's.

His father's hand landed heavily on his back. "You want a lift home?"

Griff shook his head. It was only a five-minute walk from his father's barn to the cabin he and Don shared at the end of his father's property. "I'll be fine. Thanks."

"I know you will."

BELONGING

HIS father's confidence in him had never wavered, even when his own did. Or maybe, his was strongest when Griff's was weakest. Griff didn't know. Only that he was grateful for the support, for himself, for Albert, and for Howe. Walking out of that hospital after the scene with Albert, Griff appreciated the man's mile-wide practical streak. And driving up the drive, he realized his father was probably the one who had mobilized people to get the work on two farms done when Don and Griff had gone into meltdown over Howe.

He put the car in park and listened to the morning. Sunshine pouring over the horizon would be streaming into their kitchen right now. So unlike the cool, quiet sanctuary of the tiny cabin they had shared for so long, the main house they now shared was the hub of three farms and a thriving, interconnected network of so many people that some days, Griff could barely get his head around it all.

Now, though, his lover was inside that huge home alone, and it finally sank in that everyone nudging him in this direction had been right. Even wrapped up in casts and blankets and tubes as he was, Howe was being well looked after.

Don was the one who needed him. Griff had what no one else could give him.

Pocketing Pete's keys, he hurried as fast as his crutches allowed up the front porch steps, clattered inside, and called out.

The house was deathly silent. No radio. No TV. No gregarious riot of voices discussing who was going to do what.

"Don?" He peeked into the kitchen. He was there, pouring over what looked like ledgers and bills and looking exhausted and wild around the edges. His gaze was too glassy. His curls stuck out at all angles and he was too pale.

"Hey, babe." Griff approached as if he might take off for the other end of the room like a skittish horse.

He didn't look up.

"Don?"

He slammed the ledger he was looking at closed. "Fucking hay didn't pay for itself," he snarled. "How am I so bad at this? I grew up doing this shit and I'm screwing it all up!" He grabbed a fistful of papers and threw them. A calculator smashed against the kitchen wall and the pages fluttered to the floor and into the sink almost gently.

"Don, hey." Griff hurried to him, and he started at the hand Griff rested on his shoulder.

"I'm losing my farm, Griff."

"We are not going to lose anything, you hear me?" He crouched next to him, splaying his cast out at an awkward angle to get low enough to see into his lover's face. "We aren't, I promise."

"You can't—"

"Yes, babe, I can. Come here." Griff pulled Don to him, and he nearly fell out of the chair in his rush to get as close as possible. Unable to hold his balance on one foot, they both thudded to the floor. Griff half expected him to break out sobbing, even though he wasn't a crier. He never had been. History proved Griff was the one more likely to burst into tears, but he managed to hold it together this time.

Don didn't cry either. He clung, his entire body shaking with the force of his arms around Griff's middle.

Digging fingers into Don's hair, Griff clung back and buried his face close to Don's neck where he could smell skin and diesel fuel and hay, sunshine, heat, and the sweat of fear. They ended up sitting on the kitchen floor, holding on to each other for a long time, and it brought back that Christmas, that last time Howe had come between them.

December, age twenty-seven

THEIR little cottage had barely been dug out of the storm. When Griff got inside, it was dark everywhere but the kitchen, and so quiet. Only the rustling of papers let him know Don was sitting at the kitchen table. Griff sidled in to see what he was doing.

His head lifted slightly when Griff's feet hit the creaky floorboards on the kitchen side of the threshold.

"Hey," he said without looking around. "You're home."

"I'm home. Everything okay?"

He turned then, and for a heartbeat stared up, silent and searching. Griff didn't know what to give him, so he waited.

"You're home," he said again, as though the fact of Griff's presence was taking a moment to settle into his brain.

"Yeah. Don, what's wrong?" Stepping closer, Griff itched to slide fingers into his shaggy hair, to touch him.

"I hung up on you." His voice was a soft whisper of sound in the quiet room.

Belatedly, Griff remembered his promise to call him before they had left and realized that promise had completely flown out of his head in the flurry to get a horse who didn't like trailers or traveling into the vehicle for the second half of the six-hundred-mile trip home.

"Jesus, Don, I'm so sorry."

His brow furrowed. "Because I hung up on you?"

What was wrong with him? "I was supposed to call before we left today and I forgot. I'm sorry I didn't. It slipped my mind."

He continued to look at Griff, bewildered, and Griff crouched beside his chair to see into his face. It was like he was only half present in the conversation, half trapped in some other reality Griff couldn't share with him. "Don. Babe, what is it?"

"You said you loved me and I hung up on you without saying it back, and what if something had happened, Griff?"

"Nothing happened."

"But it could have, and you would have thought I was that mad at you. If something bad happened and I hadn't said it—"

"Okay, you need to calm down. Come here." Griff stood and held out a hand. "Nothing happened, and I know you love me." He pushed all his doubts out of the way and took Don's hand when he didn't immediately take the invitation. Bullish? So what. He'd respond if Griff took control, and right now, Griff needed him to respond.

"You tell me what's going on, Don. What is it?"

"I love you."

"I know you do."

"Maybe Mom was upset when...."

His mother. He had to be referring to her car accident. He was stuck back in that horrific moment in the dead of winter when she'd been taken from them, and Griff had been worried about a fight about Howard, who they never fought about. "Why are you thinking about that?"

"I was talking to her before it happened. About Howard. She told me I should—"

"Should what?"

He shook his head. "She didn't like the idea of us. She was so sure it wouldn't work. That it would ruin us. She didn't understand, and I couldn't make her see. I yelled at her, told her to butt out of my life, that it didn't concern her. I was horrible to her. I hung up on her. And then... that." He dropped his head. "And I couldn't go into that hospital room and look her in the eye. If she was distracted, Griff, if I—"

"No." Griff took both Don's shoulders and shook until he looked up. "No, Don, don't do this. The only things responsible for that accident were shitty road conditions and zero visibility, you understand me? Your mother knew how much you loved her and she knew even if you were upset with her you would never turn your back on her. She *knew* that."

For a moment, he simply stared at Griff, and Griff waited for his words to sink in past the daze.

"When's the last time you slept?" Griff asked him, when everything he'd said had no apparent effect on his lover.

He shrugged. "Don't sleep well when you're not here."

"I know." Griff pulled him close. "But I'm here now, so we're going to get you sorted out. Come on." He steered Don from the kitchen toward the bedroom at the back of the little house.

"I do love you, Griff. And I'm sorry."

"It's okay. It's past. That was yesterday, and today I'm home, yes?"

He nodded. "You were right about Howard."

"We'll talk about Howard later. You and me right now."

Don pulled them to a stop and a tiny frown changed his face, brought his gaze from that lost, distracted distance back to the kitchen with Griff. "You want him."

Griff took Don's jaw in one hand and gripped his wrist hard with the other.

His eyes got wide and all his attention fixed upward, on Griff's face. Finally.

"I said we'd talk about him later. Right now, it's late, I'm home with you, and I owe you a few promised love bites."

"So easy," he whispered. "If I let you take over, everything else goes away."

"So let it. That's the whole idea."

And besides, he was right. This was easy. Him and Griff. It was the simplest thing in the universe.

"It will all be there tomorrow, and you and I will be here to deal with it together, yeah?"

He nodded. "Yeah." A faint smile replaced the frown. "You do all the work in bed lately."

"Who's complaining?" Griff brought his face close and kissed him until he was pretty sure Don was done with talking. They had more important things to do with the rest of the night.

They didn't talk about Howard the next day. Or the day after. Maybe they were avoiding the topic. Or, like they usually did, were letting fate dictate how that panned out. Or they were too afraid to fight. Griff had no idea, but Don never brought it up again, and so Griff let it slide away.

WELL, not that it ever really went away. There remained a Howard-shaped hole in their life together. Don was right about one thing. Griff wanted Howe. He wanted them both and was too terrified to remind Don of that fact lest it broke them apart. Since he'd been living life without Howe for months, Griff could not imagine his life without Don. Missing Howe he had grown, if not comfortable with, at least used to. He'd learned to navigate around the missing piece and avoid falling into the hole very often. Without Don, he imagined the fall would be inevitable and without end. He couldn't deal with that.

So he kept his mouth shut. He endured.

And he wondered when it had happened that the man he'd first imagined to be his rival had turned into a man he sometimes wanted so desperately everything ached. He didn't just want him in their bed. He wanted him in their lives. He wanted to bring him coffee when he had his head stuck under a truck hood or inside a combine housing, and he wanted to rub his shoulders in the bath after a long day. He wanted to be able to yell at him for leaving greasy overalls on the laundry room floor.

Griff wanted to wake up next to him on Christmas morning and see his smile burst open when he opened gifts. And he wanted to sit with his family at that Christmas Eve dinner and hold his hand, right there where everyone could see him doing it and declare he was Griff's, Don's, family. That he belonged.

Instead, standing in the Jenkins's living room that Christmas Eve after he'd been attacked, Griff whispered the wish into Don's ear in the quiet moments alone on the couch and after all the kids had piled out into the afternoon snow to feed livestock, and held his breath.

Don said nothing more than he ever said. That he'd tried. He'd failed. It sounded like he thought Griff was accusing him of not trying hard enough. He wasn't. At least, he thought he wasn't. He had to wonder if maybe all of this romanticized nonsense of the three of them he'd built up in his head was just that. Nonsense. Maybe he was, after all, the only one who believed in it.

But then an innocent, practically five-year-old kid pointed out Howe's absence and Don didn't shut him down. He looked sad. He looked defeated. And he explained the reality of three men in a mess of broken hearts to a kid in a way that made it seem painfully simple.

After leaving Alex out in the late-afternoon sunshine with his cousins, they stomped the snow off their boots and peeled out of barn coats in the mudroom as Pete admonished them for letting in the cold. Griff watched Don's face, hoping for some hint the bantering touched deeper than surface affection.

Nothing touched Don deeply lately. Not even the control and the pain in the bedroom got under his skin unless Griff pushed him hard, and lately, he wasn't responding in a way that gave Griff confidence he wouldn't let it go too far.

"We'll just make our excuses and go, okay?" Griff said, laying a hand on his back.

He nodded and offered a thin smile.

Griff didn't know if it hurt more to see him try to appease him and fall short, or not try at all.

"You two are not going anywhere," Katie told them as they entered the kitchen. "It's Christmas Eve dinner, and you are going to sit at the table and eat with the rest of us."

"Kate—"

"Besides, I brought you something from town, Donny, and it would be rude not to accept." She spun him around to face the doorway to the living room. Her voice had been calm, but she bounced in place and pressed her clasped hands to her lips, failing to hide a shit-eating grin.

"What?"

"Howe," Griff said, shocked out of his confusion at the sight of him standing in the middle of the room. Don's dad was shoving a beer in his hand, and Andrew clapped him on the back hard enough to make him take a staggering step toward the two men standing, stunned, in the kitchen doorway. In three strides, Griff had crossed the room and gathered the baffled man into a bear hug.

"Griff." He attempted, once and feebly, to extricate himself. "Everybody—" He gave up when Griff backed out of the hug only far enough to kiss him, lips engulfing his protest, hand on the back of his head, holding onto him until he gave in and kissed back.

Don had taught Griff a lot about how to take control, and he wasn't above using what he'd learned on Howe. He could suck it up, quit his complaining, and just let Griff take advantage of the fact he couldn't run off this once.

When Griff finally let him up for air, Don was standing where he'd left him, grinning. Griff glanced at Katie and Megan and mouthed *Clamato juice*?

They both giggled.

"How much trouble did he give you?" Don asked them.

Megan shrugged and crossed her arms in self-satisfaction. "Nothing we couldn't handle. Tried to tell us he preferred frozen Chinese in a box to turkey and mashed potatoes and our famous stuffing. Even said"—and here she turned to watch Griff and noted that he held on to Howe, just in case he thought he was going to put any space between them—"that Griff wouldn't want him here."

"I want him," Griff said, voice gruff, head bobbing an affirmative as he gazed into Howard's admittedly startled-looking expression. "Family," Griff told him and shook his head in warning. "Don't try and pretend otherwise."

Howard nodded and leaned on him a bit. "Okay, Griff. I'm here." His fingers dug into Griff's side. "I'm here."

"Good." Griff had to duck his head because everyone would see he was tearing up, and he would never hear the end of that. He snuck a glance at Don, though. He was watching them so closely. He knew why Griff hid his face. Griff couldn't tell what he was thinking or feeling, but he knew Don knew, because Don had his number like no other person alive did, including Griff most days.

He really hadn't expected to spend Christmas with Howe. Hadn't expected Howe would ever forgive them for that morning in the garage. The months since then had seemed like lifetimes for both of them, but here Howe was, ensconced under his arm, and no way was Griff letting go.

Everyone tried not to notice the awkwardly stretched silence between Howe and Don. Griff was about to say something, to reach for Don, to find a way to make this better somehow, when Howe finally held out a hand.

Don smiled, stroked his fingers, kissed him briefly, and stepped back. Griff couldn't tell if he was happy Howard had come. It was time to reconcile. So why did he keep his distance?

Griff couldn't ask with everyone milling around the room chatting and joking and welcoming Howe as if he hadn't been missing from their lives for almost four months. But Griff needed to know. Before he could figure out how to ask, Don turned his back and left the room.

"I shouldn't have come," Howe said, voice not quite low enough for those closest not to hear.

"Shut up," Griff told him. "Just shut up. You belong here."

"Uncle Howard!"

Alex. Thank-fucking-god for practically five-year-old enthusiasm. The kid launched himself at them and Howe let go of Griff just in time to catch him.

"I'll be back," Griff told him and Howe nodded, glancing over Alex's tousled hair to meet his eyes.

Everything Griff wanted to see was there, right on the surface, glowing in his eyes, etched in the sad worry lines across his face. He wanted to be here. It was obvious. He wanted this with everything he was, but he didn't dare hope for it. He didn't hope because it could ruin Griff and Don, and he saw that. He was terrified he'd be the cause of a split between them.

"*We* will be back," Griff assured him. "Don't worry."

He hurried after Don.

PART THREE—TOGETHER

MOVING FORWARD

December, age twenty-seven

"YOU okay?" Megan had followed Don into the kitchen and he cursed silently. So much for a moment alone to breathe through seeing his two— what did he even call them at this point?—cling together like that.

"Yeah. Fine."

"You don't lie to me, Donny. You're terrible at it."

"Don?" Griff tried to enter the kitchen, but Megan whirled and pointed the way back out. "Busy. I need to talk to him."

"But—"

"It's okay, Griff. I'll be out in a sec, babe."

Griff winced at the endearment, and Don turned to face the sink and listen to the door swing closed.

"I'm fine, Megan," Don insisted. "It's fine." If he said it enough times, he'd believe it. Or he'd get inured to the pain of hearing it, at least.

"We shouldn't have gone to get him," she said. "I tried to tell Katie—"

"Sure." Don smiled at her. "Blame the kid."

"Well." She tossed her head to flick heavy chestnut curls over her shoulder. The motion was meant to be a comical imitation of their little sister, who was, by far, the princess of the family. Megan had never been girly or wanted to be girly, and her decidedly unfeminine build only added to the absurdity of the motion. "You know what *she's* like. Little brat. Baby always gets her way."

He laughed, because she wanted to lighten his mood, but he could tell by her frown it didn't ring true. "You should have done it, Megan," Don assured her. "Howard's family."

"If he's being a douche—"

"He's not. And you have to promise me, no matter what happens, we're his family."

She eyed him sternly. "Whether you're sleeping with him or not? And what about Griff? What happens if the two of them—"

"Megan, please."

"You listen to me, Donny, you brought them together. Why should I stand around and let them hurt you?"

"If they are happy, then I'll get over it."

"Right, and you'll just find yourself another boyfriend because gay guys are a dime a dozen out here in the corn fields."

He bristled. He loved her for caring, but she was being a jerk. "First of all, you have no say over who either one of them sleeps with, let alone who they love. I didn't ever mean for anyone to get hurt, but maybe it was bound to happen. I mean, thinking we could really make a relationship work three ways." He sighed. It had seemed like the best of ideas at the time. And for years after, it had been an easy fit, ebbing and flowing through their lives as the years passed and their spirits moved them to be together or take time apart. It had seemed natural to give Howard space when he wanted it, and enfold him between them when he came back again. He always came back. Or always had. Only since Don's own mother had injected that doubt in his mind had things seemed to get more and more complicated.

Then Terrance Hawthorn had stepped in and beaten the lesson home that none of them exactly fit the mold, and everything had disintegrated.

"If any of us can take it being the odd one out, it's me," he informed his sister, sure of that one fact, at least. "I have all of you. Howe has no one and Griff and his dad... I don't want them to lose out on what we've built, either."

"You're kidding me, right?" She glared at Don. "You've been best friends with Griff for as long as I can remember! We let him into this family for *you*."

Don smiled at her, or tried, but it came off as more of a snarl. "He's been my best friend for as long as I need to remember too. Nobody let him in anywhere. He earned everything he has. He made it possible for us to keep this place when Mom had to work and Dad had to be plowing. He worked his ass off taking care of you girls, and of Mom when she miscarried, and helping his father build that house and train horses, and no one can ever say he doesn't deserve to be part of this family. I will never, ever take that away from him. That's why I'm glad you did this."

She at least had the decency to nod agreement, even if she did cross her arms over her chest and widen her stance, just like their father when he was ready to bulldog his way through an argument.

"Look, Meg, he gave me every opportunity to stop this from happening when we took this step in the first place. And when we were kids, he stood back and let me choose Howard first, and he never interfered. He stayed my best friend when he wanted more, and now it's my turn."

She snorted. "You're an idiot."

Don could only shrug. "Maybe."

"No, I'm your sister, and I know. You're an idiot."

He gathered her into a tight hug and squeezed. There was no use arguing with her. She would tell him he was a fool, and still defend him against every sort of asshole in the world, including the two people he loved the most if she thought he needed defending. There was nothing he could do or say to stop her, any more than she could dictate who Griff and Howard chose to be with.

"You can think I'm a fool if you want, Meg, but I could not have given Griff a better gift this year. So thank you."

"Well, I don't know if you're welcome yet. Jury's still out."

"Fair enough. I'm going upstairs for a few minutes' alone time. Call me when supper's ready?"

"Sure." She didn't look happy to let him sneak off, but she didn't stop him as he began a tiptoed ascent up the creaky back stairwell.

"I don't understand this, you know," she confessed. "The three of you. How it works...."

Don pulled his shoulders up and let them drop as he leaned on the railing and stuffed his hands into his pockets. "I can't explain it. It just is."

She pushed the door open to peer out into the living room again, and the sight there brought a sigh to his lips.

Griff stood close to the door, back to the kitchen and his arm possessively circling Howard's waist. Much of the initial stiffness had left Howard's shoulders. He almost looked relaxed, happy, as he talked to Don's and Griff's fathers.

"I mean, how do you explain that?"

Megan shook her head. "I used to think it was weird to have a gay brother, you know."

Don hadn't known and he cocked his head at her. "You never said anything."

"What is there to say? It's your life, and Griff is, like, hot and sweet and just—" She smiled, but it looked sad. "—I thought he loved the shit out of you. You've been happy, up until this last couple of years, and I respect that. Well, no, I mean, yeah. I do, but I mean, shit. You were happy, and so I was happy for you. Now?"

Don nodded. "We'll see."

She let the door swing closed again and gazed up at him. She looked so much like their father, but for that split second, he saw their mother looking out at him, worried, wanting to lay down enough of her own rules to make everything work out. Megan, though, was not their mother, and she pinched her lips tight over whatever objections she had.

"If I could fix this, Donny—"

"You would. I know. And I love you for not trying to, Meg. I'll be upstairs."

A COOL breath of air ghosted over Griff's back and the soft swish of the kitchen door swinging open almost made him turn, but he didn't. Howe's fingers dug deeper into his ribs and he tightened his own grip.

From this distance, it had been impossible not to overhear the argument going on so close on the other side of the door. Griff didn't think anyone but he and Howe had heard it, but then, no one else really mattered.

"We have to talk," Howe said quietly.

Griff pulled a deep breath through his nose and nodded. "Yeah."

"Before dinner. I can't sit at that table and know he feels like that and not settle things."

"Yeah." No way could Griff eat anyway. Not with the Olympic-sized puddle of sick sloshing around in his gut. He'd known Don was worried about where they all stood. He hadn't thought for an instant his lover thought Griff would leave him.

Behind them, the door opened and closed again, and Megan came to stand beside them.

"Dinner in ten minutes, you guys," she whispered. "He's up in his old room. You *fix* this." And she walked away.

"That's that, then," Howe said softly.

"We've definitely been told." They exchanged a glance and slipped up the stairs.

Griff knew the old house as well as he knew his own. Most of the bedroom doors had to be propped open to keep them from slamming every time someone opened or closed another room or went in and out of the house. The master bedroom at the top of the stairs was exceptionally tidy, not even a trinket on the dressers and only a few books on the shelves around the head of the bed. A black iron cat held the door open.

Three rooms lined up down the hallway along the railing above the stairs: the girls' room, with a painted iron lamb in front of the door; Pete's tiny boyhood room, which stayed open because he'd installed an eye and hook to hold it; and Megan's room, predictably propped open with a stack of dusty books. Probably the same ones she'd left there when she'd moved out. It was where she'd piled all the books she'd read as a kid and was ready to exchange at the used bookstore. Griff had seen that pile reach the door handle on more than one occasion. The door to Andrew's room was closed, as it had been since Megan, Talia, and Katie had boxed up their mother's belongings and stored them away in there.

Don's old room was at the end of the hallway. That door wasn't open, but it hadn't latched, either.

Griff pushed it open with two fingers and peered inside.

Don was standing by the window, looking out. As they watched, he ran a hand through his hair, rested his forehead on the glass, and let out a sound that came way too close to a sob for Griff.

"Don?"

Was that a sniff?

"Hey, Griff." Don turned from the view, and for the barest second, the look on his face threw Griff back to the first time he'd seen Don, ass on the floor in a school hallway with a bully standing over him. Then Don's gaze shifted to take in Howe's presence and a shutter closed. His expression went blank, and Griff was lost, unsure how to save him this time.

"What are you doing up here, Donny?" Howe asked, weaseling past Griff and entering the room.

Don took a step back, all the space he had before his shoulder blades hit the window. "Howard."

"Tell me you're happy I'm here. Or tell me to leave," Howe said, jumping right into the morass. "But don't back away like that. No more shying away from this"—he swirled a finger around to indicate all three of them—"or standing back and hoping it works out."

Don glanced between the two men, and Griff found he couldn't breathe. The air had been sucked from the room the moment Don opened his mouth to give Howe an answer to the question none of them could manage to ask out loud.

"Wait!" Griff strode forward, clapped a hand on the window, and pushed fingers into Don's hair, gripping tight. He had to get his say in. Before Don said something, made some irrevocable pronouncement on them, Griff had to speak up. Or something. He couldn't stand by and just let things go sideways. "You don't get to do this," he whispered, though there was no way he could keep his voice low enough Howe wouldn't hear.

"And you don't get to force—"

"I have no intention of forcing anything, Don." He did tighten his fingers more, though, until Don's eyes widened and his teeth gritted. "Just want to get your attention," he pleaded, knowing he was doing this all wrong but unable to figure out, in the panicked moment, how to do it right.

Don tried to nod, but Griff's grip didn't let him move his head. Grinding his teeth at his own bullish behavior, Griff loosened his grip, but still, he couldn't make himself let go completely.

"You've got it." For a brief instant, Don's gaze flicked up to meet Griff's, defiant and hopeful, furious and frightened and all the things Griff understood instantly, because the feelings were mutual. Then the one thing he had to give, the one thing Griff had come to cherish most, he gave. He surrendered and dropped his gaze to the floor.

"Good." Griff breathed out his relief. "Now will you listen to me?" He wished Don would also look at him, but he was willing to take this one step at a time. "You don't get to decide for all of us how this is going to go. It's never been that way, and it is not going to be that way now. Tell me what you want. And none of this bull about making sure Howe and I are happy. No one wants to be thrown over so someone else can be happy, and I don't buy that you're okay with it, so don't try to sell it." He gave Don's head a shake. "What do you *want*?"

"You," Don whispered.

"Then you have me." Instinct kept Griff holding on, though, even with that confession.

"I'll go," Howe said softly from the doorway.

"No!" Don twitched, like he wanted to rush to block Howe from leaving.

Griff didn't let him take so much as a single step. "You'll stay," Griff addressed them both with the hard edge in his voice and held his free hand out to Howe. "Come over here."

"Griff, stop this. You're hurting him." Howe reached to disengage Griff's hand from Don's hair.

But Don had ceased his struggle at the tone of Griff's voice and leaned on the window. His gaze had gone soft and Griff could feel him begin to relax at last.

"Not more than he wants," he said, feeling Don's capitulation as his lover leaned into him. "Trust me, Howe."

"I do, but...."

"No buts. Come here." He pointed at the floor directly in front of Don's toes. His heart raced, and surely Don would feel the way his hands shook. He could ruin everything if Howe balked, and why wouldn't he? Being ordered around like this didn't usually make most people want to open up. Just because it worked to get Don's attention, that didn't mean it wouldn't drive Howe further away.

"Why are you doing this?" Howe asked, glancing between them.

Don put a hand on Griff's wrist where he held him, but the touch was light, connecting rather than trying to get him to let go. "Because it worked," Don said, flipping a look up at Howe. "It always works." He smiled faintly and held his other hand out to Howe. "He only bites if you want him to."

Griff closed his eyes, as if that would keep Howe from seeing his reaction. As if the heat in his face wouldn't give away his embarrassment over having that little nugget revealed.

"Griff?" Howe's voice was quiet but roughened by whatever Griff didn't have the nerve to see in his eyes. "Fine," he said, and the shuffling sound of his feet on the floorboards was enough to make Griff open his eyes.

Howe had moved closer, though, not farther from them.

"Does it make you feel better to have your hands on me?" he asked, looking steadily into Griff's eyes.

Griff clenched his jaw, ground his teeth again, but nodded despite the risk of making Howe flee at the thought.

Howe nodded in return. "Fine." He took another step, and the moment he was within reach, Griff took him by the scruff of the neck and placed the two men face to face. "I will make you two kiss," he threatened, trying to make it sound light, knowing it sounded heavy-handed and stern. And desperate.

Don's gaze flicked to him, shock and then gratitude giving way to amusement when Howe sputtered. A grin flickered about Don's lips. It was a ridiculous threat, Griff knew, but the part of him spurred by the way Don reacted to this was already so deeply rooted. He craved the control as much as Don did, and it grounded him, the same as it grounded his lover.

Almost, Don broke into a grin. "You can let go, Griff," he said.

Griff growled at him. "Maybe I don't want to let go."

"You going to force us to kiss?" Howe asked. At least he seemed to have lost the worried frown, even if he still seemed a little off balance with Griff's demands, unsure if Griff was seriously going to make this happen or not.

"Do I have to?" Griff turned to glare at him. "You'd be kinda surprised what I can make Don do these days."

That shut Howe up for a few thudding heartbeats.

"You're enjoying this," Howe accused him finally.

"Immensely. Now kiss my boyfriend."

"So you can watch?"

"Yes." The trick was not to crack. To let Howe see he meant it, he wanted it, that he expected it, but not make him feel like he had no choice either. Don trusted Griff enough that he would kiss Howe if Griff wanted it, believing it would work out. Howe would kiss Don only if Howe wanted it. The difference was not lost on Griff. The difference was what made them separate. Whatever common ground there was left was what would keep them whole.

Howe's eyes widened and his cheeks flushed. "You really mean it."

"I'm committed," Griff rumbled. "If that's what you mean. So's Don."

Don's head bobbed affirmative, curls like silk against Griff's palm.

"You can't make me any guarantees." Howe made it sound like an accusation. "You can't make him any, either."

"I can guarantee I mean this with all my heart," Griff said, finding, at last, the one thing he could hit Howe with that wouldn't damage him beyond repair. That very frightening truth was the only weapon he had.

Howe's fingers curled around the wrist of Griff's hand where it still cupped his neck. "Does it matter what I want?"

"Of course it does." Griff manned up and looked his erstwhile lover in the eyes. "Tell me to let go, and I will."

"Just hang on to me," Howe said through clenched teeth, instead.

"Much better," Griff rumbled as he pulled at Don's hair, just to let him know he had his lover in hand, wouldn't let him go. Ever.

Hesitant, Howe leaned forward, testing how much movement Griff would allow, maybe, checking to see if this was real or if it might be a joke at his expense.

Griff had no intention of restricting his motion unless he tried to leave. That was never going to be an option. Nor was he really going to force them to do anything they didn't choose to do. But he was going to lend his encouragement in any way he could. Any way they would accept and understand.

Hopefully accepting he had no choice but to figure things out between them, Howard turned his attention to Don, meeting his gaze and trapping Don between that look and Griff's grip. "It's always been Griff," Howe said quietly. There was no amusement in his tone. Griff could feel his uncertainty snaking around and through them all. "It's been Griff standing up for me, standing with me since the day you told me I wasn't worth it—"

"Jesus." Don closed his eyes. All the playfulness drained away. Defeat replaced surrender. "I was a stupid kid, Howard. Scared of bullies."

Howe touched his face. "You're the bravest person I know. You just didn't want me like you wanted him."

Don snorted. "It's all been Griff, just like you said."

Howe frowned and the sick rose to Griff's throat again, preventing him speaking.

DON couldn't have opened his eyes to look at either of them if his life depended on it. He couldn't see what they thought about him being so dependent when he was the one who had always promised them the fairy tale.

"Don." Howard's fingers traced a warm, tender path down his cheeks. "You have to talk to me."

Swallowing a lump of fear, Don rested his head back against Griff's palm and nodded. He knew he had to talk. He had to tell them how he felt. He had to admit things he didn't want to admit, like that he didn't know how any of this was supposed to work. He'd set out to give them both the home and family he'd dreamed of since he was a kid, and all he had to offer was a failing farm and a future with no guarantees.

"So answer the question," Howard demanded. "You have to trust us. What do you *want*?"

"You," he whispered.

There was silence for what felt like forever.

"You said the same thing to Griff," Howard reminded him.

Like he needed the reminder.

"I know."

"So which is it?"

At least Howard's fingers remained, soothing in their contact with his skin. And Griff's hand hadn't left his hair. He tried to move his head, just to see if Griff would release him. Both men tightened their grips in response. Griff's hold pulled at his roots and made him groan. Howard cupped his chin, his thumb hard and calloused on the side of his jaw.

Why couldn't it be like this always? Why were they making him choose?

"Both." He said the word, moved his lips, but couldn't be sure any sound came out.

Lips touched his and his knees nearly buckled. Hands tightened on him: in his hair, on his face, wrapped around one arm, holding him up.

"Was that so hard?" Griff whispered in his ear.

Howard was still kissing him and he couldn't answer with more than a low moan.

"No one is leaving anyone," Griff continued. "I promise."

Don nodded and finally let go of the tension he'd been carrying for so long. There was more to it. If they were going to be together, they had to set boundaries. They had to make rules, and they had to live like they meant it. But Howard kissed and Griff hovered and Don gave in.

What else could he do under the circumstances?

"OKAY, stop molesting my brother, you two." The clap of hands at the doorway made them all jump. "Supper time," Megan announced. "Nice as this is to see, I need minions. Griff, you're tall. I need platters off the shelf in the kitchen."

"Mark's taller than me."

"He's helping Talia with the table settings."

"Again?" Don complained, wrapping fingers in the front of Howard's shirt when the mechanic tried to move away. "Haven't you settled all that?"

"Had to add seats, didn't I? Speaking of, Howard, there's a desk chair in my old room. Bring it downstairs, please."

Griff raised both eyebrows. "We've been dismissed, I think."

Howard nodded agreement, but fixed a look on Don. "You okay?"

Don nodded. "Yeah." He worked out how to make his limbs do what he told them, got his fingers free of his shirt, and touched them to Howard's cheek. "I'm good. We're good. Probably just let her have her way."

Howard nodded. "Okay."

"Come on." Megan clapped her hands again. "Come help."

Obedient, Griff pecked Howard's cheek and Howard hurried to do her bidding.

Griff shuffled out of the room after him.

Braving his sister's attitude, Don pushed himself upright and looked her in the eye. "I thought I told you I wanted a few minutes alone."

"Sometimes you just don't get what you want, Donny, unless you actually ask for it." She shrugged, a mannerism that exactly echoed their mother in every way. "You sometimes don't ask for what you need, and it isn't so fair to make everyone try to guess. I know you're probably pissed off at me for sending them up here. I've been pushy today. But you are a miserable, annoying wet blanket sometimes, and I am not going to apologize for keeping Christmas real for the rest of us."

Don grinned. "Love you too, Meg."

"I know. Come down and eat. The kids are going nuts to get to the gifts."

"All they get to open tonight is pajamas. They know what's coming. I don't know why that's so exciting."

"Don't you remember what it was like? Opening that package and having new PJs to wear that no one else had already worn the knees out of? Lying in bed all cozy in new fleece with our flashlights, waiting and listening for sleigh bells."

Don nodded. "I remember."

"It's a big deal."

"I guess."

"Come on." She took his hand. "Come and eat. It's Christmas."

Halfway down the hall, Don glanced into her old room to see Howard still moving books from the office chair he was meant to bring down to the table.

"Be right there, Meg," he told her.

Following his gaze, she smiled and nodded. "Don't be long. You know Dad won't start until everyone is there."

"Hey," Don called softly into the room. "Need a hand?"

Howard shook his head but didn't turn, even when Don's weight made the floorboards next to the bed creak.

"Come here," Don said softly into Howard's ear when he'd reached him. He took his hand and made him face him. "You know I didn't have anything to do with them bringing you here. I didn't want to put you under that kind of pressure. But I did want you here. Today of all days."

Howard touched his lips to shut him up. "I know. I saw your face when you came into the living room. We overheard your conversation with Megan. You had no idea. Your sisters are devious."

Don acknowledged that. "Griff and I were going to come to your place, but you're here." Leaning his forehead against Howard's, he let out a sigh. "So much we have to talk about."

"I thought we'd settled all this."

Don cupped Howard's cheek, studying his face, trying to see what he was thinking beyond his dark, wary eyes. He found himself shaking his head. "I thought I knew how this should work. And I just... decided to fix your life without asking you what you wanted. And then I got pissed off at you when it didn't work. I was an ass."

A sad smile crossed Howard's face and disappeared. "You were right, though. I blame myself for them. I want my own family back, and I shouldn't want that. I know how screwed up they were. But they were still mine."

Don bit his lip, nodded. "I was an ass to say what I did."

"An ass, maybe, but right. Don—"

"I'm sorry."

Howard smiled. "I know. I knew even when you said it that you didn't mean it the way it sounded. I just…." He waved his hand toward the sounds of happy confusion below as kids were called inside and food platters clattered as they were loaded down with meat and vegetables. "Your family…."

"God, Howard, watch me very carefully, babe." Don looped an arm around his neck, took his chin in hand, and turned his head back to focus on Don's face. "Read my lips. *Our* family. Yours, mine, Griff's. And I'll tell you what. If you want to deny that, you get to tell Alex why he can't call you Uncle Howe, because I am not up to another bout with that kid."

"He's talking? He's, like, two."

"Practically five, actually, and talking is an understatement. Trust me."

Howard laughed, and Don thought he probably had not heard anything more incredible in his life.

"Guess I missed some stuff, huh?" Howard asked softly.

"It's fine. Kids change fast at that age. We'll catch you up. But for now, we should go see about helping or something," Don said.

Howard stalked him into a corner, though, and cupped his face. "Kiss first?"

It was even better than hearing his lover laugh.

Griff had to search them out long minutes later and prod them apart and down to the table.

When Don headed for his usual place at the table, it was his father who intercepted him and brought him around to the head of the table.

"Dad?"

Donald Sr. motioned to the chair he normally occupied. "It's time, Don."

"Time for what?" He glanced where his father was pointing and saw his own nametag folded into a tent over something sitting on the plate. "This is your place."

"Everything moves on, Don. Lives change and grow and it's time for me to step aside."

"Aside from *what*?"

"Don't be dense, Donny," Katie said, slapping his shoulder. "Daddy wants to retire."

Don frowned and fingered the nametag on the plate, glanced at his dad, and finally lifted it. A single key, to the front door of the main house, with the dented metal key tag Andrew had made for their father in shop class in eighth grade, sat on the plate. "Dad, what is going on?" He faced the older man. "Retire? I don't understand."

"I'm old, son. I'm not going anywhere, but that little cottage is too small for three grown men. It was too small for the two of you. And this house is too big for just me. You run the farm in all but name." He handed Don an envelope. "It's in trust, of course. There will be a bit for everyone, but as long as you choose to live here and run the place, it's yours. Katie will be twenty-one soon. When that happens, her college fund allowance stops, and you'll decide what to do with the profits. When you sell it, it gets split, seven ways, equally."

"What do you mean 'when'?" Don looked at the thick envelope in his hands. "I'm not selling. This is our home."

His father smiled. "You might have noticed, Don, everyone has a home of their own. Except for Katie, but that will come. This is *your* home, because you've made it that. I'm only making it official."

"Why?"

His confusion received the typical fatherly pat on the shoulder. "Because it's time, Donald. You've always wanted this, and it's time. I'm not going far. Just to the cottage, and you'll live up here in the main house. I'll still be around when you need the advice of an old man." He smiled. "But the real work is down to you young folk."

"Dad." Don thought about the accounts and the stack of bills and only barely fought off panic.

"I know what the books look like, son, and there's no secret it isn't pretty. But you have ideas. Fresh new ways to make this old farm viable again, and I'm showing you my support by giving you the chance to make those calls."

Don glanced around the table at his brothers, his sisters, their kids, and finally to Griff and Howard. They were all expecting him to accept this change. It was written on their faces that they always knew he would be the one to take over one day. Not one of them doubted him.

"I don't know what to say," he whispered at last.

Pete shook his head. "No shit."

People chuckled and Don managed a smile. He'd always known this would happen someday without ever really giving much thought to how or when. Now that the key and the deed were in his hands, he had no idea how to react.

"Dad, I—"

His father pulled him into a bear hug and pounded him on the back. "I'm proud of you, Donny. Your mother would be too," he said quietly. Probably everyone could hear them, but this was meant just for him, and he squeezed his father tight.

"You think so?"

"I know so. She worried about you, but she was burstin' with pride that you stood up to everyone, including her, and followed what your heart said was right."

"I should have—"

His father pushed him away, but held on to his arms, looked into his eyes. "She understood, Don." He smiled—sad, maybe, but honest. "It's right that you don't remember her like that. She understood, I promise you. She wanted you to remember how she was, not what happened."

"We fought...."

"I know. People fight." He glanced past him to Howard. "People fight and they make up, and sometimes you have to forgive yourself when you screw up, and trust that the people who love you are tough enough to keep loving you, even when you don't deserve it." He looked back at Don. "Your mother was as tough as they come, son. There is nothing you could have done to stop the way she loved you. And she'd be so proud of you for holding on to what you believe in. For fighting for it."

Don nodded and realized he was long past tearing up.

"How long they going to hug before we can eat?" Alex whispered in a tone that would have carried to the kitchen.

Since his brother was sitting right beside him, Robbie cuffed him lightly, though the question broke the tension and everyone laughed.

"We can eat," Don assured him.

"Good." Donald Sr. winked at his grandson and hurried to the other end of the table to take the seat there, and everyone who wasn't already at the table found their place.

Don took the seat at the head of the table, with Griff on one side and Howard on the other, and contemplated the nametag beside his plate. When he looked to his older brothers, they both gave him nods of approval, along with wide grins, and he suspected everyone but him and maybe Howard had known this plan was in place.

Howard's knee pressed into his thigh and Griff took his hand.

"You okay?" Griff asked.

Don nodded. It was an overwhelming feeling to realize, even if he was the youngest Jenkins brother, and even if he had stepped way outside the bounds of tradition in his choice of life partners, no one in this vast group doubted he deserved any of it.

MAKING IT WORK

Present day

WHEN the floor got too cold and Griff's back began to ache, he roused Don. "Babe, we should go up to bed."

"It's middle of the day," he whispered groggily. "Have to harvest."

"Pete's already out there, and Robbie and Mark have the animals under control. All you and I have to worry about is us."

"Howard—"

"He's fine."

"I should go."

Griff kissed the top of his head. "Not like this. You're a mess. Too tired. If you go, you'll go when you're put back together. He doesn't need to be freaked out over you falling apart. Come on." He got to his feet and pulled Don up after him.

"I'm not falling apart." Glancing around the kitchen, though, Don nearly crumpled again. Papers lay everywhere. There was a puddle of coffee on the stove, as though the percolator had boiled over and he hadn't bothered to clean it up. A dog dish with food crusted in the bottom sat by the door.

"Where's Clay?"

Clay was the mostly gray Border Collie they'd bought after Griff's experience with the Cage's dog making it so easy to get the horse out of the trailer. In fact, Clay was a younger dog of the same parentage as the Cage's animal, and had proven to be more than up to the task of managing the animals on all three farms, once Steve Cage had trained him up and taught Griff how to handle him.

"Smarter than us," Griff muttered. "Pete probably let him out. Hang on and I'll call—"

"No, I remember now. Robbie took him when he dropped his dad off." He frowned. "Pete's on the combine?"

Griff nodded. "Come upstairs. There's nothing for you to worry about besides getting cleaned up and into bed. You're looking and acting like you haven't slept since you left for the fields yesterday."

"Maybe… I haven't." He looked up at Griff. "Howard's okay."

"Oh, babe." Griff pulled him into a one-armed embrace and closed the back door with the other. "Howe is going to be fine, I promise. And if you're very good and do everything I say, I'll even take you to see him later."

"I'm not five," Don muttered.

"You can act remarkably like it when you're this tired. Let's go." He led an unresisting Don up the back stairs and into their bedroom. He didn't even manage to get Don into the shower, though. He left him on the bed and when he came back from the toilet, Don was curled under the covers, his clothing abandoned on the floor. He snored softly and Griff took a moment to watch him before returning to the kitchen to tidy up.

It didn't take long, but among the sheaves of paper, he came across what didn't seem to belong at first. It was a university paper, and quick investigation told him Mark had written it. And received an excellent grade for his efforts. What caught Griff's attention, though, was the short note scrawled across the cover page.

Uncle Don:

Here is the paper I told you about. I appreciate you letting me use the farm as my model, and I hope you see what I did. This can work. This will save the farm, I know it.

"What can work?" Griff muttered. He settled at the table and began to read.

HOURS later, he had Don's papers organized, half a fresh pot of coffee drunk, and he was doing the math longhand on the back of a seed brochure because the calculator had been beyond repair.

"What are you doing?" Don's sleepy voice from the doorway at his back startled him, and he snapped the tip off his pencil when he jumped. "Is that math?" Don tilted his head at the work as he passed on his way to the coffeepot.

Griff pushed himself away from the table. "Yeah. Well, sort of. I was just—" He motioned to the piles of notes and papers. "Don, why didn't you tell me?"

"Tell you what?" Was he purposely not looking at Griff as he spoke? Avoiding his gaze as well as avoiding answering the question? For a moment, Griff watched him retrieve a mug from the cupboard and fastidiously remove the stem from the coffee pot before he poured.

"The farm, babe." He held up a sheet of paper. "I knew things were tight, but this… why the hell didn't you tell me it was so bad?"

Don closed the microwave where he'd placed his coffee and stared at the buttons, but he shoved his hands into his pockets instead of pressing any of them. "It's my problem. I'll figure it out."

"Your problem?" Griff stared at him. "Your problem? What the hell does that mean? This is our problem."

"My farm, my—"

"My *home*! Or was that all just so much talk? All these years you've been going on about family, was it all bull?" He stood so abruptly his chair flew and landed with a bounce on its back on the floor. He almost toppled when his cast threw him off his balance. "I *live* here," Griff snarled, poking a finger on the papers sitting on the table. "In a few weeks, I'm bringing Howe back here to heal, and you want to tell me this is not my problem?"

"I just meant—" Don started the microwave and took the sugar and a spoon from the cupboard above.

"You meant to shut me out of your life so much you weren't even going to tell me we are on the very edge of losing everything. What did you figure? You'd just wake me up one morning and say, oh, yeah, by the way, babe, we're homeless. The bank wants our land."

"I can fix this!"

"Let me help you! Goddammit, Donald, I thought we were family. I thought we were in this together. All three of us! Or does Howe know and you both just figured I didn't need to be told? Am I that close to being shoved out the door that it doesn't matter?"

"Out the door?" Don turned to stare at him, sugar pot in hand. "What?"

"You think I haven't noticed the missed calls and every time you stay out till you can't see to cut the next row, come home so tired you don't have to talk to me? How many times has he come out to the fields to fix the damn combine? How the hell does one machine even need that many repairs?"

"Griff—"

"You don't get to shut me out, Don. Dump me if you're going to, but—"

"I'm not!" The sugar bowl shattered against the wall, the shards falling pretty much where Griff had cleaned up the bits of the calculator, the contents spraying in a great, shimmering arc up the wall to sift to the floor, counter, and sink like so much snow. Don stared after it as though unsure he was even the one who'd thrown it. He clenched his fists at his sides and lifted his head enough to glare at Griff. "I am not fucking dumping anything. It's been less than a year since Dad gave me the farm and I'm letting it slip through my fingers. Less than a year since we got Howard to see reason, and we're already falling apart. All I ever wanted was to…." He threw up his hands and they fell to his sides with a slap. "I don't even know."

"Same thing you always do, Don. Try and make everything into this picture-perfect image of life that you seem to think existed when you were a kid, and it never did. My dad was a miserable divorcé, and I spent as much time here as I could so I didn't have to be there. Your mother fed me because he couldn't. Howe—that was just a nightmare, and if you really think about it, was this place ever in the black? It was never perfect. It just worked because we didn't focus on all the shit."

"We were kids."

"And now we aren't. So what?"

"So I don't know how to do this! Any of it!" Don's voice rose, his arms flew as he encompassed Griff, the house, the entire farm with a wild gesture. "I'm supposed to be a farmer. A family man. And I'm losing the farm. Losing"—he lifted both arms toward Griff—"my family. I don't know how to keep this from happening."

Griff grabbed both hands flung toward him and pulled.

Don stumbled into him and they both crashed hip first into the counter, Griff's cast once more throwing him off balance as Don's weight tumbled against his chest. Hesitant at first, he wrapped his arms around his lover, unsure if the gesture was going to be accepted. When Don didn't pull away, he tightened his arms, fitting them securely around Don's waist and resting his chin on the shorter man's head.

"Nobody knows how to do what we're doing, babe."

"My father farmed this land for forty years and never had the bank knocking on his door."

"Have you talked to him about it?"

Don snorted. "He handed me the deed less than a year ago. I've sold the entire harvest, Griff. If, by some miracle, none of it rots in the field, the revenue still doesn't even cover the cost of the seeds, planting, and harvest, let alone repairs to the combine. I'm just praying I get it all cut and baled before the thing gives up on me too, because if it breaks, who's going to repair it? Howard can't, and I'm a shit for being more worried about a forty-year-old rattletrap than him, but I'm screwed if it breaks."

Rubbing circles over his back, Griff breathed in the heady mixture of Don's scent that he'd grown so accustomed to. "*We* are not screwed. Albert can repair the combine if it comes to it. Mark's ideas in that paper about going organic are viable ideas, Don. I ran the numbers myself."

"I didn't give him the real numbers. Just some optimistic estimates and those freaked him out enough."

"I ran the real ones. It'll take more time, be riskier, we might have to tighten our belts a little more, but it can work."

For a few minutes, Don said nothing, just sagged against Griff in silence. "Albert can repair the combine?" he asked after a while.

"He's got some skills. And if he can't, he can talk to Howe, they can do it together. But you have to stop taking everything onto your own shoulders and let us help. Good God, what is that smell?"

Setting Don off to one side, Griff wrinkled his nose and followed the foul odor to the microwave. He popped the door open just in time to see Don's coffee flow over the rim of the cup in a delicate cloud of brown bubbles.

"Fucking hell! I can't even boil coffee right." Don slumped against the counter in defeat.

But Griff had to chuckle. "Actually, this coffee is pretty definitively boiled, I think." He peered into the cup to find only a finger of sludgy liquid in the bottom.

Don smiled, sighed, and wrapped his arms around himself. "That's not funny."

"Yes it is."

"Yes." He lifted his gaze to the ceiling. "God, Griff, what the hell happened?"

"I think you put it in for ten minutes instead of one."

"Not the coffee, asshole."

Griff grinned at him. "I know." He pulled Don back into his arms. "Life, babe. Life happened, and we fell behind a bit."

"A bit?"

Griff held his breath as he waited for Don to decide if he was going to wiggle free or relax.

He'd done neither when he spoke next. "Are you sure about Howard, Griff? One hundred percent sure, I mean. No reservations. It can't work if any of us are jealous." He looked up into Griff's face, and every nuance of his expression said what his words did not. *I so need it to work.*

"I am so sure about Howe and about you some days it aches all the way to my toes that he refuses to move in," Griff assured his lover.

"I think he's afraid he'll come between us."

Griff nodded. "It's a legitimate concern."

"You think he'll come between us?"

Griff ran his hands up and down Don's back. "I think, for him, it's a legitimate thing to worry about. When you went out with him in high school, I did let it come between you and me. I was jealous, just like you said."

"That was... God, fifteen years ago!"

Griff smiled. "That many already?" He rested his head on Don's. "Seems like yesterday, you know."

"I don't know. Maybe that many. Lots, anyway."

They stood there in silence for a long time. Eventually, Don pushed himself upright and rearranged himself against the counter's edge, hands deep in his pockets, gaze on the worn linoleum flooring. "I once told him I didn't think loving him was worth the risk." He glanced up through his lashes at Griff; the dark spikes had to make the view blurry. "I was so terrified, Griff. I didn't know how to love him and keep you. I didn't know how to face Terrance down, and I don't know how to look Albert in the eye now that Terrance is dead."

"You are not responsible for Terrance, for one thing. No one is." Griff reached to place a hand on Don's shoulder, but the other man tensed and he let the hand fall before he even made contact. "Let Albert come to you. He will. He has more reason now than ever to call these farms home."

Don glanced up at him again, confused.

The look brought a grin to Griff's face. "You need to pay more attention to the way he and Mark dance around each other, Don. Albert is just fine. And when the time comes, you'll see. He'll take what we've offered and make his own place. As for Howe, I only need to know you do want to keep me, even if you love Howe. Keep me and let me keep you."

This time when he lifted a hand and Don flinched, he didn't let it stop him, but he snaked his fingers into black curls and furled his fingers.

"And when I say keep you, Don, I mean *keep* you. In all the ways you need to be kept." He tugged until Don lifted his chin, and continued to apply pressure until his lover looked him in the eye. "In every way."

Adam's apple bobbing frantically, Don licked his lips three, four times before finally responding. "You think Howard will be okay with that?"

"I think Howard will have to be okay with it because some things I need just as much as you do. It's how we work best, and letting you flounder along on your own, keeping my own counsel, playing the housewife—which I love to do, don't get me wrong—but giving in to you thinking you need to call all the shots screws us up."

"Because you think I can't make decisions—"

"Because you try so hard to please everyone, you sometimes fail to take your own needs into account. You err on the side of playing it too safe. You want to convert this farm to organic produce, then that is what you do, Don. You make that decision, and trust me to stand beside you. Don't keep looking over your shoulder for approval. I do not need a partner who's afraid to stand his ground and make the tough calls. You step out there and trust me, I got your back. I need a guy who does what he knows is right and lets me hold him up when all the work and decisions and stress and fear get too much. Maybe I can't punch out every danger that comes along, but I sure as hell can be strong enough for us both. For all three of us, if it comes to that." He tightened his grip and shook Don slightly. "I didn't defend a frightened helpless little boy that day in the hallway when we were twelve. I punched a dickhead in the face because he was a dickhead. You were standing on your own two feet, facing him, staring him down, and you did it alone, without me."

"He would have wiped the floor with me."

"But I was there."

"I didn't know that. I was terrified," Don whispered.

"So the hell was I. So what? The fact is, I walked in to see this skinny little black-headed kid with tiny fists and the most stubborn scowl I'd ever seen facing down a fat, belligerent bully, and if that little kid was scared, it didn't show. I wanted to be a part of that." He grinned and felt heat flood his face. "I wanted to be a part of whatever it was that made the air around you different than what the whole rest of the world breathed."

Don's head tilted a tiny bit. "Really?"

"Well, I can look back and know now that's what I wanted. I was twelve. At the time, I knew what side of that line I wanted to be on, and that has never changed."

Don blinked at him.

"And now you know I'm here. I'll always be here." Griff relaxed his fingers and rubbed the pads over Don's scalp, as much to be touching and feeling the warmth as to soothe where he'd been pulling at the roots of his hair. "There's something else bothering you."

For long minutes, Don said nothing.

"Talk to me." The urge to shake him, to take him in both hands and somehow pry the thoughts that were swirling in his dark, troubled eyes out of his head was almost overwhelming. But that wouldn't build the trust between them. He had to show his own trust that Don would confide in him, open up to him, and not just be physically vulnerable to him, but emotionally as well. If he couldn't do that, there was nothing to salvage and all the physical surrender would be pointless, just as Griff had begun to realize over the past few months.

Finally, Don's tongue darted out over his lips again and he let out a short, hitched breath as he looked up into Griff's eyes. "Why did you first kiss Howard? Really? Was it because you thought I wanted him?"

Howard. Again, it was about Howard. He couldn't deny it was a reasonable question. "It was because… he needed kissing."

"Neanderthal," Don muttered. But he didn't sound mad. Just patient, and a small smile flirted with his lips for a heartbeat.

"If I was kissing him, he couldn't cry. If my arms were around him, he couldn't come apart. If I gave him a reason to stay there, with us, he couldn't take off and…."

"And what?" Don asked gently when Griff only finished the sentence with a shrug.

"His brother killed himself, Don."

Don nodded.

"I was scared for him. Scared for you if something bad happened to him. I didn't know how you'd react if you lost him."

Don nodded again.

"He was my friend then, and I didn't want that to change. I liked him even though I knew he was your first and might be the one you eventually chose, but"—he lifted a shoulder and ran a thumbnail along the edge of the counter—"I guess when it comes right down to it, he needed something to hold on to and I knew you would never offer it because technically, you were going out with me and you'd never do that to me. So I took the initiative."

"So you really did do it because you thought I wanted to."

Griff considered. It would be easy to allow Don to believe that. Allow them all to believe he was okay with the arrangement because both Howe and Don wanted to be together. And a part of him truly believed if that's all it was, he'd be able to live with it and deal with his jealousy. But the truth was, he wasn't only jealous that Don wanted Howe. He was just as bent out of shape that Howe wanted Don.

His thumb slipped and a loose bit of Formica jammed under his nail. He cursed and drew back, plunging the injury into his mouth.

Don reached, closed fingers over his wrist, and pulled firmly until Griff relinquished the small hurt into his lover's care. His touch was warm and roughly calloused, the pressure featherlight. "Let me see."

Griff watched him, remembering the careful way Don had cleaned Howe's wounds after that long-ago beating. Had it really been only one year since that shattering event? "It's fine," Griff whispered.

"You didn't answer my question." Don remained focused on Griff's hand as he spoke, guiding his hand to the sink and running cool water over the tiny hurt. Every move he made was calm and gentle and soothing.

"I did it because he needed it," Griff said.

Don still didn't look up as he shook his head. "He didn't need his life complicated by you kissing him and taking him to bed. He needed friends to keep him safe and sane and alive after his world ripped open and bled all over the town. We could have done that for him without bringing sex into it." Carefully, he removed Griff's hand from the flowing water and wrapped a towel around it, diligently rubbing and stroking until it was dry.

"I wasn't thinking anything at the time," Griff finally admitted, letting out the pent-up, sour air in his lungs. "Any more than I thought about punching Terrance in the face when we were kids. I just did it because that's what I wanted to do. That's the solution I saw to all the things that were hanging in the air around all of us. If I could make him stop crying and you stop worrying, it would all be okay."

Don nodded one last time, and finally looked up, directly into Griff's eyes. "You always do just what you want to do," he agreed.

Now he was sorry he'd let all that air out, because his lungs wouldn't work to bring any back into his body. His head swam and it was a good thing he was leaning on the counter.

"So why, lately, haven't you been doing what you want?"

"What?"

"You haven't been doing what you want to do. You've been sitting in the house grouching about being stuck there. You're unhappy. What do you want, Griff?"

Lifting his cast, Griff frowned. "I've been stuck—"

"You're never stuck. What's wrong? Because I don't mind admitting I've been sitting out on that combine dreading coming in every night to you sulking around and never telling me why."

Just as Griff opened his mouth to protest, as the ire rose to lend acid to his words, he saw it. He saw the way Don's hands twisted around the towel he still held. He saw the uncertainty in his gaze, though—to his credit—Don never looked away. He felt the heat of the other man's body intensify, fear making him tremble and sweat. And he saw how hard it was for Don to say what he just had. To call Griff out. To be the one to pick the fight they'd been pretending they weren't having in their silent, passive-aggressive way.

"You were lying to me," Griff said flatly. He held up a hand when Don tried to interrupt. "An omission is as good as a lie. You were worried sick about the books and the bills, and you didn't tell me. You didn't want me to know how much work Howe was doing on the equipment for free, and you just thought if you didn't say anything I wouldn't notice how you never relax anymore? How even the most demanding I can get in bed isn't enough to center you? But I couldn't force you to tell me the truth."

"It isn't your job to center me."

"It fucking is so! That's what we *do*. That's how we work. That's how I help you get through the hard parts, Don, and you haven't been letting me help."

"It isn't about Howard?"

"It was never about Howe. Not really. I think it's just about us slipping away and I need us back." There. It was out. He'd said it. "And not some lame version of us where we dance around what we really are, either."

Don stared up at him, eyes huge, face pale, head bobbing. "Me too," he whispered. Lifting Griff's big hand, Don stared into his eyes as he placed Griff's palm over his heart. Griff could feel the other man's trembling. "I need us back, too, but...." He swallowed hard, blinked.

"But what?"

He shook his head.

"Nope." Griff cupped his chin and made him look up. "Tell me."

"You're on top," Don said quietly. "Easy for you to accept... what we are."

Griff shook his head. "Not if you're not cool with it, babe."

"I am. Just... talking about it... saying it is harder than I thought."

Griff found a smile for him. "Then you don't have to say anything to anyone but me. It's about us and no one else."

"And Howard. He'll know."

"And Howe, yeah." Griff dragged his thumb along Don's stubble. "He has to know. You okay with that?"

A shrug lifted Don's shoulders. His gaze remained locked with Griff's, searching for something. What? There was a question there, but Griff wasn't quite sure what it was. Without the question, how could he offer the right answer? He'd have to wing it. Bending, he cupped Don's face, firm, gentle, and kissed him, with the best promise to protect his lover's heart he could put into a touch.

It didn't last very long. It did last long enough, because Don drew in a calm breath when they parted and a smile came to his face. And stayed there. "Okay," he said, dipping his chin once. "Okay."

"We'll bring Howe home now? No more letting him dangle out there on his own," Griff insisted. "I don't know how he'll deal with—" He hesitated, but Don's gaze didn't waver and it was time to call things what they were anyway. "—you being my sub."

A sharp gasp greeted that and Don's eyes widened. His smile faltered.

"Aren't you?" Griff asked, suddenly fearful he'd gone a step too far putting a label on it.

Again, Don spent a long time swallowing and licking his lips before responding.

"Answer the question, babe," Griff insisted, walling the fear away for the moment and pushing confidence to the fore. He tucked his fingers under Don's hair along the back of his neck. Heat rose in waves off Don's skin. Sweat slicked the curve of his spine and Griff circled his fingertips, massaging the damp skin, lightly kneading the taut muscles beneath.

A soft moan left Don's lips and he let his eyes close, his body gravitating toward Griff.

THE hand on the back of his neck felt so good. So very sure and steady. He closed his eyes. The floor seemed to tip Don toward Griff, and in seconds his face was buried in the warmth of the other man's flannel. His world, in that moment, was entirely Griffith shaped. It smelled of sunshine and horses and open sky.

"Griff." He nuzzled, wiggling his hands under Griff's shirt to find skin along the small of his back. He felt, exactly as Griff had said, *kept*.

"I'm waiting, Don," Griff said gently. His fingers stilled on Don's neck, closing tight and removing his option to move away. "I asked a question." His chest heaved under Don's cheek. "Please. I need an answer."

"Yes." Don could only whisper. "I—"

He didn't have to say another word, though. Griff's hold on him solidified into concrete honesty. He could relax. He could lean on the bigger man and be safe from falling. For the first time in a very long time, he felt like he could do anything. "I want to go see Howard," he blurted.

"Now?" Griff moved him away from his body, though Don felt no less contained than he had been, pressed up against the man.

"After a shower, yeah. I need him to know I can do that for him. So he knows we want him home, not just that we're saying it. I'm ready to make this happen."

Griff hauled Don close again and held him. "Thank you."

Don shamelessly rubbed his face against Griff's shirt, their two bodies as close as clothing and physics would allow.

HOME

"DAMMIT." Howard growled under his breath. His broken wrist had healed, but the nerve damage remained. No matter how many times he squeezed the damn tennis ball, some days the simplicity of a button defeated him.

"Let me." Next to him at the sink, Don reached to undo the fastener.

Howard slapped his lover's hand away. "I can manage."

Don's lips tightened to a white line, but he backed off. From the bedroom, Howard could feel Griff watching them. Out of the corner of his eye, he noticed Don glance in Griff's direction and yet another frustrated snarl escaped. How often over the course of a day did he see that? Don looking to Griff for guidance, like he couldn't make up his own mind about anything.

"Asking him permission to leave me the fuck alone?" he snapped.

Immediately, Don took a step back. His lips thinned more, his jaw set. His fists clenched, and Howard was sure in one second, he'd spin on a heel and stalk out of the bathroom, out of the bedroom, and out of the house. Some shit job away from the house needed doing and Don would find it. Anything to put distance between himself and the hard shit he didn't want to face.

He began the countdown in his head. Three… two… one.

But Don didn't leave. He glared. His eyes narrowed. "For your information, that isn't how it works. He doesn't make decisions for me. I don't ask permission for anything, least of all, how I interact with you. You want to know why I just looked at him? It was because I told him before I came in here that I was coming in here, and that, probably, we'd get into another fight. I wanted him to know so he could decide for himself if he was going to leave us to it or—"

"Gang up on me?"

"Support *me*," Don countered, gritting the words through his teeth.

Howard could practically see them on the air, thin and sharp-edged with Don's annoyance. "So it is the two of you against me!"

"It's the two of us *with* you," Griff corrected from behind him.

"The fuck!" Howard jumped and lost his balance, landing on his bad knee, but Griff caught him. "You were just in the bedroom." He struggled to loose his arm from Griff's grasp but gave up quickly. Griff never let go until he damn well felt like it.

Griff motioned with his thumb over his shoulder to the bathroom's public door. "Hallway," he explained, setting Howard back on his feet and holding on until Howard tried again and jerked his shoulder free.

"I'm fine," he muttered.

"No one thinks otherwise, you know," Don said.

Howard glared at him. He didn't have to sound so damn reasonable.

"I can undo my own damn buttons."

"And stand on your own two feet probably too," Griff agreed as he moved behind Howard and pressed his chest to the other man's back.

The heat and strength was too much. Howard closed his eyes. "Griff...."

Don moved in too, running his hands up Howard's chest. Through his overalls, shamefully clean because even working a screwdriver or a wrench was beyond him still, through the tank top beneath, the strength of his lover's small, nimble fingers elicited shivers. He wished he could feel it on his bare flesh.

Don's compact body and Griff's huge strength sandwiched him between his lovers and he sighed. Hot breath wafted over his face. Lips played over his earlobe. "Now can I take your clothes off you?" Don asked.

"Not fair." Howard fought the instinct to give in, clung to the anger that kept him independent.

"Not fair hiding under all that material," Griff countered. "We've been very patient with you, Howard, but it's time."

Forcing his eyes open, Howard straightened as much as he could. "Wait a minute." He pushed at Don's shoulders. The other man was too close for him to get a decent purchase on his chest and shove him away. "I'm not Don. You can't order me around."

At that point, he didn't have to shove because Don moved voluntarily, taking his hands and his touch back with him.

"Don't move," Griff ordered.

Don's gaze swiveled from Howard to Griff, and he nodded slightly and took a small step closer. He didn't look at Howard again, though, and his lips pursed, hard and unforgiving.

"I don't understand that," Howard said, lifting a hand, daring to touch what, at the moment, seemed to be Griff's property, as well as his own unhappy lover. "Why?"

Don's eyes drifted closed again. Griff reached out, right past Howard, to caress Don's cheek and he moved into the touch as Howard watched.

That was why. Because when Howard drove in a barb, Griff was there to pluck it away and soothe away the sting. Why couldn't it be the same for him? He had to always drive the barbs the world stuck in him deeper and deeper until he couldn't remember when it didn't hurt.

A callused hand smoothed over the side of his neck. This time it was Griff's lips close to his ear. "Lean on me." His gruff voice caressed that aching, stinging space inside and Howard couldn't resist the temptation to give in to the command. Just this once.

"Good," Griff crooned, continuing the easy, calming touch. "Relax." He pressed his lips to Howard's temple briefly, then rested his hand under the collar of Howard's overalls, fingers carefully slanted over his throat and collar bone. "Don, get him undressed."

Howard squirmed. "I—"

Griff's hand smoothed up his throat and his fingers touched Howard's lips. "Shhh."

Subsiding, Howard let Don pop open his buttons and ease the stiff fabric off his shoulders. Griff maneuvered his body with gentle touches and steady support to allow Don to remove his clothes. At Griff's gesture, he dragged his arms up over his head so Don could draw the shirt off. The skin of his back itched against the hair of Griff's chest and he couldn't remember when Griff had removed his shirt or if the man had come into the room bare-chested to begin with.

He still wore his jeans, though. Howard knew because the buckle of his belt and the rough fabric abraded Howard's ass just enough to send a zing of shocked pleasure racing over his skin as Griff arranged him, once more with his weight leaning on the larger man.

"Comfortable?" Griff asked.

Howard nodded, helpless to deny it. Once more, he let the weight of his lids win and they fell closed.

Griff's fingers raked through his hair and he let out a breath.

"Good. Now open your eyes and watch."

"Watch what?"

"You'll see." Griff's fingers curled and tugged the hair at his temple and Howard's eyes sprang open before he thought to actually obey. Electricity raced through him and he jerked, but Griff held him fast and the shudder passed. "Don," Griff said. "Undress."

Don's lashes fluttered as he dropped his gaze, nodded, and began to unbutton his shirt. He moved quickly and smoothly, shedding his clothes and tossing them on top of the hamper until he stood before them, naked and obviously excited by the prospect of whatever else Griff might tell him to do. He planted his feet comfortably and clasped his hands behind his back.

He was gorgeous, all pale skin, dark hair curling down his belly and around his stiff cock.

"What do you see?" Griff asked.

Howard frowned. "Don."

Griff gave his hair another sharp tug and the zing of shock was sharper, this time. More focused, and he bit his lip.

"Be specific," Griff demanded.

Howard's gaze had wandered back to Don's arousal. "Don's cock," he muttered, annoyed at the orders, even when the hot breath used to issue them licked his sensitive neck and ear with wisps of pleasure. The pull on his hair at his belligerent response wasn't short and sharp this time but a long-drawn-out, painful affair that got his attention.

"You know what I'm asking. Give him a real assessment of what you see when you look at him."

Howard nodded and the pressure eased. Griff's blunt fingertips caressed his scalp and another kind of sweet shudder eased through Howard's body, releasing enough tension to let him lean just a tiny bit more. "He's beautiful," he said this time. "The contrast." He reached and wound a lock of hair around his finger. "Fascinating."

"It's always fascinated you, hasn't it?" Griff asked.

A sudden lack of saliva in his mouth reduced Howard's response to a faint nod.

"What else?"

When he didn't answer right away, the tug at his hair returned, almost gentle, like a reminder whose hands he was in. Don watched him patiently, trust in his eyes now. All his anger seemed to have vanished with his acceptance of Griff's control over the situation, and Howard understood, suddenly, what that trust was worth. He swallowed until he had enough saliva to speak, and a thought to voice. "Home." It just might be the response that would satisfy Griff and make Don blush.

Their small lover didn't disappoint. Pink rushed up his neck into his cheeks and he blinked, once, twice, glanced between them, and licked his lips. His teeth darted out, nipped at his lower lip, and he swallowed hard a few times.

"He is," Griff agreed. "Kneel, Donald."

Something in the atmosphere changed when Griff uttered Don's full name.

Don's lips curled in a sweet, calm smile and he dropped to the bath mat in front of Howard, lifting his chin to gaze up at him.

A shiver ran through Howard at the sight. All the tension his lover carried around all day completely drained away. His limbs were loose and his back straight. His eyes sparkled.

Without thinking, Howard reached and touched the tips of his fingers to the pink flood of happiness on Don's cheek. "Look at you," he whispered.

Don smiled at him, but said nothing.

"Any objection to me telling him to suck you until you come down his throat?" Griff asked, brushing the question in intimate promise over his neck with his lips and his breath. "I know he's been dying to get you off for a very long time." He snuck an arm around Howard's waist and dragged his hand up from throat to hair.

Gazing down at Don, Howard saw in the other man's eyes all the promises they'd ever made each other shimmering on the brink. Don would never turn him out if he said no, that he couldn't go down this road. Neither of them would. The promise had been made and the fact he was here still, after everything, told him it was kept because they wanted him, and no other reason.

"I can't," he whispered, getting only half his words out before he felt the tightening of Griff's hold, saw the wavering of Don's expression. "My knee." He sank his fingers in Don's hair. "You'll topple me."

"Bed then," Griff growled, that command scraping along skin like stubble. "Now." He gave Howard a small shove, making his will clear, even though he didn't let him go until he was sure Howard was stable on his feet.

"Yes, sir," Howard grinned tentatively over his shoulder, hoping he wasn't insulting either of them, to find Griff's gaze take on a kind of snarling, animated heat.

"Like that, is it, smartass?" His lips curled into a wicked grin. "Move it." He held out a hand to Don. "Come along."

Don let Griff lift him, at ease with the idea of letting Griff take him in hand. He followed quietly, gaze hungry, lips curled into a soft, anticipatory smile.

Howard suddenly felt like a meal and wondered if he should let this pair devour him. But his feet had already carried him halfway to the bed, and not once had his good sense been consulted since Griff had asked the question. Maybe he was just that eager to get off. More likely, he liked the way they wanted him, broken bits and all.

Besides, it was worth letting Griff call the shots when it made Don look like *that*.

They had him laid out in seconds, back supported by pillows, legs wide, Don's kisses and tongue sending one shockwave after another through him even before he got anywhere near his cock.

"Jesus," he muttered, stroking fingers through black curls and fighting to keep his eyes open long enough to see Don take him in. Watching his pink, pretty lips circle his cock was worth the struggle. Seeing Griff mount the bed, finally as naked as the two of them, behind where Don's ass waved in the air was even better.

AS EAGER as Don had been to get Howard naked—he'd been waiting months for the man to heal physically, and months more for him to find his emotional balance, he took the lovemaking at the pace Griff dictated. Howard had been very right when he'd said it had always been Griff. Griff had stepped into his life, taught him how to be strong, just by being that way himself. Then he'd brought Howard into his life too, and he was determined now to keep it that way.

The slow, methodical seduction might be what Howard needed to ease into this once and for all, but it was good for Don too. He swung, at

Griff's hands, between calm seducer and pliable submissive, reminded of the latter every now and then by a sharp twist of skin between Griff's knowing fingers, or a stinging bite that left him panting.

"That feels good to you?" Howard asked at one point, as Griff shocked Don to stillness, one nipple fast between his fingers.

Don met Howard's gaze, mind singing with white noise, trying to understand the question, only able, in that breath, to be what Griff made him. Then the pain passed and he drew in a breath, and the answer came as clear as spring rain. "Yeah." He licked over Howard's abdomen and wiggled back slightly to nuzzle in his bush and smell his arousal.

Above him, Howard moaned and stroked his hair. Behind him, Griff stroked his ass, sliding his work-rough fingers over his hole. He paused in his exploration of Howard's body, stilled once more in Griff's hands. The pressure at his hole increased and he caught his breath.

"Griff?" he asked, unsure.

The finger moved on, but only a heartbeat later something warm and slick took its place. Not a dry finger this time, but one covered in warmed lube.

"Griff, what—"

Griff's dry hand ran down his back in a wide swath of calluses, strength, and reassurance. "I know what I'm doing this time, babe."

Don rested his forehead briefly on Howard's stomach as the idea of letting Griff do this sank in. He looked up to see Howard watching him, gaze thoughtful.

"You mean to tell me you and Griff never...." His brow furrowed. "Ever?"

Don shook his head. "We've done lots of things." He blushed deeper, he knew, but he couldn't help it. "Not that."

"Do you want to?" Howard asked.

Griff's slick finger traced around his hole.

Don thought about the question, about his answer as he knelt there between them. Howard's cock nudged at his cheek as Griff's finger nudged at his hole. This was one more step down the rabbit hole. One more way for Griff to make his claim.

Don glanced up at Howard. Uncertainty niggled at the warm bud of pleasure in his gut, holding its growth in suspension. What would his mechanic think if he let Griff go where he'd never let Howard? Would he think even less of this dynamic? Would he fall further in Howard's esteem?

He was already falling, though. This was new and frightening and he didn't know what his answer was.

It was Howard who reached out and saved him this time: cupping his face, lifting his chin, meeting his gaze, and finally, smiling, waiting, but not letting him avoid making the choice. "You have to answer him, Donny."

"I don't know."

Sitting up, Howard drew Don up with him, pulled him close enough with just a finger under his chin, to kiss. He drew the kiss out, long, tender, and reassuring, grounding him in the fear, making it okay that he was afraid, accepting it, and keeping it close as he pulled away. "You trust him," Howard said.

It wasn't a question. It was just fact, and Howard knew it.

Don had to accept the truth so he bobbed his head, still unable to find words.

Griff's finger pushed, entered him, and he pulled in a breath, closed his eyes.

"We'll take very good care of you, Donny," Howard promised. "Now"—he slipped his hand around to the back of Don's head, lowered back onto his pillows, and gently returned Don's attention to where it had been, between his legs—"finish what you were told to do."

Don accepted the order, as gentle as it was, because it calmed him to do so. The rabbit hole wasn't so dark and scary, after all. It was comfortable. Safe. Licking up the length of Howard's cock at last, he raised his gaze, saw Howard watching him intently, and felt the bud of warmth bloom to heat and pleasure as Griff's fingers stretched and opened him with a sharply felt burn.

GRIFF watched the scene play out between his lovers and remained silent. They didn't need him to sort out their places in this odd dynamic. He wasn't sure how he could help anyway, but when Howard spoke, confirming Don's place, accepting it, relief washed through him.

Waiting until Don's attention was back on Howe's cock, he looked across his back and met Howe's gaze.

The man smiled calmly at him. Maybe, just maybe, this whole thing could work.

Don lowered his head to the pillow, but he didn't close his eyes. Instead, he watched Howard, still, as if waiting for something.

Howard had no idea what, but the ball was clearly in his court. He touched Don's cheek, kissed his lips, moved back enough to see him clearly. "This was incredible, but now you should do as he says, babe." He ran his knuckles over Don's stubbled jaw. Darting a quick, uncertain glance at Griff, who still seemed preoccupied with Don, he drew in a breath and made up his mind. "Be a good boy, Donny, and I'll blow you next time." Pulling in another quick breath, he plunged ahead, determined to choose his place in the dynamic, to prove to them he could be what they both needed. "If Griff says so."

Don squirmed to look over his shoulder, a huge grin on his face.

"That could be fun," Griff agreed, meeting Howard's gaze at last. "If you can finally do as *you're* told."

Howard swallowed his instant, defensive reply and curled his fingers around Griff's hand. Maybe he'd be able to give the answer aloud later. Right in that moment, he hoped it was enough he didn't say no.

Griff nodded and smiled. "Good enough."

Relief washed through Howard and he sighed. Exhaustion flowed in its wake, leaving him weak and heavy. Not just the lethargy of a really good orgasm, but the kind of bone-deep tired that came from releasing anger and tension and uncertainty. The kind that came from knowing he could sleep and eventually wake to the same safe and secure feeling of being where he was meant to be. Of deserving this place and knowing he had something worthwhile to give back.

"Go to sleep." The whisper came across light-years of twilit space between his and Griff's pillow.

Don snored softly between them already and Howard blinked into the gloom. "That your first order?" he asked, carefully feeling his way through the equally gloomy spaces between what had been and what was becoming.

"If it makes you feel better, yes." Not even a pause between question and answer. No hesitation. Only promise.

Howard thought about that. If it would make him feel better.

"It makes you happy to have that sort of control?"

"Is that a problem?"

"Just a question because I want to know. Does it make you happy, or is it what you do to make him happy?"

The darkness grew, sneaking in through the blinds as night fell and late summer sounds drifted in from the yard.

"It makes me feel better," Griff said at last. "I'm good at it. I like it, yes."

"Do you need it?"

Another, shorter pause. "I have it, Howard," he said finally. "Because it works for Don and me. You and I can figure out what works for us. It doesn't have to be the same."

Howard fumbled through the dark to find Griff's shoulder, arm, and eventually, his hand. "Tonight was a good start, I think."

"I hope so, Howe."

Howard lay quietly as full dark gradually took over. Don's breathing remained steady. Griff's fingers laced with his were warm and secure. "Why did you kiss me? Years ago, I mean. Why did you start all this?"

"You were falling to pieces in front of me. Don loved you, and I—"

"You what?"

"I thought I did too. I wasn't sure until I had this thought, sitting there on the roof imagining what it must have been like for you, alone in the attic, knowing what was waiting downstairs, the end of everything you knew and loved… having to see what your dad did…. I thought I should have been disgusted that you didn't do anything. But all I could feel was fucking relieved that you hadn't completely fallen to bits before we were there to hold you together. For once, in that moment, lying in bed listening to you cry your heart out, finding and hurting the person who had hurt you was less important than keeping track of all the pieces and making sure we didn't lose you after you'd lived through it. That's all." A short, sharp breath wafted across the bed. "For once in my life, a kiss trumped a pounding and my gut told me to take the chance."

"Don didn't know you were going to?"

"No."

"He could have been really, really pissed at you."

"I know. But what you needed was more important, and maybe I realized if he was the guy I really thought he was, he'd get it."

"He did."

"Yeah."

Howard moved their hands to rest on Don's hip between them. "We're really lucky to have him. I want to be the family he's always wanted."

Griff chuckled. "Well, fuck, Howe, it's about goddamn time."

"Jerk."

"Dipshit."

Howard brought Griff's knuckles to his lips. "I love you."

"Yeah." Griff let out a long sigh that caught at the end. "Love you too. Now go to sleep. I mean it."

"Yes, sir," Howe said softly, tightening his fingers. "Whatever you say."

THE high-pitched sound of late summer filled the world. The dusty-gold smell of it filled Don's mind and soul. The heat was dry and absolute. Perfect for the combine. He ran his palm over the thick red paint, pitted and uneven from covering decades of rust patches and Bondo. The metal was already hot to the touch just from the lazy summer sunshine.

"How does it feel?" Griff's big hands curled over his shoulders. Strong fingers dug into flesh and Don sighed.

"Not sure actually."

"Well, I, for one, will not miss dashing out there to fix the damn thing every other day, I'll tell you that right now," Howard said, joining them and handing out coffee cups.

"It's got a lot of memories," Don confessed. "I'm sort of sad to see her go."

"Please tell me you aren't still thinking we shouldn't have done this," Griff said. "Converting is the right thing to do. We don't have to carry the debt of this thing anymore." He slapped the side of the offending machine. "Renting Manning's combine for the hay fields we have left is a good expense, Don." He grinned. "And you still get to go out there and ride the damn thing, though I have no idea why you like it so much."

Don nodded. Approaching their neighbor and offering to help the old man harvest his hay in exchange for a few days' use of his much newer combine had actually been Mark's genius idea. All they had to do was pay the diesel bill for the fuel they used and any maintenance costs that occurred while they had it on their property, and make sure it was properly cleaned and stored after. The financial burden of not having to use or replace their own ancient combine was lifted, and Manning's fields got harvested without the old man having to pay for it in weeks of physical recovery afterward.

"I don't think I ever thought it was a bad idea. Just a scary one."

Howard draped an arm over his shoulders. "Well, let's see. This week, I moved the last of my things over from the apartment, gave the garage's manager keys to Albert, Griff took over running his dad's place, and you put your ass in the air—"

Don slapped a hand over Howard's mouth. "Fuck, dude!" He glanced around, but only Abe and Albert were in the yard, and neither of them was close enough to hear what Howard was saying.

Beneath his palm, Howard grinned.

"All I need is for Megan or Talia to overhear you say something like that."

"Like what?" Talia sauntered out of the house, coffee in hand and grin on her face.

"Nothing," Don snarled. "I have work to do."

She snickered.

"Are you, like, going home any time soon?" Don muttered at her.

Sliding a hand over her obviously swollen belly, her face turned serious and she shrugged. "I guess I'll have to, eventually."

"You know you can stay as long as you need to, Talia," Griff told her.

She nodded.

"He's right." Don turned to face her. He hadn't consulted either of his lovers, but in the face of his sister's misery, he couldn't stop the offer flying from his lips.

"Just come home, Tali."

She stared at him, mouth open.

"I mean it. To hell with that jerk. Why are you waiting around for him to do the right thing? He fired you for getting pregnant, Tali, he is not going to marry you for it."

"Don!" Howard glared at him.

"I'm sorry, Tali, but you know I'm right. So come home. You won't be doing it alone here. Meg is close, Pete and his... brood. Us." He glanced between his slack-jawed partners. "Let us help you. For now, you can live here. You'll find a better job, and an apartment if you want one. Just come home and stop being so stubborn."

She smiled and laughed a bit as her eyes watered. "You're a dunce. You don't want a kid running around here."

"Of course we do. Dozens of them."

"Now wait a minute!" Griff laughed out loud.

"This is the place for kids, Tali, not some dingy basement apartment in a bad part of the city. Now I know Andy offered you a place and you told him no."

"How did you know that?"

"Mark mentioned it last time he was down. But this is different. This is home. So you can't say no. And besides, think how thrilled Dad will be to have his own grandkid around to spoil."

"He's already got dozens."

"Well. That's true." Don smiled. "Besides, we have enough room for you to have a studio, and you can use up Mom's stockpiles of wool while you're at it. Dad will be happy to see it get used. We'll get some sheep again. Please. Think about it."

She nodded and pulled in a deep breath. "I'll think about it."

"Good." He let her go, and she wandered back into the house.

"You're out of your mind," Howard crowed. "A kid? Really?"

"She's my sister."

"And you're a pushover," Griff said. "I'm going over to look at the horses. Shouldn't take all day. I'll clean out Andrew's old room this afternoon. It's the biggest, and we can set up Pete's for the baby. It's small, right next to hers, and also the warmest in the winter."

Don grinned. "I have hay to cut."

"Albert!" Howard called, lifting his mug in salute. "Let's get moving, kid! We have cars to fix." To Don he said, "We can give you a lift to the Mannings'."

"How am I going to get home?" he protested.

"You'll come home when we pick you up at five. Surely you don't think Griff and I are going to swamp out that room on our own. Come on."

He pounded him on the back and the weight of his thumping blow reminded Don instantly of the night before and the long, red nail marks Howe had left down his back. Howe grinned. "Hay isn't going to lie down all on its own, now is it?"

"Five o'clock it is," Don said to himself, thinking how much he loved his family. His life, hell, even his job and the prospect of ten hours bouncing along on top of the combine sounded good to him right then. Taking the cooler of lunch and thermos of coffee from Griff, he kissed his cheek and headed for Howard's truck. It was going to be a good day.

JAIME SAMMS has been writing her stories between men long enough to know better, but not nearly long enough to have told all the tales she has to tell. She splits her time between a day job that pays the bills and her writing that feeds her soul. She's also a mom with a saint of a husband, who keeps the kids fed and clothed and home schooled and herself on a schedule that keeps her sane. She also reviews yaoi novels for Kuriousity, http://www.kuri-ousity.com/. The three cats in residence seem to approve of this arrangement enough to warm her toes at night and keep up a supply of mice from the backyard they think the family needs for survival. Who are we to argue?

Visit her web site: http://www.jaime-samms.net
Blog: http://jaimesamms.blogspot.com
LiveJournal: http://dontkickmycane.livejournal.com/

Also from JAIME SAMMS

Jaime Samms

OFF STAGE: RIGHT

Also from JAIME SAMMS

ANGEL
ELEGY
Jaime Samms

Also from JAIME SAMMS

http://www.dreamspinnerpress.com

Also from JAIME SAMMS

Still Life

JAIME SAMMS

http://www.dreamspinnerpress.com

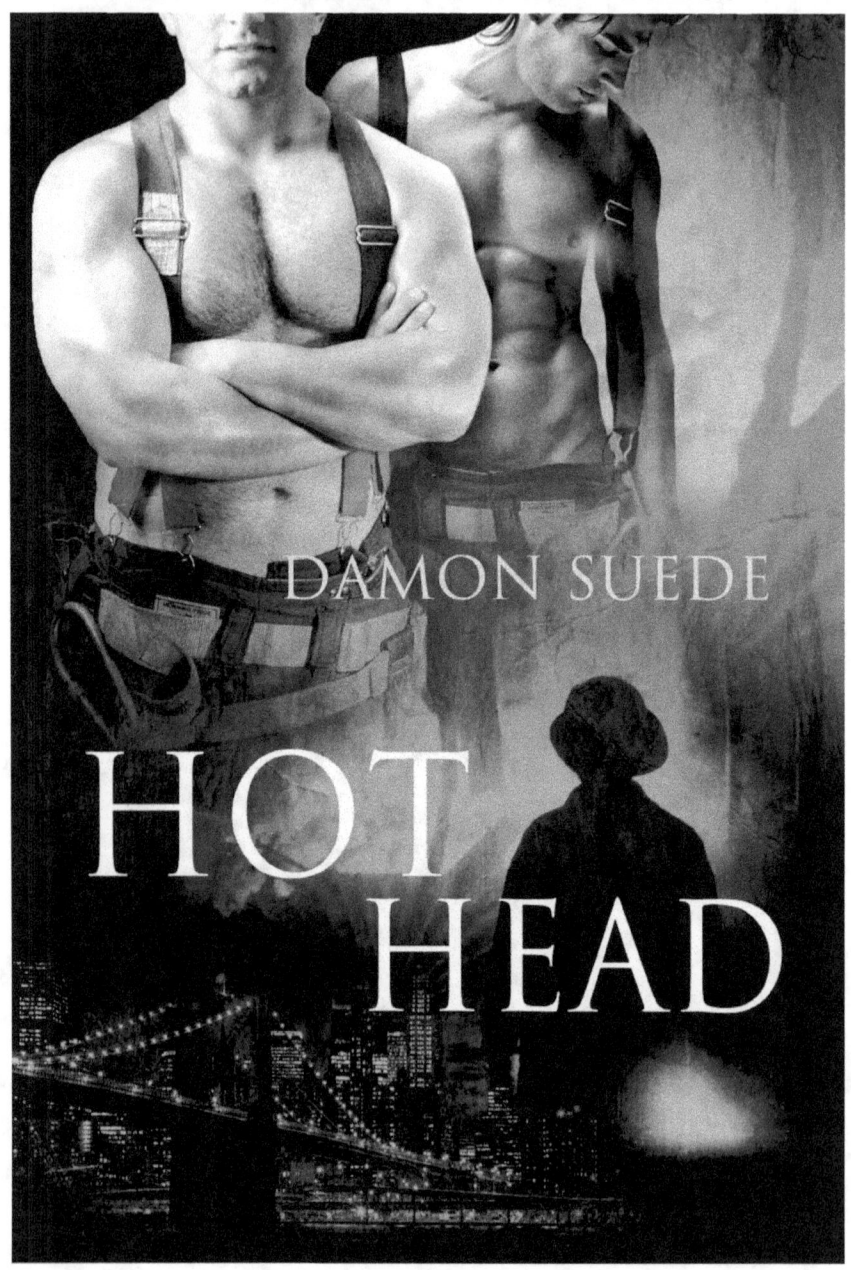

COMING
HOME

M.J. O'Shea

www.ingramcontent.com/pod-product-compliance
Lightning Source LLC
Chambersburg PA
CBHW070114260626
47160CB00004B/1466

Readers love KIM FIELDING

Motel. Pool.

"It made me believe. This isn't so much a ghost story as a love story, and it will break your heart"

—My Fiction Nook

"I've always enjoyed Fielding's stories, but this has to be one of my favorites from her."

—Love Bytes Reviews

"I really enjoyed this novel. Author Kim Fielding took us deep into the minds of both her main characters. In doing so, she made the possibility of ghosts a reality and gave them a depth of emotion beyond what I ever expected. Torn and weak, her men sprung to life on the page and made for a strong story straight to the end. All in all, *Motel. Pool.* by Kim Fielding is a wonderful paranormal story not to be missed."

—Joyfully Jay

The Tin Box

"When I started this book I simply could not put it down."

—Watch and Word Society

Pilgrimage

"An endearingly fun and charming read that kept me engaged and entertained from beginning to end."

—Gay List Book Reviews

"I didn't want to put it down!"

—The Blogger Girls

By KIM FIELDING

Alaska
Animal Magnetism (Dreamspinner Anthology)
The Border
Brute
Don't Try This at Home (Dreamspinner Anthology)
A Great Miracle Happened There
Housekeeping
Men of Steel (Dreamspinner Anthology)
Motel. Pool.
Night Shift
Pilgrimage
The Pillar
Snow on the Roof (Dreamspinner Anthology)
Speechless • The Gig
Steamed Up (Dreamspinner Anthology)
Stitch (with Sue Brown, Jamie Fessenden, and Eli Easton)
The Tin Box
Venetian Masks
Violet's Present

BONES
Good Bones
Buried Bones
The Gig
Bone Dry

Published by DREAMSPINNER PRESS
http://www.dreamspinnerpress.com

BONE DRY

KIM FIELDING

Dreamspinner Press

Published by
DREAMSPINNER PRESS

5032 Capital Circle SW, Suite 2, PMB# 279, Tallahassee, FL 32305-7886 USA
http://www.dreamspinnerpress.com/

Cover Art
© 2014 Christine Griffin.
alizarin_griffin@yahoo.com
http://christinegriffin.artworkfolio.com/
Cover content is for illustrative purposes only and any person depicted on the cover is a model.

ISBN: 978-1-63216-270-0
Digital ISBN: 978-1-63216-271-7
Library of Congress Control Number: 2014945897
First Edition October 2014

Printed in the United States of America
♾
This paper meets the requirements of
ANSI/NISO Z39.48-1992 (Permanence of Paper).

CHAPTER 1

"I DIDN'T take you for the skulking type, Ery." Chris grinned and held out a glass of white wine.

Ery realized he was clutching an empty, and willingly exchanged it for the new one. "I'm not skulking."

"Lurking?"

"Someone's been cuddling up with a thesaurus." Ery took a sip of the wine. It was good stuff. No doubt more expensive than his usual Trader Joe's find. "Anyway, I'm resting. Relaxing."

"Didn't know you did relaxing, dude."

Chris tugged at his dress-shirt collar and tie as if they were strangling him. The only other time Ery had seen his friend dressed up was at Chris and Dylan's civil commitment ceremony, when Dylan had somehow cajoled the guy into a tux. That afternoon Chris had probably been too emotional to care what he was wearing, but this evening he clearly would have preferred his usual ancient T-shirt and faded jeans.

Ery had another swallow of wine. Chris might look uncomfortable and out of place, but Ery felt like beetles were crawling under his skin and through his stomach. He was not relaxed. "Where's Dylan?" he asked.

Chris waved vaguely across the crowded room. "Chin-wagging with his boss and some big-shot client. I got tired of hearing about gambrels and porticos and whatever the fuck else they were goin' on about." Despite Chris's complaint, Ery saw his pride for Dylan, who'd recently made partner at the architectural firm.

"Dylan's moving in pretty fancy circles nowadays, isn't he?"

"Yeah. But when he gets home, I make sure he ain't gettin' too full of himself."

Despite Ery's general unease over the evening, he couldn't help but laugh at Chris's leer. "You remind him of his real priorities, huh?"

"Always."

Chris had somehow managed to find a bottle of beer instead of wine, and he leaned against the wall next to Ery, sipping slowly. They watched as a man in an expensive suit and a woman wearing a necklace undoubtedly worth far more than Ery's annual salary peered at a large bronze statue.

"I love it!" the woman cooed. "It's a perfect conceptualization of global climate change. Brilliant!"

Her companion nodded gravely. "Exactly. The way the texture over here depicts the melting of the glaciers and the impact on coastal cities…. And look over here, where the artist—"

"Global warming is bullshit." The interruption came from a thin woman of indeterminate age and considerable surgical enhancement. "It's just another liberal scheme to control corporate freedom."

The necklace lady frowned. "We've been through this, Jenn. The vast majority of scientists agree—"

"The vast majority of scientists used to agree that people were controlled by humors and that sperm had teeny tiny human beings inside them. That doesn't make it true." Jenn tucked a lock of hair behind her ear. "Besides, they're all getting paid to produce those reports. The media eats it up."

The man shook his head. "That's not true. And you can't deny climate change is happening already. What about the drought we're having?"

"Some years we have drought and some years we flood." Jenn shrugged. "It all evens out. Anyway, I *enjoy* this weather. Warm and not so goddamn dreary all the time."

"That's just because you're from *California*," the necklace lady shot back. She enunciated the location as if it was something terrible, and the man nodded his agreement.

2

Jenn snorted. "And you're just mad because ski conditions are going to be crappy this winter."

Still squabbling, the three of them wandered out of earshot.

"Jesus," Chris said after another sip of beer. "No wonder you ain't mingling. Times like this, I kinda wish Dyl could go all furry right here. I'd love to see this crowd panic."

For a moment Ery entertained himself with a mental image of a rampaging werewolf growling at Jenn and pissing on the climate-change statue. But of course Dylan wouldn't. He only turned into a wolf when he was safely on his farm or the adjacent forest land, and he wouldn't let anyone near him but Chris. Which was sensible enough but disappointing under the current circumstances. What was the point of being pals with a supernatural creature if he couldn't terrify a few idiots?

While Ery remained up against the wall, Chris walked over to give the statue a closer look. He spent a minute or two tilting his head this way and that before returning to Ery's side. "I think it looks like a sperm whale giving birth to a piano."

Ery tried not to giggle but lost the battle. God, he liked Chris, who wasn't like any of the people Ery hung out with. And he certainly wasn't the type he'd have pictured getting together with Dylan, but Ery was really glad those two had hooked up.

His good humor swiftly faded. "That statue sold for forty grand."

Chris made a sour face. "Morons."

"At least some of it will go to a good cause." That was true. All the artists were donating a chunk of their sales toward a new shelter for homeless teens.

"If I had $40K burning a hole in my pocket, I'd just hand it over to the kids and not waste it on an ugly piece of shit." Chris blushed slightly and shot Ery a quick look. "I don't mean your stuff, man. Your paintings ain't ugly."

"They're not selling either."

"That one did." Chris waved his bottle in the direction of a large canvas Ery had painted in sky blue with cloudy little streaks. There was a heavy jagged line across the center, like a seismograph recording or an EEG. Small spots of red and subtle green shading completed the effect.

Ery sighed. "Stender bought it." The senior partner in Dylan's firm. Ery should have been pleased that his work would soon be hanging in one of the city's top architectural offices, where a lot of people would see it. But he was fairly certain Dylan had talked Stender into the purchase out of pity or solidarity or friendship. Ery wanted people to buy his work because it spoke to them, because they loved it.

Chris must have noticed Ery's glum look, because he gently pried the empty wineglass from his hand. "I'm gonna see if I can wrestle Dylan outta here. Then I'm gonna let you take us to a club where you can find yourself a guy and dance 'til you puke."

Ery tried to perk up over that. He was constantly trying to drag Dylan and Chris someplace fun—if for no other reason than to show the world he was friends with the hottest-looking couple in the Portland metro area. But tonight he was more in the mood for someplace quiet and sober, where he could emo to his heart's content. He patted Chris's shoulder. "Sure. I'll wait here." He plastered himself against the wall again, as if he were a piece of art on exhibit.

He wasn't usually such a wallflower. At most art shows, he buzzed around, checking out the other pieces, talking to friends, flirting with the cute guys. Usually he had fun. Not tonight.

The thing was, his usual shows were at a bar or restaurant, or maybe in the kind of community space that was jammed between a yoga studio and a bicycle repair shop. Everybody drank beer and nobody wore a tie—unless she wore it ironically. There were generally a lot of tats and piercings, but no plastic surgery and no necklaces worth tens of thousands of dollars. And if he sold a few pieces, great— a few extra bucks in his pocket. But he didn't sweat it one way or the other. It didn't matter.

Tonight mattered. There were art critics and people with seriously deep pockets. The show was out of Ery's league. He'd only gotten the invite via Dylan, whose firm was a major sponsor. But tonight was a chance to make a name for himself, to fulfill his dream of quitting the evil day job and becoming an artist instead of a hack.

And it just wasn't happening.

Nobody was throwing rotten vegetables at his canvases, which should have been a consolation. But nobody was paying his work much attention either. They were too busy emptying their pockets for climate-change sperm whales.

He was staring morosely at his feet when a hand landed on his shoulder. He looked up to find Dylan smiling at him. Jeez, Dyl looked good. He had his arm around Chris's shoulders.

"The two of you look like a magazine cover," Ery said.

Chris snorted. "What magazine is that? *Overdressed Homos Quarterly?*"

Dylan rolled his eyes. "Let's get out of here before Jack Everson finds me and tries to discuss his façade in more detail."

"His façade, huh?" Chris waggled his eyebrows. "Should I be jealous?"

"Do you have to make everything into a dirty joke?"

"Yes. I do."

They were adorable together. Ery heaved his tenth sigh of the night. "Let's go, guys."

They had to stop first and say good-bye to the couple chairing the event. But the hosts were clearly a lot more interested in Dylan than Ery, so the interchange was short. A few minutes later, the three men walked out into the unseasonably warm October night.

"We're parked in that garage," Dylan said, pointing. "You?"

"Same."

"I'll drive and we'll take you home after. You can come downtown in the morning to get your car, right?"

"I guess." Another deep sigh. "Look, can we just… I don't know. Go have coffee or something?"

Dylan and Chris exchanged a quick look. "Sure," Chris said. "But it means you're gonna miss seein' Dyl get his groove on."

"Has his dancing been enhanced too?" When Ery first met Dylan back in college, Dylan had been cute in a geeky, gawky sort of way. But for some reason, becoming a werewolf had buffed up his body and beefed up his… magnetism, so now he turned heads wherever he went. He only had eyes for Chris, though.

Chris laughed. "No, he's still a spaz when he dances."

"Hey!" Dylan protested, but not very vigorously.

Ery shook his head. "I'll have to save it for another night. I'm kinda wiped, I guess."

With Chris muttering something about hell freezing over if Ery was out of energy, and with Dylan looking worried, they walked down the sidewalk until they came to a Starbucks. Not exciting, but it would do. Ery staked out a good seat in the back corner while Dylan and Chris ordered drinks. The place was pretty crowded and noisy enough that Ery couldn't hear the sound system, which was just as well. He wasn't in the mood for retro pop or bossa nova or whatever corporate wanted the baristas to push this week. If he were home, he'd probably listen to Stravinsky or Bartók. Something depressing and eastern European. The kind of music that should be accompanied by vodka and unfiltered cigarettes.

"Here you go," Dylan said, setting a paper cup in front of Ery. "Three sugars, right?"

Ery smiled. "Yeah."

Chris and Dylan sat across from him, which made Ery feel a little like he was at a job interview. Dylan had something venti and blended, and Chris had just a small paper cup. Dylan plopped down a couple of paper bags. "Chocolate chip cookies and some kind of berry loaf. Help yourself."

"Thanks." But Ery wasn't hungry and didn't need more calories. The goodies wouldn't go to waste, though. Dylan ate all the time—the result of his weird metabolism, he said. Ery wished *he* could eat nonstop without gaining weight.

"I'm sorry your grandmother couldn't make it tonight," Dylan said as he broke off a chunk of cookie.

"Yeah. She wanted to. She would have enjoyed it too. But… she's getting old, you know? She said it would be too much for her." Ery didn't want to think about it. Although his parents were cool, he'd always had a special relationship with his grandma. She was an amazing lady. Even now that he'd passed thirty, he still felt as though she could answer all the questions in the universe.

He decided to change the subject. "What have you guys been up to, anyway?"

"Usual," Chris answered. Then he frowned, loosened his tie, and pulled it off. He shoved it at Dylan. "That's better. We're almost finished with the bathroom, and then I'm gonna put in some new shelving units in the living room. Built-ins. We're gonna get that fireplace workin' too." Dylan and Chris's old farmhouse was in a constant state of restoration and repair, which neither of them seemed to mind.

Dylan chuckled. "And Chris bought this... this *thing*, which he claims he can get running."

"It ain't a *thing*. She's a '70 Olds 442, and she's gonna be a thing of beauty when I'm done with her."

"It's like *Christine*," Dylan stage-whispered. "Only instead of killing people, the car eats all his time and money."

Ery sat back in his chair and listened to his friends bicker. No matter how snarky their words, they touched each other all the time: shoulder bumping shoulder, a hand giving another a quick squeeze, a fond ruffling of hair. And whatever Chris did under the table, hidden from Ery's view, sure made Dylan jump and then blush.

Dylan finished the first cookie and started on the second. "We haven't seen you at the studio for a while."

Chris and Dylan had turned the farm's small barn into a studio for Ery. They'd made it clear Ery was welcome to use it whenever he wanted, unless there was a full moon. At first he'd gone there almost every weekend and even after work now and then, and he'd happily slathered paint over his canvases. He liked the building, which still smelled slightly of hay. During the day there were barn swallows, and in the evenings, bats swooped out from the rafters.

But his visits to the farm had tapered off over the past months. He hadn't been there at all in several weeks.

"Have you been busy at work?" Dylan prompted.

"I guess. I've been working on a new account, redesigning logos and signage for a grocery chain. Which is every bit as exciting as it sounds. And I'm illustrating a manual for nursing students."

"Oh."

While Dylan slurped and chewed and avoided eye contact, Chris unfastened the top few buttons of his shirt and folded a napkin into origami shapes. Ery watched a group of college kids at a nearby table.

7

They all had textbooks and laptops open in front of them but seemed to be spending most of their time on their phones. His attention strayed to the counter, where one of the baristas looked vaguely familiar. A brief hookup from long ago, maybe. Or maybe not. The guy didn't seem to notice Ery at all.

For no reason Ery could discern, Dylan gave a sudden violent jerk. He glared at Chris, who raised his eyebrows expectantly.

"We're, uh, going on a trip in a couple weeks," Dylan said.

"Camping again?" The previous year Dylan had surprised Chris with a shiny new Airstream trailer, and they liked to take it to the coast or up into the mountains now and then.

"Nope. Chris has this passport without a single stamp, so we're going to do something about that. Europe."

"Wow! That sounds great! Have you decided where in particular?"

Chris answered. "Barcelona. That's in Spain." For some reason he snickered and Dylan scowled. "Also Paris. We're doing a week in each."

Ery's grandmother had sent him to Paris for his twenty-fifth birthday. The guy he'd been dating went too, and they had a blast. They spent hours at the Louvre, but it was the Musée d'Orsay that truly captured Ery's heart. He'd stared at the impressionist paintings with awe, imagining that someday his work might hang in a place like that. Hah. Fat chance.

"Remind me to give you the names of a couple clubs in Le Marais," he said. "You can't fly all the way over there and miss out on the real Gay Paree."

"I'm gonna come off as an even worse hick there," Chris said morosely.

But Ery shook his head. "Are you kidding? Those French boys will eat you up. They'll eat *both* of you up."

Now his friends looked skeptical. Dylan remained perpetually unconvinced that he had evolved into sex on legs, and Chris seemed to think the entire world viewed him as a hopeless redneck instead of a bright, talented, and caring man. Their low self-esteem should have annoyed Ery, but he found it slightly endearing. "You guys'll have a lot of fun," he said.

8

They chatted for a while about Paris and Barcelona. Dylan pretended to despair of sitting next to his restless partner for an eleven-hour plane trip, and Chris went on about how Dylan was going to want to try every snooty, weird food in Europe. The college kids went away, and soon a middle-aged lady with a pink streak in her hair took their table. She had a laptop too, but instead of staring at her phone, she clacked madly away at her keyboard. Ery wondered what she was writing.

Chris and Dylan started shooting significant looks at each other again. They were probably thinking it was time to hit the road for the hour's drive home. If Ery had been a better friend, he would have given them a graceful out. But he wasn't in the mood to go back to his depressing apartment—it was always too cold or too hot, and the neighbors had crappy taste in music. So they all simply sat there for a while.

Chris finally exploded. "Oh, for fuck's sake! Gettin' Lon Chaney here to talk about anything important is goddamn impossible." He bonked Dylan hard enough on the shoulder to make him wince. "We need to talk about something besides croissants and berets, Ery."

Dylan chewed his lip and looked as if he were about to undergo a painful dental procedure. "What's wrong, Ery?" he said at last.

"What do you mean?"

"I mean... you seem kind of off lately."

Now it was Ery's turn to look away. "The show tonight was kind of a bust. It bruised my ego a little."

"I don't mean just tonight. You haven't been using the studio. You haven't been...." Dylan waved his hands helplessly.

Chris stepped in to translate. "You haven't been flitting."

Ery blinked at him. "Flitting?"

"Yeah. Normally you're zooming all over the place, talkin' a mile a minute, smiling at everyone. You're Mr. Congeniality. But now... well, look at yourself. You're not even dressed like normal."

Glancing down at his clothing, Ery shrugged. "I'm wearing a suit. I think that's pretty normal."

"That's pretty normal for someone else. *You* usually look like you stole your clothing from fuckin' Oz. Technicolor."

Chris had a point. Ery's suit was a sober charcoal and his shirt was powder blue. The only real color came from his tie, a bright red with a hand-painted surfer.

Dylan and Chris looked worried. This time, at least, Ery managed not to sigh. "My job ate my soul." He couldn't quite resist a dramatic swoon, toppling slowly forward until his forehead was on the table. It smelled like cookies and cleaning fluid.

"Is it that bad?" Dylan asked gently.

Ery lifted his head from the table. "You know what I did today? I drew a picture of a guy with a catheter in his dick. And I tried to decide between fifteen nearly identical shades of green for the leaf in the new grocery store logo. Used to be I could spend the day on stuff like that, and when I was on my own time, doing *real* art, I could work it right out of my system." He'd been happy then, paint splattering everywhere like a rainbow drizzle. It was a little like the feeling a kid got on the first day of summer vacation. But lately that feeling had faded.

"Can you find a different job?" Chris asked.

"No. I mean, yeah, maybe. But I don't think it would help. It's too late. I murdered my muse."

At the show, a silver-haired man with a companion who was either a grandson or a much younger lover had paused in front of one of Ery's paintings. Ery hovered nearby, ears cocked. "I like the palette," the older man said. "And the way the balance is just slightly off. But overall... eh. It lacks originality. The artist just isn't saying anything to me."

The younger man nodded. "It's too derivative. It doesn't say anything new."

The words had hurt—mostly because they were true. Ery hadn't felt the old joy when he'd painted that piece. He'd *thought* about the painting a lot, planned it carefully, intentionally included a few sly references to de Kooning and Gorky. But in the end, the work had felt almost as clinical as sketching a dick with a tube in it.

"It sounds like your creative wellspring's gone dry," Dylan said, then winced. "Sorry. I've been listening to Stender too long."

"No, no, you're right. Ideas used to flow out of me so fast I could hardly keep up. And now? Nada."

"Sucks, man," Chris said while Dylan shook his head sympathetically. And Ery felt a tiny bit better for sharing. He hadn't even told his grandma how he'd been feeling lately, although he'd caught a few of her worried looks. He wasn't usually a complainer, and he didn't want to whine. But lately he'd been feeling like something important had broken inside, like a piece of himself had gone missing.

"Hey," said Dylan. "Maybe a change of scenery would help. Come to Europe with us."

Ery snorted. "Third wheel much?"

Chris smiled. "Nah. I bet you're fun on a trip. You could take us to those clubs you were talkin' about."

Honestly, the idea was tempting. But although Ery had some vacation time saved up, he didn't have much money. He couldn't afford to jet-set. "Thanks, guys. You're sweet. But I'm gonna stick around here." A new idea struck him. "But maybe I'll take some time off work. You don't mind if I hang out at the studio, do you?"

"We built it for you," said Dylan. "Hang out all you want. In fact… while we're out of town, would you mind keeping an eye on the place for us? Kay offered, but that means she'd be bringing the baby with her, and that kid is a terror. She's walking now." He shuddered.

Chris nodded eagerly. "Yeah, good idea. Besides, the sister-in-law probably wouldn't want the rug rat around if we got invaded by ghosts or werewolf packs again." He was grinning, but he wasn't exaggerating. The previous year, the farmhouse had been haunted, and a bunch of extremely unfriendly werewolves had tried to kill Dylan and Chris.

"Ghosts I can handle. I don't know what to do about werewolves, though."

"I've faced 'em twice," said Chris. "If they ain't Dylan, I recommend screaming like a little girl and running like hell. That's what I did."

Dylan squeezed Chris's shoulders. "You did not. You saved me."

"First I screamed and ran. Didn't save you 'til Uncle Frank powered me up."

"Nuh-uh. Your dad told me. You were already heading toward me and that pack when Frank chipped in. If the ghost hadn't helped, you'd have run right in there and gotten yourself torn to pieces. Dope," he added fondly.

They continued to squabble for a moment, but they were all googly-eyed over each other while they did it. Ery had to admit it—he was 99 percent thrilled that they'd found each other and made such a good life together and 1 percent jealous as hell. Not because he regretted that, after a little experimental fooling around back in college, he and Dylan decided they made better friends than lovers. That had been the right decision by far. It was only… jeez, he wanted what they had.

Maybe Dylan was right. Maybe a vacation and a little change of scenery would help. Couldn't hurt. "Sure, I'll keep an eye on the place. I'll just camp out there while you're gone, if that's okay."

"Anytime," Chris and Dylan said almost in unison. All three of them laughed.

"You guys are adorable. You're gonna be one of those old married couples that finishes each other's sentences." Ery smiled at them. "Thanks. This'll be good. Heck, maybe some supernatural creatures *should* show up. That might knock me out of my rut."

"Be careful what you wish for," Chris warned. "Weird shit happens around Dylan."

Dylan protested. "Hey! The ghost was *yours*."

"Right, sure. You're only responsible for the murderous lycanthropes."

"Fancy word there, country boy."

"I know a lotta fancy words, city boy. Like *retribution* and *penance*." Chris waggled his eyebrows meaningfully.

Ery sat back in his chair to watch his friends, the merest hint of a squiggle in his heart—a squiggle that meant maybe things were going to get better. He smiled and ate a big piece of Dylan's remaining cookie.

CHAPTER 2

ERY HAD named his Mini Cooper Bea because she was bright yellow with a black roof and bonnet stripes. Today he felt like Bea was happy to be escaping the constant stop-and-go of city streets. She buzzed contentedly down the county road, the unseasonable sunshine making her sparkle.

Ery was happy too. He'd shoved a bunch of clothes and food and books in the back of the car, locked up his apartment, waved good-bye to the neighbors who listened to polka music at full blast, and headed out to the farm. After weeks of moping and stagnation, it felt great just to be moving again. Leaving the office the day before had been particularly satisfying. He felt like he was playing hooky, like those times in eleventh grade, only now nobody was going to rat him out to his parents and he wasn't going to have to face a meeting in Principal Morris's office.

Poor Principal Morris. What kind of karma landed a guy a job as a high school principal?

Ery turned off the county road onto Dylan and Chris's bumpy lane. Theirs was the only house in sight now that the frumpy little shack where Chris used to live had burned down. Where the shack used to be, the guys had planted a vegetable garden. They had a fancy grape arbor that Dylan designed and Chris built. They planned to put in a bunch of fruit trees too but had skipped it this year due to the drought. The garden still looked nice, though. Ery wondered which of his friends had decided on the sunflowers and roses.

On the other side of the lane, golden wheat awaited harvest, with its backdrop of rounded green hills. Ery had never been much for country living, but he could understand why Dylan had fallen in love with this property. Probably his hunky next-door neighbor had helped with the infatuation.

Dylan and Chris stood on their front porch. Chris was smoking a cigarette and sipping from a brown bottle. Dylan was fussing with his phone, but he looked up at Ery and waved as Ery parked. No cramped parallel parking for Bea, and no risk of door dings. Aside from the Airstream, Dylan's truck, and Chris's collection of questionably functional vehicles, Bea had the acreage all to herself.

After getting out of the car and opening the boot—you had to call it that if you owned a Mini; it was a rule—Ery grabbed a bag of groceries. "Hey, guys. All packed and ready for your adventure?" He walked toward the house.

"We're packed," Chris said. "OCD Boy here is triple-confirming all our flight times."

"Sometimes they change at the last minute," Dylan replied somewhat defensively.

Ery grinned. "You sure you don't want a ride to the airport? We'd have to take your truck, but—"

"Nah," Chris interrupted. "It's a hassle. The truck can stay in the economy lot for a couple weeks. And you can enjoy getting back to nature quicker."

To be honest, Ery wasn't sorry to be missing the drive. But he'd had to offer, at least.

"I'm gonna go put this stuff away," Ery said. "You guys aren't leaving yet, are you?"

Dylan checked the time on his phone. "Half an hour. And hey, you're welcome to stay in the house if you'd rather. Whichever room you want." He shrugged. "Or the apartment. Your choice."

Ery had to grin at that. When Chris and Dylan converted the old barn into a studio, they surprised Ery by making part of the structure into an apartment. The small space contained pretty basic furnishings, but it had everything he needed: a bedroom/sitting room with a view down to the pond, a kitchenette, and a bathroom with a nice shower. They'd even hooked up a small washer/dryer set. They told him the setup was so he could spend the night whenever he wanted and really feel at home. He'd cried a little at the time, which made Dylan hilariously uncomfortable. Jeez, he was lucky to have such great friends.

"I'll stay in the barn. That way, in the unlikely event my muse revives in the middle of the night, I'm all set."

It took Ery three trips to lug all his crap to the barn, and then he had to put the perishables in the fridge. He decided to unpack the rest later, after he said good-bye to his friends. He got to the front of the house just as Dylan and Chris were arguing over who had packed more useless shit.

"He has, like, ten different charger cords in there," Chris said, pointing at Dylan's suitcase. "It's like traveling with a Radio Shack."

"At least cords are light. You're the one with all the books."

"Gotta have somethin' to read, and I ain't gonna learn French or Spanish."

"They have books in English over there. Or you could get a Kindle."

Chris snorted. "That'd be another cord."

Ery gave Dylan a hug, then Chris. "Have a fab time. Send me pictures so I can be suitably envious. Bring me back a hot Spanish boy."

Dylan smiled. "Help yourself to whatever in the house. We pretty much cleaned out the fridge, but there's frozen stuff and dry goods and all that."

"And every appliance ever invented," Chris muttered. He was the household cook, but Dylan couldn't resist gadgets.

Dylan pretended he hadn't heard. "There's more towels and things if you need them. Keys are on the counter. So're emergency numbers—Rick and Kay, and Chris's dad. I mean, you should be able to call me, but just in case."

"I'm sure everything will be fine. I'll be fine. I'll be Picasso." He thought for a moment. "Is there anything I need to take care of on the land?"

"Nope," Chris replied. "Got drip irrigation on the garden, and it's on a timer. Everything else takes care of itself."

Dylan looked a little uncomfortable. "Um… the pond. You might want to kind of… be careful if you go in it." He glanced at Chris, who nodded.

Ery was puzzled. "Be careful of what? Is it shark-infested?"

His friends sort of hemmed and hawed for a moment, and finally Dylan answered. "It's just weird. Chris and I go swimming in there sometimes and it's fine. But one time, when I was looking for something at the bottom—when we were dealing with Uncle Frank—I found out it's a hell of a lot deeper than it should be. And one of the wolves who was after us got… um…."

Chris finished for him. "She jumped in and never came out. Maybe she got caught in some of the crap that's down there, but maybe not. Dunno."

Okay. That *was* weird. Ery shrugged. "I don't know how to swim. And nobody should be swimming in Oregon in late October anyway. It goes against nature."

They climbed into the truck with Chris behind the wheel and Dylan still listing things he thought Ery ought to know, like where they kept extra toothbrushes and the fact that the nearest grocery store had a crappy selection of organic produce. Ery wasn't sure whether the guy was having a fit of OCD or trying to distract Chris from being nervous about the trip. Possibly both. The truck's big engine roared to life, and Ery waved as they pulled away. He coughed a little on the cloud of dust they kicked up and then went off to the barn to unpack.

THE FIRST thing Ery decided after putting away his clothing was that the barn apartment needed decorating. The walls were interesting— reclaimed barn wood from a falling-down structure on a farm a few miles away. They had a lot of texture and character, but they were gray. As was the polished concrete floor. The furniture was sort of charmingly old-fashioned. The pieces had once belonged to Kay's grandmother, and Dylan had stored them in his basement before putting them to use in the barn. But the entire apartment had about as much color as an old black-and-white print.

When he finished some paintings, he'd hang a few of them here. Brighten up the place. Now all he had to do was paint.

Right.

First he made himself a salad for lunch. He was about to eat when he realized it would be improved with truly fresh veggies, so he ran over to the garden and picked several tomatoes. But then he decided it was a shame for all those flowers to go to waste, because he couldn't see them from the barn and surely by the time Dylan and Chris returned, rain and cold would have arrived. So Ery picked some flowers. And a few herbs he found tucked in one corner. Then he paused for a while to admire a spiderweb with a beautiful spider in the center. And to watch a caterpillar munching on a leaf.

He finally returned to the barn, where he spent a long time trying to find a suitable container for the flowers. The apartment wasn't furnished with vases. Eventually he discovered an old canning jar half-hidden under some boards in the studio space. He dumped out the dead bugs and scrubbed the glass before arranging the blooms to his liking and setting the bouquet in the middle of the table.

The salad was delicious. It would have been even better with a homemade dressing instead of the splash of balsamic he'd brought with him. He googled salad dressing recipes, found a good one, and made a shopping list. He also checked his e-mail, Twitter, and Tumblr accounts. That took a while. He got distracted.

Finally it was time to paint... after staring out the window for a bit. Beauty of nature and all that. Trying to prime the creative wellspring, right?

Chris must have had the Bobcat out recently, because the blackberry bramble was diminished enough to allow a view over the slope and down toward the pond. Ery couldn't quite see the water due to the angle of the hill, but he could certainly see the almost impenetrable evergreen forest behind the pond. The forest didn't belong to Chris and Dylan—it was state land and it went on for miles. Dylan liked to roam there when he was a wolf. To hunt there, in fact. Ery shivered slightly, imagining his mild-mannered friend turning into a deadly predator.

What was it like for Chris to have a supernatural lover? Ery was fairly comfortable with the paranormal, since his grandmother was a spiritualist. But it was one thing to talk about otherworldly creatures or even to chat with them; it was something else entirely to date one. To love one.

Something moved down near the pond, but Ery couldn't quite make it out. Despite Dylan's monthly midnight munching, a lot of wildlife passed through the farm. This was something good-sized, like a deer or a coyote. It made the brush rustle. He squinted through the glass, but all he could see were moving leaves and a very quick flash of something buff colored.

He gave himself a little shake. If he procrastinated any longer, he was going to lose the light.

He wandered into the studio to take inventory of his supplies. He had several primed canvases in a variety of sizes, most of them large. A good selection of paints and brushes on the shelves Chris had built for him. An easel, although Ery sometimes preferred to work with his canvas flat on the floor or propped against a wall. Back when he was using the studio more regularly, he'd also schlepped over some sketchpads and pencils, a few palettes, a wide selection of acrylic mediums and acrylic and oil paints, and a couple jars of varnish. He had everything he needed to get started—except inspiration.

"Dammit, airhead!" he said aloud. Kids used to call him that when he was in school—Ery the Airhead. He hadn't actually minded that name too much, in part because he knew he was actually fairly smart and in part because the other names they called him were a lot worse. Ery the Fairy was one of the milder choices. Ery might have been comfortable with his orientation since grade school, but his peers sure weren't.

He'd go home in tears and his parents would hug him, tell him they loved him exactly the way he was, and ask if he wanted them to discuss the bullying with school officials. Their support was wonderful, but again the next day, he'd have to brave those hostile faces and would end up heartbroken over their refusal to accept him. By high school he'd finally accumulated a group of good supportive friends and had stopped giving a shit what anyone else said. But jeez, getting there had been hard!

That wasn't a good memory. But maybe that was what he needed right now: a little roiling emotion to fuel his work. Art is pain, right? Everybody knew that the best artists were tortured souls. People with perfectly happy lives probably sat at home and did cross-stitch kits of kittens in baskets.

He chose the biggest canvas, four feet by five. He would have liked something even larger, but that got expensive. This would have to do.

He didn't plan or sketch anything beforehand. He chose some colors almost at random, squeezed them onto his palette, and blended. Then he began to paint. He didn't let himself pause, not even long enough to stand back and take a look at the whole picture. This was brainstorming, an attempt to build a direct pipeline to his emaciated, neglected muse. "Are you in there?" he asked her as he worked. "Can you hear me?" He always pictured her as an older lady with a slightly beaky nose and hair badly in need of conditioner. She wore clothing unsuitable for her age simply because she wanted to, dammit, and she swore like a longshoreman. She didn't give a flying fuck what shade of green Planet Foods used in its logo. She wouldn't shop there anyway—she ate nothing but Ben & Jerry's and Snickers, because muses didn't have to worry about calories or nutrition.

He didn't hear her answer his call, but that didn't mean she wasn't there. The secret was to keep slapping paint on canvas and hope genius was flowing through him.

It wasn't.

He had to stop to get more paint, and when he turned back to the canvas, he moaned at what he saw. He hadn't covered much of the canvas, actually—his brushes had been too small for great washes of color. The section he had painted was complex, full of multicolored squiggly lines bisected by a wide column with two oblongs hanging below.

He'd painted someone's junk.

It was *pretty* junk, with bright colors and lush pubic hair. It was a little difficult to tell without the rest of the body to give a sense of proportion, but it was probably fairly ample junk, with a long wide shaft and generous balls. It was happily erect. It was more or less anatomically correct, colors aside. But jeez, it was a crotch, and it had absolutely no artistic value. It wasn't even sexy, what with the greenish tinge of the glans, not to mention the twisty yellow line emerging from the tip, which was either an extremely narrow and creatively aimed stream of pee or else a catheter line.

"Fuck!"

If Ery's muse was still alive, she was far too pissed off at him to be of any help.

CHAPTER 3

ERY ABANDONED his polychrome penis and spent the afternoon and evening reading a mystery novel. He had more salad and some curry for dinner. He went to bed early but didn't fall asleep for a long time. Through the open window, he heard bats winging and owls calling. A leafy rustling could have been critters or perhaps a light breeze. The barn rafters creaked a bit as the temperature cooled.

He woke up several times during the night with the blankets twisted around his legs and the last wisps of unsettling dreams escaping from his mind. Once he had to get up to use the bathroom, and while he was at it, he detoured to the fridge for a drink of water. He stopped to look out the window, but although the moon had just begun to wane, he couldn't see much besides shadows. Werewolves had really good night vision, Dylan said. That would be kind of nifty.

He got back into bed but had trouble falling asleep again. He felt as if he was forgetting something, but he couldn't imagine what. Or as though he should be noticing something. But he'd spent the night in the barn before, and he couldn't discern anything special about tonight. He plumped the pillow and straightened the blanket, and then he dragged out his old childhood trick of counting his breaths.

The trick must have worked, because the next thing he knew, sunlight was pouring through the window glass and warming his face. He hadn't bothered to close the curtains the evening before. Privacy wasn't a big issue out here in the boonies. When he checked his phone, he was surprised to discover it was after ten. He hadn't intended to sleep so late.

He got up, showered and shaved and dressed, but didn't bother styling his hair. He wore an old pair of paint-stained jeans and an equally stained red T-shirt. Instead of scrounging some breakfast, he decided to call his grandmother.

"Are you settled in, dear?" she asked when she picked up the phone. She didn't have caller ID or anything—just good intuition.

"Yeah. It's a comfy little place. Nobody's playing polka."

"I should hope not. It's not too quiet, is it?"

Her slightly concerned tone made him smile. "No, it's just right. Exactly the perfect setting for an existential crisis."

She blew a dismissive puff of air. "You're always overly dramatic about these things. I know you're unhappy, Ery. Everyone has rough patches. But you are strong and far too spirited to stay down for long."

"But I can't paint, Grandma. I mean, I can't paint anything *good*." He blushed slightly at the thought of her seeing what he'd produced the previous day. She was no prude, he knew that, but she was his grandmother, for goodness' sake.

"Do you remember when you wanted to be Peter Pan for Halloween? You wouldn't let your parents buy you a costume and you spent days trying to make one. You came to me in tears because you couldn't get it exactly right."

"I was seven."

"And you were trying too hard. Once you finally relaxed and allowed yourself to be satisfied with something less than perfection, you had a wonderful time. Everyone thought you were adorable. I still have the photos."

"Grandma, I was *seven*. I'm thirty-one now."

She chuckled. "And you're still the same stubborn fellow. Hard work and perseverance are admirable, but you can't force things. When the time is right for something special to happen, it will."

"Are we talking about my art or my love life?" he asked suspiciously.

"Both, my dear."

She'd been telling him this same story for years, and he wasn't convinced. But he was comforted a little.

"Do you need anything, Grandma? I can come into town."

"No, I'm just fine. Edna's picking me up soon. We're going out for lunch and then we have a card game, and we'll stop at the market on the way home. But you're a sweet boy to ask. Now, go enjoy the farm. Perhaps a little outdoor exercise will do you good."

"Right." He rubbed his face with his free hand. "Call if you need anything."

"Of course. I love you, Ery."

"You too, Grandma."

Munching on an apple, Ery shuffled to the studio. It was a space any artist would envy. Chris and Dylan had installed a couple of skylights in the barn's tall ceiling and some large windows facing north, toward a stand of Christmas trees gone feral, so the light was fantastic. The studio had lots of room to move around, plenty of shelves, and even a deep sink up against one wall. As soon as the studio was ready to use, Ery had installed a sound system so he could listen to music while he worked.

Maybe, he thought as he entered the room, the previous night's painting wouldn't be as bad as he remembered. After all, Keith Haring painted bright-colored erect penises, and everybody loved his work.

Slowly, Ery turned to face his painting.

It was worse than he remembered.

It looked like the Jolly Green Giant had used his dick as a paint mixer and then stuck a tube in it. It was grotesque, and not in an interesting Bosch-Ernst sort of way. Just looking at it made Ery want to cry. "Thanks a lot, muse," he muttered.

He slapped three coats of primer over the ugly thing, which made him feel slightly better.

Instead of trying a new piece, he left the studio and settled down in the apartment with his iPad. After watching three episodes of *Lost* on Netflix, he ate the leftover curry and checked his e-mail and social media accounts.

Back in the studio, the blank canvas mocked him.

Maybe the thing to do was get outside. He grabbed his sketchbook and a couple of pencils, slipped into his sneakers, and ventured out into the sun. It was a glorious day, with a sparkling blue sky streaked ever so faintly with jet trails. Birds twittered. A line of deciduous trees across the wheat field blazed with autumn glory. He thought he could smell the pond, damp and green and, after Chris and Dylan's cryptic warning, slightly mysterious.

He headed in the other direction, though, past the house and garden and down the gravel lane toward the county road. He liked to walk. He lived about two miles from his office, and unless the weather was truly miserable, he walked to and from work every day. The exercise was good for him, and it saved some wear and tear on Bea. He wasn't a hiker, really. He preferred sidewalks and the possibility of stopping for a coffee along the way. He liked to peer in store windows and check out restaurant menus, and he enjoyed pausing to pet people's dogs. Especially if the people were male and cute.

Here there were no cafés, no dog walkers, no interesting window displays. But it was still pleasant to stroll along, examining the roadside plants and listening to insects hum. The road was quiet; when he returned to the farm over an hour later, he'd seen only a half-dozen or so cars and some mildly curious cows.

He intended to head back to the studio, but he found himself walking right past it and around the remains of the blackberry bramble, then down the slope to the pond. He could tell the water level was lower than normal, but a couple of mallards didn't seem to mind. They paddled around contentedly, stopping every so often to dip their heads into the water. Their raised tails struck Ery as funny for some reason. He sat on the soft ground, put the sketchpad on his lap, and did a quick cartoon of bobbing ducks. The cartoon made him smile, so he made another drawing—this time with more detail—of the ducks standing on the opposite bank, the female curled up in a nap while the male kept an eye out for trouble. You had to like ducks. They were pretty, and they conversed with endearing little quacks.

When the second drawing was complete, Ery scooted backward a little and leaned against a fallen tree. He set the sketchpad down beside him. The sun warmed his head and shoulders, and he closed his eyes against the light reflected off the pond's surface. He drowsily realized he was dropping off, then decided he didn't care. He let sleep wash over him like a warm wave.

WHEN ERY woke up, at first he thought he was dreaming.

He was slumped against a tree trunk with the late afternoon sun throwing long shadows. His legs were cramped and his ass was sore. He had the sneaking suspicion there were bugs in his hair. None of which mattered, considering a naked man was standing over him.

The man had sleek muscles under skin pale even by Pacific Northwest standards. If he had any body hair, it was too light to see, but droplets of water glistened on his soft uncut cock and glided down his torso. His wide eyes were a startling, clear green, and even wet, his long hair was white. But his handsome face was youthful—early twenties, perhaps—with a slightly pointed chin, a wide mouth, and prominent cheekbones.

He was standing so close that he was dripping onto Ery's sketchbook. His head was tilted slightly, as if he were thinking very deeply about the drawing of the ducks.

"This is private property!" Ery squawked inanely.

The man startled as violently as if he'd been shot. Without a word, he spun around—*spectacular ass*, Ery couldn't help but notice—sprinted the few steps to the pond's edge, and dove into the water.

Ery lurched to his feet and followed in the man's footsteps, but even though he waited for several minutes, the man never reappeared. The ducks across the water quacked disapprovingly at Ery.

"Fuck! Fuck, fuck, fuck, fuck, fuck." Ery paced back and forth at the pond's edge, soaking his sneakers but not venturing any deeper than his ankles. Had the guy drowned? There was no sign of him anywhere. Ery had only a vague idea how the pond was formed, although he knew it had something to do with a stream and an earthen dam. He couldn't see a stream or a dam—everything was too overgrown except for the little beachy area where he stood.

Ery had no idea what to do. He didn't have his phone, and even if he did, emergency help was far away. Much too far to be of any help rescuing someone from drowning.

Jesus, what if the thing in the pond—the thing Chris and Dylan warned him about—had grabbed this guy just like it grabbed that werewolf? What if it grabbed Ery too? Not that he was planning to go into the water. He could barely dog paddle.

"Hello? Hello?" he called.

The only answer was the echo of his own shouts.

After several more minutes of fruitless and frantic running back and forth, Ery sprinted up the hill. The man must have come from somewhere; the farm had no near neighbors. As Ery ran around to the gravel lane, he expected to find the stranger's car. But he didn't. Just Bea, the Airstream, and Chris's junkyard. He couldn't hear a motor nor see a dust cloud left by a departing vehicle.

He had to act; he couldn't do *nothing*. Jeez! He was a grown man who ought to be able to handle these things on his own. He thought about calling Dylan and Chris, but it was something like three in the morning for them, and what the hell were they supposed to do from halfway around the world? Then he considered calling his grandmother, but that was just ridiculous. Grown man, remember? He mentally ticked off a list of his friends and family members, but he couldn't think of anyone who had special knowledge for a situation like this. Well, his cousin Gina had been a lifeguard once, but that probably wouldn't help. And she lived in Denver; she wasn't exactly in a position to save the pale stranger.

Ery ended up running into the house, finding Chris and Dylan's landline, and dialing 911. He had to explain several times to the dispatcher what had happened, and then he had some difficulty giving directions. Street addresses were a lot easier in the city.

He heard the sirens approaching almost fifteen minutes later. A sheriff's car got there first, and a fire truck followed close behind, bouncing and rattling over the gravel. Under different circumstances, Ery would have been thrilled to pieces with the array of buff uniformed masculinity that swarmed around him. But as it was, he was flustered and sort of freaking out.

26

Everyone ran down to the pond. The sky was growing dark, so the rescue personnel shined the beams of their flashlights over the water and into the trees. Naturally, there was no sign of anything unusual.

One of the cops was a tanned young guy who looked like he'd been plucked straight off a tractor. With his beefy physique and earnest expression, he would have looked more at home in overalls and a John Deere cap than in his khaki uniform. He held Ery's sketchbook. "This belongs to you, sir?"

"Yes."

"And you didn't remove anything from the scene?"

"No, nothing. I didn't touch anything."

The deputy nodded. "And you didn't see or hear any vehicles?"

"No."

"Sir? How much have you had to drink today?" The cop came a few steps closer.

"Nothing! I mean, I had some coffee and… and water, I guess. That's it."

"Uh-huh." The cop was younger than Ery, for Christ's sake, but somehow he managed to sound paternal. "And have you taken any prescription or nonprescription medications recently?"

Ery sputtered slightly. "I'm not on drugs! I don't do drugs." Well, he *had* dabbled, especially back in his student days. But usually he didn't need chemical help to have a good time, and he hadn't even smoked a joint in over a year. "And I'm not crazy either," Ery added before the officer could ask.

Deputy Junior didn't believe him. "Sir, there's no sign of anyone else here. No clothing or shoes. Are you positive this isn't just a case of, um, overactive imagination?" He lifted his eyebrows and waved the sketchbook as if to suggest that everyone knew artists were nuts.

"He was here," Ery replied stubbornly.

They stayed another hour. Since getting to the woods on the other side of the pond was nearly impossible without getting wet, nobody tried it. But they looked around the farm, scoured the barn and the house, even poked around in the trailer and the cars. And they found nothing.

Finally the older deputy handed Ery a card. "If you see him again or find anything, give us a call."

"But aren't you going to… drag the pond or something?"

"Sir, search and rescue costs a lot of money, and there are only a few of us to serve this entire county. We can't go on wild goose chases."

"He wasn't a wild goose."

"*If* you find something more, call us. If more evidence turns up somewhere, we'll consider further investigation. But for now we're just going to have to make a report." The expression on his face conveyed his low enthusiasm for that activity.

Ery couldn't think of any arguments or inducements to get the cops and firemen to stay and keep looking. He reminded them to keep an ear open for missing-persons reports, thanked them for their time, and watched them roll away.

CHAPTER 4

ERY SPENT the evening debating whether to call or text Dylan and Chris. He eventually decided not to, mainly because he didn't want to ruin a trip that had only just begun. He certainly would have had a hard time enjoying Paris and Barcelona if he knew some guy had drowned or disappeared on his property.

He couldn't possibly paint tonight, and more episodes of *Lost* had little appeal. He surfed aimlessly instead and paced the studio and found a bunch of small and unnecessary chores to perform. He almost broke down in tears when he realized he might be responsible for a man's death: he'd startled the stranger with his shout, causing him to jump into the water. And maybe if Ery had leaped in right afterward, he could have saved him despite his lack of swimming skills. But what the fuck was the man doing there in the first place?

Ery swung a broom around the barn, cleaning up spiderwebs, his stomach roiling with guilt and anger. When he went to bed—early again—he made sure to close the curtains.

He had strange dreams that he couldn't remember when he awoke. He got up early and lingered over coffee and toast. He felt calmer than he had the previous evening, but he was still uneasy. He kept looking at his sketchbook and the small spots on the paper where water droplets had landed and then dried.

He eventually went into the studio, put away the big canvas with the painted-over penis, and set up a small canvas instead. He worked on it all morning and afternoon, pausing only for a few bites to eat and an occasional stretch. He finished the work just as the sun went down. It was a detailed, almost photo-realistic depiction of a male mallard. It reminded him a little of a Renaissance-era still life, except his duck was still alive instead of hanging on a hook or arranged lifelessly atop a table. And his wasn't exactly Great Art. It was more like a very time-intensive doodle.

At least it wasn't a penis.

The following morning he called his grandmother but didn't mention the possible drowning. She didn't ask him how things were coming along, which was nice of her. They chatted instead about her friend Marianne's upcoming surgery and a book his grandmother had just read about the bubonic plague epidemic in nineteenth-century San Francisco. She told Ery that his parents were thinking about selling their house in Minneapolis and moving back to the West Coast. That would be nice, Ery thought. He liked his folks.

After he got off the phone, he drove to pick up some groceries. The other customers in Fred Meyer stared at him. He wasn't dressed in one of his more colorful outfits—just skinny red jeans, a tight Alice in Wonderland tee, and a black cardigan. And yellow high-tops. All right, so maybe he was a bit exotic for the location. Looks he could handle. As long as they didn't run him out on a rail.

He returned to the farm and put the food away, then went to the studio and gazed at the duck painting for a while. He was suddenly seized by a very strange compulsion. He grabbed the completed duck, plus a blank canvas and some of his painting gear, and trudged down to the pond. Where, he noted, there were no naked men.

He propped the duck painting on a handy tree branch. Yes, it was totally ridiculous, and the painting would be destroyed when it finally rained. But in the meantime, he liked the whimsical notion that the real mallards would have art on their wall, so to speak. They watched him from across the pond, and he imagined they were thankful.

"It the latest thing," he told them. "Fowl art. We're totally cutting-edge here. You can tell all your pals you were into it before it was cool. In case you're hipster birds. I can't really tell."

If Deputy Junior overheard him now, he would cart Ery away.

He set up his easel on the little beach. He'd brought a medium-sized canvas and a selection of expensive oil paints and brushes.

Instead of creating one of his usual abstract works, he was in the mood for a landscape. Which was odd, but he wouldn't complain about finally feeling a little inspired. He picked up his pencil and did a rough sketch of the pond and trees before starting in with the paints.

"I'll call it *Scene of a Possible Crime*," he told the ducks, who didn't seem impressed.

The beginning of the project went smoothly. He chose one particular tree to paint in detail, and this time he actually enjoyed working with the various shades of green. He painted a few of the nearby trees too, but only their vague shapes, as if the one specimen could suggest the particulars of the rest. He liked the effect, which was an interesting combination of realistic and abstract.

But as he prepared to work on the water, he instead found himself mixing shades of yellow ochre and ultramarine, along with titanium white. The result was a very light skin tone—just right for a pair of smoothly muscled bare legs.

"Shit." Ery hadn't intended to paint the crime scene, or the victim. But once he began, he couldn't stop himself. He created a beautiful nude man with dripping white hair and slightly puzzled green eyes, standing with his feet just barely covered in the pond.

Ery was still working when he lost the light. The painting wasn't complete, but when he looked at it in the dimness, it felt *right* to him, like a puzzle just on the verge of being completed. He hadn't felt that way about his art in a long time.

He muttered to his muse as he dragged his supplies back up the hill. "So *that's* what you needed to wake the hell up—a death. Maybe you think we're in ancient Greece and you needed a sacrifice." Oddly conflicting emotions stirred within him—joy over finally painting something good, sorrow and guilt over the source of his inspiration.

After putting away the supplies and setting the new painting on the easel, Ery washed up, sautéed a chicken breast, and boiled some pasta. It was a good dinner. He read his mystery novel while he ate. After he'd tidied up the kitchenette and started a load of laundry, he curled up on the old-fashioned sofa with his book and a glass of wine. The stereo played Debussy. For a man in crisis, Ery felt pretty good. He stayed up fairly late and fell asleep almost right away.

THAT NIGHT'S dream was unusually vivid. Maybe that was a side effect of his muse's revitalization. He knew it was a dream even as he experienced it: as he walked noiselessly across the cement floor of the apartment, wearing only the purple flannel sleep pants he'd worn to bed; as he opened the door to the studio and approached the glowing white figure that stood in front of the easel.

The naked man turned to look at him. He was dry in the dream, and in the moonglow that spilled through the skylight, his hair looked like liquid silver. "Do you belong here now?" the man asked, his voice hoarse, as if he seldom used it, and tinged with a slight accent.

"I'm watching the place while Chris and Dylan are gone."

The man cocked his head slightly. "Do you love Chris Nock like Dylan does?"

"Uh… no." Jeez, did this mean he subconsciously had the hots for his friend? "We're platonic pals is all. Good pals."

"What is your name?"

"Ery."

The man laughed delightedly and fluttered his hands near his face. "Airy?"

"With an E. Who are you?"

"Stroemkarlen." He smiled, revealing even, white teeth. "Karl, I suppose."

Fantastic. Ery's subconscious housed dead foreigners. But it occurred to him that maybe the point of the dream was to help expiate his guilt. Well, he'd give it a try. "I'm sorry I scared you. I was startled. I didn't mean to harm you."

Karl seemed unconcerned. "You were protecting Nock land. And you didn't harm me. You see?" He held his arms out to the side as if to display his very healthy-looking body.

"Uh, good." So Ery's brain was trying to worm out of responsibility. Well, whatever worked.

"Thank you for the gift. It is very beautiful. I used to like the motorcycle best, but now this is my favorite." Karl smiled a little shyly. "You're a very good artist."

It took Ery a moment to make the connection—although he still didn't understand the bit about the motorcycle. "You mean the duck."

"Yes. I'm sorry the water will ruin it so quickly, but I'll have my memory of it. Nobody's ever given me anything so pretty." He turned slightly to gesture at the painting on the easel. "And now you're painting me?"

"I… I guess."

Karl bowed deeply. When he stood upright again, he had captured his lower lip between his teeth and his eyes glistened. "Thank you. I'm honored."

"I'm…. It's…." Ery tried to respond, but Karl was walking slowly toward him—he was heartbreakingly beautiful—and Ery was completely frozen in place.

Karl didn't stop until he was close enough to settle his hands on Ery's bare shoulders. The two were almost exactly the same height. Karl's palms were chilly and he smelled sort of earthy and green, like springtime. His lips were a very light pink, but they looked soft and slightly wet, as if he'd just licked them. "I like the bright colors you wear," Karl said. "Like a butterfly or a flower." He reached up to lightly stroke Ery's head. "And your hair is very interesting."

When he was younger, Ery had often dyed red or blue or green streaks into his hair. Now, however, it was its natural dark brown, aside from a bleached bit in front. He hadn't been bothering with sculpting it since he came to the farm, and in his dream he was suffering from bedhead. "Thank you?" he said uncertainly. He wasn't at all comfortable with the direction this dream seemed to be heading.

"It's been a long time since I touched someone," Karl said sadly. "Is it all right that I'm touching you?"

"I don't, um, don't know if that's such a great idea."

Karl let his hands fall to his sides and bowed his head. His hair hid his face. "I'm sorry. I didn't mean to offend you."

"I'm not offended. I just don't want to dream about having sex with a dead man."

That made Karl look up again. "Is that what you think this is?"

"Well, yeah."

After a brief pause, Karl shook his head slightly. "Maybe I should come to you in the sunlight again, so you know I'm real. You won't yell next time, will you?" His tone had been light, as if he were joking, but then his expression turned serious. "Please, Ery. Come down to the water tomorrow. I want... I would like someone to talk to for a little while. I'd like to talk to *you*. Please?" He raised his hand and seemed about to brush the fingers against Ery's cheek, but stopped.

It was silly to make a promise to a man in a dream, but Ery couldn't refuse. Karl looked so vulnerable. "Okay," he said.

Karl's smile bloomed wide. "Thank you!" And before Ery could brace himself, Karl leaned forward to kiss him.

Ery had always loved making out. Sometimes he suspected his mouth was one of his major erogenous zones, second only to his dick. He liked the intimacy of kisses—the shared breaths, the closeness of the other man's face, the way he could taste his partner as well as feel him. So maybe it wasn't a surprise that the man in his dream was an excellent kisser. Those lips were as soft as they looked, and Karl's tongue was slippery and agile, slightly mint tasting. His teeth felt sharp. And *Jesus*, he made these breathy little whimpers that traveled from his mouth, through Ery's, down his spine, and straight to his cock.

If it had been possible, Ery would have survived on nothing but a kiss like this for every meal.

Somehow his fingers ended up tangled in the waterfall of Karl's hair, which felt like strands of cool silk. Karl put his hands on Ery's hips, drawing their bodies closer, allowing Ery to know that Karl's cock was as hard as his own.

Ery gasped when Karl pulled away. "That was very nice," Karl said. "But sleep, Ery. I'll see you tomorrow." He headed toward the door that led outside.

"Wait! Who *are* you?"

His hand on the doorknob, Karl looked back over his shoulder with a sad little smile. "I told you. Stroemkarlen. Good night, Ery." An eddy of cool air blew in before he closed the door firmly.

Trancelike, Ery shuffled back to bed. He wondered whether he would remember the dream in the morning. He wondered whether his balls would stop aching by then. Jeez, he hadn't had a wet dream since he was a kid, but just now he'd come awfully close. He lay down, pulled the covers up, and slipped into complete unconsciousness.

He woke up with the dream still so vivid that he could almost taste Karl, could almost feel his hair. "This is probably worse than painting penises," he told himself. "Now you're having weird sex dreams." Maybe he should visit a club or something—hook up with someone and get really, really laid.

Groggy and rubbing his face, he wandered into the studio, intent on inspecting his work in the morning light.

Something sat on the easel in front of the canvas—something he couldn't recognize from across the room. He was almost close enough to touch it when he realized what it was: a fist-sized stone with red and gray flecks, polished and worn very smooth.

CHAPTER 5

FOR THE second time in less than forty-eight hours, Ery freaked out. He paced back and forth through the studio and the apartment, sometimes peering out the windows. Probably twenty times, he picked up the business card the deputy had given him, but he always put it down again. The cops weren't likely to be any more helpful this time than they were the last, and he couldn't begin to craft a story that wouldn't get him arrested or hauled away. *Remember the naked drowned guy from the other day, officers? Well, he came back—still naked—and we sucked face and he left me a rock.* Yeah. That was just great.

Wherever his frantic circling took him, Ery always ended up back at the easel, holding the stone. It was the perfect size and shape to nestle in his palm, and when he held it in the beams of sunlight, it seemed to have a hundred shades of gray and red. If he were to paint it, he'd have to do a lot of color mixing.

Ery reconsidered contacting Dylan and Chris, and again he rejected the idea. Let them have their joie de vivre while they could. Besides, Ery wasn't especially eager to share last night's adventure with his friends or his grandmother, all of whom would at least raise eyebrows over the gratuitous making out.

But seriously, what the *hell*? Who was this Karl guy and what did he want?

And jeez Louise, but why did even the thought of him make Ery's toes curl and heart pitter-patter?

He finally decided that the most direct route—although maybe not the wisest—was to go down to the pond and see if Karl appeared. Ery had very mixed feelings about this, however. He was anxious about what might happen if Karl showed up and suspicious he'd feel stupidly rejected if Karl didn't show.

He finally compromised, pulling on a pair of jeans and not bothering to do anything with his hair, thereby making the statement that he didn't give a damn whether he saw Karl and certainly wasn't trying to impress anyone. And yes, Ery might have put on a pink-and-green argyle sweater, which *might* have been bright colors like Karl had admired, but that was a coincidence. It was a little chilly this morning and the sweater was one of the warmer things he'd packed.

Nobody was waiting for him at the pond except the mallards. Ery stood for a moment, watching a dragonfly skim the water, before it occurred to him that the duck painting was gone. He checked near the base of the tree in case it had fallen, but it wasn't there. He wasn't sure what to think of that. "I can make you another," he told his feathered friends.

He sat on the fallen log. It was strange. People went on and on about the peace and quiet they sought in the country, but it wasn't really quiet at all. True, there were no honking horns or squealing brakes, no people shouting into cell phones, no sirens or blaring music or screaming kids. But birds called from the treetops and insects buzzed. Very faintly, far away, a motor droned. Maybe the guy who rented the wheat field was running his tractor. A bit of breeze made the leaves rustle and branches creak, and when something moved just beneath the surface of the water—fish?—it made small *plip-plop* sounds.

A loud splash made Ery startle, and Karl emerged from the pond.

He walked right out of the water, smiling broadly, as naked as ever. He shook his head to gather his hair behind him, sending glittering droplets flying into the air like jewels. "You're here!" he announced as he stepped onto the beach.

"Uh, yeah." Ery fought the urge to stand up and back away. "Where did you come from?"

Karl gestured behind himself.

"No," Ery said. "I mean before that. How'd you get in the pond to begin with?"

"I dove." Karl grinned as if Ery had asked an amusing question. Then he walked closer and sat beside him.

Absently, Ery wondered whether the tree bark was uncomfortable on Karl's bare ass.

"Did you like my gift?" asked Karl.

"I… yes. It's very pretty. Thank you. Where did you get it?"

Again, Karl pointed at the pond. "I've had it a long time. It's one of my favorites because of the colors. I thought it suited you."

"Thank you."

Karl scooted closer, so his hip was almost but not quite touching Ery's. He seemed happy just to sit there for a bit, both of them watching the ducks.

"Last night…," Ery began, but he wasn't sure what to say next.

"I'm sorry. I'm not allowed in the house, but I thought maybe the barn doesn't count." Karl sounded hesitant and uncertain. "Maybe. And I couldn't… I saw you, and you're so beautiful. And I wanted to see what you were painting. I didn't expect it to be me! That was a good surprise."

Ery was still stuck on Karl's opening statement. "Who says you're not allowed in the house? What do you mean?"

"It's the rule. Can't go where people live unless they invite me."

Vampire! Ery thought, which was ridiculous. He was willing to concede the possibility that vampires existed—after all, one of his best friends was a werewolf—and Karl was certainly suitably pale. But the sun was shining on him and he wasn't emitting a single wisp of smoke. Unless that part of the vampire mythology was untrue. Ery's only sources of information on the subject were *Nosferatu* and *Buffy*.

"You're not a vampire, are you?" he asked. Now there was a sentence he never thought he'd utter in earnest.

Karl laughed. "No, I am definitely not undead. And bloodsucking? Yuck." He twisted slightly on the log so he was facing Ery. "How about you? What are you?"

"I'm an artist. Which is way less interesting than being a vampire, and only slightly better paying."

Again, Karl laughed. "All right, then. Tell me about yourself, please. About your life. Do you live near here?"

"My life is really boring. I live in Portland and—"

"The city!" Karl's eyes widened. "All those people! I went once, just to see, but it was too busy. All those boats, big and little, and the bridges and the… the concrete walls along the river. It was interesting, but I was very glad to get back home again."

"And where *is* home?"

Karl ignored the question. He settled his hand on Ery's knee and squeezed lightly. "Will you tell me more, please? About, oh, about what you do every day in the city. And do you have family?"

Ery almost answered him. There was something so compelling about the closeness of Karl's body and the intensity of his gaze. Ery was no stranger to another guy's interest, but he couldn't recall anyone ever looking at him quite so intently, as if Ery were the most fascinating creature to walk the planet. And he couldn't help but remember how nice that kiss had been. How soft Karl's lips were, how silky his hair.

But dammit, he needed to know what was going on!

"Who *are* you?" Ery asked. He sounded more plaintive than demanding.

Karl sighed and the corners of his mouth twitched downward. "Nobody. Stroemkarlen. I never do anything interesting and nothing ever happens to me—well, almost never—and I never have anyone to talk to. I don't have pretty colors like you and I don't know how to… to make things. Like you do. I don't think anyone even believes in me anymore."

Overcoming the urge to hug Karl and soothe him, Ery squeezed his eyes tightly closed. When he opened them again, he looked down at the ground. His sneakers were muddy. Karl's feet were muddy too, but the muck was drying and flaking off. Karl's feet were as pale as the rest of him and a little short and wide.

And his toes were webbed.

"You're not human, are you?" Ery whispered.

Karl pulled away. He sat with his shoulders hunched, his head hanging so that his hair hid his face. "No."

"And you're not a ghost or a vampire or a werewolf, and that about does it for my knowledge of… supernatural beings."

After a moment, Karl raised his head to look at Ery. His fine, pale eyebrows were drawn together. "You don't seem… I would have expected you to be more surprised. People usually are."

"Well, people usually don't have a grandmother who sees dead people or a good pal who turns furry once a month."

Karl nodded. "Dylan makes a handsome wolf. Some of my kind can shapeshift too, but I can't." He paused and said very quietly, "I can't play music either," as if it were a shameful secret.

"What is your kind?"

"I've told you. Stroemkarl. Fossegrim. Nix."

Only the last term sounded familiar. "Nix?" Ery chewed on his lip, trying to remember what that meant.

"Water spirit," Karl supplied helpfully. "Have you heard of us?"

"Maybe. A little." There hadn't been any nixes on *Buffy*, so Ery didn't know the stories. Then a thought occurred to him. "So Stroemkarlen is your, uh, species. But what's your name?"

Karl stood and walked toward the water. With his feet submerged and his bowed back toward Ery, he said, "I don't have one."

"You don't…. What do you mean?"

"Who called you Ery?"

"My parents. They went through a huge baby name book and came up with lists, and Ery was the only name they agreed on." If his father had gotten his way, Ery would be Sam, which sounded flat and squashy. But better than his mother's first choice, which had been Sativa. *Way to tell the world you spent the seventies stoned, Mom.*

"I don't have parents."

Ery was pretty familiar with the birds and the bees, but they'd skipped water spirit procreation back in junior high sex ed. "How were you, um…."

"Created. I was created by a sorcerer to guard a harbor. He didn't bother to name me. And he didn't make me very well. When I found others of my kind, they...." He looked briefly disturbed but quickly recovered. "So I came here."

Somehow Ery found himself standing, walking across the little beach, wading right into the pond. He settled his arm around Karl's shoulders. "So is it okay if I keep calling you Karl?"

Karl twisted around to embrace him and settled his head on Ery's shoulder. His hair was still very wet. "Yes, please," he murmured.

Ery hugged him back. He liked giving hugs as much as he liked getting them. Even a platonic embrace was comforting and energizing. Wet feet and a wet sweater didn't matter. "I don't know anything about water spirits," he said. "But you seem pretty well-made to me."

Holding Ery a little more tightly, Karl managed to shake his head. "No. I told you, I can't shift or play music as I ought to."

When Ery woke up this morning, he hadn't expected his agenda would include consoling a nix. But Karl felt comfortable in his arms, and when Ery stroked his back, he discovered that Karl's skin was very soft over taut muscles. Somehow Ery managed not to be shocked when Karl began to kiss his neck instead of just leaning against it.

"You're very nice to me," Karl purred.

Were all these creatures so mercurial? Ery felt dizzy. And his feet were getting cold. "Can we, uh, go to shore?"

Karl peeled himself away, grasped Ery's hand, and tugged him to the beach. Instead of sitting on the log, however, Karl pulled him to the ground and sat cross-legged beside him, leaning against Ery's shoulder. The ducks watched them from across the pond, appearing slightly scandalized. Maybe they were homophobic fowl. Or just prudes.

Wet sneakers were uncomfortable, so Ery toed them off. The action apparently met with Karl's approval, because Karl chuckled. "You can take off your other clothing too. I'd like to see you."

"It's, um, kind of chilly. Aren't you cold?"

"Cold doesn't bother me. Where I come from, a pond like mine would be iced over all winter, and the banks would be covered in snow. It rarely snows here," he added wistfully.

41

"How did you end up here, in this pond?"

Maybe that was the wrong question to ask, because Karl wilted again. "The other stroemkarl didn't want me to stay. They chased me out into the sea. But the sea… oh, it's very big, and I was just one small spirit, and I was so lonely. I followed ships. For years and years I followed them, and I swam so many places, but none of them were home. I followed one ship into a river and I stayed awhile. I liked all the green on the shore."

The Columbia River? Ery wondered how long ago this was—how old Karl was—but didn't want to interrupt now that Karl was finally telling his story. Besides, details like that weren't important at the moment, not with Karl sounding mournful. Ery squeezed his shoulder, which made Karl press a bit closer.

"I was wandering up a stream one day when I found this pond. I might not have stayed, but I was tired and it was a safe place to sleep. And when I woke up in the morning, there was a boy—a young human man—and he was very pretty. He was washing some clothing. I spied on him for a time."

"Who was he?"

"A Nock. Henry Nock. Well, I didn't know that yet. But I watched, and I learned that he lived here with his family. The house was new then, and the Nocks farmed, and I…. One day I showed myself to Henry." He shook his head ruefully. "I couldn't resist, just as I couldn't with you."

Dylan had once mentioned that his house was over a hundred years old. Ery hadn't realized Chris's family had owned the land for so long. He wondered if Henry resembled Chris. If so, no wonder he'd caught Karl's eye.

Karl sighed. "It was Henry who called me Karl. And he… we became lovers. I had never imagined how nice it would be to touch someone like that." He turned to look at Ery. "Have you had lovers too?"

For no good reason, Ery blushed. "Uh, yeah."

"Good! Then you know. It was *wonderful*. But even better was when we would sit and talk and he'd tell me about, oh, books he'd read.

Funny things his family had done. We had to be careful. None of Henry's family could know about me. About us. But we always found a little time together. I made the pond my home."

When Karl went silent, Ery knew this tale wouldn't have a happy ending. How could it? But he had to ask. "What happened, Karl?"

No answer came for a long time, and when Karl did speak, it was in a quiet rasp. "After a while, Henry came to the pond less often. He said he was busy. Maybe he was. Humans are very busy creatures. But then he stopped coming at all. I waited... I would creep around near the house, all around the farm, but I didn't see him. And one day I heard his mother talking to his father, telling the old man that Henry's wife was expecting a baby."

"Wife!"

"Henry had moved away and begun his own family. I never saw him again."

Ery was angry. "That's terrible! How could he do that to you! I understand that same-sex unions weren't exactly a thing back then, but I don't care. That's a shitty thing to do."

Karl's eyes glittered, but his tears didn't fall. "Henry told me once that I couldn't love because I don't have a soul. I think that's why he left."

"Bullshit!" Ery leaped to his feet. "That was just a coward making excuses. Look, my grandma is sort of an authority on... well, she doesn't call them souls. But it's all the same thing. She says every living thing has an energy—even the tiniest little fungus or gnat or whatever. Energy isn't just what makes us alive. It's what makes us... us. You have energy too."

Looking delighted, Karl stood. "I do?"

"Of course. And... how did Henry make you feel? Not physically, but here." Ery pointed to his heart and then his head.

"He made me happy. Whenever he came to visit, nothing else mattered to me. I don't own very much, but if I had a treasure, I'd have given it to him. I'd have died for him."

"Sounds like love to me," said Ery, who loved his family and friends but had never truly been *in* love.

Karl hugged himself. "Thank you, Ery. For believing me."

Ery smiled at him.

"It hurt when Henry was gone. I thought about leaving. But I knew I'd be lonely wherever I went, so I ended up staying. I like this place." Karl spread his arms to indicate the pond, the trees, the entire area. "And the Nocks have never known that I was here, but sometimes they left things in the water and I told myself they were gifts. That made me feel a little better."

Remembering what Dylan and Chris had told him, Ery asked, "Is your pond sort of… extra deep?"

"Yes. I like some room."

"Ah." Ery decided not to ask whether Karl had actually excavated the bottom or whether he enlarged the pond via magical means. "Dylan told me that."

Now Karl looked upset. "I thought he was going to take my motorcycle away. I didn't realize Chris loved him. I almost… I almost hurt him. I'm sorry." He hung his head.

"And that other wolf? The one who disappeared?"

Karl snapped his head up, his eyes fierce. "This land belongs to the Nocks. She wanted to hurt Chris and his father. I protected them."

"Like… like you protected the harbor."

"Yes."

Ery shivered, and not from his chilly feet. Karl didn't look dangerous, but Ery wondered what he might be capable of. The nix didn't seem evil by any means, but Ery had already learned that ghosts often operated according to a moral system very different from humans'. Maybe the same was true for water spirits.

"Are you angry at me?" Karl asked, looking almost like a child who expected punishment.

"No, of course not. You saved my friends."

"Oh." Karl beamed.

Ery had never met anyone so emotionally fluid, and he felt more than a little dizzied by his own jumbled feelings, which zoomed around inside him. Maybe sitting back down was a good idea.

As soon as Ery was on the log, Karl plunked down too, this time very close. "I'm glad you're here," Karl said. "We're not supposed to show ourselves to humans. But you're different. You're… you're good. Kind."

The truth was, Ery tried to live up to his grandmother's expectations. He did try to be nice to other people, and as someone who was himself a bit out of the norm, he was tolerant of all sorts of eccentricities. He volunteered for various good causes and donated to charities when he could. But he was certainly no saint. He could be selfish and petty. He'd been accused more than once of being a drama queen. He used to kind of sleep around. "You don't even really know me," he told Karl. "I could be a serial killer. Or a Tea Partier."

"I can tell you're good. I thought so when I saw your paintings— they have a little of your spirit in them, I think. And I knew for sure when we kissed." He smiled coquettishly. "It was a very nice kiss. Can we do it again?"

"I…." Ery blushed. "I don't think that's a good idea."

"Why not?"

"I only did it last night because I thought I was dreaming."

For several moments Karl was quiet and thoughtful. "Henry told me about dreams," he finally said. "But I don't think I understand them."

"You don't… you don't dream?"

Karl shook his head. "Henry said it's because I have no soul."

The more Ery heard about Henry, the less he liked him. But he didn't say so, since obviously Karl had cared a great deal for the schmuck. Ery could understand that—he'd occasionally become infatuated with complete bastards himself. "Well, I thought you were a dream last night. And sometimes in our dreams, we do stuff we'd never do when we're awake. It's all very Freudian and everything."

"Why wouldn't you kiss me if you were awake? Because I'm male?"

"Uh, no. That's a plus for me, actually. I'm a Kinsey six."

"Then because I'm not human?"

"Not… no, I guess that's not really a deal breaker for me." After all, Chris and Dylan had proved to him that a partner who was not entirely human could be just as loving and wonderful. Dylan had staked his own life to save Chris—twice.

Karl crossed his arms and looked in danger of sinking into a full-fledged pout. "Don't tell me you don't find me attractive. I felt you last night. And I see the way you look at me."

The thing was, Ery was having trouble explaining his reluctance even to himself. Last night's kiss had been amazing. If they'd made out a little longer, he possibly could have come just from the lip-lock and the little bit of dry humping. And it wasn't as though he asked for an engagement ring before hooking up with some guy. For the past decade, his love life had consisted almost entirely of quickies and one-night stands, with a few short-term and overwrought flings thrown in for good measure.

But maybe *that* was the problem. For a while now, he'd been hoping for something more than just a scratch for his itch. His grandmother kept telling him that someday someone special would come along, and fuck if he hadn't believed her. He'd cooped himself up in a goddamn tower lately, waiting for Prince Charming to come prancing up on a unicorn to whisk him away.

"It's just not a good idea," Ery repeated. He stood and brushed imaginary dirt off his jeans. "I think I'm going to head back inside."

Karl slumped, the picture of dejection. Ery idly wondered if the nix's mood swings were more melodrama than real, but he couldn't help a little lump in his throat when he looked at those bowed shoulders. "I'm sorry, Karl. I'm a little overwhelmed, okay? And I'd like to get back to my painting."

"Will you tell Chris and Dylan to chase me away?" Karl asked very quietly.

"No! Of course not! This is your home too."

Karl looked up at him somewhat hopefully. "You're not angry with me? You don't hate me?"

Jeez. "No, and no. Look, we can still talk." God, he was giving the poor guy the we-can-still-be-friends speech. "This evening, maybe?"

"Yes!" Karl grinned and jumped up from the log. "Yes, please!"

"Okay, then." A bit awkwardly, Ery walked past him and started up the path to the house.

Before he reached the top of the rise, Karl called out. "Ery?"

Ery turned to see Karl standing at the edge of the pond, looking beautiful and wild and sad.

"Will you really come back?"

"I promise."

Karl smiled, waved, and dove into the water with barely a splash

CHAPTER 6

A WATER spirit is living in your pond.

Ery felt only slightly guilty as he sent the text to Dylan. He wasn't asking the guys to *do* anything about it, after all. It was just kind of an FYI, like *I think the kitchen faucet is dripping a little* or *The mailman left you a package.* And it wasn't even very late in Europe.

Within a few minutes, an answering text arrived: *????*

Water spirit, Ery typed back. *Nix. Name is Karl.*

Dylan and Chris probably discussed that one for a while, because it took Dylan some time to respond. *Dangerous?*

Pretty sure not. He killed that wolf though. Says he protects Nock land.

More Nock trouble. And I thought I was gonna be the one with the weird supernatural issues.

Ery smiled to himself, picturing the way Chris was probably grinning and whacking Dylan on the shoulder over that one. He pecked out a response. *You're both weird. It's why I love you.*

Need help with the Nocks' nix? Jesus, I've turned into Dr. Seuss.

No, all is well. You guys having fun?

Paris est magnifique. Be careful, Ery.

Middle name is careful.

He put down the phone and thought about what to do next. Honestly, he wanted to paint. His fingers itched to hold a brush. But his thoughts kept straying to the extraordinary creature down in the pond. Finally Ery booted up his laptop and did a little research.

48

It turned out that although the Internet was full of information about water spirits, none of it was particularly useful. Yes, some of the stuff he read confirmed what Karl had told him, but a lot didn't seem to apply. For example, Karl hadn't indicated any particular interest in snuff or vodka, and he certainly didn't look like a horse or a dragon. But there were some interesting bits too, like one source that referred to water spirits as nocks, and another that quoted a poem about a nix who was sad because he had no soul. "Bullshit," Ery muttered.

He found a painting of a nix, created by some Swedish guy in the nineteenth century. The Swedish guy was crazy and had syphilis, which wasn't especially comforting. But the art itself was nice, and the stroemkarlen looked a little like Karl. Maybe the artist really had seen a water spirit.

Although some of the Internet sources talked about nixes luring people to their deaths by drowning, Ery wasn't especially alarmed. Karl hadn't seemed inclined to drown him so far. Besides, some of those same sources claimed werewolves were ravenous, murderous monsters, yet Dylan was mostly kind of quiet and anal-retentive.

Ery gave up on the Internet and called his grandmother instead.

"Hello, dear. It's nice to hear from you."

"Hi, Grandma. How was the card game?"

"Oh, I don't know. We're a bunch of old ladies. Everyone wants to talk about their diagnoses and dead husbands. I'm tempted to spice things up a little. Next time maybe I'll borrow one of those magazines you used to hide under your mattress, and I'll share it with the girls."

"Grandma!"

She laughed. "Oh, I know. It's undoubtedly all videos nowadays. Nobody reads anymore."

He sputtered helplessly for a moment before he could reply. "If you do that, you have to invite me."

"It's a deal, darling. How is your farm stay going?"

He noticed she didn't ask specifically about the painting. "Pretty well, actually. I think I found my muse."

"Oh, that's wonderful! I knew you would."

For a moment he considered telling her about Karl over the phone. But no, in person was better. She'd probably be really excited to discover something new, and he wanted to give her time to ask lots of questions. And he was kind of hoping she'd clue in to his own conflicting feelings and give him advice. Jeez, he was pathetic. "How about a lunch date tomorrow?"

"Are you planning to return to the city?"

"Yeah," he lied. "I need more art supplies."

"Well, lunch would be delightful."

"I'll pick you up at eleven thirty?"

"Perfect. Have a good day, dear."

He felt a little better after he hung up, as if he'd actually *done* something. He headed to the kitchen to make himself lunch.

HE SPENT the entire afternoon working. He became so absorbed in his work that the time slipped by quickly, and he was surprised to glance up and discover that the sun had almost set. The painting was nearly complete. He'd captured Karl's longing in fine detail, and a realistic pair of ducks paddled on the water, but much of the background remained abstract.

"I think it's better than the Swedish guy's," Ery said aloud. But it wasn't the best he could do. What he really wanted was to revisit the biggest canvas, only instead of a penis, he'd paint a landscape that combined abstract and realistic elements, suggesting the blurred line between the real and the imagined. He'd create a beautiful water spirit, tempting the viewer but maybe causing a little unease as well. "The nix will have a penis, actually. But it won't be rainbow colored."

And thinking about Karl's dick was not such a great idea, as it turned out.

Ery took a shower, and while he soaped and scrubbed, he also jacked off quickly, thinking about Karl and feeling like he'd regressed to his teenage years. Afterward, he ate a quick dinner. Then he threw on a light jacket, grabbed his flashlight, and set out for the pond.

This time Karl was waiting for him, sitting on the little beach and playing with something small in his hands.

Ery sat cross-legged, facing him. The flashlight cast strange shadows onto the ground and made Karl's skin glow eerily.

"Did you paint today?' Karl asked.

"I did."

"Why do you paint?"

Scratching his head, Ery considered the question. It was a little like someone asking him why he breathed. "I have to," he finally said. And he would continue painting, even if he never again produced anything better than multicolor penises or boring grocery store logos.

Karl nodded. "That energy you were telling me about—your soul? I think you put a little of it in your art."

"Maybe. When it's good, anyway."

"People do that. Chris does, when he fixes things. I've watched him. Henry was good at building things too. And I've seen men who loved to sail like that, or to fish. I've seen Dylan when he's hunting as a wolf. It must be nice to… to put yourself into something like that." He sighed. But then his mood changed again and he grinned. "I brought you a present."

"You don't have to give me anything."

"I want to. Put out your hand."

Somewhat hesitantly, Ery obeyed. Karl set something light in his palm, and Ery angled the flashlight so he could see better.

It was a shell. It was beautifully curved, and it glowed a pearlescent white with delicate orange bands. "Is this a nautilus shell?" he asked.

Karl shrugged. "I don't know what the creatures are called."

"It's not from the pond." Ery wasn't exactly an expert on marine life, but he was fairly certain nautiluses—nautili?—lived in the ocean.

"No, it's from far away. I brought… I brought a few things when I came here. I had a little net bag I wore tied to my waist."

Ery pictured Karl swimming for thousands of miles, picking up a few little treasures as souvenirs, saving them for decades while he remained alone in his little pond. The shell remained on Ery's raised open palm. "I can't take this from you."

"Why not?" Karl asked, frowning.

"It's too valuable. You can't—"

But Karl beamed. "It is! I knew you'd see that. I think most people would say it's only a shell, nothing important or special at all. But *you* see. That's why I want you to have it."

Realizing that he couldn't refuse the gift without causing offense, Ery set the shell carefully on the ground beside him. "Thank you. I'll find a safe place for it." *And*, he didn't add, *I'll think of you every time I look at it.*

Seemingly pleased with himself, Karl lay down on his back with his head close to Ery's lap. He took the flashlight and aimed the beam here and there, tracing light patterns on the trees across the water. He smiled in amusement like a young child.

"It must get really dark down here for you," Ery commented. Because of the contours of the land and the absence of development, the only light at night would come from moon and stars.

"I have good vision. It helps when I swim very deep. I hear well too."

"Oh. Well, that's good."

"Hmm." Karl set the flashlight in Ery's lap and moved a little closer, so that a few strands of his hair spread over Ery's jeans. He looked a little sleepy, Ery thought, or maybe just lazy. Languid. He settled his hand on Ery's knee. "Is this what dreams are like?" he asked.

"Um… I don't know. Most of my dreams are pretty weird."

"Oh, but this is very strange for me! A beautiful man who talks with me. It's as if I have a friend." He paused and blinked for a moment. "*Are* we friends, Ery?"

"Yes, I suppose we are."

"Thank you. Henry was my friend too, but that was so long ago…."

Ery wanted to touch him. Specifically, he wanted to run his fingertips across Karl's pale, hairless chest, to see if his skin was as soft as

Ery remembered, to paint invisible designs across shoulders and between pink nipples. So Ery sat on his hands instead. He listened to the water lapping softly at the shore, and somewhere far away, a coyote called.

"Don't you have other friends?" Ery asked. "Are there other nixes here?"

"No. And they wouldn't have me anyway. It's the sorcerer's fault."

"The one who, uh—"

"Who made me." Karl sat up quickly and positioned himself so close that his knees pressed against Ery's. He put his hands palms-up on his thighs. He had unexpectedly broad fingers, but they weren't webbed. "I've never been able to shapeshift. I don't know if he did that on purpose or out of carelessness. Doesn't matter. But other nixes, they would become dolphins and outswim me, or they'd turn into birds and fly away. Or become squid and speak to each other in flashing colors I couldn't understand.

"Then there was the music. The others, they play… well, a sort of flute. The music is very beautiful. And it's important too. It's how lovers court each other and how friends relax. But if I try, I produce nothing but twisted notes."

Ery had been the only openly gay kid in his junior high. That wasn't exactly the same thing as not being able to turn into an octopus or participate in cultural music performances, but he knew how it felt to be an outsider. "I'm sorry," he said.

"But it was more than that. I was created to guard the harbor. The sorcerer told me to watch the ships as they came and went, to listen to the sailors talk. And most nights he would come down to the water's edge and call me, and he'd ask me what I'd heard. Were there smugglers or pirates? Did any of the sailors mean the prince harm?"

"You were sort of a spy."

Karl gave a small shrug. "I suppose. Honestly, I think a big part of it was simply that the sorcerer was lonely. People tend to shy away from his kind, I think."

That made sense to Ery. It would be tough for a wizard to have a normal social life. "So he just wanted to chat?"

"Partly, yes. He'd listen to my reports and then he'd tell me about a pretty girl he'd seen at the market or a potion he was working on. And the problem was, I *liked* it. I liked listening to his human ways and I liked watching the other humans on their boats and at the piers. Most of my kind want little to do with your kind, Ery, but not me. Yet few humans are willing to be friends with something like me." He smiled sadly and gave Ery's hand a quick squeeze. "Except you."

Ery's insides felt warm and twisty, like a pretzel straight from the oven. It was an uncomfortable sensation, but not entirely unpleasant. He cleared his throat. "Do you want to live among humans, then? Pass as one?"

"I can't. I mustn't be too far from water or spend too long out of it or I'll die." The corner of his mouth twitched. "I suppose maybe I could find a house somewhere very close to a river, but the neighbors would wonder why I kept jumping in. Besides, how would I live? People need money. I have nothing but... but stones and shells. And a few odds and ends that have been tossed into my pond over the years."

Well, that was a good point. A water spirit probably didn't have many marketable skills. And there were other complications too, like the fact that Karl apparently didn't age. People would notice that.

Karl patted Ery's leg. "Don't look so sad. I love my home here. I'm happy to have it. I just get a little lonely is all."

"You know, Chris and Dylan are really great guys. And neither of them is any stranger to... stuff that's a little unusual. You guys could hang out."

"Thank you. Maybe we will. But they're very busy. And they have each other, don't they?"

"Sure. But they have other friends too. Like me."

Karl gave a low chuckle. "I'll bet they have no other friends like you."

Ery squirmed uncomfortably. "I can't... I'm only staying here for a little while. Pretty soon I have to get back to my place and my job. But I can come visit sometimes if you like. I come here to use the studio anyway."

Lifting one hand almost to Ery's face and then letting it drop, Karl nodded slightly. "Please. Please do."

"I will," Ery promised.

He wished he could promise more than that, but he wasn't that stupid. He couldn't guarantee Karl anything but his casual friendship. Jeez, why did he feel so bad about that? He'd only just met Karl, plus this entire situation was… weird.

"I have to go," Ery said. He picked up the shell and the flashlight and rose gracelessly to his feet. "I'm getting kind of cold."

Karl stood too. "Will I see you tomorrow?" he asked hopefully.

"I don't know. I have to drive into the city, and I really want to paint some more. I have all these ideas in my head."

Maybe it was because Karl looked so disappointed. Maybe it was because the shell felt smooth in Ery's grip. Or maybe it was just because Karl was naked and ethereal and stunning. But when another idea leaped into Ery's head at that moment, he acted on it without even thinking: he leaned forward and kissed Karl's smooth cheek.

Karl seemed startled, but only for a brief moment. Then he made a quiet sound—a sort of whimper—and gently gathered Ery in his strong arms. This time the kiss was lip to lip. Ery's full hands made their position slightly awkward—but Karl's salty taste was more important, and the soft brush of his hair against Ery's neck, and his heartbeat thudding hard against Ery's chest.

By the time a breathless Ery pulled away, Karl's hard cock was digging into the hollow of his hip, while his own dick ached unhappily within too-tight jeans. It would have been easy to peel off those jeans and take a lot more from Karl than a kiss. But Ery stepped back, breaking their embrace.

"Gotta go," he rasped.

"Good night, Ery," said Karl before disappearing into the darkness.

CHAPTER 7

ERY WOKE before dawn, which was unheard-of. He hadn't slept well—he kept waking from dreams he couldn't remember—but he felt strangely energized. Without bothering to shower or exchange his sleep pants for jeans, he threw on a sweater and socks and headed for the studio.

Chris and Dylan had installed a heater in the apartment, but the studio was cold. Ery set out his paints and brushes as he brewed an oversized cup of coffee. He held the mug and let his hands warm up a little. As soon as he could clutch a brush properly, he attacked the painting of Karl and the pond, adding the strokes of blue and green to finish it. He squinted at the completed work before nodding. "That'll do, Ery," he said. It was good. Probably the best he'd ever painted. But his mind was already busying itself with plans for the big canvas.

During conversations with other artists, Ery had learned that many of them saw a piece clearly in their head long before they set brush to canvas. His friend Lilli, who did mostly Warholesque female nudes, told him, "It's almost like doing paint by numbers. I just fill in the blanks."

But Ery's work had always been more spontaneous. He would begin with a spark of an idea—maybe a color or a shape, or sometimes a bit of movement that had caught his eye—and he'd expand on that. It was a method that had always suited him, in part because it was such a departure from his paying gig, where he had to do everything to precise commercial specifications. And usually the impromptu methodology worked pretty well, although lately not so much. The technicolor dick was a good example of that.

Today, though, Ery knew exactly what he was going to paint. He could see the scene as vividly as if it already existed in reality. He knew every detail, even though the only model for the composition was the rounded nautilus shell that sat on a nearby shelf, gleaming in the morning sun.

He was so jazzed to begin that he almost called to cancel his lunch date with his grandmother. She'd understand. But no, he really needed to get off the farm for a little while before he flung himself straight into Karl's strong and naked embrace.

BEA SEEMED happy to be buzzing along in traffic again. Maybe she'd felt neglected or feared Ery would abandon her to Chris's quasi-junkyard. "Never, honey," Ery said, patting the dashboard. It occurred to him, however, that the big canvas was never going to fit in his car. Dylan had brought it to the farm in the back of his truck months earlier; if the work went as well as Ery hoped, he'd have to ask his friend to drive it back again soon.

As the highway grew more congested, Ery realized he missed the city. Dylan and Chris might be happy in the boonies, but Ery could take only so much peace and quiet. He needed activity and color and a dash of chaos. He needed people to talk to.

Right now, he needed to pee.

He parked crookedly in front of his grandmother's house, thundered up the sidewalk, and rang the bell. He barely resisted the urge to dance from foot to foot as he waited for her to make her slow way across the house. As soon as the door swung open, he bent to drop a quick peck on her cheek, then rushed past her. "Be right back!" he called.

She was waiting patiently for him in the parlor when he returned with his empty bladder. "You should have gone before you left," she said with a smile.

"Traffic was slower than I expected." He gave her a hug. He remembered when she had seemed impossibly tall; now she was several inches shorter than he was, and her skin looked fragile. She still stood very straight, her clothing still elegant—today she wore a cream suit with a green blouse—and her hair was as carefully coifed as ever. But she was well into her eighties, and now she used a cane when she left the house.

"Are you ready to go, Grandma?"

"Almost. Just let me put away my breakfast dishes and fetch my purse."

"Can I help?"

"Don't be silly. I have to feel useful for something, dear. I'll be just a few minutes."

She walked to the kitchen, where Ery heard dishes rattling and water running. He wandered to her bookshelf and picked up the cloisonné seagull he'd loved when he was a kid. Really, he loved his grandmother's whole house. True, the decorating scheme was a little old-fashioned for his taste, but it managed to pull off sophisticated without being stuffy. The knickknacks and prints were things his grandparents had picked up during their youthful travels: blown glass from Murano, a copper coffeepot from Istanbul, a pottery vase from San Francisco. The house itself was a tidy bungalow from the 1920s with beautiful woodwork inside and a colorful cottage garden out front. Ery's happiest childhood memories were made in this house.

"I see you're trying to make off with my bird again."

Ery grinned and replaced the figurine on the shelf. "Someday it's going to fly right over to my place."

"I'd have let it fly long ago, but then I wouldn't see my grandson anymore."

"I love you for more than your bird, Grandma."

"Yes, I know. You like my silver candlesticks too." Her eyes glittered with amusement. "Do you need to visit the restroom before we leave, Ery?"

"I think I can hold it."

He resisted the urge to help her down the single step from the porch to the sidewalk. She hated being fussed over. But when they got to the car, he held her cane while she lowered herself into the passenger seat. He always felt a little guilty that Bea was hard for his grandmother to get in and out of, but she said she liked the car. "It has personality, dear, just like you."

"Where to?" Ery said before he started the engine.

"Anywhere but that mausoleum."

A year or so ago, Ery had taken her to a sedate place where subdued classical music played over the sound system and the menu hadn't changed much in fifty years. His grandmother had not been pleased and had teased him about it ever since.

"Someone at work was raving about a Vietnamese place off Foster," he offered.

"That sounds delightful."

They didn't chat as he maneuvered through traffic, because she was of the opinion that a driver ought to pay close attention to steering the car. But she didn't mind the radio, so they listened to NPR. The reporter was interviewing a scientist about the drought. Ery's grandmother made unhappy little clucking sounds over the bad news.

The restaurant didn't look like much from the outside, but at least there was handy parking. And when Ery and his grandmother entered the place, it smelled good. Plus the waiter was very cute, and he looked at Ery with more than casual interest. He sat them at a good table near the window and handed them plastic-coated menus. "Let me know if I can help you with anything," he said, his smile turned suggestively on Ery.

After the waiter left, Ery studied the menu. "Do you want some spring rolls as an appetizer?"

"I don't think so, but you go ahead if you'd like some, dear."

"Meh. I'm not that hungry."

The waiter returned very quickly. He nodded politely at Ery's grandmother. "Have you decided, ma'am?"

"I'll have pho, please. The combination. I'd like a small bowl, and also some hot tea."

Now the waiter turned to Ery. He bent close as if he wanted to hear better. "I have specials for you today," he said.

"I'll just have the same as her, please, only a big bowl. And a lot of ice water. Thanks." The dry weather and the drive across town had left him parched.

The waiter looked slightly disappointed as he walked away, and Ery's grandmother reached across the table to hold Ery's hand. "Are you all right, darling?" She looked worried.

"I'm fine."

"But that very handsome boy was flirting with you and you weren't flirting back. What's wrong?"

He sat back in his chair and scowled. "I don't have to flirt all the time, Grandma. I'm not a slut."

"I never said you were." She looked at him as if he'd reverted to that small boy sneaking candies from the little glass jar in her parlor. "But I know you well, Ery Phillips, and if you're not paying attention to a boy like our waiter, something is wrong." Her voice softened. "Is it your painting?"

"No, actually that's been going well. Really well. I finished a fantastic painting this morning and I'm about to start another." He didn't mention the duck. Or the penis.

"That's wonderful! But why so glum?"

"I'm not glum. I'm just… thoughtful. I have things on my mind."

She raised her eyebrows but didn't say anything. They sat there silently for a few minutes, both of them looking around at the other customers. At the next table, young parents were trying to get their toddler to eat her noodles instead of wearing them, and beyond, three men in button-down shirts were loudly discussing a coworker named Chuck, who had recently received a promotion they didn't think he deserved. The rest of the crowd represented a broad spectrum of people, from the Pepsi delivery guy in the corner to the fashionably dressed young women across the room.

The waiter appeared with their teapot and cups. He tried for eye contact with Ery again, and Ery gave him an apologetic little frown. He *was* really cute. Under other circumstances, Ery would have made sure they'd exchanged phone numbers before the soup bowls were removed. Now he just watched the waiter's tight ass as he walked away.

Ery took a sip of his tea, burned his tongue, and set the cup down. "Grandma? Do you know anything about, uh, supernatural creatures besides ghosts?"

"Spirits, dear." She believed that the term *ghost* was misleading and a little pejorative.

"Well, yeah. But I mean, what about spirits other than the dead-people kind?"

"I'm not sure what you mean."

He sighed. "Have you ever heard of a nix? A water spirit?"

She sipped at her tea and, of course, did not burn her tongue. "I assume something more than idle speculation lies behind this question."

"Pretty much."

She waited, but when he didn't offer additional details, her expression turned thoughtful. "Let's see. I have heard of them. They're a bit like fairies, I believe." Ery snickered, which made her shake her head. "*Really*, Ery. You're not twelve years old."

"Sorry," he said, although he wasn't. Considering the facts that he and Karl had kissed twice and that Karl was clearly as turned-on as he was by the making out, *fairy* seemed a completely appropriate term.

"Well, I know there are quite a few legends about nixes, but I haven't any idea how accurate they are. I wasn't even aware that they were real. But then, until last year I would have told you that werewolves were a myth." She drained her teacup and poured some more. "Have you met some nixes, Ery?"

"Just one."

He was trying to decide what details to share when the waiter returned with their pho and an expression that was polite, professional, and slightly disappointed. "Can I get you anything else?"

"Not now," Ery answered. "Thanks."

Silence reigned as he and his grandmother slurped and chewed. She was better with chopsticks than he was. He wondered how and when she'd learned to use them. Had she traveled in Asia when she was young, or was it just a sign of her fondness for Chinese restaurants? He really should ask more about her youthful adventures. He didn't even know when or why she'd decided to become a teacher, or whether she'd dated anyone before settling down with his grandfather. Did she want more children than just the one she'd had? What did she do with her free time when she was a teenager? She always seemed so content and self-assured, but she must have experienced struggles in her life. What were they?

But today was a day to discuss nixes.

"A nix lives in Chris and Dylan's pond," Ery said. "His name is Karl."

"I see," she replied, unruffled.

"He's old. He came from somewhere far away, but he's been there since the house was new. He's not supposed to show himself to people, I guess, so mostly he doesn't. Chris and Dyl didn't know he was there."

She nodded and ate a sliver of meat. "But he showed himself to you."

"Yeah. I was painting and I think that intrigued him. I think he's sort of attracted to… pretty things. Bright colors, stuff like that."

After a long and fairly significant pause, his grandmother asked, "And he is attracted to you?"

"I…. Yeah." Ery set down his chopsticks and rubbed his face. "He's really lonely, Grandma. His last friend dumped him, like, a hundred years ago. He's had a sad life, I think. But he's interesting and… and sweet. He gave me presents. He might also be deadly, under some circumstances. He killed a werewolf, but that was good because he was saving Chris at the time. He says he protects Nock land. And jeez, he's really, really gorgeous and he doesn't wear clothes. And we kissed twice, but the first time I thought I was dreaming. And he can't shapeshift or play the flute like other nixes because this sorcerer sort of screwed up, which really sucks because it means his own kind won't let him hang out."

He stopped to catch his breath.

"You kissed?" his grandmother said, her face neutral.

"I just vomited, like, fifty-seven nuggets of information, and that's what sticks? Not the killing part?"

"Don't say *vomit* during a meal," his grandmother scolded. "And Ery, are you concerned about your safety when you're near this nix?"

62

"No. Karl wouldn't hurt me." Ery wasn't sure why he was so positive about this, but he was.

"I trust your judgment. And I'm fairly certain it's the kissing that's troubling you."

He viciously poked a chopstick at a bit of floating vegetable. "It's really good kissing," he mumbled.

She smiled at him. "It *has* been a very long time for me, and perhaps fashions have changed. But in my day, dear, really good kissing was considered a *good* thing. Your grandfather, for instance… I used to tell him he was handsome and had a good sense of humor, but it was his kissing that won me over. And other things that kept me."

Ery looked down at his pho as he blushed furiously. Ew. Yes, he had wanted to know more about his grandmother's past, but the only thing in the world worse than being confronted with your parents' sex life was being confronted with your grandparents' sex life.

"You know that's not the point, Grandma."

"Then what is?"

Ery struggled to find words to explain a problem he couldn't quite put his finger on. "He's a good kisser. Lots of guys are. I've never had any difficulty finding guys to make out with. Like him." He pointed at the waiter, whose back was to them as he delivered some food to another table. "And fine, maybe most of my dates have been a little more mainstream than Karl, but whatever. I'm just not sure if that's what I want to keep on doing. Loving and leaving, I mean. Maybe I want more. Except I'm not *finding* more, and maybe I'm never gonna, so I probably shouldn't be so… so *picky*. I should be thrilled to have a waterside fling on the farm."

His grandmother looked at him for a long moment. Then she pointed her chopsticks at him. "I'm going to tell you something, dear, and you're going to take it the wrong way. But it needs to be said. It's time for you to grow up."

"Grow up?" he squawked. "I have a real, fairly respectable job. I pay all my bills on time. I'm registered to vote. I separate my recyclables from trash and do my tax returns and visit the dentist regularly. I listen to National Public Radio!" He realized how loud he was being and made an attempt to moderate his volume. "I have a retirement account," he hissed.

"See? I told you you'd take it wrongly." She took a deep breath and let it out. "You are a very responsible young man. But darling, there is more to being an adult than being responsible. You also have to decide who you want to be."

"I want to be an artist." He was aware that he sounded a little sullen.

"Not *what*. Who. What kind of a man are you, Ery?"

He was pondering this question when the waiter came by. "Anything else?" he asked.

Ery shook his head. "No, thanks. Just the bill, please."

"Sure. Can I take your dishes or are you still working on them?"

Ery's grandmother put her chopsticks across her bowl. "I'm finished, thank you."

After the waiter left, Ery frowned at her. "Didn't you like it? You didn't eat very much."

"It was delicious. It's only that my appetite has become rather small."

A curl of worry twisted in his stomach. "Are you all right, Grandma?"

She laughed. "I'm fine. I'm just old. And I'm afraid I'm reaching the point where this ancient body is becoming more of a nuisance than it's worth." He must have looked as appalled as he felt, because she took his hand. "Oh stop, Ery. You know very well how I feel about death. I have lived a long, fortunate, and happy life, and when the time comes for my spirit to leave this body, I will greet the event with joy. I'm looking forward to moving on."

Intellectually, Ery could accept this. His grandmother believed that all living energy got recycled, and so death was really just a chance to be reborn—an opportunity for new adventures. Ery's own experiences, as well as what had happened with the ghost of Chris's Uncle Frank, led him to think that what his grandmother said was true. But dammit, Ery didn't want his grandmother to get reincarnated into a rosebush or a jaguar or someone else's newborn baby. He wanted her here, with him, giving advice.

Speaking of which, she hadn't forgotten where their conversation was going. "Ery, you are a good man. I am so proud of you! Your parents are too. I want you to know that. Whatever path your life takes, we will always love you very much."

He ducked his head and tried not to sniffle. "Thanks, Grandma."

"So, when it comes to your personal life, do you truly want to settle down? Or is it just something you feel you *ought* to do because many of your friends are doing it?"

"If they jumped off a cliff, would I jump too?" He sighed. "I remember when Mom used to say that to me."

"Well, it still applies. If you are happy as a free spirit, keeping your sex life casual and, well, adventurous, there's nothing wrong with that. As long as you're safe, of course. Not everyone needs to be half of a monogamous pair, not by any means. If you want to search for something more permanent, that's fine too. Just make sure it's what you want, and not what you *think* you should want."

"What if I don't know?" he asked. He tried not to whine.

She chuckled slightly. "Well, you could try therapy. That works for some. But honey, do what feels right to you—as long as you don't harm anyone else. In the end, it's our own expectations we have to live up to."

Ery paused while the waiter, with a final smile and a wink, dropped off the bill and then left to tend other customers. There was a short struggle between Ery and his grandmother over who would pay; Ery won. He left a hefty tip, just because.

"You won't think I'm a skank if I sleep around? Even if I sleep around with nixes?"

"No, dear. I might be a tiny bit envious, but I will *not* think you're a skank."

ERY DROPPED off his grandmother at her house. As he walked her to the door, she leaned slightly on his proffered arm. "See?" she said as she searched her purse for her keys. "One little lunch out on the town and I'm done. I need a nap now."

"A nap sounds good to me too."

"Are you going back to the farm today?"

"Yeah. I want to paint."

She reached up to ruffle his hair. "Good. But drive carefully." She unlocked the door and went inside. "Do you need to use the restroom, dear?"

Ery rolled his eyes. "I'm good."

"Well, enjoy your day. And thank you for lunch. It was delightful."

"Thanks for your advice, Grandma."

"Oh, you'll reach a good decision one way or the other. Just remember—don't settle. Don't be afraid to try things out a little! Everyone should try something impossible once in a while."

He leaned down to kiss her papery cheek. "Thanks, Grandma. I love you."

She ruffled his hair again. "And I love you, my very bright spirit."

He hadn't been kidding about the nap. He'd awakened much too early. As he pulled away, he thought about driving the short distance to his depressing apartment for a little snooze. But instead he headed over to Hawthorne, found a parking spot, and wandered around for a little while. People were taking advantage of the unseasonable weather, sitting at sidewalk tables with dogs or strollers at their sides as they drank coffee.

When Ery was in college, he spent a lot of time in this neighborhood. He and his friends would hang out over coffee or beer, bitching about school or bragging about their sex lives, solving all the world's problems over slices of pizza. They'd catch films at the Bagdad. He remembered sitting across the table from Dylan in a café on Hawthorne as Dylan said his parents had died in a car wreck a few days earlier. Dylan had been dry-eyed and grim-faced; his parents had recently discovered he was gay, and they hadn't been at all happy about it. But Dylan's reserve didn't allow him to talk about his grief and guilt. So Ery had held his hand and cried for him, and damned if Dyl hadn't left with a little less tension around his eyes. Dylan had been younger then, of course, and prewolf, so he was more geeky than sexy. But he was still the same person—solid, a little cautious, loyal, smart.

Ery remembered a few dates on this street too. Not many. Usually he'd hook up with a guy at a club or a bar, and while they might make it back to someone's apartment, they didn't exactly hang out afterward. But once in a while he'd meet someone while grocery shopping or through a mutual friend, and they'd have a cup of something while they got to know the basics about each other. Those meetings were always a little awkward, though. Ery tended to fear he was talking too much or coming on too strong. What if the other guy thought he was weird? Maybe they wouldn't like his slightly eccentric taste in clothing. Probably they just wanted to get laid and go home.

Anyway, there were coffee places and bars closer to his current apartment, spots he could walk to instead of hassling with parking. One of them, P-Town, had occasional live music, and once a week, his friend Drew played guitar there. Ery often went to listen, usually sharing a table with Drew's partner, Travis. They were great guys. Drew couldn't speak because of a brain injury, but Travis talked enough for the two of them and had an uncanny ability to communicate with his man. Ery doubted *he* would ever understand anyone that well.

So even though he'd walked this street many times before, today Ery strolled with fresh eyes. After a while he bought a coffee and sat, watching the colors and shapes of the cars that went by. He eavesdropped on the conversations around him—the drought, the economy, bands, movies, kids—but the discussions all felt alien, as if he were an anthropologist from another planet.

Ery had a lot of friends, and he could call one or more of them. It was a weekday, but some of them had jobs they could blow off for a while. They could give him advice. Heck, he could take a poll on his life.

But he kept his phone tucked in his pocket, and he sipped his coffee.

Nobody stopped by the table to offer answers to his conundrums.

He stopped at a gourmet grocer for a few things, and only as he was paying did he wonder what Karl ate. Seafood? Ery once dated a guy who was so allergic to shellfish he could die if he ate a single shrimp. Eating out was like running the gauntlet, with Tony interrogating the waitstaff about ingredients and food handling. Which was reasonable enough, Ery supposed, but then Tony would always send things back because they were cooked too much or not enough, or because the sauce was wrong, or because the vegetables weren't fresh enough. After three weeks of going out, Ery was surprised a chef hadn't yet snuck just a little bit of crab into Tony's fettuccine. Surprised and slightly disappointed, because it would have saved Ery a messy breakup.

On the way from the grocer to his car, Ery paused in front of the window display at a music store—sheet music and drums, mostly. Ery's feet led him inside.

"Help you?" asked the hippie-looking guy behind the counter. He was leafing through a thick catalog.

"Um… I don't know." He hadn't exactly planned this. "I have a friend who… who'd like to play an instrument. He tried the flute but it didn't work out. Any suggestions?"

"What kind of music does he want to play, man?"

Ery listened to classical when he was working and whatever he could dance to when he went out. "I don't know. It has to be something that doesn't plug in, though." Because there weren't any outlets near the pond, and electricity and water didn't mix.

"Percussion? Wind? Strings?"

"Uh…." Ery looked around the room quickly, and a display on the far wall caught his gaze. He thought about how expressive his mute friend Drew was with his guitar. The guy could have a whole conversation via bits of song, and when you listened to him play, you could feel every one of his emotions as if they were yours. Travis had once confided that in the years after Drew's accident, before he and Travis met and fell in love, the guitar playing had probably prevented Drew's isolation from driving him crazy.

Ery pointed at the display. "One of those, maybe?"

"Yeah, that's a good choice. It's versatile. Doesn't take a lotta skill to play a few basic chords so you can impress the chicks." He twitched his head slightly. "Or the dudes." Leaving the catalog open, he came out from behind the counter and walked across the room. He stood for a moment in front of the guitars, stroking his graying beard. "How much you wanna spend?"

"Not too much?" Ery was hoping his muse would stay active, which meant shelling out bucks for art supplies.

The salesman nodded. "Look. If you're not sure whether your pal's gonna take to it, buy him something cheap to start out. He can always upgrade if he digs it."

That made sense. So ten minutes later, Ery was walking up the sidewalk, wondering how to fit a guitar case into Bea's limited interior.

Chapter 8

He hit rush-hour traffic on the way home, and by the time he got to the farm, the sun was setting. *No more painting today*, he thought unhappily. But he smiled when he unloaded the car.

He ate a quick pasta dinner, threw on his coat, and grabbed the guitar and flashlight. The night seemed unusually quiet, making his footsteps very loud. Karl claimed to have good hearing—did he hear Ery coming?

He must have, because when Ery came within sight of the pond, there was Karl standing in the shallows, dripping and smiling widely. "You're here!" Karl called as Ery approached. "And—oh! What's *that*?"

Ery practically skipped down the hill. "A surprise."

"For me?"

"Well, you're the only one here, so yeah."

Karl actually hopped with excitement. But when he came rushing forward, Ery put out a hand to stop him. "Wait! I think you'd better dry off a little first."

Karl looked down at himself as if it had never occurred to him that he was wet. Then he shook himself like a dog, making Ery duck and laugh. Karl gathered his long hair into a rope and wrung it out over the ground, then flipped it behind his back. "Dry enough?"

"I guess so." But Ery held on to the case. Maybe a wooden instrument wasn't the best present for a water spirit. Maybe *any* present was a bad idea. It might hurt Karl's feelings or dredge up painful memories. There might be some kind of nix cultural taboo about string instruments. Or maybe— Oh, *stop.*

"Here," Ery grunted, holding out the case.

His grin still stretching from ear to ear, Karl took the case carefully and looked it over. "It's nice!" he exclaimed. "I like the shape."

Jeez. "It's only the case, Karl. To carry and store it. The real present's inside."

"Oh!" Karl set the case gently on the ground. He crouched in front of it. After a moment he found the latches, opened them, and slowly lifted the lid. His eyes went very wide and he gasped. "It's beautiful, Ery!"

It wasn't, really. It was a very basic model. It certainly didn't have any of the fancy wood or shell inlays that the pricier instruments boasted. "Do you know what it is?" Ery asked.

Karl shook his head. But then he reached out and touched one of the strings, and it twanged softly. He made a startled *meep*, followed by a laugh. "It makes noise!"

"It makes music. Um, if you learn how to play. It's a guitar. Here, let me show you." Ery set the flashlight down, aiming the beam more or less at himself. He lifted the guitar out of the case, draped the strap over his shoulder, and held the instrument as if he intended to play. He didn't actually know how, but he quickly demonstrated how plucking the strings made notes, and how pressing the strings to the neck with the fingers of his left hand changed the sounds.

Still on his haunches, Karl gaped. "I've heard men play these before. But I didn't know the name or what they looked like."

"Now you do." Ery slipped the strap off his shoulder and replaced the guitar in the case. "There are some picks in the case if you want to use them. I could get you some sheet music or some instruction books, or...." He didn't even know if Karl could read. Were nixes literate?

"Why did you bring me this?" asked Karl.

"Because...." He let his legs fold and sat facing Karl, the guitar between them. "I knew this girl when I was in college. Mary Lynn. She wanted to be an artist, but she just wasn't that great at drawing or painting, and she totally sucked at sculpture. She was trying really hard, though. It was a little heartbreaking. Then one day someone gave her this camera—this old Russian analog thing. And she started taking these amazing photos. I mean, like, wow. Last I heard she was a big shot with shows in New York and everything."

Karl looked puzzled. "So… you brought a guitar?"

"Mary Lynn wanted to be an artist. She *was* an artist—she just needed a different medium and she went from bleh to brilliant. Maybe to be a musician, you just need a different instrument." He ducked his head to avoid eye contact. "You don't have to like it. I can take it back. Or we could try something else. Bongos?"

"You did this for me?"

Ery nodded. When he looked up again, Karl's faced glowed with joy as streaks of moisture ran down his cheeks. Ery was pretty sure they weren't leftover pond water.

"You are a wonderful friend," Karl said hoarsely. "May I?" He gestured at the case.

"Of course. It's yours."

Nobody had ever handled a sacred object more reverently than Karl lifted that cheap guitar. He sat cross-legged on the ground and, moving slowly, settled the guitar in place on his lap. He ducked his head so he could put the strap on his shoulder. Then he spent several minutes just stroking the wood with his fingertips and delicately touching the strings.

"You use those screw things to tune it," Ery offered. "I can buy you a tuning fork if you need one, I guess."

Karl shook his head. He was a naked water spirit, sitting in the dark by the side of a pond. Yet the guitar looked strangely fitting on him. He plucked tentatively at the strings and seemed delighted with the results. "So beautiful," he murmured, more to himself than Ery.

Ery leaned back with his palms on the soft earth and watched. He'd always liked giving gifts, but he'd never seen any recipient quite so thrilled. Then he remembered his eleventh birthday, when his parents had bought him a wooden box full of *real* art supplies—not cheapy kid stuff—and he had an inkling how Karl must feel.

For a long time, neither of them spoke. Karl was absorbed with his guitar, testing different combinations of finger and hand movements. And Ery was absorbed with watching him. He liked the way Karl's hair kept flowing forward, only to be pushed impatiently back. He liked the way the space between his pale brows made a little V of concentration and the way Karl's pointed tongue sometimes peeked from the corner of his lips. But best of all, he liked the way Karl glanced over at him periodically, his green eyes filled with happiness.

And then something weird happened. Well, something else weird. Ery realized that the random twangs and plinks had evolved into notes, and those notes were beginning to twine together into a melody. It was a simple tune, but there was no doubt it was a song.

"I'm making music," Karl whispered. "Real music."

Ery's throat felt thick. He had to swallow twice before he could answer. "You are. I like it a lot."

Karl suddenly removed the guitar from his lap and returned it to the case. Then he scurried over so quickly that he knocked the flashlight sideways, sending the beam aiming off into the trees. Which didn't matter anyway, because when Ery stood, he found himself with an armful of sobbing, squeezing nix.

"Thank you, Ery. Oh, thank you. You can't know...." Karl sniffled. "This means so much to me. You are so kind."

"I'm really glad you like it." Ery gave the side of Karl's head a quick kiss, just because he couldn't help it.

"And I can keep it? Truly?"

"Of course. Do you have a place to keep it dry? I don't think it should get wet."

"I can make a shelter from branches."

Ery wasn't sure that would be enough, but he'd think about it; maybe he could come up with something better. Maybe one of those plastic sheds intended for gardeners. But since rain was still not in the forecast, branches would do for now.

Karl sighed loudly and leaned a good part of his weight against Ery, which was not at all unpleasant. "I've never been so happy. Do you feel like this sometimes too, Ery? Like your heart's too big for your chest?"

Ery was pretty much feeling that way right now, but he didn't say so. He hugged Karl tightly and gave his damp hair another kiss. "I'm pleased it worked out." Then he pulled away slightly. "How about if I give you some time to play with it? I'm kinda wiped, anyway."

"All right," Karl said, and in the darkness, Ery couldn't read his expression.

They said their good-byes—Karl added several more thank-yous—and Ery retrieved the flashlight before trudging up the path. Inside the apartment, he got ready for bed. He hadn't been lying—he really was exhausted.

The night was a little chilly, but he acted on a whim and cracked the window open. He was rewarded when a stray breeze brought with it a few strummed notes. The tune was at once mournful and beckoning, which reminded Ery of a watery legend. "Jeez," he mumbled. "I think Karl's a mermaid. Mer*man.*"

He crawled onto the mattress, tugged up the blankets, and turned out the light. He wasn't any closer to making decisions about his life, but as he lay there listening to the bits of songs that floated his way, he knew one thing for sure. Making Karl happy was important to him.

ERY WOKE up early again and headed into the studio right away. He set the biggest canvas on the easel and mixed some paints on his palette. Almost instantly, he became completely fixated on his work—not feeling the morning chill or the empty ache in his stomach, not even engaging in conscious thought. He'd once had a psych prof who gave a lecture on the creative process and discussed *flow*, during which a person was completely immersed in writing or building or dancing or playing ball. Ery didn't often achieve that experience, but he did this morning. It must have been flow that led the Greeks to assume there were muses, because the ideas and creative energy seemed to come from nowhere at all, almost without effort, and poured out onto the canvas.

Only when Ery's hands cramped and his back became sore did he take a break. He'd painted nonstop for most of the day and was shocked to discover that the afternoon was nearly gone. He couldn't remember ever being quite so focused. The work was going well, and he could actually *feel* his success in his fingers. It was a wonderful sensation. Maybe Karl would experience flow on his new guitar.

He made himself a thick sandwich and some soup, and only when he was seated at the little table in the kitchenette did he look at his phone. He had a couple of messages from friends and an e-mail from work, but what caught his attention was a text from Dylan.

Everything ok? No problems with knock nix?

Ery smiled. *I bought him a guitar*, he texted back.

Although it was very late in Europe, Dylan replied quickly. *You send most surrealistic tests. Locking forward to explains when we bet buck.*

Maybe you'll get a concert when you return. And then he added, *Having fun?*

Chris mad me dance st one of those clubs. I'm kinda drink. And I'm suck at French dancing too.

Ery doubted that. Dylan had always been too self-conscious to enjoy clubs when he was in college. He was convinced everyone else in the place was way out of his league. Which was stupid, because although he *had* been sort of hipster-geeky, he was always cute. And now that he'd been turned into some sort of vulpine sex god, he made men drool. And he moved with an easy, unconscious grace that was probably an asset on the dance floor.

I bet you and Chris had to beat the gay population of Paris off with a stick. Un baton.

Beat off. Hahaha.

Okay, French booze didn't improve Dylan's sense of humor. *Go to sleep Dyl.*

Can't. Chris just got out off shower and is trying to seduce mee.

Ery snorted with laughter. Oh, he was definitely going to save this conversation to share with Dylan when he was sober. *Then shouldn't u stop texting and go get him?*

No reply arrived, so Ery assumed Dylan had either taken his advice or passed out. But just before Ery stood to clear his dishes, the phone buzzed again.

Chris here. Wolfman's wasted. I got pix.

I'd pay good money to see them. Ery cackled.

May use for blackmail later.
Good plan. Now go molest ur boyfriend.
My partner you mean. Night Ery.
Night.

Ery recalled the commitment ceremony and how handsome his friends had looked in their tuxedoes, although Chris kept pulling at his bow tie as if it were choking him. Drew played love songs on his guitar until Chris's father began the ceremony—he'd gotten himself ordained through some mail-order ministry just for the occasion, and how adorable was *that*? Chris and Dylan's faces had been filled with such heart-wrenching, bone-deep joy that Ery had begun to cry. His grandmother had handed him a tissue. Chris's voice had broken during his vows. The love, the commitment, the permanency... clearly those things meant the world to Chris, who'd spent a good chunk of his life alone.

But Ery had never been alone. He had family who loved and accepted him, and he had a lot of friends. He didn't need a partner to be complete.

He washed the dishes, then decided there wasn't enough remaining light to make picking up his brushes worthwhile. He pulled on a coat and headed down to the pond.

He heard the music as soon as he went outside. It wasn't loud, and it didn't resemble any song he'd ever heard before, but *oh*, it was sweet. It pulled Ery quickly down the path, past the blackberry brambles, over the crest of the hill, and down to the pond.

Karl sat on the fallen tree, playing. His eyes were closed and he didn't notice Ery approaching. Ery felt a little guilty for spying on him in such an unguarded moment, but nonetheless he stopped to watch.

Karl was crying. His hands moved steadily on the guitar, coaxing mournful chords, and his face was wet with tears. He was so beautiful, so sad, that Ery's heart clenched almost too tightly to beat. *I should go back.* But his feet wouldn't move. Even his breathing felt forced.

The song went on for a long time. It made Ery think of cold gray water and empty gray skies. He shivered and pulled his coat closer around him. A few nearly harsh tones called out like the cry of a gull, long deep notes resonated like a foghorn, and a flurry of chords crashed and rumbled like a mighty storm.

Then Karl opened his eyes and saw Ery, and the music stopped.

"Don't...," Ery began, then cleared his throat. "You can keep playing."

But Karl set the guitar carefully in the case near his feet and walked up the slope to Ery. Without saying a word, he folded Ery into an embrace. They'd hugged before—several times, in fact—and not always with platonic intent. But this was different. Karl felt so cold that he burned Ery right through his clothing, and he groaned as he tried to burrow himself into Ery's skin.

"Please," Karl whispered into the shell of Ery's ear.

It was possible that Karl's music had cast a spell over Ery, like the tempting songs of mythical sirens. But Ery didn't feel bewitched. Had he wanted to, he could have removed himself from Karl's grip, muttered something apologetic, and run back to the barn. But God, he really didn't want to.

Ery laced his hands around the back of Karl's neck, twining his fingers in long, damp hair, and pressed his lips to Karl's. Karl opened his mouth at once so that Ery's tongue could enter and dance with his. The inside of Karl's mouth was salty and slick. He tasted a little like miso soup, which was a good thing. Ery liked miso soup. Karl's mouth was as cold as the rest of him, but it soon warmed as he stole some of Ery's heat. Ery gave up the heat willingly, because in return he saw fireworks against his closed eyelids and swallowed Karl's moans like bites of rich dessert.

As the kiss continued, Ery untangled his fingers and allowed his hands to drift down. He kneaded muscular shoulders, taut muscles, and the knobs of Karl's spine. Soft skin warming under his touch, and then the firm rounds of Karl's ass.

Karl bucked against him a few times, then pulled back a little, wild-eyed and breathless. "Can we, Ery? Please, say yes!"

Well, yeah.

Ery didn't actually say anything, but he gave Karl's ass a good affirmative squeeze. The two of them collapsed onto the path—fortunately avoiding the reaching blackberry canes—with Karl's body blanketing Ery's. This gave Ery a dizzying view of Karl's curtain of hair and smiling face, and of the blue evening sky above him. Maybe it was because of the tilt of the ground, but as Karl nuzzled Ery's face and neck, Ery felt like he was falling upward, tumbling with Karl into a vast, airy void.

"Ery?" Karl said. He was struggling with the zipper on Ery's coat. Obligingly, Ery unzipped it for him, then gasped when Karl pushed up his sweater and laid icy palms on Ery's chest. He gasped even louder, though, when Karl began to suckle on his nipple while tugging gently at his chest hairs.

Ery ran his hands over every bit of Karl that he could reach. Karl didn't stop what he was doing with his clever mouth and nimble fingers, but he leaned eagerly into Ery's touch, squirming and wriggling like some boneless sea creature—only way, way sexier. He scattered kisses over Ery's stomach and licked Ery's belly, taking the time to dip into his navel as if lapping at a tiny cupful of something delicious. But the button and zipper of Ery's jeans stumped him. He made a growling, frustrated noise and looked up into Ery's face. "Help."

Chuckling, Ery unfastened the jeans and shoved them, with his briefs, down past his knees. He couldn't take them off completely because his shoes were in the way, and with Karl back on top, he couldn't untangle the mess around his ankles. No worries, though, not with all that glorious skin now pressed against his.

"You're beautiful," Karl said as he rose enough to get a good look at Ery's body. "Why do you cover yourself with so many clothes?"

"I thought you liked my bright outfits."

"I like this better," said Karl, undulating against Ery—who liked it too.

"Well, it's kind of a cold climate for human nudity. And then there's the whole getting arrested thing."

"If you were stroemkarlen, you could be naked all the time and you'd never mind the cold."

"I'd make a terrible nix. I can't even swim."

Karl stopped stroking Ery and looked down at him, shocked. "You can't swim?"

"I can flail. I used to be really prone to ear infections when I was a kid, so I never really learned."

"I'll teach you. When the weather's warm again, you'll come swimming in my pond. I'll show you my home."

That implied a sort of permanency that made Ery uncomfortable, but Karl looked far too happy for Ery to express any misgivings. "I'd like to see your home," he said, which was true.

Karl applied himself to Ery's body with renewed enthusiasm. The ground was scratchy under Ery's bare ass, a sharp stone was poking between his kidneys, and he was cold. Also, there was the possibility that mosquitoes could this very moment be homing in on the tastier parts of his anatomy. But when Karl kissed him again and pressed his groin tightly against Ery's, all those concerns disappeared. Ery kissed back so fervently he could hardly breathe, and he set his hands where he could feel Karl's heavy glutes flex and strain.

It was strange. Ery could have felt a little helpless, fettered by his clothing and pinioned under a supernatural creature. Karl was clearly very strong. Stronger than Ery, who was kind of wimpy, but also possibly stronger than any human. He'd killed a werewolf. He'd apparently nearly drowned Dylan, and Dylan was a good swimmer and very powerful. Yet Karl's caresses were gentle and sensual, and Ery felt completely safe beneath him.

Karl mouthed along Ery's jawline, then his collarbone. He teased his nipples, pinching them very lightly. "Is this good, Ery? What do you like?"

"Very good. I like this."

Karl went still, his face tucked against Ery's chest so Ery couldn't see his expression. "It's been... a long time. And I haven't... I want to make you feel good, Ery."

"This is how good you're making me feel, Karl." Ery took Karl's hand and moved it to his cock, which was desperately hard and already slick with precome.

"Oh."

And it turned out to be a wise strategy, because aside from giving Karl a little more confidence and getting him moving again, it meant his hand was conveniently located for some very nice stroking. His fingertips were smooth. Would they form calluses from his guitar strings? That thought didn't matter, because Ery and Karl were back to kissing now, and Karl cleverly lined up their cocks, which was brilliant. He was powerful enough to balance on his legs and one arm so he could jack them both at once, and *that* left Ery free to buck up with his hips and play with Karl's magnificent ass.

When Karl spread his legs a little, Ery took that as an invitation. He pressed the fingers of his right hand into the tight space between Karl's cheeks and touched ever so slightly against Karl's hole.

Karl cried out in a language Ery didn't recognize. It sounded like he was swearing. He arched his butt up, clearly eager for more. Ery obliged by sticking his longest finger ever so slightly into Karl's body. A few neurons in Ery's brain were still functioning enough to worry about whether the dry intrusion was hurting Karl. But Karl solved that conundrum by swearing again and speeding up the movements of his hand and hips.

Flow could happen with sex too, although Ery's psych prof never mentioned that. Usually Ery was too mindful of who was doing what to whom, and where he was, and what was going to happen after he and the other guy got off. But not now—now he moved without thinking or planning. He just *felt*, and it felt so *good*! Karl must have thought so too, because his words devolved into babbling and then drawn-out cries that were somewhere between a song and a scream.

Karl climaxed first. His come was cool and very slick, and the lubrication it provided was exactly enough to send Ery flying over the edge as well. He didn't come back to earth for a while, and when he did, the landing was unexpectedly gentle.

Breathing harshly, Karl had collapsed on top of him. He clutched Ery's hips hard enough to bruise, but Ery didn't mind. It felt as if Karl's grip was an anchor.

"Is it… raining?" Ery said after a while.

Karl lifted his head and they both looked up at the sky. Ery hadn't registered that it had grown dark while they were having sex; if he had noticed, he'd have assumed it was just dusk. But in fact, although the orange tint of sunset was still visible near the treetops across the pond, a heavy cloud had appeared overhead. Fat raindrops pattered down on their bodies.

"The guitar!" Ery cried.

Karl leaped up and ran to where he'd left his instrument and hurriedly closed the case. He looked around and then shoved the whole thing into a berry bramble. "The rain will stop in a few minutes," he said.

Ery stood and, shivering and brushing off debris, tried to get dressed. His crotch and belly were wet and sticky. "Can nixes predict the weather?"

"Not really. But the sky will clear when I'm a little calmer." He gave a rueful sort of grin. "I didn't mean to do it, but you were so good...."

"Wait." Ery squinted at him as he fastened his zipper and button. Ick. Clammy underwear. "What do you *mean*, the sky will clear when you're calmer?"

"I got sort of excited. And when I get really intense...." He shrugged.

"Are you trying to tell me that when you get worked up, you bring *rain*?"

"Yes. When I realized Henry was never coming back, I made a storm so big the pond flooded almost all the way up the hill." He frowned. "I think I ruined some crops. I didn't mean to. I can't always control it."

"Holy shit."

"It's not very special. All my kind can do it. It's just calling to water."

Ery shook his head in disbelief. His hair was getting wet. "Not very special? Do you have any other superpowers?"

He meant it lightly, but Karl drooped. "I'm sorry," he mumbled, staring at the ground. "I'm sorry I upset you."

Nearly stumbling over his own feet, Ery hurried to him and set his hands on Karl's shoulders. "I'm not upset. Just surprised. I've never slept with someone who can affect the weather."

After a moment of looking searchingly into Ery's face, Karl relaxed. A grin slowly crept over his face. "I've never made it rain during sex before. Not even with Henry. This was... you were really good."

Honestly, Ery felt like Karl had done most of the work. He smiled back. "You were amazing. But jeez, I really need a shower."

Karl glanced up. "Rain's stopping already. But you can clean up in my pond."

"Thanks." Ery squeezed Karl's shoulders. "But I think I need hot water, you know?"

"Oh. Of course."

"But I could hang out for a while here first, if you want."

That brought a smile from Karl. "Thank you. But you're cold and I'd like to go back to my guitar. Is that all right?"

"You know, if I keep my window open, I can just barely hear you play. It's nice."

Karl's smile widened. "Really? It'll be nice to know you're listening."

They cradled each other's heads as they kissed good night. But then Karl grew concerned that Ery might stumble in the growing darkness, so he took Ery's hand and led him up the hill. That gave them the chance for more kissing, which might have progressed to another round of clothing removal except Ery really was cold. His teeth chattered. And now the ground was muddy.

Karl waited at the top of the hill until Ery was about to disappear around the corner of the barn. Ery turned and waved, and he could just barely make out Karl's pale arm waving back.

CHAPTER 9

THE HOT shower felt wonderful, and Ery stayed in until the water started to run cold, but he was still achy and fatigued when he got out. Also hungry; he hadn't eaten much all day. He was getting a little tired of cooking for himself. In the city, he went out for lunch or dinner a few times every week. But now he made a couple of eggs, scrambling them with some ham, cheese, and chopped veggies. As he sat down to eat, he wondered why Chris and Dylan didn't have chickens of their own; Dylan used to lecture him on the merits of organic free-range eggs. But then the obvious answer occurred to Ery.

"Duh," he said, scooping up a forkful of food. Werewolves probably loved organic free-range chickens.

Being a supernatural creature would be kind of nifty, what with the cool powers and the sexy and all. But there were downsides too. Dylan worried a lot about hurting people. He was lucky to be able to craft a lifestyle in which he could work around his monthly problem, and he was luckier still to have found Chris as a partner. But even then, Dylan could never forget what he was. And because he was a werewolf, he and Chris had twice come very close to being killed. Even things like a vacation to Europe had to be carefully scheduled so he didn't end up in a real-life enactment of *An American Werewolf in London*, or in this case, Barcelona. So yeah, definitely a downside there.

Then there were those who couldn't hide their supernatural nature, couldn't pass for human twenty-seven days out of twenty-eight. Like, say, nixes.

Even as Ery finished his dinner, he couldn't keep his thoughts from drifting to Karl. Jeez, even after a shower and over an hour later, Ery still felt little electric zings running down his nerves and across his skin. And despite the eggs, he could still taste Karl in his mouth.

Ery hadn't been a virgin since he was sixteen and had visited his friend Tommy's house for a study session that didn't exactly involve trigonometry. In the past fifteen years, he'd done just about everything one man could do with another—and occasionally with two or even three others. Answering the immortal question posed by Jimi Hendrix, Ery was Experienced.

And tonight's interlude with Karl hadn't involved anything more than what he'd done during those first early fumbles with Tommy: just a little half-dressed frotting. But sitting here in the barn apartment, he knew it had been more than some forgettable little hookup. He just wasn't sure what to do with that knowledge.

Well, for tonight, maybe avoidance would work. After cleaning up his dinner dishes and brewing some decaf, he booted up the laptop and logged into Netflix. But even before he chose a movie, he stood, crossed the room, and cracked open the window.

The scent of rain was gone. Karl's little downpour had already sunk into the thirsty ground. Soft guitar chords wafted up the hill, in through the window, into Ery's heart.

"Should've bought him bongos," he grumbled.

EITHER HIS muse was making up for lost time or she was punishing him for neglecting her. Whatever her motive, she woke him up just as the sky was turning indigo. She relented enough to allow him a cup of coffee and some toast, but even then he was desperate to get to work. Very soon he was stationed in front of the big canvas, palette and brush in hand.

It was an undersea tableau. He rendered the water itself in medium tones of blue, gray, and green, the lack of sunlight suggesting that this was deep below the surface. The bottom of the canvas depicted sand, with angular little shapes representing rocks and streaks and dabs of muted color implying various small sea creatures. A few fish swam by, elongated ovals with wavy triangular fins, but they weren't the focus of the piece.

In fact, the painting had two focal points, although so far he'd completed only one: a nautilus shell that lay on the ocean floor, gleaming so temptingly that a viewer might believe they could grasp it. Ery had painted the shell in such intricate detail that it could have been taken from a naturalist's guide. The precision was a marked contrast to the rough outlines and simple washes of color he'd used for the other items, and Ery hoped such treatment conveyed the shell's importance.

And then there was the other main focus, which he had only begun. Like the shell, it would be painted in great detail. It was a man—or more accurately, a water spirit. He would be shown with flowing white hair and pale skin. Naked, of course, and floating near the bottom of the sea with no fish or other living things immediately around him. Surrounded by sea life, yet alone. One arm would be outstretched, the fingers almost but not quite touching the shell. It wouldn't be clear whether he was about to pick up the nautilus or had just placed it on the sand. The nix would face the viewer, his expression neutral, his eyes layers of vivid green. Viewers would be left to interpret his thoughts and feelings as best as they could, influenced by their own desires and needs.

Ery was positive the whole thing was going to be really frigging amazing, and his brush flew over the canvas. He didn't need a model—he *knew* the body he was painting. He knew how the skin flowed over smooth muscles, how that upper lip was bowed just so, and how the chin came almost to a point. He knew those broad fingers, and how they felt—

"Oh!" said a voice behind him.

Ery startled so wildly that the brush flew out of his hand and clattered to the floor halfway across the room. He might also have screamed.

Karl stood inside the barn, bending over slightly to inspect the other painting, the one of him at the pond. His guitar hung on his back by its strap, and he was beaming.

"I didn't hear you come in," Ery said. He went to fetch the brush.

Karl didn't even glance at him. "This is…. Ery, this is so beautiful! Do I truly look like that to you?"

"Actually, I was thinking that one didn't do you justice. The new one will be better." He waved toward the work in progress.

Although Karl seemed reluctant to abandon the smaller painting, he walked closer to the easel and then around to the front. This time he gasped and went very still.

"It's not done yet, of course," Ery said, suddenly nervous. Usually nobody saw his work until it was completed. "I've really only got your feet right so far, but I'm kind of—"

"I've never seen anything so wonderful. This looks just like swimming in the ocean feels. When the water is so very large around me, and there's no…." He looked over at Ery. "In the sea, I never had a home. Not like my pond. It's a small pond and maybe not very interesting—most of my kind would never live in such a place. But it's *home*. You understand that, don't you?"

"I think I do."

Karl turned his gaze back to the painting. "Why are you painting me, Ery? There are so many other things you could work on."

"Does it upset you?" It had never occurred to Ery to ask permission.

"No!" Karl shrugged. "I never thought I was that interesting."

"Yeah, Karl. You are definitely interesting."

Karl looked down at himself. "Because I'm pleasing to the eye?"

"No. I mean, yeah, you're pleasing, all right. But it's more than that. You're just… special." Ery couldn't think of a better word than that.

And maybe it was a good word after all, because Karl smiled widely and his eyes shone. "I've never been special before," he whispered.

Fuck. One of these days Ery really needed to learn to keep his mouth shut. He managed a weak grin as he walked back to the canvas—and to Karl. "My work's going really well. I'll be finished with this one in a couple days. Before I return to the city."

"Oh." Now Karl's face was serious, and he nodded. "You have to go home soon."

"Yeah. I have a job. But Dylan and Chris will be back. I told them about you and they're looking forward to meeting you."

"They don't mind that I'm here?"

Ery shook his head and inspected the brush bristles for debris. "No, of course not. They don't know the whole story yet, of course, but they already suspected something was a little weird about the pond. I think as long as you promise to stay out of Dylan's way when he's a wolf, they'll be happy to have you as a neighbor."

Karl didn't look as relieved at this news as he might have. He pushed his hair behind his ear and glanced toward the door. "Do you want me to go so you can get back to work?"

Ery intended to say yes and then maybe offer to meet up after the sun set. But Karl was looking vulnerable again, and really, Ery didn't want to be alone. But he did want to paint. Then an idea struck him. "Hey. Would you mind playing your guitar while I do my thing? Usually I listen to music in the studio, but I didn't turn it on this morning. Besides, you're better than anything on my playlist."

Apparently nixes could blush, because a faint tinge of red colored Karl's cheeks and he dropped his gaze shyly. "Really?"

"Really. I'd like it a lot."

At first Karl sat on the floor. But Ery worried that he would be uncomfortable like that; the concrete was hard and cold. The only chairs in the barn were the straight-backed ones from the kitchen, and the couch was far too heavy to drag out of the little apartment. So Ery compromised, fetching a couple of cushions from the couch instead.

As soon as Karl sat on them, he bounced up and down happily. "They're so springy!"

"I guess. They're just cushions."

"I've never used human things before."

That made Ery blink. "Never?"

"Well, sometimes people toss things into my pond. Like the motorcycle. But I can't really use them. I just sort of… pretend."

Ery licked his lips. "Have you ever been in a house before?"

"Only this one. I've, uh, peeked in the windows of Dylan and Chris's house, though—but before they lived there. It was empty for a long time. That made me sad. Do you think homes get lonely?"

"Maybe." Because jeez, he was having this conversation with a rain-inducing water spirit. Anything was possible. "Do you want a tour?"

The corners of Karl's mouth lifted. "Not now. I want you to finish the painting."

"Okay." Ery went back to the canvas and dabbed his brush onto the palette.

Almost as soon as the bristles touched the canvas, Karl began to play. The music was surprisingly soft, and the notes bounced around the rafters in a way that seemed to please Karl, because he managed to incorporate the echoes into his song. Again, the tune evoked the ocean. Although the painting had been going very well before, the guitar seemed to help Ery find some new details to include: a ripple of water here, a half-hidden frond of seaweed there. But mostly the music helped him paint the nix, because in some indefinable way, the song *was* Karl. A little of his spiritual energy leaking through, maybe, just as Ery's was into his painting.

Ery could have kept on painting all day, but his stomach gave a loud gurgle that made Karl laugh and pause his strumming. "You should eat," Karl said. Somehow he managed to sound just a little bit like Ery's grandmother.

"Let me just get this bit…."

Karl stood and walked closer. "You need to take care of yourself."

Crossly, Ery plunked the brush down. "Fine. Don't nag." And then in a softer voice: "Come on. We can do the ten-cent tour."

He led Karl into the apartment. Even though it was a pretty simple place, Karl's eyes went wide as he took in the surroundings. He walked slowly over to the end table and eyed Ery's laptop. "What's *that*?" he asked breathlessly.

So Ery ended up explaining nearly every object in the room, which reminded him so much of a scene in *The Little Mermaid* that he had trouble controlling his giggles. Karl didn't take offense at the laughter. He was chuckling too over some of the items he found. "You have so many clothes!" he exclaimed when he opened the dresser drawers. He fished out a pair of Ery's briefs—lime green and fairly minimalistic—and shook his head. "And not just to keep you warm."

"It's… fashion, I guess."

"Like the fish who like to show off to one another with flashy colors."

"Maybe." Ery gently took his underwear and shoved it back in the drawer.

Karl found the kitchenette especially fascinating. He oohed and aahed over the stove and the microwave and laughed delightedly over the sink. "Water whenever you want it! See, you can call it even better than a nix can."

"It's just plumbing, Karl, not magic."

Splashing a little of the water on his chest—but carefully avoiding the guitar strap—Karl shrugged. "It seems like magic to me."

Ery opened the fridge. "I'm going to make a sandwich. Do you want one?"

"It's… something you eat?"

"Yep."

"I've never tried human food."

Ery turned to look at him. "What do you eat, anyway?"

"Nothing."

"*Nothing*? But then how do you…?" Ery waved his hands vaguely at Karl's body.

"The water sustains me."

"Oh." Well, that made some sense, Ery supposed. He grabbed his sandwich fixings, and Karl watched closely as Ery assembled his meal. Then they sat opposite one another at the small table.

"It's, um, a little weird being observed while I chew," Ery said.

"I'm sorry. I can leave."

Ery grabbed Karl's hand. "Stay. It was a comment, not a complaint. Does it gross you out that I eat, uh, stuff?"

"No. It's interesting." Karl grinned. "And strange. You start with… with bread and meat and whatever that white stuff and yellow stuff was, and you put it in your body and it becomes… Ery."

Well, Ery had never thought about it that way before. Put like that, eating *was* a little strange. "I guess today I'm a turkey," he said.

Karl patted his hand. "You make a very pretty turkey."

After the food was gone and the tour resumed, Karl was completely entranced with the little bathroom. He had a vague idea about human excretion—which he also found strange but not disgusting—but he'd never seen a toilet before. When he was friends with Henry, he said, there had been an outhouse behind the big house. He decided the toilet was much nicer. And he was especially enamored with the shower. So much so, in fact, that he set his guitar on the bed and then spent a happy twenty minutes under the spray, toying with the temperature and water pressure.

Ery watched, amused and slightly aroused.

"The warm is *wonderful*!" Karl enthused. He gave Ery a watery leer. "But not as nice as *your* heat."

Jeez. Ery shifted uncomfortably. "I should get back to work. Will you play some more for me?"

"Yes!"

Ery handed Karl a towel to keep him from dripping everywhere. Ery would have liked to dry off that beautiful body, but he kept his hands at his sides. *Just because you want something doesn't mean you should have it*, he reminded himself.

Karl settled happily on the cushions again and resumed his song as Ery picked up the brush. Sometimes Ery glanced around the edge of the canvas, and Karl would smile at him. Even aside from the music, it was nice having company. The few times Ery had attempted to paint with a friend nearby, the friend had either interrupted him constantly with chatter or grown impatient with waiting. But Karl did neither. He just sat and played, and as far as Ery could tell, Karl was as perfectly content as anyone could be.

Only when the sun set did Ery stop painting. Karl stopped playing as well. "Are your hands as tired as mine?" Ery asked, flexing his fingers.

Karl looked down at his hands. "I suppose. I hadn't noticed." He looked up at Ery. "It was a very good day."

"I agree."

"Can I come back tomorrow?"

Ery's heart beat a little faster. Stupid heart. Keeping his voice steady and as casual as possible, he answered, "Sure. I'd like that."

When Karl stood, it seemed natural for them to move into a hug. And very soon, that hug turned into something more active—so much so that Karl set down the guitar and Ery forgot how tired and sore he was. Karl smelled good, like the beach. Why hadn't Ery noticed that before? He'd almost forgotten how delicious Karl tasted, how smooth his skin was.

They seemed destined to end up on the floor, which wasn't a great idea. The concrete would be even less comfortable than the path to the pond. Ery *should* have escorted Karl to the door. But instead he found himself taking Karl's hand and tugging him to the bed.

Karl liked the bed. He bounced on the mattress and exclaimed over the softness of the bedding. He laughed at the pillows. But the bed proved only a brief distraction, because very soon he pulled at Ery's shirt. "Can I see all of you this time?" he asked.

With slight hesitation, Ery began to undress. He wasn't exactly ashamed of his body, but nobody had ever called him buff. He was skinny, always had been. He didn't like the gym and didn't often lift anything heavier than paintbrushes. He liked to walk, sometimes even hike, but that was about it. Karl, on the other hand, had the perfect swimmer's physique—not surprisingly. And yes, Karl had already seen most of Ery, but that was in the great outdoors. In the little apartment, everything felt closer and more intimate.

But Karl didn't look disappointed as Ery stripped. Far from it, in fact. He sprawled on the mattress with his torso propped up by pillows, his eyes wide open. He chewed on his lower lip, and Jesus Christ, now he was stroking his hard cock. Slowly and firmly, never taking his eyes off Ery.

Ery wasn't a size queen. As far as he was concerned, any dick was good dick. He was reminded of that old saying: *It's not the size of the boat that matters, but the motion in the ocean.* Actually, though, Karl's boat was no dinghy. His cock was fairly long and... elegant. Slender, but with a nice flare where the rosy glans peeked out from beneath the foreskin.

"Ery?" Karl said, and Ery realized he'd frozen in mid-undress. He kicked off his shoes and peeled off his jeans and bright multicolor-striped briefs. That left him in nothing but his socks, and if there was any sexy way to take off one's socks, he'd never learned it. But he'd always thought that keeping socks on during sex was kind of dorky, so he bent and tugged them free.

"I like your hair," Karl announced.

Self-consciously, Ery looked down at himself. He wasn't naturally very hairy, but he had a sprinkling of dark hairs on his chest and a treasure trail leading to his groin. "I got tired of manscaping," he explained.

"I don't know what that means."

"Never mind."

"What does the tattoo mean?"

Ery had managed to escape art school with surprisingly little ink, but he had drawn his grandmother's cloisonné seagull and had it tattooed over his heart. "It's just... I don't know. It's a bird."

"Come here, please, Ery. I want to touch you."

Well, Ery wanted that too. He walked to the bed and collapsed beside Karl, who immediately rolled onto his side and wrapped Ery in a close embrace. They began to kiss, which was as nice as Ery had come to expect, but this time they let their hands roam all over each other. Ery loved the silky skin just above the swell of Karl's ass, and Karl apparently had a special fondness for Ery's body hair.

Then Karl suddenly pulled back a little, his eyes intense. "Taste," he said gruffly and proceeded to lick Ery's neck and shoulders, suck on his nipples until Ery whimpered pathetically, and lave his tongue down the center of Ery's body. He nibbled very lightly on the skin over Ery's hipbones. And when Ery spread his legs, Karl settled between them, nosing Ery's balls.

"You taste good," Karl said. "Salty. Like the sea."

"Mmm," Ery replied, actual words a little beyond him at the moment. When Karl slipped Ery's cock into his mouth a moment later and began to lick and suck, Ery found some words, but they were mostly things like "Oh God" and "More please" and "Jesus, yes!" Karl's mouth was as cool as his skin, but that in no way diminished Ery's enjoyment.

Karl was good at giving head. Ery didn't know whether that was because he was a water spirit or whether the skill was unique to Karl, and really, it didn't matter. Karl could swallow him down without gagging, and he made a humming noise that drove Ery crazy with need.

Desperately, Ery grabbed Karl's hair and tried to tug him up. "Gonna…. God, gonna come…."

But Karl didn't budge. If anything, he worked harder. He bobbed his head, petting the hairs on Ery's thigh with one hand, stroking the sensitive skin behind Ery's scrotum with the fingers of the other. Ery couldn't move much, but he thrust with his hips, and Karl happily took whatever Ery gave him.

"Karl…." Ery moaned. He squeezed his eyes shut to avoid sensory overload. But it wasn't enough—with a drawn-out sound, Ery came, emptying himself down Karl's throat.

Karl continued sucking him until the stimulation became too much and Ery batted weakly at his shoulders. When Karl lifted his head, he was licking slightly swollen lips and looking a little smug. "You're delicious."

"I thought…." Ery's heart was still racing and it was hard to breathe. "I thought you only ingested water."

"Your seed's not so different from seawater." Karl grinned. "And much more fun." He moved up until he was draped halfway over Ery's body, settled his head against the crook of Ery's neck, and sighed happily.

"Uh… I can return the favor," Ery offered.

Karl chuckled. "No need." He grabbed Ery's hand and moved it to his crotch, where his cock was wet and soft.

"You came just from blowing me?"

"Mmhmm."

Wow. That was really hot.

Karl seemed content to remain where he was, and Ery didn't mind. They drifted together in a postorgasmic doze for a little while. And then Ery's phone rang.

"Dammit. That's my grandma." Although she might have some weird psychic way of knowing when he was calling her, he recognized her by the special ringtone.

Karl rolled out of the way so Ery could get up and hurry to fetch his phone. If it had been anyone else, he would have let it go to voice mail.

"Hi, Grandma. Is everything okay?"

"I'm fine, dear. But you sound a little out of breath. Is everything all right?"

He glanced at Karl and blushed. "Yeah. I just had to run for the phone."

"You should get more exercise."

"Yes, Grandma," he said, rolling his eyes.

"I spoke with your parents tonight."

His stomach cramped. "God, are they okay?"

"They're *fine*," she said with a sigh. "Everyone is fine. But they say you haven't spoken with them in a while."

"Mom stalks me on Facebook." Which was true. She "liked" every single one of his posts and periodically posted recipes and news stories to his wall. It was like the olden days, when she used to send him newspaper clippings and coupons, only this way all his friends got to see too.

"Ery Phillips, Facebook is *not* the same as a genuine conversation. Your parents care about you. They worry. I know an actual letter is far too much to ask, but surely you can manage a phone call."

He loved his grandmother, but she was really good at guilt trips, and sometimes she seemed to forget he wasn't twelve anymore. No point in arguing, though. "Fine. I'll call tomorrow."

"Good. And everything else is going well?"

He didn't know if she was fishing for information about his painting or his nix. In either case, he didn't want to get into it right now. "Yeah. My muse has been cracking her whip."

"I'm glad to hear that, dear. Well, I'll let you go, then. I love you."

"I love you too, Grandma. Maybe we can have lunch again when I'm back in town."

"It's a date."

When Ery set down the phone, Karl was watching him with a slightly tilted head. "Your family?" he asked.

"Yeah. Grandma likes to remind me of my familial obligations now and then."

"Is it nice to have family?"

Ery crossed the room to the bed and sat next to Karl. "It is. Mostly. But I'm lucky 'cause I have a good pack of relatives." He laced his fingers with Karl's. "Does not having one make you sad?"

"I don't know. My people, we don't…. Water spirits have trysts with one another. Sometimes they may stay together for a few weeks. But then they move on. And offspring, they come into the world already grown and they depart at once. They flow, like water. Most nixes won't even live in ponds, you know. They like rivers and seas."

"But you?"

Karl turned his head to look at him. "I like my pond."

After several minutes of silence, Karl gently extricated his hand from Ery's and stood. "I should go."

"You don't have to."

"I need to get back to water." He glanced toward the studio. "Can I still come back tomorrow?"

Ery jumped to his feet. "Of course! I wish you would."

"Good. And can I leave my guitar here tonight?"

"You don't want to play anymore?"

"I'm tired." Karl cupped Ery's cheek in his palm. "You wore me out."

Together, they walked out of the apartment and through the studio, where the cold made Ery shiver. Nudity was a lot easier for nixes. But he wasn't too cold to trade a last kiss at the door, or to watch Karl disappear into the darkness.

CHAPTER 10

KARL ARRIVED midmorning. This time he made enough noise as he entered the studio that Ery wasn't startled. Karl headed straight for his pile of cushions and his guitar, and he began to play. Every time Ery peeked around the canvas, he saw Karl's troubled expression. But he didn't ask about it until he took a break from painting.

"I'm gonna brew some coffee," he said. "Do you need anything?"

Still strumming distractedly, Karl shook his head.

Ery filled the studio's coffeemaker at the sink he used for cleaning brushes, measured some grounds into the filter, and leaned against the sink while he waited.

"Are you okay?" he finally asked.

"Yes," Karl answered, although his eyes were haunted.

Abandoning the coffeemaker, Ery crossed the room and crouched in front of Karl. He set a hand on Karl's knee. "What is it? Did I fuck up somehow?"

After setting the guitar aside, Karl smiled. "No. You're wonderful. It's only...."

"What?" Ery wanted to strangle him. *This* was one of the many reasons Ery and Dylan hadn't worked out as boyfriends back in college. Trying to get Dylan to share feelings and worries was like digging for gold with a toothpick. It drove Ery nuts. He honestly didn't know how Chris could stand it. Maybe Chris was better at digging.

Karl looked down at his lap, where his hands lay open. In a tiny voice, he said, "I think I had a dream."

For a crazy moment, Ery thought Karl meant a *wet* dream—which, well, was fitting for a water spirit. Ery remembered the first time he'd come in his sleep and the panicked way he'd stripped his sheets off the bed, changed his pajamas, and shoved everything in the washing machine. His mother, of course, had suspected immediately what was going on. Fourteen-year-old boys weren't generally so eager to launder their bedding. Both parents sat down with him that night for a birds-and-bees talk that, seventeen years later, *still* made him squirm with discomfort. But that was also the night he'd admitted to his parents that he liked boys instead of girls. They hadn't exactly been surprised.

And then Ery remembered something Karl had said to him several days earlier. "I thought you said nixes don't dream."

"We don't."

"But…."

"I was asleep. Drifting in my pond. And—"

"Wait. I've been meaning to ask this. How do you breathe underwater?"

Karl gave him a look that said it was a stupid question. "Gills." He sort of squirmed his skin and deep, bloodless slashes appeared on the sides of his neck. He squirmed again and they vanished.

"Holy shit!" Ery placed his fingers on either side of Karl's neck and stroked. He'd kissed that neck quite a few times already, and just as during the kisses, all he found now was smooth, uninterrupted skin. "How'd you do that?"

"Gills in water, lungs on land," Karl replied. "It's easy."

"Jeez." Ery collapsed so that instead of crouching, he was sitting on the floor and facing Karl. "I'm sorry. I interrupted. You were drifting in your pond…."

"And I was asleep. But then I wasn't. I was back in the harbor where I was created, and I was trying to listen to men on ships, but I couldn't understand them. It was strange. Things kept… shifting." He huffed out a breath. "I was scared."

He still looked distressed. Hoping it would help, Ery grasped both of Karl's knees and squeezed gently. "Dreams can be scary even when you're used to them."

"I heard the sorcerer calling me, so I swam to the shore. Only, when I got there, it wasn't him. It was you, Ery, and you were wrapped in the long fur coat he used to wear. But you had your phone. You were speaking into it, but I couldn't understand you either. I think you were saying something important. You asked me a question and got angry when I couldn't answer."

"God, Karl. I'm sorry."

Karl tried to smile. "I know it wasn't really you. You don't have to apologize. But in the… in the dream I thought you were real. You walked away from the water with another man. He turned to look back at me and I saw it was Henry. You both left, even though I called for you. And then… then the water… the water in the harbor started to drain away. Like it does in your shower. I woke up choking."

"Fuck. That's awful." Ery sometimes had dreams that started out as good ones, with him soaring and flying high. But then he'd begin to plummet to earth and he'd jerk awake in his bed, drenched with sweat and with his heart beating madly.

"I thought I was dying," Karl said gravely. "But after a while, I calmed down and I realized what had happened. Ery, I'm not supposed to dream. I never have before. I've never heard of *any* nix dreaming."

Ery felt almost as unsettled as Karl looked. He tried to keep his voice steady, because there was no point in both of them freaking out. "What do you suppose it means?"

"I don't know!" Karl wailed. Then Ery realized Karl was shaking—not from cold—and Ery drew him close in an awkward hug. He smoothed his hand in circles over Karl's back.

Maybe it was predictable, but after a few minutes Karl seemed to want more physical comfort than an embrace could provide, so they kissed instead. Soon they were back on Ery's bed, engaged in an enthusiastic sixty-nine.

Afterward, there was cuddling. Then they each took a shower—it wasn't big enough for them both—and Ery fixed himself some lunch. Karl tried a tiny bite of cheese, declared it interesting, and spit it out. His mood had lifted, at least. He even laughed when Ery demonstrated his awesome ability to juggle apples for about ten seconds before fumbling and dropping them all. "That's why I don't juggle knives," Ery said, bending to retrieve the fruit.

Karl helped him wash the dishes. Not very well, but it was sweet of him to try. He liked the soap bubbles, and he playfully flicked some at Ery. "Did you call your mother and father?"

"What? Has Grandma recruited you to nag?"

"Well? Did you?"

Ery sighed and wiped a bowl dry. "Yes. We had a thrilling conversation about the weather, the boots my mom bought on sale this week, and the furnace repairman who tried to talk them into a new furnace after the valve broke."

"They love you."

After putting the bowl down, Ery turned to look at Karl. "Yeah. They really do."

When the dishes were done, they returned to the studio. Ery worked on painting the nix's face—the eyes were really complex—and Karl played his sad, compelling tunes. The time flew by.

When night fell, Ery cleaned his brushes and Karl set his guitar down. Ery walked him to the door. "Will you be okay?" Ery asked.

Karl sighed loudly and leaned against him. "Yes."

"But what if you have another dream?"

"I don't mind dreaming. It just… it was very strange."

Ery tried to imagine going a long lifetime with uninterrupted sleep, only to have a nasty dream zap him out of the blue. It would be frightening and disorienting at best. "Hang on," he said. As Karl looked on curiously, Ery ran into the apartment, grabbed something from the bathroom, and zoomed back. "Here," he said, putting something into Karl's hand.

Karl looked at the object. "A… a chain?"

"A necklace. It's not expensive or anything. But it's stainless steel, so it won't rust." The chain held a small pendant: an enamel unicorn with a rainbow-hued horn. It had been a gift from his mother years ago, when she was trying to demonstrate how much she supported her son's sexual orientation and fashion choices. He liked it a lot. It was a good way to tell the world, *Yeah, I'm queer. So the fuck what?* But he hadn't worn it for a while. Still, he'd been dragging it around in his toiletry case as sort of a talisman of those warm memories.

"It's very pretty," Karl said. He was smiling but still looked a little confused.

"You don't have to wear it if you don't want to. You can just keep it in your pond."

"I'd like to wear it."

Ery clasped the chain around Karl's neck. The irony of a real mythical creature wearing a fictional one around his neck wasn't lost on Ery. Assuming unicorns were fictional. He was no longer sure.

"It looks good on you," Ery said, because it did.

"Thank you. I've never owned jewelry."

Ery kissed Karl's smooth cheek. "When I was a kid, I went through this period when I had a lot of nightmares. I thought a wicked witch lived on my ceiling fan." He shrugged at Karl's raised eyebrows. "Yeah, it was weird. Anyway, I used to wake up screaming my head off. So one night when my dad tucked me in, he set this Han Solo action figure on my bed. Uh, a little plastic man doll. Jeez, maybe it's Dad's fault I turned out gay."

Karl was waiting patiently but was probably wondering where the hell this story was going. Ery patted his shoulder. "Dad told me that Han Solo would protect me from the witch or any other monsters. I was old enough to know it was just a doll, but you know what? After that, anytime something was chasing me in my dreams, Han Solo would show up and shoot the crap out of it."

"You have good parents," Karl said.

"I know. But my point, Karl, is that this unicorn is your Han Solo. If you have another shitty dream, maybe you can just ride off on your magic unicorn."

It was a silly idea. But Ery felt oddly responsible for Karl's nightmare—he had played a starring role, after all—and this was the best comfort he could think of.

Karl rubbed the unicorn and then smiled at Ery. "Can unicorns swim?"

"This one can."

"You give the most wonderful gifts."

Ery glanced over at his paintings—one of them complete, the other nearly so. He returned the smile. "You too."

WHEN KARL came bouncing into the studio the next day, he was jubilant. "It worked! The unicorn worked!"

Ery was in the middle of mixing some paint, but he put down the palette so he could give Karl a hug. Karl was still a little damp. "Did you have another dream last night?" Ery asked.

"Yes. I was in the middle of the sea, but there was nothing around me—nothing but water. Not a single fish or plant. I swam, but I was lost and was swimming in circles. It was awful. But then the unicorn appeared! Her name is Skuld."

"Oh. Okay." Considering that Ery had named his car, he couldn't exactly criticize Karl for naming the imaginary magic unicorn. "She helped you?"

"She swam with me. She led me to a river, and that river narrowed to a stream, and then we were back at my pond. She ran off into the woods, but I don't think she went far." He frowned slightly. "I'll have to warn her to be careful of the werewolf when Dylan returns."

Ery blinked at him. "Uh… she was just a dream, Karl."

Karl shrugged, unconcerned. "Maybe. But I think dream creatures have their own energy too. Just like us."

Arguing with a water spirit about the dubious existence of a unicorn that needed to avoid a werewolf was the pathway to insanity. Ery smiled and patted Karl's arm. "I'm really glad she helped."

"Me too!" And then Karl surprised Ery by grabbing him around the waist and spinning him in an impromptu dance. His joy was contagious, and Ery wasn't surprised when the dance eventually led into the apartment and ended with them collapsing on the bed. Their lovemaking that morning was exuberant and playful, with tickling and laughter blending nicely with the naughty touching.

Afterward, as they lay tangled together on the mattress, trying to catch their breath, Ery realized he'd never had so much *fun* during sex before.

Karl's head was cradled against Ery's shoulder and he was playing with Ery's chest hairs, tugging them gently, twisting them with his fingers, tracing them into shapes. "Maybe now that you've given me Skuld, I'll have good dreams too."

"I hope so." Ery stroked Karl's hair, teasing loose a few little tangles. "But why do you think you're dreaming at all?"

Karl hesitated a moment before answering. "I think it's you."

"Me?"

"Your... human energy. If you can give a little of it to your paintings, why not to me?"

Ery wasn't sure what he thought about that. It made some sense, but it also gave him a fluttery feeling in his chest, and he didn't know quite why. "But then why didn't you dream when you were with Henry?"

"Because I never spent as much time with him as I do with you."

"But I thought...."

Karl stilled his fingers, but he kept his palm on Ery's chest. "He'd come down to the pond. We'd talk a little and have sex. Quickly, because someone might find us, or because he had work to do. Then he'd go away." He propped himself on an elbow so he could look at Ery's face. "Sex is nice. But your company is even nicer."

Shit. More with the flutter. "Karl... you know I can't stay here, right? I have to go back home in a few days."

"I know. But you'll visit sometimes? To use your studio?"

"Yes."

"Good. And when you do, you'll come down to the pond and call me?"

Jeez. "Of course. We're friends, Karl."

Karl smiled widely, but his expressive eyes held a hint of sorrow. "And even when you don't—when you can't be here, I'll have some lovely memories. And Skuld. And my guitar! I never imagined I'd have so much."

If Karl had so much, why did Ery suddenly feel so empty?

WORK ON the big painting went very well. Karl arrived every morning to play while Ery painted, and at some point each day, they ended up in bed. When Ery took breaks to eat, Karl sat with him at the table, taking tiny tastes of everything, talking about his dreams or some of his travels. He helped Ery wash the dishes afterward. At sunset every evening, Karl headed back to his pond. Ery used the time to catch up on his e-mails, social media, and texts; to call his grandmother; to assure his friends that he hadn't dropped off the face of the earth. He watched movies. And when he went to bed, he dreamed of Karl. When he woke up, he told himself that it didn't mean anything. Of course he dreamed of the guy—they spent all day together, Ery was painting him, and Ery hadn't seen anyone else in days.

They were good days, and they passed very quickly.

During the evening on the day before Chris and Dylan's return, Ery and Karl stood in front of the big canvas. "It's amazing," Karl said, his voice reverent. "You painted exactly how I feel."

Ery was a little overwhelmed. He knew deep in his gut that this painting was very good. It wasn't just the best work he'd ever done—it was Art with a capital A. "You should have it," he said quietly.

"But don't you want other people to see this? People need to see this, Ery."

"It's… I think I stole some of your energy, Karl. It's not right for me to take it."

Karl snaked his arm around Ery's waist and gave him a squeeze. "You're not taking anything except what I'm willing to give. I want everyone to see what you can do. Besides, it would only get ruined if I took it." He conked his head lightly against Ery's. "You can't hang a painting in a pond."

Ery thought about the duck painting but didn't mention it. "All right, then. There's a gallery I'd like to show these to." He waved to indicate the smaller canvas as well.

"Will you do more?"

"Yeah." He had a lot of ideas; his muse had made a list. "But I'm gonna need more paint, and I'll have to borrow Dylan's truck to haul more canvases out here."

The previous day, Ery had shown Karl Internet images of some his favorite artists, and he'd explained how some of those men and women were remembered and admired long after they died. Karl had been mildly impressed by the Swedish guy's stroemkarlen portrait, but he'd been more enthused over Hokusai's *Great Wave* and some of Monet's watery scenes. He was also fond of Hockney's swimming pools.

"Will you be famous?" Karl asked.

"Dunno," Ery replied. "I'd just like to earn enough to quit the evil day job."

"And to be happy?"

Ery glanced at him. "Yeah."

Although the sun set soon after, Karl didn't seem eager to leave. Ery was thankful for that. He used up most of his remaining food to make a strange dinner: cold cereal, sliced cheddar, an orange, and a nuked potato. Karl tasted everything but seemed most surprised over the tang of the orange. After they washed up, Ery transported the couch cushions from the studio floor to the couch. He and Karl sat down and squashed close together, watching *Finding Nemo* on the laptop. Karl loved it.

When Ery started yawning, Karl smiled at him. "I should go."

"You don't have to." Ery looked pointedly at the bed. They'd already wanked each other that morning, but Ery was up for something a little more involved. In fact, what he really wanted was one thing he and Karl hadn't done. "Will you fuck me, Karl?"

Karl's eyes went wide. "You mean...."

"I want you in me. Please."

"I… I've never…." Karl swallowed so loudly Ery heard him.

"You and Henry never did this?"

"He did. He didn't want me to."

Of course. "And other nixes?"

Karl shook his head. "No."

In what he hoped was a comforting move and not a molesty one, Ery caressed Karl's knee. "It's fine. What we've been doing is great. Or I can top if you don't—"

"I want to." Karl's voice had faded to a whisper. "But what if I'm not good?"

Ery had to bite his lip to suppress a laugh. "I promise you, whatever you do is gonna be great. Jeez, you can almost get me off just by kissing me."

A sparkle appeared in Karl's eyes and a leer on his lips. He slammed himself into Ery almost hard enough to hurt—"Ugh!" Ery grunted—and tried to remove Ery's clothes while also maintaining some major-duty lip-lock.

Maybe they wouldn't make it to the bed after all.

With both of them fumbling at Ery's buttons and zipper, they eventually managed to strip everything from his body. Karl, of course, wore nothing except his necklace. He pushed Ery flat on the cushions before lying on top. God, all that skin against skin was pure heaven. Plus Ery had easy access to Karl's ass. *I should paint this ass*, he thought blearily. *It's a masterpiece.*

They made out for a while, letting fingers wander and sharing moans. Their cocks were nestled nicely against each other, but Karl was taking care not to thrust his hips, and Ery didn't have the leverage to move much at all. It was good to concentrate on other parts of the body instead. With Karl on top of him, every bit of Ery became an erogenous zone. His frigging *eyebrows* felt good when Karl stroked them. And good God, those broad, smooth fingers played him like a guitar and brought forth a tune of whimpers, grunts, and drawn-out vowels.

Ery had come before with sex play just like this, his spend pulsing against his belly and Karl's, the scent of Karl's briny seed mixing with his. But tonight he wanted more. He pushed up at Karl's shoulders. "Gonna roll over, babe."

Karl scrambled quickly, with little sign of his usual grace. He almost landed on his ass on the floor, in fact. Ery flipped onto his belly, spread his legs as widely as the couch allowed, and looked over his shoulder to smile at Karl. "I've been told this is my best side."

With a small snigger, Karl lightly patted Ery's ass. "It *is* very pretty."

Ery wiggled appreciatively. "Do that some more."

Obligingly, Karl squeezed and stroked. Then he knelt, laid his body along Ery's back, and began to lick. He began on the tender nape of Ery's neck, then moved on to his shoulders and worked his way down the spine. After a few swipes of tongue, he would blow softly, making Ery shiver. Sometimes Karl nibbled instead—very lightly—or scraped his teeth across skin. It was slow and erotic, and even when he stayed above the waist, Ery had to fight to not hump into the cushions.

But then Karl finally reached Ery's ass. Ery couldn't actually see what Karl was doing—the angle was wrong, and anyway Ery's eyes were squeezed shut by then. But he would have been willing to swear under oath that Karl's tongue could do things a human's couldn't. Ery almost lost it completely when Karl stuck that wonderful, agile appendage into his body. But Ery had been hoping for a larger, harder appendage.

With a tremendous effort of will and a fair amount of brute strength, Ery twisted onto his back. He looked up at Karl, whose eyes had gone very dark and whose hair hung down like a silk sheet. "Let's move this to the bed," Ery said. "More room."

Karl climbed off, then offered Ery a hand up. Ery couldn't help a little groping as they walked, which meant they nearly tripped over one another but ultimately made it safely. After a bit of mutual wriggling and squeezing, Ery decided he wanted a good view of the action. He arranged himself on his back with his knees bent and a pillow under his ass. Karl stared down at him, mouth slightly open, as if he wasn't quite sure what to do next.

"There's lube right there," Ery said, pointing at the nightstand. They'd used the stuff a couple of times before as an aid to wanking each other or rubbing off. Karl said he didn't like the taste, which made Ery wonder whether he'd prefer the flavored stuff. But the nearest drugstore was a good half hour away, and Ery hadn't had a chance to go out and buy any.

Prior to this evening, Ery had also thought about safer sex. He was usually careful about it, in part because his parents and grandmother had made him promise. He didn't do buttsex without protection, and he had himself tested periodically. But he didn't have any rubbers at the farm. He'd only brought the lube because he assumed he'd be jacking off. He had no idea whether Dylan and Chris kept condoms in their house—they'd been exclusive for over a year and, well, werewolf.

Ery had tested fine. And in addition to Karl being a water spirit, the last time Karl had had sex, Ery's great-grandparents hadn't even been born yet.

Bareback it was.

Karl uncapped the bottle of lube. "Squeeze some on your finger," Ery instructed him. "It's been a while since I've done this. I'm gonna be tight."

"Oh." Karl's voice was about an octave higher than usual. He grinned, followed Ery's instructions, and then very carefully traced around the edge of Ery's hole.

Too carefully, actually. Ery was already pretty worked up. "I'm not that fragile, Karl. Or immortal."

Karl slid his finger inside, and *oh*, that was good. But not good enough. "Another," Ery rasped impatiently.

For a guy who claimed not to know what he was doing, Karl did a great job loosening Ery up. He watched Ery's face avidly, and whenever Karl discovered a specific angle or movement that was particularly nice, Ery's expression must have showed it, because Karl did more of the same. By luck or accident, he found Ery's prostate, and that just about sent Ery rocketing off the mattress. "I-I'm ready now," Ery panted.

"Are you sure?"

"For God's sake, Karl. Fuck me!"

With a distinctly devilish gleam in his eyes, Karl squirted a little slick onto his own cock and stroked himself very, very slowly. At that moment, if he'd suddenly claimed he was a demon instead of a nix, Ery would have believed him. Ery watched as a droplet of clear fluid appeared at Karl's slit and slowly dripped onto the blanket. "Ohh, fuck…." Ery whimpered.

Maybe Karl took pity on him, but more likely Karl himself couldn't hold out much longer. He positioned himself between Ery's legs, lined up his cock, and moved his hips forward.

Ery truly was ready. As Karl sank into his body, Ery felt only a good, *good* stretch and just the nicest touch of burn. The sensation of a cock inside him without a latex barrier was novel enough that Ery couldn't tell whether Karl's dick felt different from a human's. In any case, Ery was not complaining.

"*Herrejävlar*," Karl moaned. He looked down at where their bodies joined and then up at Ery's face. Karl looked like a man who'd just found religion. "Th-that's so good."

"It's even better when you move," Ery hinted.

"I… I don't think I'll last long when I do."

That made Ery laugh. "I'm gonna go off like a rocket, so no problem."

Karl laughed too, which felt a little strange with him inside, but then he began to thrust slowly. He closed his eyes, and if Ery were to paint that exact expression, nobody would be able to tell whether it was a depiction of exquisite pain, intense pleasure, or religious rhapsody. Maybe Ery *would* paint it. He'd title the piece *Ecstasy*.

And then he stopped thinking and simply felt. He was flying through the air like a jet, or maybe torpedoing through water. Didn't matter—either way he was floating somewhere off the ground, and every inch of his body tingled and hummed. His vision, normally sharp, had gone two-dimensional and gray at the edges, so that the only real thing left was Karl, beautiful Karl.

He heard a loud pounding and assumed it was his heart. Maybe it was, but it was also, he realized, rain falling hard on the barn roof.

Ery's hands were fisted in the bedsheets. Neither man was touching Ery's cock, which was fine—he didn't think he could withstand any more sensation. It was plenty to feel Karl moving inside him, to hear Karl's grunts and foreign blasphemies, to see the look of rapture on the heavenly face above him.

Ery's eruption took him by surprise. He arched his back and neck, and he let out a noise that sounded inhuman to his own ears. Within moments Karl fell over the edge too, losing his rhythm and then freezing with his cock fully sheathed in Ery.

Karl collapsed onto Ery with a noisy exhalation, at which point Ery straightened his legs and was a little disappointed when Karl's softening cock slid out of him. He made up for the loss by holding Karl tight.

"All right?" Karl croaked.

Ery mustered just enough energy to tug lightly on Karl's hair. "Perfection."

"You're amazing."

"Hmm. Back at you."

Of all the places in the world, there was nowhere Ery would rather have been at that moment than in bed with Karl. With considerable effort, he yanked the pillow out from under his ass and tugged the blankets over them both.

Karl sighed into Ery's neck. "Should go."

"Not yet," Ery protested sleepily. He yawned. "Don't wanna let go."

Maybe Karl didn't want to let go either, because he didn't move. His breathing had been raspy during and after sex, but now it evened out and slowed, and together he and Ery drifted away.

CHAPTER 11

ERY HAD seen photos of the Dust Bowl, when winds lifted all the parched topsoil from farms on the Great Plains, and that was what he dreamed of this night. He wandered through choking clouds of dust, searching for something precious. As he walked, coughing and stumbling, a great sense of urgency filled him. He tried to hurry, but layers of sand sucked at his feet, slowing him down.

He woke with a gasp and a pounding heart. *Where the hell was Han Solo?* He turned his head, intending to awaken Karl with a comment about borrowing his unicorn.

Next to him on the mattress lay a desiccated corpse.

Ery shrieked, jerked backward, and fell out of bed with the blankets twisted around his feet. He tried to untangle himself, but it was just like in his dream: every movement was molasses-slow. He couldn't breathe. Horrible choked sobs tore from his throat like shards of glass, and he shook uncontrollably.

Once he finally freed himself and stood, he was afraid to look at the bed. But he *did* look, and Jesus Christ, what he saw made him so dizzy he nearly fainted. It was a male body with long white hair. The body was shrunken—like a mummy—the skin as dusty and wrinkled as an ancient parchment. A chain hung around the neck, and on the chain was a small colorful unicorn.

"Oh God! Karl! Karl!"

Karl didn't even flicker an eyelid.

Ery wanted to collapse. He wanted to wake up and discover this was just a terrible nightmare. What he did, though, was reach forward and lay his hand on Karl's chest.

The skin was no longer soft. It felt like dried-out leather. But very faintly, Karl's heart still beat.

"Karl? Jesus, Karl, please!" Ery shook Karl's shoulders, but the only result was Karl's head flopping sickeningly on the pillow.

God, what was he supposed to do? He searched frantically for his phone, but once he found it, he froze with it cradled in his palm. If he called 911 and Deputy Junior and the hot firemen showed up, what would Ery tell them? *Take him to the nearest nix hospital!* Somehow Ery doubted that the ER was going to know how to deal with Karl.

Ery had never been good in emergencies. His mind tended to go blank. He couldn't afford that right now, couldn't slip into the luxury of panic. "Think, goddammit!" he yelled.

Water.

Dropping his phone to the floor, Ery rushed to the kitchenette. He grabbed a glass, filled it to the brim at the sink, and ran back to the bed, sloshing water as he went. "Karl? Please, drink." Ery propped Karl's head up and held the glass to his dried-out lips. But the water simply ran down Karl's chin and neck.

Ery was crying. "Swallow, Karl. Please! You have to swallow!" But no matter how loud he shouted or how firmly he pressed the glass to Karl's mouth, Karl didn't respond.

A funnel. If he had a funnel maybe he could force some water down Karl's throat. But when Ery pulled everything out of the kitchen drawers and cupboards, there was no funnel. Maybe there was one in the big house, but the kitchen there was enormous, and Ery couldn't stand to leave Karl long enough to search.

He was agnostic at best, but if there really *was* a God—or gods— now was the time to pray for a miracle. Ery babbled something pleading and desperate and probably unintelligible, but the words didn't matter, because it all came down to one thing: *Don't let Karl die.*

And then he noticed something through his tear-blurred eyes. Where the water from the glass had dripped, Karl's skin looked a little less dry, a little more… lifelike. Maybe… maybe Karl didn't actually have to drink the water for it to work.

Ery upended the entire glass on Karl's head.

Almost immediately, Karl made a tiny whimper. His eyes moved beneath closed lids, and his fingers twitched atop the sheet.

Despair turned to hope in Ery's chest, and that hope triggered a release of adrenaline. Lifting weights was not his thing, and his upper body strength was negligible. But he jammed his arms beneath Karl's body, lifted him, and rushed to the bathroom. When he got there, he dumped Karl in a fetal position on the floor of the shower and turned on the spray full blast.

For a long time, nothing happened. Ery collapsed to his knees and tried not to fall apart. But then Karl moaned and began to stir. Ery squashed as much of himself into the shower cubicle as would fit, and he propped Karl's head on his lap. He pushed Karl's hair out of his face and lightly stroked his cheek. "Karl? Karl, how can I help?"

Slowly, Karl opened his eyes. His gaze was fuzzy and confused, but it gradually sharpened. "Ery," he wheezed.

If Ery hadn't already been sitting down, he would have collapsed with relief. As it was, he began crying again and could barely speak. "What do you need, Karl?"

Karl gestured weakly at the showerhead. "This."

"Okay."

Ery sat, Karl lay, and the water ran. Soon the small water heater reached its limits and the stream became icy. Karl didn't seem to mind, but Ery was naked and soaked, and he began to shiver. Slowly, and clutching at Ery's leg for assistance, Karl managed to sit up. He tried a small smile. "You're wet."

"Jesus, Karl." Ery wrapped his arms around him. "What the fuck happened?"

"I was… away from water too long." Karl kissed Ery's cheek. "Get dry and warm, Ery. I'll be all right."

Ery didn't want to let go of him, but his body was about to shake itself to pieces. He scrambled awkwardly to his feet, grabbed a towel, and rubbed himself vigorously. Keeping the bathroom door open, he hurried to the main room, where he found last night's jeans and sweater crumpled on the floor. He put them on quickly before returning to the bathroom.

Karl sat in the shower, leaning against the wall. He no longer looked cadaverous—just wet and exhausted. "I need to return to my pond. I can't…. Could you help me get there?"

"Of course! But are you sure you…." Ery glanced worriedly at the showerhead.

Karl tried to stand. He waved away Ery's offered help and used the shower wall for support. He rested there a moment. "Shoes, Ery. The path will hurt your feet."

Ery's feet were not his foremost concern at the moment, but he rushed over to his sneakers and jammed them on. "Isn't there anything else I can do?"

"No. I'll be fine after a few hours in my pond." Karl shook his head. "I'm sorry, Ery."

"You're sorry! I almost killed you." Ery wiped his damp and slightly snotty face with his arm.

Karl shuffled over and settled his arm around Ery's shoulder, letting him bear a good part of his weight. Not knowing how long he could last as the support, Ery started walking toward the studio.

"You didn't almost kill me," Karl said as they moved. His breath came in short pants and he stared at his feet, as if he needed to concentrate on them in order to walk.

"I did. You were going to leave last night and I asked you not to."

"I'm hundreds of years old, Ery. I'm responsible for my own choices." Softly, he added, "I liked sleeping with you."

"Jeez, I liked it too. But it's not worth dying over, is it?"

Karl didn't answer.

They walked past his guitar, out the studio door, and down the path, their progress slow. The ground was muddy from the previous night's downpour, and Ery didn't want to lose his footing and send them both sprawling down the hill. Fortunately they made it to the bottom without mishap.

Karl looked drawn and weak, but he stood on his own and enveloped Ery in an embrace. "Thank you, Ery. For everything."

"For...." Ery's voice broke. He sniffed. "Are you positive you're okay?"

"I will be soon. I just need to float for a while."

"I... I'll come back later to check on you." And to say good-bye.

Karl squeezed him. "Good. Just call me. I'll hear."

"I'll bring your guitar. And do... do you want me to introduce you to Dylan and Chris? They'll be here in a few hours."

Pulling away slightly, Karl gave him a small smile. "Yes, please. I'd like that."

Ery wanted to say much more but couldn't find the words. Besides, Karl didn't look like he'd be able to remain standing much longer. "Last night...," he began.

"Was the best of my life. Making love with you, and then... it felt so good to sleep with you, Ery. Maybe I'll dream of it now."

Ery nodded and stepped back. "Sweet dreams, Karl."

After giving his beautiful smile, Karl turned to the pond. He didn't so much dive in as fall. He disappeared entirely, and soon even the ripples died away.

Across the pond, the two ducks watched Ery reproachfully. "Keep an eye on him," Ery rasped. Then he turned to head back to the barn.

THE APARTMENT was a mess. The bedding was wet and smelled like sex, the contents of the kitchen were strewn on the counter and floor, and the entire bathroom was soggy. Ery spent a good chunk of time cleaning everything up. He washed and dried the sheets and towels and ate the very last of his food. He tidied up the studio, organizing paints and brushes. With the perspective of a new day, the paintings still looked as good as he'd hoped.

But while Ery kept his hands busy, his mind was on Karl. Ery was still nearly sick with self-blame over what had happened. Even worse than that, his mind kept replaying their conversation. *I'm responsible for my own choices*, Karl had said. Did that mean he'd opted to sleep with Ery *knowing* he might die? If Ery had slept just a little longer, if that nightmare hadn't woken him when it did…. He couldn't bear to finish the thought.

Why the hell would Karl risk death just to spend the night in Ery's bed?

Ery didn't want to think about the answer to that one either.

As Ery worked, his gaze kept straying to the door. He wanted to go down to the pond and check on Karl. He knew he shouldn't—Karl needed to remain undisturbed so he could rest and recover. But what if he *wasn't* recovering? Ery kept picturing a pale body floating facedown in the green water, the metal chain at its neck gleaming a little in the sun, the ducks swimming worriedly nearby. He pushed the image away.

Ery was sweeping the studio floor and adamantly not thinking when he heard the rumble of a big engine. He put down the broom and slipped into his jacket, then left the barn and took the path leading to the big house. He turned the corner of the house just as Dylan and Chris were beginning to unpack the truck.

"Hey!" Dylan called, waving.

Ery waved back as he walked to them. Dylan had a few days' growth of whiskers, and Chris's hair was sleep-rumpled. But they both looked happy and relaxed.

"How was it?" Ery asked.

"Fuckin' amazing," said Chris, lifting a heavy suitcase. "We're goin' back."

Dylan gave his partner a goofy adoring smile before facing Ery. "It was really fantastic. God, I want to build a house like one of Gaudi's. You think this place would look strange with a mosaic tile roof?" He waved at his typical late-nineteenth-century farmhouse.

"It would definitely be unique," Ery replied. "But hey, it's your house. You should do whatever you guys want. It's not like the neighbors will complain."

"Speaking of neighbors, what's up with, uh…." Dylan jerked his head in the direction of the pond.

Ery winced. "He's, uh…. He'd like to meet you. I can introduce you before I take off, if you want."

"You don't have to leave just because we're home."

"Thanks." Ery smiled weakly. "But I gotta head back to the coal mine."

Chris put the suitcase down and walked a little closer. "You okay, man? You look a little… dim."

Ery didn't want to talk about it, not right now. If he started, he was likely to end up in a complete breakdown, and neither he nor his friends wanted that. He'd just hold it together until he got back to his own place. Then he could put on *Brokeback Mountain* and sob himself into snotty, red-eyed oblivion.

"I'm just a little tired," Ery said. "I've been doing a lot of painting."

Dylan and Chris exchanged a look—one of those life-partner psychic transmissions—and Ery had no idea what they were thinking. Nor was he in the mood to ask.

Dylan had been carrying his messenger bag and two small suitcases, but now he set them on the ground. "Can we peek? And then you can introduce us to… him." Another anxious gesture at the pond.

Ery would have thought that after a very long flight and with jet lag and all, the guys would have preferred to just go inside and crash. If he was a good friend, he would tell them to rest and unpack, and he'd do the introductions later. But he wanted to get things over with and go home. "Sure. C'mon."

Abandoning their luggage, Dylan and Chris accompanied him to the barn. Inside the studio, he waved them toward the canvases and looked up at the dusty rafters as he waited. When he didn't hear anything for several moments, he got brave enough to look. Both men were staring at the bigger painting in stunned silence.

Chris glanced at him. "Holy shit," he whispered, then turned back to the painting. Dylan didn't say anything at all, but his eyes were very wide and his mouth hung slightly open.

Ery gnawed at his fingernail. "Um…."

With an expression akin to shock, Dylan finally looked at him. "Holy *shit*, Ery. Just… holy shit."

Apparently that was the limit of his friends' critique. Ery was pretty sure that was a good thing; he didn't often see Chris at a loss for words. "I, um, want to do a few more. I need more canvases. Then there's a guy I want to show them to. Julio. He owns a gallery, and…." He chewed his lip. "Would you help me transport the paintings when they're ready? Or I could rent a truck."

"Fuck, Ery," Chris said. "Your gallery guy's gonna cream himself when he sees these. Course we'll drive 'em there."

Dylan nodded vigorously. "These are brilliant, Ery. Really fucking brilliant."

Despite the difficult start to the day and the storm of emotions in his head, Ery basked a little. Dylan didn't swear all that often, so his praise seemed sincere. "Thanks. My muse reported back for duty."

"This, uh, guy in the paintings." Dylan waved his hand. "Is it…?"

"Karl. Come on. He's looking forward to meeting you guys."

Dylan and Chris exchanged another significant look, and when Ery bent to put the guitar in the case, then straightened with the case in his hands, his friends both had their eyebrows raised. "It's his," Ery said, slightly defensively.

After a few more moments of art appreciation, the three of them headed out the door. "Uh, Dyl?" Ery said as they started down the path. "I know this sounds a little strange, but there may or may not be a dream unicorn in the woods and—"

"Sounds like you been doing shrooms," Chris said.

"I haven't even had a beer in weeks."

But Dylan only looked thoughtful. "A dream unicorn?"

"Yeah. Her name is Skuld. I think she has a rainbow horn."

Chris snorted, so Dylan bonked his shoulder. "There are other strange things in those woods. A couple months ago I saw a sasquatch."

Stopping in his tracks, Ery gaped. "Sasquatch?"

"Yeah, I thought Dyl was full of shit too," said Chris, earning a glare from his partner. "But he was pretty damn adamant about it, so…." He spread his hands and shrugged.

"But… Bigfoot lives over there?" Ery said, pointing.

Dylan rubbed his neck. "Dunno. Maybe he was just visiting. I only saw him that once. I haven't, uh, smelled him before or since." He looked a little embarrassed over the last bit, as if there were something shameful about his enhanced senses.

"You didn't try to eat him or anything?"

If anything, Dylan's embarrassment intensified. "He's too big for me. I go after smaller prey."

"He's more a Thumper guy than a Bambi guy," Chris interjected helpfully, which earned him another glare.

But Ery was feeling a little relieved. "So if you do come across this unicorn?"

"I don't think it'll be a problem," Dylan said.

They started walking again, although Chris did mutter, "Unicorn. It's what's for dinner."

The pond was peaceful, and there was no floating corpse. The ducks quacked softly at them—maybe welcoming Dylan and Chris home—and a few insects skittered over the surface. The ground was still a bit muddy, which seemed to puzzle Chris and Dylan slightly, but Ery didn't bother to explain. A crow landed in a nearby tree and scolded them.

Ery set the guitar case atop a blackberry bramble. "Karl!" he called. "Dylan and Chris are here."

At first, nothing happened. But just as Ery's gut began to churn with worry and he prepared to call again, ripples formed on the water. For a heart-stopping second, Ery thought *Black Lagoon*. But it was Karl who emerged, with his hair dripping and his necklace shining. He looked tired and hesitant, and he stopped while the water still lapped around his shins. "Hi, Ery," he said quietly.

Dylan and Chris were gaping again. Ery didn't know why—he'd warned them. And they'd seen the paintings. "Hi, Karl. How are you feeling?"

"Better. Thank you. I've been resting all day."

Ery hovered close to the edge of the water. "Karl, meet Dylan and Chris. You've seen them around. And guys, this is Karl. He's lived here for a really long time."

Consciously or not, Chris had placed himself protectively in front of Dylan. It was a silly gesture, considering Dylan's werewolf strength, but so sweet it made Ery's chest ache a little. "Hey," Chris said gruffly.

After glancing uncertainly at Ery, Karl nodded. "Hello. You look a little like Henry."

"Who?"

"One of your... ancestors, I guess," Ery explained. "He was Karl's friend." And a selfish asshole, he didn't add, in part because who was he to talk?

"Shit." Chris looked over at the far bank, where trees and brush clustered thickly. "The time when that bitch of a wolf was after us and she...." He used his hands to mime something being sucked down really fast. "That was you?"

"Yes."

"And when Dyl was diving for the saddlebag and he just about drowned?"

Karl looked down at his submerged feet. "I'm sorry. I thought he was—"

"Lay off him," Ery interrupted, surprising everyone—including himself. "He thought Dylan was an intruder trying to steal his stuff." He sighed. "And he's had a rough day, so be nice. He's... he's really good."

Karl came splashing out of the water, and Ery braced himself for a hug, but then Karl stopped an arm's length away. He was smiling widely. "Thank you, Ery. And I am sorry, Dylan. I won't do it again. If you want the motorcycle back—"

"Keep it," Dylan answered quickly. "It's no big deal. Besides, you saved Chris and his dad. But why?"

"They're Nocks. It's what.... Is it all right if I stay here? I know it's really your pond, not mine."

At those words, Ery's heart broke. This was the only true home Karl had ever known, and yet he apparently didn't feel as if it belonged to him. Ery hadn't realized Karl was so insecure about it, and he certainly couldn't bear the worried look on Karl's face. So he stepped nearer and wrapped his arm tightly around Karl's waist, drawing him close. He stared expectantly and a little challengingly at Chris and Dylan.

Who exchanged one of their looks again. "Of course you can stay," Dylan said as Chris nodded.

"It's a weird neighborhood but friendly," Chris added.

Karl slumped a little with relief. "Thank you."

"Maybe one of these days you could tell me a little bit about my family. Don't really know much about the history."

"I'd like that."

This was good, Ery told himself. Dylan and Chris would warm up to Karl soon. Karl would remain safe and housed, and he'd have a couple of friends nearby. All was well.

So why did Ery feel all twisted up inside?

He gave in to an irresistible urge and turned his head to kiss Karl's cheek. "I told you. They're good guys."

Sneaking a quick look at Chris and Dylan, who were watching intently, Karl kissed him back. "You don't mind if they see?" he whispered.

"No," Ery whispered back. More loudly he added, "Guys, me and Karl are good friends, okay?"

"Friends with benefits?" Chris asked.

Ery blushed, which was silly. "Something like that. Just... he's special. Really special. I want you to know that."

Karl still looked tired, but now he was glowing in a way that might have been faintly supernatural. "You're special too," he said.

Chris grinned and rolled his eyes. "Jesus. Two of 'em. No wonder there's a sparkly unicorn in the woods. I'm surprised there ain't any dancing gumdrops. Is Tinker Bell gonna move in across the road?"

"Let's give them a couple minutes," Dylan said, tugging at Chris's arm. To Karl he said, "I'm glad to meet you. I hope we can chat later."

"Yes, please."

"I'll look forward to it. Ery, we'll meet you up at the house, okay?"

Ery nodded. He and Karl watched as the two men started up the hill. Ery waited until they were out of earshot before he turned to Karl. They placed their hands on each other's backs and rested their foreheads together. "Thank you, Ery. For not being embarrassed to tell them we're friends."

Ery felt a whole bucketful of feelings about Karl, but embarrassment wasn't one of them. And he thought it was important for Chris and Dylan to know that Karl wasn't a run-of-the-mill water spirit—he was someone precious.

"I bet you could use some more R and R," Ery said. "And I have to get back to the city."

"I know. Ery, I know you have a home somewhere else and a job and friends and family and... I've known all along that you couldn't stay here. I'm just... just a nix. You have your whole human life to live."

"You're not *just* anything. You're amazing."

When Karl sighed, his breath chilled Ery's skin. "I know humans fall in love and find partners. Like Dylan and Chris. I know you will too." He stroked Ery's cheek with his thumb. "Another man who will be good to you and love you. You need that. You deserve it."

"But Karl—"

"I knew from the beginning. You can't stay with a stroemkarlen. But it's been a wonderful time, Ery. You've given me so much."

Ery had already cried today. He was *not* going to do it now. "I'll be back, Karl. I mean, my studio's here and... and you're here too."

"Good. But if you can't come back... when you meet your someone... I understand. I want you to know that. You've already given me so much, Ery. You've filled my heart. See?" He moved one of Ery's hands to his chest, as if Ery could feel what was inside.

What Ery felt was smooth skin, hard muscle, and a steady heartbeat. And about fifty tons of grief and guilt. He wanted to say this was all a lot of BS, that he'd always return to the farm and Karl, that they'd have each other always. But that would be a huge lie, and they both knew it. Karl deserved the truth.

"I want to come back," Ery said.

"Good. Maybe we'll dream of one another."

Of course they kissed after that. This kiss tasted of longing and regret, of joy and sadness, of unfulfilled wishes and miso soup. It was a very complex kiss. But it had to end eventually. Ery watched Karl sink back into the water, and then Ery walked away.

DYLAN AND Chris must have taken the luggage inside. Now they stood on the porch, Chris smoking a cigarette and each holding a bottle of beer. "Want one?" Chris asked Ery, waving his bottle slightly.

"No, thanks. I'm gonna hit the road."

But he didn't, at least not yet. He didn't even go to fetch his stuff from the barn. He stood next to Chris, leaning forward against the porch railing, staring out at the wheat field across the road and the green hills beyond that. He wondered what sorts of creatures were hidden in those trees, and he thought about how strange the world was.

Chris stepped off the porch and ground the cigarette butt under his heel. Then he dropped the butt into a coffee can kept on the porch for that purpose. He took a long swallow from his bottle. "So you and Davy Jones...."

"We're kind of a thing," Ery said. "I'm just not sure *what* kind of thing."

"A new thing," Dylan offered.

"Yeah. That."

"He's real pretty," Chris said. "You two look good together. And you don't have to worry 'bout him stealin' your clothes."

Ery sighed. "Yeah. We're totes adorbs, right? Look, I'm gonna go."

But Chris grabbed his arm. "What's up, dude?"

"It's... it's way too long and dramatic for now. Later, okay?"

"'Kay." Chris let him go.

Putting an arm around Chris's shoulders, Dylan asked, "You'll be back soon to paint?"

"This weekend, probably. Unless my muse jumps off a bridge on the way home. You want me to bring anything with me?"

They shook their heads.

"Okay. And, uh, if I order some canvases and have them shipped.... UPS does come out here, right?"

"We ain't on the moon," said Chris. "Dyl orders shit all the time. He's got a hard-on for those catalogs with all the expensive shit nobody needs. And... what's that website with all the fancy kitchen crap? It's got a French name to prove to everyone how hoity-toity it is. Should just call it Things Dylan Doesn't Know How to Use But Buys Anyway."

Unperturbed, Dylan grinned. "But I know *you* know how to use them. And shall we discuss some of your Amazon indiscretions, Mr. Nock?"

"I'm not even in the same league as you, Mr. Warner. But anyway, yeah, UPS knows where we live. Just give 'em our address and I'll let you know when your stuff gets here."

Ery thanked them. He gave each of them a hug too, just for good measure. Then he trudged to the barn for his belongings.

CHAPTER 12

ERY LIVED on the second floor of a converted Victorian. He'd rented this particular apartment because he liked the neighborhood and because it was an easy commute to work and to his grandmother's house. The rent was reasonable, but the house wasn't in the best repair, the temperature was always wrong, and the walls were thin. He got decent light in the living room, which had a big window facing the street, but the bedroom was like a cave, the kitchen hadn't been remodeled since the 1970s, and the bathroom tended to mildew. With the landlord's permission, he'd used bright paint on the walls and hung multicolored curtains. Several of his paintings adorned the walls. He'd created a sort of canopy over his bed with pink, yellow, and green silk scarves, and his thrift-store furniture pieces were slathered with acrylic paint and reupholstered with stripes or dots.

Every time Chris came over, he claimed the décor gave him a headache. Dylan would counter with a pointed comment, saying men who had formerly lived in ugly shacks and peed off their porches should not throw stones. Jeez, Ery really enjoyed those two guys together.

Ery's apartment was considerably larger than the little one in the barn, yet when he unlocked the door and dumped his suitcase on the floor, it felt cramped and a little claustrophobic. He sighed as he kicked the door shut behind him.

He'd stopped at the grocery store on the way home because, after two weeks away, his cupboards were pretty bare. So now he trudged to the kitchen and, after drinking about a gallon of water, put everything away. He knew he should go back downstairs to check his mail, but it seemed like too much effort. The bills and sales circulars could wait until later.

He collapsed on his couch with the remote control in his hand and a big glass of water nearby and stared at random crap on TV until it was time to go to bed.

"DID YOU have a good vacation?"

Myra Acker was close to sixty, but she dressed like a twenty-year-old. She was offbeat enough that she could almost get away with it. Ery was willing to overlook her fashion faux pas because, while he found his job dreary, he liked his boss. She was sweet without being cloying, and she tried her best to assign projects based on each artist's interests.

Ery pulled the stool up to his drafting table and smiled at her. "Yeah, I did."

"Did you do some painting?"

He wasn't ready to share just yet, so he simply nodded. "And I relaxed. I was kind of house-sitting for my friends who have a farm."

"Ooh! Did you have to milk cows?"

That made him laugh. He didn't have the faintest idea how to milk a cow, and if he tried, he'd surely end up embarrassing himself and the bovine. "No livestock. Just some nice land and a barn with a studio." And a pond with a nix—plus a neighboring forest with a unicorn and Bigfoot. Yeah, there were some things you just didn't say to your boss, no matter how great she was.

"I've always dreamt about buying a farm. I'd grow all my own vegetables. Oh, and did you know there are miniature donkeys? I think I'd want some of those."

He winked at her. "I've always preferred my asses on the larger side, thanks."

"Oh, Ery." She clapped his shoulder. "We've missed you around here. The office is always duller without you. Are you ready to get back into it?"

He let out a long breath and tried to sound enthusiastic. "Sure. Hit me, Myra."

A stool nearby was currently unoccupied, so she rolled it over and perched. She always sat with her back very straight. She'd mentioned once in passing that she'd been a model when she was younger. He could believe that. Now, though, she wrote copy for a lot of their customers and oversaw the artists. Three other people worked full-time in the art department, and a few worked on a part-time or contractual basis.

"I'd like you to finish that nursing manual. I tried giving it to Paula, but she's just not as good as you at anatomy."

"Are you telling me I'm better with penises than Paula is?"

"I'm telling you that exactly. But I have a couple other projects for you too, honey. We have a calendar to design for an architectural firm. They asked for you specifically."

Great. Dylan was throwing more bones his way. Ery suspected that Dylan was trying to work off some guilt, having completely blown off their friendship for a couple of years after turning into a werewolf. "Okay. A calendar."

"They're top-notch, Ery. They're going to want something special."

"I'll do my best."

"I know you will. And then we have a new restaurant. It's over on Northwest Twenty-Third, and this will be a bit of a rush job, okay? They want a logo, menus, business cards, web page—the whole shebang. You can go over there today to get a feel for the physical space and talk to the owners. And I bet we can get you a meal or two out of the deal."

Free food. Goody. "What's the cuisine?"

"Eastern Europe."

"Seriously?" He raised his eyebrows at her. "Someone thinks borscht and pierogies are gonna bring in the crowds?"

"You never know, honey." She stood. "I'll send you all the files." With another friendly tap to his shoulder, she walked away.

He booted up his computer and tried to get himself enthused. "Dicks, dates, and goulash. Let's go, muse!"

After reading over the files and sending off a couple of e-mails, he decided to tackle the manual first. "Huh huh huh," he chuckled to himself in his best Butt-head impression. "I said tackle." As it turned out, though, he wasn't illustrating anyone's junk, with or without tubes. Today was all about muscles. That was kind of fun at first, until he realized the guy he was drawing had narrow hips and a strong, wiry build, like a swimmer. And then he daydreamed about how those muscles felt when they bunched and flexed over him, under him.

"Concentrate," he chided himself. But he got to the sartorius, which ran sinuously from the knee, up the inner leg, and across the upper thigh. And then the external oblique, which caressed the anterior ilium and formed that sweet furrow where Ery so loved to run his tongue, and then licking a bit farther south, over to the pectineus muscle, and then, jeez, to those firm hairless balls or—

He picked up a file folder and fanned himself. He needed lunch.

HE COULD have driven to the restaurant, but parking was often a pain in that neighborhood. Besides, other than his aerobics in bed, he hadn't had enough exercise lately. So he took the light rail across the river and through downtown to the Goose Hollow stop and walked from there. It was good weather for a walk, actually—crisp and sunny. Which wasn't normal for early November, but he wouldn't complain.

The restaurant was still under construction. Workmen bustled around, doing things with saws and hammers. Normally Ery would have enjoyed ogling a few of them, but today his heart wasn't in it. He looked around for the owners, who'd promised over the phone to meet him there.

"Ery Phillips?" someone called from the dimness at the back of the room.

He followed the voice to a table where two men and a woman sat, all with a clear family resemblance. They were all roughly his age, and all very attractive.

A brief round of introductions confirmed what Ery had guessed: this was a family business. Helena Kamski was the chef, and her brother Marek would run the front of the house. Ery wasn't sure exactly what their cousin Aleksy's role was, apart from flirting shamelessly with everyone in the room he wasn't related to—including Ery.

The four of them sat around a shabby, dusty table and smiled at each other. "I am sorry for the mess," Marek said, waving his hand slightly.

"It looks like a big project."

"We can show you some concept drawings of what everything will look like when it's complete." Marek patted the iPad in front of him.

"Great. But why don't you tell me a little about the general idea first?"

Helena answered. "We came here from Poland when we were children. And we know about the American stereotypes: grouchy fat ladies in babushkas eating nothing but cabbage."

Aleksy sat next to Ery. He waggled his eyebrows. "We're not all Borises and Natashas, you know." His sandy hair was spiked with even more product than Ery used, and he wore a tight navy sweater that brought out the color of his eyes. His plump lips were such a bright pink that Ery would have suspected lipstick, except Helena and Marek had the exact same mouth.

"Okay, got it," Ery said. "No Borises or babushkas. I'm guessing you don't want Lenin grinning from the front of the menus either."

Aleksy laughed, but his cousins made faces. Whether at his attempt at humor or at communism, Ery couldn't tell. Then Helena tucked a strand of hair behind her ear. "We will call our restaurant East by Northwest. We will serve traditional dishes from Poland and nearby countries, but with local ingredients and a bit of a local twist."

"Polish-Northwest fusion. Interesting. Can't say I've ever had that."

"I thought not. The kitchen here isn't ready yet, but I brought a few dishes from home so you could try them. All right?"

He was hungry. "Sure. Sounds great."

While Helena and Marek disappeared into the back, Aleksy scooted his chair a little closer. "Are you from Portland?" he asked.

"Born and raised."

Aleksy pointed toward the kitchen. "Those two have lived here for years. But I just moved from Chicago. I don't have a real sense of the place yet."

"Well, our winter's gonna be a lot warmer than you're used to."

"Good. I like it hot." Aleksy dropped a slow wink. He had dimples. "So I was wondering, what are the good clubs?"

"It depends what you're into," Ery replied, although he had a pretty good idea what this guy wanted. He wished the siblings would hurry back so he could finish his business and get the hell out of there. He wished he didn't have to be polite to Aleksy. He wished…. Well, it didn't matter.

"I'm into a lot of things," said Aleksy. "I really like… going deep."

He was going to double-entendre Ery to death. Ery tried to derail the conversation by admitting the one thing that had horrified him a few years ago. "I'm kind of old for the scene, really. I'm not the best person to ask."

But darling Aleksy with the long eyelashes and the angelic mouth was not in the least put off. "No, that's not true. You look like *exactly* the best person."

Ery was glad to be saved by a loud crash and clatter from near the front door, followed by a barrage of swearing. Aleksy jumped up to investigate. By the time he returned, Helena and Marek were setting the dishes—fragrant steam rising—on the table in front of Ery.

"This is only to give you some ideas," Marek said as he placed cutlery in front of Ery. "Of course the menu will be much more varied."

Ery nodded. "Sure. I wouldn't expect you to make me everything today. So, um, what am I about to eat?"

Helena pointed at a bowl of deep red soup with dumplings. "Borscht. It's pretty typical Polish food, but with a few added greens and parsnips as well as beets. The dumplings are filled with wild-gathered bolete mushrooms."

Ery tried a spoonful. It was sweet and sour and rich. "This is delicious!"

She beamed. "It was our grandmother's recipe. I only changed it a little."

Besides the soup and some terrific rye bread, Ery also got to eat blini with smoked coho salmon and sturgeon caviar, some kind of stew made with sauerkraut and elk kielbasa, and mussels in oil with onions. "In Poland, we would make that with herring," Marek said, pointing at the mussels.

Ery was getting full. He wiped his mouth on a paper napkin. "Well, it's really yummy like this."

They insisted on giving him dessert: some kind of dryish rolled cake with a filbert filling, and pierogi stuffed with blueberries. "I haven't eaten this well in a long, long time," he said honestly. "Once you guys open, I'll definitely be back." Maybe he'd bring his grandmother. He'd bet that she'd like the place a lot.

Marek leaned back in his chair with a satisfied smile. "We will have a liquor license, of course. We'll be serving microbrewed vodkas as well as local wines."

"Can you show me what the dining room will look like?"

While Marek scrolled through a series of images on his iPad, Aleksy pressed close to Ery, ostensibly so he could see too. The siblings didn't look surprised or annoyed with Aleksy's behavior. Probably they were used to it. Ery tried to ignore the other man's proximity and focus instead on the drawings. Already a few vague design ideas were floating through his head. This was a lot more fun than a grocery store logo, mostly because it was unique and a bit of a challenge. After all, East by Northwest might very well be the only place on the planet to serve this particular cuisine. It could start a new trend.

All three of the owners walked Ery to the door. They had to dance around plywood and coils of wire as they went. Once they were out on the sidewalk, Ery shook Helena's hand, then Marek's, and promised to send them some ideas soon. After they went back inside, Ery stuck out his hand for a third time. Aleksy took it and didn't let go.

"It's been a pleasure, Ery," he purred.

"Yeah, me too. Thanks for the meal."

Aleksy waved his hand as if that was irrelevant. "I can get your phone number from Marek. Maybe I'll call sometime soon and you can show me around a little."

"I'm pretty busy. I just got back from vacation and—"

"Come on. I'm sure you can spare one evening. Just a few hours."

He had to admire the guy's persistence. Not so long ago, Ery would have given in at the first lingering eye contact. Aleksy was cute. He was built well too, with nice muscles in his chest and thighs. He had just the tiniest trace of an accent. Ery had never felt one way or the other about accents, but now that he'd spent time with a Scandinavian water spirit—

Who he was *not* going to think about, dammit.

"Maybe," Ery said. He wasn't sure for whose sake he was hedging. He didn't even know whether he wanted to say yes or no.

As it turned out, Aleksy was one of those guys who interpreted *Maybe* to mean *Definitely yes, after you persuade me some more*. He dimpled. "Good. I'll call you soon, then." He finally let go of Ery's hand, but only after one more squeeze.

CHAPTER 13

ERY WORKED hard all week. The nursing manual was really time intensive, plus he was doing research on Poland. He had the calendar to complete too, and for that project, he needed to learn a little more about architecture in general and Dylan's firm specifically. His days zoomed by, and in the evenings he was too tired to do more than veg with his laptop and loll in the bathtub. He stopped by to visit his grandmother one evening, and during lunch he did a lot of aimless walking. But other than that, it was work and Netflix and warm soaks.

And thinking about Karl.

Aleksy called him twice. First he left a message, and the second time Ery picked up the phone. Aleksy invited him out that night, but Ery begged off. Too busy, he said. Which was sort of true.

He wasn't planning to visit the farm that weekend. Although he had some ideas he wanted to get onto canvas soon, he had a lot of work to catch up on. But when he came back to his apartment Friday evening, the first thing he saw was the living room shelf where he'd placed a certain black-and-red rock and a certain nautilus shell. His eyes felt prickly.

So he went online and ordered some canvases to be delivered to the farm. They wouldn't get there for several days, but he had some smaller ones at the studio to work with.

Saturday morning he woke up earlier than usual, threw a few things in a duffel bag, and jogged down to Bea, who waited patiently for him at the curb. "Up for a spin in the country, old girl?" he asked her. She seemed to buzz her approval when he pushed her start button.

It was another glorious autumn day. No storms had come to knock the leaves from the deciduous trees, so roadsides and hills were painted in swaths of reds, oranges, and yellows among the deep greens of the conifers. If Ery hadn't had a definite destination in mind—and if he'd had the necessary supplies in Bea's boot—he would have pulled over to the side of the county road and painted a corny landscape like those on the walls of mediocre motel rooms.

He hadn't told Dylan and Chris he was on the way, and when he arrived, there was no sign of them except for Dylan's truck parked out front. Ery didn't have to check in—his friends had told him long ago that he could drop in whenever he wanted, except for full-moon night. But he figured it would be polite to say hello; besides, they hadn't talked all week. So he parked Bea beside the truck, where she looked ridiculously small, and then jogged up to the porch and rang the bell.

Several moments passed before he heard footsteps thunder down the stairs, and then the door swung open. Chris stood there wearing a pair of rumpled sleep pants—backward, it looked like—and nothing else. His hair was a mess. Judging by the flush that suffused his tanned chest and face, his heavy breathing wasn't due to the exertion of racing to the door.

"You look like someone zapped you straight out of a porn video," Ery said. "A really good one."

Chris grinned. "Yeah? Well, you oughtta see Dyl."

Ery leered. "Can I?"

"No!" came the immediate shout from upstairs.

"My, what good ears you have," Ery said, laughing.

Chris chortled too, and Dylan yelled, "Laugh it up, country boy. See where *that* gets you."

Chris leaned in close to whisper in Ery's ear, "If I'm lucky, it'll get me punished."

Jeez, Ery loved these guys. "Well, I'll let you get back in the saddle, then. Just wanted you to know I'm here."

"Cool. Is it okay if me and Dyl come by later?"

"That'd be great. I want to hear about your trip."

Chris nodded. "You spending the night?"

"Yeah, I think so."

"Good. Have dinner with us tonight. Don't worry—I won't let Dyl cook."

"Hey!" Dylan shouted.

"You're gonna get yourself in trouble for sure," Ery said to Chris. "And thanks—that'd be nice."

"Gonna bring Karl?"

Ery flinched slightly. "I don't…. He doesn't eat, you know."

Chris's gaze was razor-sharp. Sometimes he liked to play up the hillbilly act, but in truth he was a smart guy who had an easy time seeing through smokescreens. "Bring him anyway. I ain't never had a nix guest. And he's real pretty to look at." He winked.

An ominous growl rumbled down the stairs.

"I'm in for it now," Chris said, looking pleased.

"Have fun."

Ery grabbed his stuff from Bea and walked to the barn. As he reached the door, he was tempted for a moment to keep on walking. He could just stop at the pond to say hello. Maybe Karl would like to come up to the studio and— No. Ery had come to paint.

And paint he did. First he peeked at his completed work. After a week's absence, he liked it even better than before. He grabbed one of the medium-sized blank canvases and his paints and brushes. This painting wouldn't include Karl or any water. It was his bedroom back in Portland, actually. And yes, he realized the irony of coming out to the farm to depict his city apartment, but a little distance was a good thing in this case. Complete accuracy wasn't his goal—he wanted to paint how his bedroom *felt*.

So there was the bed, done in careful detail. But the colors of the canopy and bedding swirled around the empty mattress like a very bright whirlwind, and the room's other furniture was misshapen, warped, dark. *Nightmare* would be the title of this one. In one corner he painted the muzzle of a gun and the tip of one shiny black boot, both of which might belong to Han Solo. Or not.

He painted so furiously that he was almost done when Chris and Dylan showed up. They were bundled against the chill but shed their coats when they came inside. Dylan held up a bag. "Beer and sandwiches. Want some?"

"Just a sec," said Ery. "Let me just finish this."

His friends didn't seem to mind. While they waited, they looked at his other paintings. When Ery put down his brush, Dylan smiled and pointed at the big canvas. "You've painted Karl to look like a Renaissance-era saint. Like something from Giovanni Bellini." He turned to Chris. "Next time we're going to Venice, okay?"

"Is that in Italy?" asked Chris mockingly. This was obviously part of some long-running in-joke Ery didn't understand. Dylan didn't even bother to glare very strongly.

"Bellini," Dylan repeated. "But the other sea life in the piece is almost more like Matisse. It shouldn't work, but it totally does. And the shell—it's almost three-dimensional. Just pops out. And God, I love the way you have the dim light hitting your subjects."

"Thanks."

While Dylan and Chris laid out lunch, Ery cleaned up a little. He smiled when he joined them and saw the spread on the table. "Just sandwiches and beer, huh?"

Dylan looked fondly at his partner. "Chris has been baking again."

The bread was homemade, and the sandwiches were piled high with thinly sliced roast beef, tomatoes, and some kind of tangy sauce that had a little kick to it. Chris had made potato salad, and the beer was likely Dylan's choice, some microbrew Ery had never heard of.

They exchanged a little small talk over the food, mostly about the European trip. Dylan steadfastly refused to discuss his drunken night of dancing in Le Marais, but he couldn't hide a smile. Chris raved about the big market in Barcelona—La Boqueria—and the motorcycles that clogged the streets. He'd enjoyed living in the center of big cities for a couple of weeks. "But it was real good to get back home," he drawled.

Then Ery remembered something. "Hey, thanks for the work, Dylan."

Dylan frowned. "What work?"

"The calendar."

"Huh?" Dylan furrowed his brow, clearly clueless.

"Your firm hired mine to produce a calendar, and they asked for me specifically. You didn't do that?"

"Nope. This is the first I've heard of it." He shrugged. "Stender liked that painting he bought at the show. He hung it off the side of the mezzanine, right over the reception lobby."

"It's not that great."

"Well, he likes it."

That was some solace, Ery supposed. "Anyway, I've been kicking around some ideas. Could I pick your brain later about some of the firm's recent projects?"

"Sure."

Chris and Dylan sat at the table while Ery cleared the dishes and rinsed them at the sink. He remembered doing this small task with Karl, and he frowned.

Hating himself slightly for doing it but unable to stop, he sat down at the table and asked, "Have you guys talked to Karl this week?" He didn't meet his friends' eyes.

After a brief pause, Chris answered. "Couple times. He's interesting. And what the fuck's going on with you two, Ery? He misses the hell out of you."

Ery groaned and sank his face into his hands. "Dammit. Damn, damn, damn."

Chris gently kicked his foot. "Spill, man. You're doin' this fucking amazing work, but you look like shit."

"Thanks," Ery grumbled into his hands. "Guys, you don't really wanna hear my crap."

To his surprise, it was Dylan who leaned over and put a hand on his shoulder. "Sure we do, Ery. You're our friend." He squeezed lightly. "C'mon. You helped us out when we were haunted. We can at least lend you an ear."

It would feel good to discuss it. Ery sighed and then began to talk. Over a couple of bottles of beer, he told his friends all the details of how he'd met Karl, how'd he'd thought their first kiss was a dream, how they ended up spending days together in the studio and in bed. And how Karl had come close to dying when he spent the night.

"I'm afraid he might have done it on purpose," Ery admitted miserably. "I mean, me, I was too busy getting laid to even think about the consequences to him. But he knew. And maybe he wanted... I don't know."

Dylan looked slightly pained. "God, I wish Kay was here. She'd straighten everything up in about five minutes."

"And make us a pie after," Chris agreed.

Ery smiled at that. Dylan's sister-in-law made truly awesome blackberry pies. "This might be too big a job even for the mighty Kay."

Chris had been slowly peeling the label from his bottle and rolling the paper into little balls, which he arranged in lines on the table. "So what do you want, dude?" he asked.

"I don't know. But whatever it is, I can't have it."

"Because?"

"Because.... Look. I know you're... a little unusual, Dylan. But you guys can make it work. I mean, most of the time you're a pretty normal guy, really. And you can live out here and telecommute. But Karl can't just go tromping around the city, and I can't stay near him."

"You can live in this apartment, Ery," said Dylan, and Chris nodded. "It's fine with us."

"You guys are great. But I can't commute from here to work every day, and I don't have the money to quit. And it's not fair to me *or* Karl if I do this thing half-assed."

"Why not?" Chris asked, crossing his arms over his chest. "I bet he'd be cool with it. And do nixes even give a shit about monogamy and that kind of crap?"

"I don't know."

"Well then, why don't you ask him, dipstick? Here you are, mooning all over the place, and you might not even have a problem. If Karl's all right with it, you can be together here on weekends, and during the week...." He shrugged. "You can do whatever you wanna in the big city."

It was a tempting scenario, but Ery wasn't sure it felt right. The plan was a little like the mediocre paintings he'd been doing until very recently—nothing wrong, exactly, but also nothing to get excited about.

Well, maybe Karl would want nothing to do with him anymore, in which case the problem was solved.

Right.

"I guess Karl and I need to talk," Ery said unhappily. But he wanted to do more painting first. So he promised his friends he'd head to the big house for dinner at seven, possibly with Karl in tow. Then he thanked them for lunch, walked them to the door, and returned to work.

This far into autumn, the sun set early. Ery lost his good light before five o'clock. But that was okay because his painting was finished. He'd never worked so fast before, and it was a little overwhelming. He cleaned up for the second time that day. Then he put on his coat over his paint-splattered jeans and tee, grabbed the flashlight, and headed down the path.

He heard Karl's guitar before he actually saw him. But the strumming stopped when Ery was halfway down the path, and as he reached the pond, Karl was standing with a face-splitting smile. "Ery!" he cried before launching himself into Ery's arms.

Well, that answered the question of whether Karl was completely through with him, at least.

And jeez, it felt so good to hold Karl again. It was like the times Ery got so absorbed in his work that he forgot to eat. He wouldn't even realize how hungry he was until he got a little food in his stomach.

"You came back," Karl said.

"I said I would."

"I know."

"Are you all recovered from… from what happened last weekend?"

Karl nodded against him. "Yes. I'm sorry I worried you."

"You scared the shit out of me! I thought I'd lost you."

Karl pushed Ery slightly away so they could look at one another. "I'm old, Ery. I can think of much worse ways to die than at your side."

Ery shook his head. "You don't have to die at all."

"Maybe it's time to. Didn't you tell me I have a soul? Or… energy, you said. And when I die, I'll be reborn as something else. That wouldn't be so bad."

Not liking the direction of the conversation, Ery pulled him close again. "I'm selfish. I want you right here."

When Karl sighed, Ery didn't know whether it was due to resignation or relief. "I'll stay here for you, Ery."

"Promise me—promise you'll take care of yourself." Because Ery couldn't stand the thought of Karl going for a stroll some weekday and walking until he turned to dust.

"I promise."

Ery didn't feel very assured. But he didn't feel as if he could press for more. He broke the embrace but kept hold of Karl's hand and led him over to the fallen tree where they could sit. "Have you been playing your guitar very much?" he asked.

"All the time. Oh! And Chris and Dylan said they'd build me a little shed to keep it dry. I may be the very first nix in history to possess his own shed."

"Good. But watch out—knowing Dylan, he won't keep it simple. You'll end up with a shed Taj Mahal or something."

Karl hummed happily and leaned against him. Ery shut off the flashlight. The illumination from the waxing moon was just enough to make Karl glow faintly. Karl stroked Ery's arm, which was nice even if Ery could barely feel him through the layers of fabric. "Will you go home tonight?" Karl asked.

"No. Tomorrow night. I'm painting. I was hoping maybe you'd spend tomorrow with me while I work."

"Of course. And... tonight? Can I be with you? I'll take showers often!"

Ery hesitated a moment before answering. He wanted Karl with him tonight, he truly did. But a nagging little voice was telling him that none of this was fair to Karl. He decided to slightly reroute the discussion. "The guys invited us for dinner tonight. Want to go?"

In the darkness, Karl's gasp seemed especially loud. "In the house?"

"Yeah, of course."

"I've never been in there. I've never been *in* anywhere except the barn. But I'd like to see. Are you certain it's all right?"

"They invited you specifically."

Still sitting, Karl managed to bounce a little. "Good! Are there rules?"

"What do you mean?"

"When you're a guest in someone's house—are there rules? When one of my people visits a place where another nix is living, he must ask permission to enter. And there are things he must and mustn't do." He sighed. "I wasn't often allowed to stay, once they realized I was odd."

Nix etiquette wasn't a subject Ery had previously considered. He patted Karl's knee. "Don't worry. Dyl's pretty laid-back, and Chris is hardly Emily Post." He remembered the story his friends had told him of the first time they'd seen each other. Dylan looking out an upstairs window at Chris, pants-free, peeing off his deck next door. "They'll be tolerant of any mistakes."

"But you'll tell me if I do anything terrible."

"Refrain from homicide or indoor rainstorms and you'll do just fine."

They sat on the log for a long time after that, mostly chatting about Ery's week. Ery thought his life was pretty boring, but Karl liked to hear the details about mundane things like buses and electric bills. He was interested in Ery's job too. In exchange, he told a couple of amusing short tales from his days in the harbor when he eavesdropped on sailors.

When Ery checked the time, it was nearly seven. "Ready to go?" he asked as he stood.

"Can I bring my guitar to the barn?"

"Sure." The barn was on the way anyway.

But when they were in the studio, Karl detoured for a quick peek at the newest painting. "Oh! Is this a real place, Ery?"

"More or less. It's my bedroom."

"I should have guessed from all the colors. How come you're not in it, though?"

The last self-portrait Ery had done was when he was forced to, back in school. "I'm not as nice to look at as you are."

Karl rolled his eyes. "You're wonderful to look at, and you know it."

"I'm just an ordinary guy, Karl."

"You're really not."

Karl seemed nervous and excited as they walked to the house. He held on tight to Ery's hand. As they stepped onto the porch, Ery realized belatedly that his companion was naked except for the necklace. Well, he hoped that didn't violate any dress codes.

Chris smiled widely when he opened the door. "Hey, guys. C'mon in."

"It smells good in here," Ery commented as they entered. He was looking forward to the meal—he'd learned months earlier that Chris was an exceptionally good cook.

But Karl was looking around the foyer, wide-eyed. It wasn't a very remarkable entryway. Chris and Dylan's remodeling energies hadn't taken them this far yet, so the wood floor needed refinishing and the dingy and scuffed green walls needed a coat of fresh paint. But to Karl the place seemed a wonder.

"Hey, Chris? I bet Karl would like a tour. He's never been in the house before."

Chris raised his eyebrows. "All these years and you ain't never been inside? Not even when it was empty?"

"No," said Karl.

"Then lemme show you around." He yelled up the stairs. "Hey, Fido—you decent? 'Cause we're comin' up." He turned to grin at Ery and Karl. "Or, y'know, we could all do clothing optional. Dyl would have a cow."

Still chuckling, he led them up the stairs.

Dylan was dressed, and he greeted them happily. He didn't seem fazed by Karl's nudity. Then he took over the tour, explaining everything in so much detail that Chris almost eye-rolled himself to death. Karl was fascinated by everything, though. He loved the bed in the master bedroom. It was a king, much bigger than the full in the barn apartment. But when he saw the enormous bathtub and Dylan explained what it was, Karl came very close to swooning. "It's like having a tiny pond inside a house!" he exclaimed as he turned the faucet on and off. Ery wondered what he'd think about whirlpool jets.

They eventually worked their way downstairs. Chris and Dylan had gotten rid of the original dining room during the remodeling, incorporating that space into the impressive eat-in kitchen. Karl sat at the table politely, sipping from a glass of water, but Ery could tell he wanted to examine the countertop appliances. And there were a lot of them.

It was a nice meal. The chicken and veggies were delicious, and Dylan and Chris were good company. Ery loved how easily they accepted Karl's eccentricities.

After dinner Karl insisted on helping Dylan wash the dishes. Ery sat at the table with Chris, nursing a beer, enjoying the view of Karl's ass. Chris seemed to be enjoying a similar view, only his gaze focused on the back of Dylan's jeans. "I never figured how good it would be to settle down," Chris said. "'Cause it's *damn* good."

Ery made a sour face. "For some people."

Chris shrugged. "Guess so. You know, Dyl's a big hotshot at his job. He's in magazines. Me, I'm just a handyman. But I wouldn't give up this life to be king of America."

Dylan looked over his shoulder to give Chris a smile.

"So love trumps professional success?" Ery asked.

"It's all about what makes a guy happy—and makes the people he loves happy too."

Ery appreciated the advice; he just didn't know what to do with it. He wasn't sure what made him happy. "I'm glad for you guys, I really am. I know it wasn't easy for either of you to get here, but it's so great you made it."

"We're a work in progress," Dylan offered from the sink. "I guess everyone is. Like Rick and Kay? They've been married almost ten years, but they had to revamp everything now that the baby's here."

"My grandma says when you stop changing and adjusting, your energy starts dimming. You might as well die, I guess." And then he added, "Karl's been around a long time, but he's still… in flux. In a good way."

It was Karl's turn to twist around with a smile. "Like the dreams. And the guitar."

"Exactly."

142

They lingered in the living room for a while afterward. One of Ery's paintings hung over the fireplace; Karl noticed it at once. He liked the books too. He couldn't read, but he enjoyed leafing through the illustrated books on architecture and home improvement. His favorite, though, was a book on the Impressionists.

"I've been dragging that one around since college," Dylan said to him. "Do you want it?"

"Really?"

"Sure."

Karl clutched the big volume to his chest for a moment before replacing it on the shelf. "Thank you. But it would get ruined now. Can I have it after the shed is built?"

"Of course."

Just a few weeks earlier, Karl had seemingly been content to submerge possessions in his pond, even knowing they'd be ruined. Like the duck painting. Ery wasn't sure what to make of his new concern over keeping things dry. Maybe it didn't mean anything.

It was a good evening, but Ery began to worry about Karl being away from water too long. "I think it's time to hit the hay," he said, stretching. "Gotta get up early to paint."

Chris and Dylan walked them to the door, where Karl and Ery thanked them for dinner. Dylan smiled at Karl. "Ery already knows he's welcome anytime, but so are you, okay? Anytime but the night of the full moon."

Karl nodded. "Thank you. I've seen you as a wolf, you know. You swim across my pond."

Dylan frowned. "Is that a problem?"

"No! You're a beautiful wolf."

"Thanks," Dylan said, ducking his head.

Ery was a little jealous. *He* never got to see Dylan go furry. But he said his good-nights pleasantly, and he and Karl held hands as they returned to the barn. It was hard for Ery to see in the dark, so Karl played guide dog.

"That was fun," Karl said. "I didn't do anything wrong."

"You make a great dinner guest. Better than most of my human friends. Even my grandma would be impressed."

"I'd like to meet her."

Ery didn't answer because that was never going to happen. Not that his grandmother would disapprove—she'd probably find Karl delightful. But she wasn't about to drive out to the farm and then tromp down to the pond.

In the barn apartment, Karl took a long shower while Ery sat on the closed toilet so they could chat. And so he could watch, because Karl with streams of water sheeting down his body was a beautiful sight. If the stall had been big enough for them both, Ery would have stripped and joined him, using his fingers to trace the path of the water over pale, smooth skin. Maybe using his tongue as well.

Karl caught him drooling. "I'm almost done," he said with a laugh.

"Hmm." Ery's jeans were uncomfortably tight. He should have taken them off before the shower. And then they *really* became too tight because Karl grinned and began to stroke his own cock.

The garbled noise that tumbled from Ery's throat didn't resemble human language. *This* was something he wanted to paint: an exquisitely handsome man leaning back against a shower wall, his white hair hanging very straight, his green eyes alive with lust and humor, his legs slightly spread so he could better fondle his hardening cock. Maybe sometimes there was a fine line between art and pornography, but if painting was ever meant to capture beauty and strong emotions, Karl in the shower made a very suitable subject.

Ery fumbled at his jeans button. He had to stand to peel his clothing off, and because he didn't want to remove his gaze from Karl for even a second, the undressing was less graceful than usual. He kept his shirt on. Then he sat back down and watched Karl's grin widen when Ery began to stroke himself.

"I dreamed about you this week," Karl said. His voice was a low purr, barely audible over the sound of the shower.

Ery swallowed. "Good dreams?"

"I didn't need Skuld's help. I like this kind of dream very much. But the real thing is better."

It was weird how hot mutual masturbation was. To feel his own familiar hand on his dick but to watch Karl mirroring his motions, to realize they were stroking and breathing to the same rhythm, to hear a moan and not be sure who'd made it—all of these things made Ery a little dizzy. Add to that the slight feeling of naughtiness he got over doing a private action under someone else's gaze—and watching Karl do the same—and Ery got worked up very fast.

Karl did too. His eyes had gone slightly glassy, and he slid down the wall until he was sitting on the shower floor with his legs spread and knees bent. But when he slowly inserted a single finger into his pink little hole, Ery had to close his eyes.

"Are you wet enough yet?" he squeaked.

"Yeah."

Ery stood on unsteady legs. He leaned in to turn off the water and then gave Karl a hand up. But they didn't make it to the bed, because Ery attempted to towel Karl dry, until the rubbing got to be too much for them both. They collapsed to the floor and rutted against each other, their bodies sprawled halfway out of the bathroom. Their actions had no finesse, no slow sensuality. This was all about raging, urgent need. Wet skin slid against dry until they were both damp. Karl pushed impatiently at Ery's T-shirt, which ended up bunched around his neck, still caught on one arm. The floor was cold and so was Karl, but they warmed under Ery's body. Legs tangled with legs, and Karl and Ery kissed so hard that Karl's teeth bit slightly into Ery's lip, adding the salty, coppery taste of blood. Karl's hair wound around both of them. Hands crept across bodies like starfish on the ocean floor. And when Ery climaxed with a rush of heat and Karl followed almost immediately after, the world was a goddamn perfect place, even if only for those moments.

CHAPTER 14

KARL SLEPT in Ery's bed again. But this time when Ery woke up, Karl was propped on an elbow, smiling, not the least bit dried out. Ery had a vague memory of him getting up once or twice in the middle of the night, and each time Ery had fallen asleep to the sound of the shower.

"Good morning," Karl said cheerfully.

"Very good."

"Could be even better." And Karl ducked beneath the blankets.

Oh God, Ery thought as suction surrounded his morning wood. *Much, much better.*

Later, after they'd each showered and Ery had some breakfast, they settled in the studio. Ery painted and Karl played, just like before, and it felt right. They spoke a little, but even when they weren't talking, the atmosphere in the room was companionable. It reminded Ery of Sunday mornings during his boyhood, when his parents sat at the kitchen table in their pajamas, drinking tea and reading the Sunday paper. His mother always did the crossword, sometimes asking his father for help with a clue or two. His father liked to read the want ads, dreaming about cars he'd never own and houses he didn't really want to buy. Ery sat there too, eating cereal and looking at the comics, and the entire world felt warm and comfortable and safe.

Eventually the sun set and Ery had to put away his paints and brushes. "I have to head back to town," he said. "Work starts early."

Karl tucked his guitar into the case. "All right." He flashed a smile. "This was a good weekend."

"It was."

"I saw the way you watch Dylan and Chris. You wish you had what they do."

"No," Ery said defensively. Then he sighed. "A little, maybe."

Nodding and carrying the guitar case, Karl walked closer. "I understand. And I told you—you deserve it. Can... can I suggest something?"

"What?" asked Ery, a little warily.

"Keep coming here on weekends to paint. And be with me. But during the week, you can look for your... your partner."

"You think I should have it both ways, huh?"

Karl shrugged. "I think I'm selfish and I don't want to give you up until I have to. But I also want you to find what you need."

Ery reached up to touch Karl's face but then let his hand drop. "It sounds so reasonable, doesn't it? Logical. But it's not fair to you."

"It's fair. Ery, I am stroemkarlen. I know the truth more than you do: for a creature like me, things flow. The bright colors wash away and the shining metal rusts. So I enjoy while I can, and later I have the memories."

"Does it make you happy?" Ery asked, remembering Chris's words.

"It's my nature."

Which wasn't exactly an answer, but Ery didn't push it. They kissed, he promised to return on Saturday, and Karl returned to the pond.

OVER THE rest of November, the skies were gray and rain fell, but not enough. All the pundits were still talking drought. Ery barely noticed. He was too busy with work during the week and his paintings and Karl on weekends. He was glad when his parents flew in for Thanksgiving weekend. They all had a big dinner at his grandmother's house, with his dad's homemade cranberry sauce and his mom's apple pie. But although he tried to be polite and attentive, his family remarked a few times on how tired and distracted he seemed. He left before dark so he could spend the long weekend at the farm.

Aleksy called once more, and again Ery made excuses.

Ery moved from his apartment, to the office, to the apartment, to the farm, to the apartment… and he felt like an automaton or as if he was acting a part in a play. Only his time with Karl felt real, but that was brief. Sometimes Karl asked if Ery had been dating anyone. He didn't seem worried or jealous about it. Either he genuinely wanted Ery to be happy—even if it meant having to share and maybe eventually to give up Ery entirely—or he had recently improved at hiding his feelings.

The weird part was that Ery's work was going exceedingly well. Paintings seemed to flow off his brush as if by magic. His shipment of canvases arrived, and he soon generated a decent collection of finished work, pleased with every piece. His day job went well too. Dylan told him that Stender was uncharacteristically loquacious in his enthusiasm for the calendar. Ery came up with a logo for East by Northwest: the Polish white eagle sitting at a table with a Native American thunderbird. The Kamskis loved it.

On a gloomy Sunday evening in December, Ery kissed Karl good-bye and walked to the big house, where he knocked on the door. Dylan answered with a grin; he had a pen stuck behind one ear. "Working on a Sunday night?" Ery asked.

"That's the problem with telecommuting. No weekends. You want to come in? Chris is watching TV."

"No, I need to head home. I was just wondering if I could get you guys to bring a truckload of my paintings into town this week. I'm gonna set something up with Julio at the gallery."

"Sure. Our schedule's open for the next few days." Dylan smiled. "An upside of the flextime. Maybe we can go out to lunch or dinner after. Chris and I haven't eaten in civilization for a while."

"I'd like that."

Dylan pursed his lips and scratched the back of his neck. "Um…."

"What?"

"We like Karl. He's a nice guy."

Ery nodded.

"He, um…." Dylan looked so uncomfortable, Ery would have laughed had the subject of their conversation been anything but this. "He's really into you," Dylan finally said.

148

"Not like there's a lot of other fish in his sea, Dyl."

"Does that matter?"

"I… I don't know." He wanted to bonk his head against the door. "I don't know," he repeated. "It's so complicated. Why can't I just find a nice, ordinary, *normal* guy?"

Dylan raised his eyebrows slightly and tilted his head.

"Jeez, Dyl, no offense intended. But you're not a water spirit."

"Nope. But seems to me, even ordinary humans come with plenty of complications."

"Maybe. Look, I gotta go. I'll give you a call about the paintings, okay?"

Dylan clapped him on the shoulder. "Take care, Ery."

MONDAY WAS a busy day. Ery called Julio and arranged for him to take a look at the paintings on Wednesday afternoon, then followed up with a call to Dylan. He worked on a few more illustrations for the nursing manual; he was in the bones section. After lunch he had a meeting with the Kamskis to review his final drafts for the menus and website art. The weather was raw, but he bundled up, took the light rail, and walked to the restaurant. When he got there, his cheeks felt numb and his nose was running.

The place was almost ready for its grand opening. He liked the look of the dining room, with lots of weathered cedar painted with the bright motifs of Polish folk art. He knew the food would be served on blue-and-white Polish pottery. An identical blue appeared as lettering in the menus and in the restaurant logo on the front. Interior pages included faint contour drawings of Mount Hood and Douglas firs.

Marek stood behind the bar, frowning over some stapled papers, but he smiled as Ery approached. "Good to see you," he said, coming around to shake Ery's hand.

"The place looks great."

"Thanks. We still have a few details to finish, but we should be ready to open on time." He pulled out a chair at a bare table and motioned to Ery to do the same. "Helena can't make it, I'm afraid. But that's okay. I can make these decisions."

"Sure." Ery placed his messenger bag on the table and pulled out his drawings. He was about to begin explaining them when Aleksy appeared from the kitchen, grinning widely.

"Ery! You're here!" While Marek rolled his eyes good-naturedly, Aleksy hurried over and plopped into the chair beside Ery. Today he wore a white button-down, a closely tailored blazer, and a bright blue scarf that looked very soft. "I like your bag," he said, patting the item in question. It was decorated with glittery pink skulls, which meant it probably wasn't the most professional accessory Ery could own, but he was very fond of it because, well, glittery pink skulls.

"Thanks," said Ery, spreading out his drawings as Aleksy leaned close. Marek seemed very pleased with everything, which was great, but Aleksy was apparently more interested in trying to squish practically onto Ery's lap. Aleksy smelled good—some kind of sandalwood cologne—and he sported an artful bit of stubble.

"So you see," Ery said, trying to soldier on despite the distraction, "you'll be able to change the menu and website design seasonally. Same basic theme, but different touches of color to tie in with the time of year."

"This is very good," Marek said.

Ery smiled. "Do you have any questions? Does this meet your needs?"

"You could meet *my* needs," Aleksy said.

Marek snorted. "This is excellent, Ery. We'll get a few versions of the logo for different purposes?"

"Of course. You'll probably want to go simple on business cards, but with more detail on your menus."

"Perfect. Thanks for your hard work."

Ery stood to shake Marek's hand. "I've enjoyed it. My boss'll be in touch over some of the nitpicky stuff."

Marek rose and nodded. "Anytime you want a table here, just call me. We'll give you a discount."

Aleksy waited for Ery to gather his things, then walked him to the door. "So now that you're through with us, you're less busy, right?"

"I've got a lot of projects lined up. And, uh, other stuff."

Aleksy leaned in close. He was a few inches taller than Ery, probably around six feet. His shoes were shiny and looked expensive. "Come out with me, Ery. Please. I promise I won't bite." He waggled his eyebrows.

He was cute, and dammit, Ery had only so much strength to refuse. "I'm booked all weekend."

"Tomorrow, then."

That was the night before Ery met with Julio. He was going to be really nervous. A distraction might be good. "Fine."

Aleksy beamed as if he'd won the lottery. "Good! Great! I'll drive! Where do you live?"

Uncomfortable with giving out his home address, Ery squirmed. "How about if we just meet somewhere? I have some errands to run."

"Okay. How about JayJay's at ten?"

Well, it certainly hadn't taken Aleksy long to find the clubs. Ery was very familiar with JayJay's. Up until about a year ago, he'd gone there often. "Ten is too late. I have to work the next day."

"Nine, then."

BY EIGHT thirty the next evening, Ery had decided 100 times to call Aleksy and cancel. But he'd decided 101 times to go through with it. He'd already showered, so he pulled on a very tight pair of yellow jeans and an equally tight white T-shirt with a deep V-neck. He wore his black blazer with the cobalt stripes on the sleeves and back. He teased and gelled his hair into gravity-defying spikes and drew on just a trace of eyeliner. When he was younger, he put a lot more effort into what he wore to go out, but he figured this would do for tonight.

He didn't want to hassle with a coat or parking, so he ended up taking a cab. It deposited him in front of JayJay's at just past nine. Even though it was Tuesday, a crowd of people spilled out the door and down the sidewalk, most of them shivering in the cold and smoking cigarettes.

"Ery!" Aleksy came running over in a shiny shirt that showed off his muscles. He hugged Ery and kissed him on the cheek. "Do you want something to eat before we go in?"

"No, I'm good." Ery blew on his hands to warm them. "I could use a drink, though."

Aleksy took Ery's hand and dragged him to the door. There was no cover on a weekday, so they just nodded at the bouncer and headed in. Ery remembered being annoyed when he used to be carded; now he was slightly miffed that he wasn't.

The temperature inside was at least forty degrees warmer than outside, and the scents of booze, cologne, sweat, and sexual tension were strong. Music pounded through the sound system, making Ery wince.

They sat at a wobbly little table near the half-full dance floor. "I'll get you a drink," Aleksy offered. "What'll it be?"

"Um... mojito?"

When Aleksy laughed, Ery wasn't quite sure why. "Sure. Be right back."

While Ery waited, he looked around. The crowd was young, and despite the early hour, people seemed geared up to party. In the center of the dance floor, five shirtless pretty boys ground against each other. So far their pants were on, but Ery was willing to bet they'd strip down to their Andrew Christians pretty soon. One of them wore body glitter, which he'd shed all over his pals, and another had an interesting jungle vine tattoo that swirled the length of his spine before disappearing into his ass crack. A lot of the other customers were watching these boys too, probably deciding which one to swoop in on first. Ery sighed. He'd been like those kids once, lithe and young, desirable and carefree. But he was too old to revel in his twinkdom any longer—too old and too burned-out, maybe.

"You want to dance?" Aleksy asked when he returned with a mojito in each hand.

"Not yet. Drink first."

They clinked glasses and sipped.

Conversation really wasn't the point at JayJay's, and Ery didn't feel like shouting. He and Aleksy sat, ogling the eye candy, slurping their booze, nodding to the music. When the glasses were empty, Aleksy brought refills.

When the second round was gone and Aleksy again tried to lure Ery to the dance floor, Ery agreed. He shucked his blazer first, though; he was already feeling warm.

Ery wasn't the best dancer, but he tended to throw his full energy into it. Aleksy was a little clumsy too, but with those goddamn dimples, who cared? Ery and Aleksy moved well together, spinning and gyrating around the half-naked twinks and the other dancers. And when Aleksy moved behind Ery and held him close, rubbing up against Ery's ass and kneading Ery's chest, that was all right. As they danced, Aleksy kissed and sucked on Ery's neck, and it was obvious as he thrust his hips that he was hard. So was Ery. Ery didn't complain when Aleksy squeezed a hand down the front of Ery's jeans and briefs so he could massage Ery's dick.

"God, you're sexy," Aleksy breathed into his ear.

"Mmm," Ery responded. Aleksy had big hands with long fingers. His body felt very solid behind Ery's. It felt good.

By then, just as Ery had predicted, the twinks had shed their pants. One of them was dancing nearby with a somewhat older guy in a pink polo shirt. The twink's hair was bleached almost white, and either his underwear was very flattering or he was really well hung. He watched Aleksy groping Ery, licked his lips, and dropped a friendly wink at Ery.

Ery knew how the night would go. A few more drinks, some more dancing. A cab ride to his place or Aleksy's. As soon as they arrived wherever, clothes would come off. The night would end with Aleksy fucking him. And there might be a sleepover, but probably not; Ery had to get up early. They'd kiss as they parted. And they wouldn't likely hook up again. Because even as they danced, Aleksy was flirting with the boys around them, checking them out without even trying to hide his interest. Ery didn't blame him. He'd done the same himself, back in the days when the only thing more important than getting laid was getting laid *next*.

The lingering taste of mint and lime was bitter in the back of his throat.

After gently pulling Aleksy's hand out of his jeans, Ery walked to the table and grabbed his blazer. Aleksy followed close behind, out into the cold night air. "My flat's not far," Aleksy said. "We can walk from here."

Ery shook his head. "I'm gonna head home."

Aleksy frowned. "I'm sorry, Ery. Did I do something wrong?"

Jeez. Ery moved close enough to set a hand on Aleksy's forearm. They were both shivering slightly. "No, you're great. I'm the asshole here."

"Why?"

Ery had probably sighed more in the past few months than he had over the previous thirty years. "I'm not in a good headspace right now. There's… kind of this guy, and… and I'm basically all screwed up."

To Aleksy's enormous credit, he looked disappointed but not angry. "I pushed you too much. I'm sorry for that."

"No, it's okay. I mean, usually you wouldn't have had to push at all. You're really hot, Aleksy. It's just that the timing sucks."

Aleksy nodded. "I get it."

"Really, I'm grateful to you. Tonight's helped me… decide a couple things."

"Like what?"

"Like… I think I want a thing with someone. A long-term monogamous thing."

Grinning, Aleksy shuddered. "Then I'm really sorry, because I'm not the settling-down type."

"I kinda guessed that," Ery said with an answering smile. He wrapped his arms around himself, which didn't cut the chill very much. "I've got a few friends I can hook you up with, if you want. They're cute, and they're more about the fun than the commitment. Want me to give them your number?"

"Thanks. I'd like that. I bet they're not as cute as you, though."

Gamely, Ery batted his eyelashes. "Nobody's as cute as me, honey."

They kissed—almost chastely. Aleksy went back into JayJay's, and Ery set off in search of a cab.

CHAPTER 15

"I FUCKIN' hate driving in the city," Chris grumbled. The three men were crowded into the cab of Dylan's truck, Chris at the wheel and Ery squashed against the passenger door. Chris glared at the road as if the other drivers were there solely to torment him.

Ery didn't care about the traffic because his stomach was too busy trying to turn inside out. He knew his paintings were good. Karl admired them. Chris and Dylan admired them. But that didn't mean Julio wouldn't hate them. God, maybe he should have waited a few more weeks. Maybe he should have given it up entirely and stuck to catheters and grocery store leaf logos. Maybe he should have slept with Aleksy the night before, quit his job, and spent the rest of his life flitting from bed to bed.

"I can hear you worryin'," Chris said as he tailgated a poky little Fiat. "You worry even louder than Dyl. You know, handymen never get all choked up like this. I don't chew my fingernails and wail, *Oh no, what if the client doesn't like the way I fixed her broken hinges? Woe is me!*"

Dylan bonked him. "Leave him alone. It's stressful."

"Bullshit. Look here, Ery. Gonna tell you the same thing I tell Dyl every time he gets his panties in a twist. You do great work. You're a fuckin' genius. And if some kinda art snob can't see that? Well, screw him. Just means he's a moron."

"Thanks," Ery said. And he did feel better with his friends' support, even if they were pretty much obligated to be in his corner. "It's just that Portland might be a small pond, art-wise, but Julio's the biggest fish here." He immediately wished he hadn't used that particular metaphor. Goody—trading one source of nausea-inducing anxiety for another. Way to go, Ery Phillips.

Dylan must have looked up the gallery address ahead of time, because he quietly directed Chris to the former warehouse at the edge of the Pearl District. If the navigation had been left to Ery, he might have sent them all to Idaho. But no, here they were, sitting in silence in front of Stumptown Gallery. Ery took a deep breath and opened the truck door.

Julio and his partner had kept the industrial feel of the building, leaving the brickwork and pipes exposed. White walls with strategically placed lighting gave plenty of space for hanging works, but the polished concrete floor also allowed big open places for large sculptures. Julio noticed Ery and Dylan as soon as they walked in. Chris had remained leaning against the truck, smoking a cigarette and cultivating his country bumpkin persona.

"Ery Phillips!" Julio exclaimed as if the visit were a surprise. He was a tall thin man, like a Giacometti statue come to life. He always wore expensive suits with colorful silk ties, and he kept his slightly graying hair slicked back from his face. He grabbed Ery's shoulders and air-kissed both his cheeks, and then settled his gaze on Dylan.

"Julio Delgado, this is my friend Dylan Warner."

Julio shook Dylan's hand and, thankfully, didn't try to kiss him. Dylan tended to quietly freak out at that kind of casual affection. But although Julio had been with his partner for years, he gave Dylan a very obvious lascivious assessment. Most gay men—and even some who thought they were straight—did the same. Dylan was an eyeful for sure.

"So? You have something new for me?" Julio rubbed his long, skinny fingers together.

"I do. You just want us to drag the canvases in here?"

"Please. But if you'll excuse me, I have a call to make. I'll be back shortly."

So while the busty and heavily tattooed receptionist looked on with interest, Ery, Dylan, and Chris brought the paintings inside. They propped them against the nearest wall, which made for a less than elegant presentation, but it would have to do.

The gallery owner reappeared just as they were setting down the final piece—the big one of Karl and the shell. Julio was still jabbering on his phone, but when he caught sight of the paintings, he stopped in midsentence. "I'm sorry," he said to whomever was on the other end of the line. "I'll have to call you back later. Ciao."

He didn't so much walk across the gallery as swoop like a ship in full sail. He surprised Ery by heading first to the painting of the bedroom. Julio moved along to the next one, which depicted Karl stroking himself in the shower. "Madre de Dios!" Julio exclaimed, his palm pressed to his chest. He continued to work his way through the paintings, exclaiming softly to himself as he went. When he reached the last one, he reversed course and examined them again.

Finally he turned to Ery. "What happened to you, my friend?"

"I was inspired."

Julio glanced at Karl jacking off. "I can see why." He shook his head. "These are wonderful. I could sell them all today with only a few phone calls."

Ery's heart sped. "Really?"

"Of course. But that's not the best course for you now, is it? No, people need to *see* these." He whipped out his phone and mumbled to himself as he poked the screen. Then he looked over at Ery. "January 19. It's very short notice, but we can manage."

"Um… what's January 19?"

"Your show, of course. Ravi will begin working on the invitations and social media at once. We'll get the word out to the press. I have a few friends at the magazines…. Perhaps I can persuade Priscilla to come up from LA if I send her a few preview photos."

But Ery's head was spinning and he felt three steps behind. "Show?"

Poking at his phone again, Julio spun around and rushed to his receptionist, then began chattering rapidly at her in Spanish. Ery might have swayed a little on his feet, but luckily Dylan steadied him with a hand to his arm. "Show?" Ery squeaked at him pitifully.

"I think he wants to host a one-man show of your work," Dylan explained gently. "Soon."

"But... but... I didn't...." Ery's best hope had been that Julio would like the paintings and agree to hang some of them in his gallery. The possibility of a solo exhibit hadn't even entered Ery's mind.

Chris had been stalking the room, frowning at the art that wasn't Ery's. Now he came close. "Dude, you hit a home run. You can calm down now."

But Ery could not calm down. When Julio returned a few minutes later and nattered on about dates and guests and agents and... and God knew what, Ery lost track of the conversation completely. He nodded a lot and hoped Dylan and Chris were noting some of the details for him.

Eventually, with Julio cackling like an evil witch, they carried the paintings to a large storage area in the back. Ery was relieved that he wouldn't have to engage in the artist's walk of shame, pitifully dragging away the rejected canvases. Julio shook everyone's hand, then kissed everyone for good measure, making Dylan squirm. Chris thought it was hysterical, though, and was still laughing as they piled back into the truck.

"Do you want an early dinner?" Dylan asked Ery.

Ery blinked at him. His head was still buzzing. "Yes. Dinner."

Clearly his friends realized that asking him where he wanted to eat was a lost cause. Dylan quietly navigated, and they ended up at a Spanish restaurant not far from Dylan's office. "I used to come here for lunch," he explained. "Haven't been in a while, but Matty mentioned it not too long ago. She says the food's still good."

Maybe it was. Ery didn't taste a thing, not even the three sangrias he guzzled. He didn't register much of the conversation either, although he occasionally managed a nod or a grunt in response to a question. He perked up enough to insist on paying the check. It was the least he could do to repay Dylan and Chris for their help.

It was still early when they finished dinner, and somehow the three of them ended up at a bar. It was definitely not JayJay's but instead a laid-back neighborhood brewpub. Ery had a pint of whatever Chris brought him, and he sat in the padded booth, still feeling stunned.

"Are you all right, man?" Chris asked for probably the tenth time.

"Just... a little verklempt, I guess," Ery replied. "I never expected...."

"You didn't think Julio would like your stuff? 'Cause Ery, we *told* you it was great."

"I know. It just seems real now."

Dylan nodded. "I know what you mean. But, um, are you going to come to the farm this weekend and paint?"

"Why?"

Chris and Dylan exchanged glances, and eventually Dylan answered. "Karl. He really looks forward to seeing you."

The anxiety over Julio had allowed Ery to push thoughts of Karl aside for the day, but now they came rushing back. Suddenly he felt ill. He squeezed his eyes closed. "Shit. I gotta call Grandma and tell her how it went. I...." He scooted out of the booth and stood. "I'm gonna walk home." It was less than a mile, and he didn't want to ruin his friends' time out. He knew they didn't make it into the city that often, and there weren't any places closer to the farm for them to hang out.

"Don't be stupid," Chris said with a frown. "We'll drive you."

Ery shook his head. "No. I need the exercise. Maybe it'll clear my head." And before they could argue, he leaned down and kissed Dylan's cheek, then grabbed Chris so he could kiss him too. "Thanks, you guys. You're the best."

He fled into the night.

ERY'S GRANDMOTHER sat across the table from him, poking at her pasta with a fork. "You don't look as happy as I would have anticipated," she said, her voice raised slightly over the din of the lunchtime crowd.

He'd had only a bite or two of his salad. "I *am* happy," he insisted. "Just sort of in shock, I guess."

She looked skeptical but didn't press the subject. She hadn't asked about Karl at all, although there wasn't a chance in hell she'd forgotten about the water spirit. "Well, I hope you intend to invite me to the show."

That brought a smile, at least. "Are you kidding? I'd refuse to do the show if you weren't there."

"It's been some time since I attended a gallery show. What does one wear to such an event nowadays?"

"Grandma, you always look fabulous. You could show up in your nightgown and slippers and still be the most beautiful woman there."

"You're ridiculous. Now, I know your parents would love to attend, but I don't know if they can make it on such short notice."

He thought of the painting of Karl in the shower and his cheeks burned. He could maybe handle his grandmother looking at that while he was nearby, but his mother? No way. "I understand. We can send them photos. I'll Facebook it for Mom."

"Good. She'll want to brag about you to all her friends, I'm sure. And your father… he won't say much, but you know he'll be nearly bursting with pride."

"I know."

"He's so much like your grandfather in that way. Always very logical. As if logic precludes emotion! I'm glad you're freer with your feelings, darling."

He wasn't sure whether that was intended as a chide over his reticence about Karl, so he simply gave her a small smile and speared a forkful of spinach and radicchio. He continued to peck at his food while he and his grandmother discussed a few details of the upcoming show: guest list, advertising, and so on. He told her of his plan to ask Julio whether East by Northwest could cater the event. People would love those blini.

After the meal was cleared, while he sipped an espresso and his grandmother drank decaf, she began to rummage through her purse. He expected her to come up with a packet of tissues or maybe some of the pills she had to take, but instead she pulled out a small cloth bag and a white envelope with his name on it. "Open that first," she said, pointing at the bag.

"It's not even close to my birthday, Grandma."

"I am aware of that. This is something else. I'd intended to give it to you anyway, but now we can consider it a celebratory gift."

He liked gifts. He took the bag and upended it gently onto the table. He almost gasped when he saw what tumbled out: the cloisonné gull he'd always loved so much. "Grandma?" he squeaked.

"Don't look like that, dear. As far as I know, I am not going to die anytime soon."

He relaxed with a whoosh of air and picked up the bird. "But why?"

"I've been going through my things. A good bit of them I plan to give away, and there are some items I'd like you and your parents to look over. One of you might want them. But I knew you'd want the seagull." She smiled fondly at him.

"If you're not dying, why are you getting rid of stuff?"

She pointed at the envelope. "Open this and you'll see why."

He tore into the envelope carefully. All that was inside was a check. Made out to him, and for a sum that literally made him choke. His grandmother waited while he drank some water and caught his breath.

"What... what the *hell*, Grandma?" He didn't usually swear around her. But the check was made out for half a million frigging dollars. He drank more water and tried not to hyperventilate.

"I sold my house, Ery." When he gaped wordlessly, she went on. "It's too big for me, and frankly, keeping up with it had become just too much. I'm moving into one of those assisted living places in Beaverton. It's a very nice place. I'll have my own apartment, of course, but they have all kinds of activities and excursions. I won't need to rely on you to do so much for me."

"I *like* doing things for you."

"I know." She patted his hand. "We can still have our little outings. But you have your own life to live, dear."

"But... but... your house...." Jeez. Now he was struggling not to cry.

She must have known that, because she dug in her purse again, and this time she produced a tissue. She handed it to him. "I love that house, and I know you do too. But it's not your style. Besides, I found some very good buyers." She grinned wickedly.

"Who?"

"Your parents! They've already sold their place in Minneapolis, and they'll be moving back in March."

He digested that information for a moment. He knew his folks had been talking about the move, but he had no clue they'd already made a decision. He was glad they would be living close again. And to know he'd still be able to visit his grandmother's house—well, that was comforting. "But why give me the money, Grandma?"

"I didn't give you all of it. My word, I had no idea what real estate values had climbed to! If your grandfather only knew.... Well, I've saved quite a bit for my own use. But I don't need that much."

"But Mom and Dad—"

"Your parents can easily afford it, especially now that they have the profits from their Minneapolis house. And your mother says they're much better off if they continue to pay a mortgage—for tax purposes, I suppose." Ery's mother was a CPA.

Ery looked down at the check as if it might grow fangs and bite him. Since he'd never imagined having this kind of ready money, he had never dreamed of ways to spend it.

As usual, his grandmother picked up on his feelings right away. She tucked the check back into the envelope and slid it across the table to him. "Ery, this isn't just money I'm giving you."

"Uh... no?"

"It's something much more valuable—something I am so very pleased to offer you. I'm giving you a choice, dear."

He shook his head. "I don't get it."

"With this much in your bank account, you can now be ruled much less by *have to* and much more by *want to*. Invest it for when you retire. Buy a house. Quit your job and live off your savings while you paint full-time. Take yourself on a wild spree across the globe. Follow your dreams, dear."

"I'm not... I'm not even sure anymore what my dreams are." He blew his nose into the tissue.

"Then the money can sit there and collect interest while you decide."

She looked so calm and sure of herself. Ery was positive that even if he lived to be three hundred years old, he'd never gain that level of serenity. And he sure as hell wasn't anywhere near it right now. "I don't know what to say," he murmured.

"You say, 'Thank you, Grandma.' Then you give it some thought and make a good, grown-up decision."

He looked over at her and gave a watery smile. "Thank you, Grandma."

HE COULD probably be excused for being a wee bit distracted on Friday morning. Not only had the entire week been filled with emotional bombshells, but his neighbors were up late the night before, blasting polka music at full volume, and Myra assigned a bunch of ad illustrations for a yoga place. Also, the guy who worked at the next desk over—a beefy-looking blond who looked like he'd be more at home on a football field than in front of a drafting table—was eating something stinky.

Ery turned his head to glare at Jason. "What *is* that?"

Jason held the paper bowl in the air. "Soup."

"What's in it?"

"Dunno. Garlic, this fish stuff…. My girlfriend made it. It's really good. Want some? I got a thermos full."

Complaining about food that someone's beloved had prepared was a bad idea. "No. Thanks."

"She says it's supposed to keep you from getting sick."

Yeah, probably because nobody would want to get close enough to share their germs. "That's thoughtful of her."

Jason beamed. "Yeah, she's really great. You sure you don't want any?"

Ery was still trying to craft a polite refusal when he was saved by his ringing cell phone. He gave Jason an apologetic shrug, then slid off his stool to head to the closetlike room where Myra made them have their non-work-related phone conversations.

"Hello?" The number was from New York. He didn't know anyone in New York.

"Is this Ery Phillips?" The woman on the other end had a crisp, businesslike voice. Ery's stomach contracted, as it often did with mystery calls. What if it was someone telling him his parents had died—in New York, oddly, instead of Minnesota? What if it was a lawyer wanting to sue him for something? Or the IRS questioning those paints he'd written off on his tax returns?

"Yes?" he answered cautiously. He'd reached the closet, so he ducked inside, shut the door, and sat on the padded chair that constituted the only furnishing.

"My name is Amanda Watanabe. I am the director of the Lonetree Foundation in Brooklyn."

The name was familiar, and after a moment, he remembered why. Lonetree ran a truly fabulous artist-in-residence program. He'd applied for it several years ago—he'd even included letters of support from Julio and a couple of his professors—but he wasn't chosen. He hadn't even been disappointed, because he knew it was such a slim chance. "Are you asking for a donation?" he said, thinking of the check he hadn't even deposited yet. He could certainly afford to give to charity now, but he wanted to think for a while before committing.

But Ms. Watanabe was laughing. "No, that's not what I have in mind. Although we always welcome gifts, of course."

He felt silly. Why would the Lonetree director call *him* to ask for money? "Oh," he said.

"Mr. Phillips, I'm calling because yesterday I had a long conversation with Julio Delgado. He told me he'll be hosting a show of your paintings very soon."

"Uh, yeah. Later this month."

"He's impressed with your work. He sent me some photos, and frankly, I'm impressed as well. Very." She put a lot of emphasis on that word. "I think your work is groundbreaking. Visionary."

Wow. "Uh… thank you." *Dazzling response, Airhead.*

"Mr. Phillips, I understand that you applied for our residency program some time ago."

"That was… five or six years, I think."

"Yes. We still have your application. And in light of what Mr. Delgado has shown me, we'd like to offer the residency position to you, beginning as soon as possible."

He needed to sit down. Jeez, he *was* sitting down. He needed to *lie* down, but there wasn't enough room in the closet.

"Soon?" he squeaked. He wasn't entirely sure he was making sense.

"As you know, our mission is to promote and support extraordinary creativity. The residency is a two-year program, although we have extended it on occasion. We will provide you with an apartment and a small stipend, and of course you'll have full access to our studio here in Brooklyn. It's a wonderful space. Your obligations will be minimal—just talking to an occasional visitor and participating in some shows."

"Shows," he echoed. He was turning into a goddamn parrot.

"Just two or three," she said. "You'd need to contribute only a few pieces."

"I... I... I...." He closed his eyes, which didn't help a bit.

"I'm sure you'd like a little time to think about it. I'll e-mail you the details. But we'll be needing an answer by the end of next week."

With an enormous effort, he managed to connect his tongue to his brain. "Thank you, Ms. Watanabe. This is a real honor. I'm... well, I'm kind of shocked."

She laughed again. "I understand. Judging by your recent pieces, Mr. Phillips, you should expect quite a few of these kinds of shocks in the near future."

Somehow he managed to thank her again, give her his e-mail address, and promise he'd get back to her soon. Then he spent a very long time sitting in the closet, staring at the blank screen of his phone.

CHAPTER 16

ERY WASN'T sure how long he spent in the closet. At one point someone knocked on the door, but he told them to go away and they did. It was quiet in his refuge—so much so that he could hear his heart beating and lungs working, and when he shifted even slightly on the chair, his jeans made a loud scraping sound.

He didn't consciously decide to get up, but at some point there he was, with his legs under him and his hand reaching for the doorknob. Jason stared as Ery walked by, but didn't say anything. He'd finished his smelly soup.

Ery sat at his table, where he'd been in the middle of a sketch for the yoga place, and picked up his pencil.

It had been Myra's day to choose the office music, which meant a station that played hits from the seventies and eighties. When Ery stood, clutching his drawing, A-ha was crooning "Take on Me." Ery had a vague impression that the band was from Sweden—or one of those countries. He wondered if they knew about stroemkarl.

Myra smiled as Ery approached her desk. "Got something to show me?" she asked brightly.

Wordlessly, he handed her the paper.

She took a quick glance and her eyes widened. "Ha-ha, Ery. Very funny." She gave it back to him, and he looked at it too, as if he'd never seen it before. There was a leotard-clad lady in a yoga pose who was about to become very good friends with an improbably large leaf-green penis with a catheter hanging from its tip. The catheter bag was balanced on the lady's upraised foot.

Ery set the drawing on Myra's desk. "I quit," he said.

"But…. What's wrong, Ery?"

"Nothing. I just… I just can't do this anymore. I'm sorry." As she gaped at him, he spun around, marched back to his table, and gathered his things. He didn't have much, really. Just his laptop and messenger bag, some favorite pens, and a mug depicting two multicolored tropical birds perched on a tree branch. Ery put on his coat. "Bye, Jason," he said. Then he walked out the door.

He didn't feel free and light as he dumped his stuff into Bea and drove away. He wasn't sure *what* he felt—but then, he'd experienced a lot of that lately. This week in spades. Maybe by now he felt nothing at all. He'd probably used up his month's allotment of emotion around the time his grandmother handed him that check.

Although it was early afternoon when he got home, his neighbors were blasting polka. Accordions were instruments of the devil. He was glad he hadn't bought one for Karl.

Karl. That was exactly the direction he didn't want his thoughts to flow. And when he sat on the couch and his gaze caught on the rock and the shell, that was against his will too. "Stop being chickenshit," he said. He scooped the cloisonné bird off the shelf—he'd set it next to the shell the day before—stuffed it in his coat pocket, and tromped down the stairs to the ground floor.

He imagined Bea was surprised to see him again so quickly. "Time for a spin in the country," he told her as he climbed behind the wheel. But first he had to get to the country, and traffic was heavy. He sat there numbly, rolling slowly forward, not hearing whatever was on the radio. He almost missed his exit.

When he arrived at the farm, Dylan's truck wasn't there. Of course, one of the guys might still be home, but Ery didn't knock on the door. He didn't stop when he walked by the barn either.

He didn't see Karl when he got down to the pond. Ery sat in one of the wooden patio chairs that Dylan and Chris had brought down several weeks earlier. He liked to think of his friends hanging out near the pond, having neighborly chats with Karl. In addition to that, though, they'd also built him a little storage shed. As predicted, Dylan

167

hadn't been satisfied to merely slap a few boards together. Instead he'd created a miniature Swedish fishing hut with board-and-batten siding painted a rusty orange. The little structure cantilevered over the edge of the pond and had a small deck as well. Karl had proudly told Ery that he'd helped build the shed. Later, though, Chris had privately confided to Ery that there was a reason there were very few nixes in the construction industry.

For just a few minutes, Ery enjoyed the peace and quiet of the pond. The ducks were there, quacking softly, and a few brown leaves floated lazily on the water's surface. The pine woods on the other side looked especially dark and dense today. Ery could well imagine Bigfoot, unicorns, werewolves, and all sorts of mythical creatures passing under the evergreen boughs.

Finally he took a deep breath. "Karl?" he said. He didn't shout; he knew Karl would hear him. And sure enough, within seconds Karl appeared out of the water. He was as beautiful as ever—a vision come to life—and he smiled brightly. He splashed a little as he hurried over, but even when Ery stood up, Karl paused just out of arm's reach.

"I'll get you wet," Karl said.

"My coat's waterproof."

That was good enough for Karl, and he launched himself against Ery in a tight embrace. "Is it Saturday already?" Karl asked against Ery's cheek. "I thought it was Friday, but sometimes I lose track."

"No, it's Friday."

"How did it go at the gallery? He loved your paintings, didn't he? Of course he did."

The meeting with Julio had been so many events ago, Ery had practically forgotten his anxiety over it. "It went well. He's giving me a show later this month. I think his favorite was the one of you in the shower."

Karl laughed. "I think you enjoyed painting that one the most." He glanced toward the shed. "Would you like me to get my guitar?"

"I'm not here to paint."

"Oh." Karl moved away slightly. "Are you here for something else?"

All those feelings Ery thought he had used up came rushing in at once—well, the bad ones, anyway. He was glad he'd eaten very little, because otherwise he would have been sick. As it was, his face burned and his mouth was drought-dry. "I have to go," he said.

Karl grinned slightly. "But you just got here."

"No. I mean… go away. From… from Oregon." He couldn't look Karl in the eyes. Just couldn't. "I've been offered this thing in Brooklyn. It's for two years and it's a really big deal. Very prestigious. They'll pay all my expenses while I paint full-time, and I'll get to meet all these important people."

"Is Brooklyn far from here?"

"It's in New York. On the other side of the continent."

Karl nodded gravely. "Is there much water there?"

For a moment Ery allowed himself a mental image of Karl swimming around in the East River or Jamaica Bay, eagerly waiting for Ery to take breaks in his painting and gallery-hopping and schmoozing. But he pushed that image away so violently that he grunted with the pain of it. "You can't go, Karl. This is your home."

"I've moved before, and for less reason."

"But not in a long time. And you love it here—we both know that. Besides, New York—there are millions of people, and a lot of noise. The water's full of both traffic and filth and… and it's no place for you. I'm sorry."

Karl pushed his hair behind his ear, then settled a hand on Ery's shoulder. "Going there is important to you."

"It's the chance of a lifetime. Plenty of artists would sell their grandmothers on the black market for this opportunity."

To Ery's surprise, Karl smiled at him. It was a sad smile, to be sure, but a genuine one. "I knew this time would come. I'd hoped it wouldn't be so soon."

"Karl, I—"

"I'm grateful to you for coming to say good-bye. Henry…. Henry just stopped visiting. That was hard. I waited for him for a long time."

Oh jeez. Ery searched his coat pockets in hope of finding a tissue. There weren't any, but he dug out a paper napkin, which would have to do. He was a douche bag who deserved to have his nose and eyes rubbed by scratchy paper. "I'm so sorry, Karl. If there was some way…. But it was never going to work out between us."

"Because I'm not a real man."

Ery dropped the napkin and grabbed both of Karl's arms. "Don't! You're as real as anybody I've ever met. Realer. It just won't…. It can't…. God, it's too complicated! I had an epiphany this week. No, I had, like, ten epiphanies. But one of them is I can't do casual anymore."

"I didn't think we were casual," Karl said softly. He shouldn't be saying anything softly, Ery thought. Karl *should* be yelling and screaming and calling him an asshole.

"We weren't. We really weren't, and that's a big part of the problem, cross-country moves aside."

Karl looked puzzled, and Ery had to resist the urge to smooth away the resulting line between his brows. "I don't understand," Karl said.

It was time. "I'm falling for you, Karl. Really hard. I've never fallen before, not once. I was kinda wondering if I knew how to love someone like this. I guess I do."

A tear trickled from the corner of Karl's eye and down his cheek, where it mingled with the dampness from the pond. But he was smiling. "I'm so glad to hear that. I can love too, you know. I do. I love you."

"God, Karl." Ery choked back a sob. He was not going to lose it. He was a grown-up. He shook his head. "If we were just… just fucking around, it wouldn't be so bad. We could have fun. But we have… really different lifestyles." He laughed slightly hysterically. "And I'll get old and wrinkled and you'll stay beautiful and—"

"You will *always* be beautiful." Karl stroked Ery's cheek. His finger must have gathered some moisture, because he licked his fingertip. "I don't care about wrinkles."

Ery was willing to give Karl the benefit of the doubt—maybe he wasn't as shallow as most humans. But a true relationship between them was still impossible. He shook his head miserably.

"I think I understand," Karl said after a few moments. "I've been thinking about this, actually. You need to paint the way I need to swim. These are our natures."

Ery nodded. That was it exactly. "I wish it wasn't mine. I wish I was a… a plumber! And I wish you wouldn't be so goddamn understanding about this. It's making me feel even worse."

The corners of Karl's mouth twitched. "You want me to yell?"

"Please."

"You don't deserve it, Ery. You've always been honest with me. You've given me… so much." He waggled his eyebrows in a very Chris-like fashion. "I can spank you, though, if you want."

Laughing and crying at the same time sucked. This all sucked. Ery felt like someone had taken a Brillo Pad to his heart. "You are the most amazing person I've ever met. Will ever meet." He stuck his hand in his pocket, hoping for another napkin but instead encountering the gull. He pulled it out and held it toward Karl. "Here."

Karl took it and turned it over in his hands. "It's the same as your tattoo."

"It's just a bird," Ery explained. "It was my grandma's. I remember playing with it when I was really tiny. See all the colors? All the intricate little lines? I think this bird is what made me want to draw. I was, like, wow! Maybe someday I can make something pretty too. So it's special to me."

"And you want me to have it?"

"I really do."

Karl let out a noisy breath. "Thank you. It will be special to me too." He stroked the gull's back as gently if had been an actual newly hatched chick. Then he looked up at Ery. "Can we make love once more? Please?"

"I… I don't think that's a good idea."

"Well, I think it's a wonderful idea. Don't worry. I understand— after this you're gone. But I'd like just one more chance to feel you and taste you."

It was a terrible idea, actually. But Ery wanted it too. "Yes," he said. It was the most foolish decision he'd made all week yet the one that made him happiest. It made Karl happy too. He sprinted over to his shed, yanked the door open, and carefully set the bird inside. Then he slammed the door and ran back to Ery.

They held hands as they ran up to the barn. They weren't giddy— the event was too solemn for that—but a little of the pain inside Ery lifted as he bumped shoulders with Karl.

The barn apartment was cold; he didn't leave the heater on when he was gone. So he flipped the switch and listened to the fan blow while Karl stood close behind him, nuzzling his neck. Even as Ery's body began to warm, the lips on his skin made him shiver.

It was clear that Karl wanted to undress Ery, pushing Ery's hands away if he tried to do it himself. So Ery indulged him, holding out his arms so Karl could slip off his coat and his purple plaid flannel shirt, then waiting as Karl pulled off his green T-shirt too. Over the past weeks, Karl had become a pro at buttons and zippers, so he didn't struggle with the jeans, and Ery balanced himself on Karl's shoulder as Karl took off his shoes, socks, pants, and briefs.

By the time he was nude, Ery was already hard. So was Karl. They spent a while standing face-to-face, carefully tracing each other's bodies with their fingers as if this were the first time and everything was new. They both knew the opposite was true—this was the *last* time. But it was still wonderful to explore, to feel smooth skin over taut muscles, to stroke the solidity of Karl's cock and the sweet fullness of his balls.

"Bed," Ery said hoarsely when his knees became a little wobbly.

He'd made the bed the previous Sunday before he headed back to Portland, but he hadn't bothered to change the bedding. So when he and Karl tumbled into it, the sheets already smelled like sex, like them—which made Ery's pulse pound a little harder and made Karl groan against Ery's shoulder. "Do you think Dylan and Chris will let me visit here when you're gone?" Karl asked.

"Of course."

"Good. This barn has good memories." He looked into Ery's eyes. "In the water, nothing ever stays. Memories float away. But here… I think a little of your spirit will always be here."

Ery smiled. "Like Uncle Frank's ghost?"

Karl had heard the story of the farm's haunting, so he knew what Ery was talking about. "Better than a ghost. You... you buzz in here." He patted his own chest, right over his heart. "You're much too alive to be a ghost."

To prove how alive he was, Ery kissed him, long and hard. He might kiss someone else in the future—probably would—but he'd always miss Karl's salty-rich taste, the extraordinary softness of his lips. Oh, and Karl's nipples, stiff and pink and delectable—he'd miss those too, along with the muscular ridges of his hairless chest, the little divot of his navel, the slightly sharp points of his hips. And God, his lovely cock, with the turgid veins, the seawater taste of the droplets escaping its tip, the foreskin Ery so liked to play with. Ery licked, stroked, and suckled until Karl was nearly wild beneath him, tossing his head from side to side and swearing in foreign languages.

But then Karl pushed him gently away. "Not too soon, Ery. Not yet. I want to be inside you."

Oh God, yes. They'd experimented with a variety of positions over the weeks. They liked them all. Sometimes Ery nearly lost himself in bliss when he sank into Karl's tight and welcoming body, and when he did, endearments and pleas tumbled from Karl's lips. But they both had a favorite arrangement: Ery on his side, Karl behind him, in him, caressing Ery's cock while he thrust with torturous, delicious slowness. At times Karl would lick at Ery's skin while they fucked. Once he bit Ery's shoulder hard enough to leave teeth marks. Afterward, when he realized what he'd done, Karl had been embarrassed and appalled. But Ery had touched the sharp edge of Karl's teeth and told him—quite honestly—how good it had been.

Now, Ery slithered up Karl's body, dropping random kisses as he went. When he reached Karl's face, he grinned wickedly. "Will you loosen me a little, baby?" Then he turned around and straddled Karl's torso, presenting his ass to his lover.

Karl actually chortled. He tugged at Ery's hips, moving him up the bed until Karl could bend forward and lick at the crease between Ery's cheeks. When Karl slipped his tongue into the ring of tight muscle, slicking everything up, Ery had to struggle to remain still. The tongue was good. Really good. But he wanted more.

After a moment or two of fumbling with the bottle of lube, Karl gave him more: a long, thick finger that moved within Ery just right. Karl had long since learned exactly the right angle to drive Ery crazy, and he didn't hesitate to use that knowledge now, probing and twisting until Ery was panting with need.

Ery pulled himself out of reach and looked over his shoulder. "Not too soon, remember?"

But it wasn't too soon, not anymore. Although Ery could stay longer—could spend the night, the week, could remain in the barn with Karl until it was time for the gallery show—he knew he shouldn't. His body could wait no longer, and his heart couldn't bear more delays.

He flipped around again, positioned himself and Karl just right, and sank down over Karl's cock. When Karl was fully engulfed, when the curves of Ery's ass settled in the cradle of Karl's hips, they froze, just looking at each other. They were like a painting, a single moment of shape, color, and emotion captured out of time. If Ery could *be* an artwork, this was the one he'd want to be.

But living flesh—be it human or stroemkarlen—was not a painting. Karl raised his hands to stroke Ery's chest and flick his nipples, to tug gently on the hair on his pecs, belly, and groin. And when he wrapped his hand around Ery's cock and began to pump, Ery could no longer keep still. He flexed his thighs, moving slowly up and down, feeling the way his body took Karl in like a gift, hating the brief feeling of emptiness when they were almost detached.

Oh jeez, and the look on Karl's face! Green eyes open wide as if in amazement, full lips slightly parted. Even if he lived as long as a nix, Ery could go the rest of his days knowing exactly what love looked like, because that was what he saw right now. He fervently hoped Karl saw the same in him.

Ery's thighs started to burn a little as he sped his movements, but he was well past caring. Someone could set fire to his feet and he'd barely notice for the heat in his belly, the energy that sparked and crackled everywhere Karl connected with him.

"Älskling," Karl whispered. "My Ery. My beloved." He closed his eyes and arched up with his hips as much as Ery's weight would permit, and he opened his throat for a long, ragged cry.

Ery's climax came soon after, rushing through his body like a tempest. Only after he collapsed and laid his cheek on Karl's shoulder did he realize he was crying again.

They remained together in bed for a time, kissing and cuddling. Standing up—separating himself physically from Karl—was the hardest act Ery had ever performed. But he pulled on his clothes and walked with Karl to the door of the barn.

Night had fallen while they were making love, but Ery didn't need the light to know what Karl looked like. He'd memorized him weeks before. Karl cradled Ery's face in his hands for a bittersweet last kiss. They leaned their foreheads together.

"Karl? Promise me you'll take care of yourself." Ery flashed to a memory of Karl dried up and dying. "Promise you won't... you won't stay out of the water too long."

"I won't. Promise me you'll open your heart to love when you get... wherever you're going."

"Okay."

"Fly away, Ery," Karl rasped. "Fly well."

They turned and walked in separate directions.

Up at the main house, warm light spilled from windows and bathed the porch. Dylan's truck was parked in the gravel nearby. But Ery didn't have it in him to talk to his friends, so he got into Bea, turned on the engine, and pulled away.

He was nearly to the county road when the windshield began to be pelted by raindrops.

CHAPTER 17

ERY HATED social media.

With less than a week before his first solo show, he was supposed to be breathlessly tweeting and tumblring and facebooking everyone he knew, and everyone *they* knew, telling them how awesome and cool and astounding his exhibition would be. He didn't want to. What he wanted to do was curl up on his couch in his overly bright living room and wallow in his self-imposed misery. No, first he wanted to go next door and shove the neighbors' speakers up their asses. It was really hard to be in an appropriately despondent frame of mind to the tunes of Harold Loeffelmacher and the Six Fat Dutchmen.

Reluctantly, Ery did his social-media best. He pimped the show to the entire population of the Pacific Northwest. When friends asked him how he felt about the exhibit, he e-mailed them back with a studied mix of excitement, pride, hipness, and humility, and he told them he hoped they could come. He *did* hope they could come. It would be awfully shitty if he and Julio spent the night talking to nobody but Ery's grandmother.

When he wasn't online, Ery was looking around his apartment, wondering what would go to New York with him and what would stay packed in boxes in the basement of his grandmother's house. Or now, the basement of his parents' new house. Aside from his clothing, laptop, and a couple of favorite books, the only items he knew he must take with him were a smooth black-and-red stone and a gleaming nautilus shell.

He sat on his couch, trying to get his Schubert and Shostakovich to drown out the goddamn accordions. He'd made decisions just like a grown-up was supposed to. And they'd been *good* decisions, leading him places he'd dreamed of since he was a kid scribbling on notebook paper. So why did it hurt so fucking much?

He hadn't said much to his grandmother over the past number of days. He didn't want sympathy or advice, and he certainly didn't want her warm, discerning gaze.

When Ery's phone rang, he almost ignored it. But he glanced at the screen and saw it was Dylan, and then a fresh wave of guilt flooded in to join the existing toxic emotional cocktail.

"Hey," Ery said when he answered.

Dylan grunted back.

Then they both sat there, listening to silence on the other end of the line. Silence, that was, until Chris growled something in the background, took the phone from Dylan, and said to Ery, "For Christ's sake, if you start clamming up too, I know the end of the goddamn world is nigh."

"Hi, Chris."

"Hi yourself. What the *fuck*, Ery?"

Ery had a pretty good inkling what Chris was asking about, but pretended ignorance. "What?"

"What did you do to your nix?"

"He's not my nix."

Chris snorted. "Well. Your not-nix has been sending us buckets of rain for days. Rest of the state's still talkin' drought, and we got so much water here I'm ready to build a fucking ark."

Shit. "I'm sorry, Chris. I am. But Karl and I, we can't... we can't see each other anymore. He's gonna have to work through this. I'll pay for any damage to your property." He didn't mention that if he were a water spirit, things would be pretty damp in Southeast Portland too.

This time, Chris sighed and swore under his breath. "There's no damage. We got a good roof. And even if there was damage, we wouldn't care. It's Karl, Ery. He's brought so much rain his pond's

177

flooded. That shed? It's most of the way underwater. His guitar's wrecked and probably whatever else he had in there."

A sharp new pain bloomed in Ery's heart. "His guitar?"

"Yeah. We offered to buy him a new one, maybe keep it in the barn 'til things dry out, but he says no. Says he doesn't want to play no more."

"I don't know how to deal with this. I sure as hell didn't want to hurt him."

After a pause, Chris asked in a quiet voice, "Hurt yourself too, didn't you? You got yourself in pretty deep with him."

"I love him."

There. The truth. He wasn't falling in love—he'd already fallen. Not that it mattered.

"Why don't you come out to the farm and we can—"

"No. I can't."

"Then—" Chris was interrupted by some rustling noises.

Dylan spoke next, and his tone was oddly firm. "Here's what we're going to do, Ery. About five miles west of our road, as you're driving down the highway, you'll see a sign for Hawkins Canyon Road. Turn south there. Go about three and a half miles and you'll see my truck parked off to the side. We'll meet you there."

"But—"

"You need to do this, Ery."

Ery didn't even know what *this* was. "I don't want to talk to Karl. It'll only prolong the pain."

"He won't be there. Just Chris and me."

Dylan and Chris had done so much for him, Ery couldn't in good conscience refuse. "Fine. I'll leave in a few."

"See you there," Dylan said before hanging up.

AS SIMPLE as Dylan's driving directions were, almost as soon as Ery turned off the highway, he started to wonder if he was lost. Only steep, thickly wooded hillsides appeared in the beams of his headlights. "Buck up, Bea," he said, patting the dashboard. "We can't be *that* far from civilization." Still, he was relieved when he finally spied Dylan's Silverado pulled off on the shoulder. Ery parked behind it.

The night was clear, with more stars than he was used to seeing. But when he got out of his car, he could smell rain. He wondered about the radius of Karl's depression storm and how long it would take before someone noticed the weather anomaly. If Karl ever needed cash, maybe he could rent himself out. He could park himself somewhere that needed precipitation and get himself emotionally worked up.

"Not funny," Ery growled at himself. And it wasn't. The knowledge that Karl was so upset over the breakup was killing Ery. The last thing Karl needed was more sorrow.

Dylan and Chris weren't standing near the truck, but Ery could see a light shining among the trees, and he heard low voices. He followed a narrow pine-needled path toward the light, and there were his friends, standing in a small clearing. They'd set up a few of those oversize flashlights and pointed the beams toward the center, like a weird stage. Karl wasn't there, which was a big relief and a small disappointment.

"Hi," Dylan said. He looked uncharacteristically jittery, chewing on his lip and messing up his hair with his hand. Chris was missing his usual easy smile.

"What's up, guys?" Ery asked. "I'm not about to be the victim of a satanic ritual, am I?"

"Not quite," Chris muttered.

Well, that was reassuring. Mostly.

Dylan crossed his arms over his chest. "We want to talk to you."

"And we couldn't talk somewhere where there's... less nature?"

"No."

Ery sighed noisily. "I'm really glad you guys are worried about Karl. It's great he has such good friends. I don't think he's ever had friends before. And I promise, you can tell him as many awful things about me as you want. This whole mess is totally my fault."

Dylan had begun to pace while Ery monologued. He didn't say anything in response, but Chris walked a few steps closer to Ery. "Look, man. Dylan kicks ass at his job. He could be a fucking superstar if he wanted. You should see some of the offers he's gotten from New York, LA, London… all over the place. The amount of money some of those guys are willin' to pay, you'd think Dylan was the goddamn Second Coming. But he tells 'em all no, and he sticks around here in this backwater. Wanna know why?"

"Because he's a werewolf."

"That's not it," Dylan said quietly. He still paced. "With the kind of salary I've been offered, I could easily afford to go somewhere isolated once a month. I stay here because I love Chris."

Now Ery saw the point of this discussion, if not the location. "But Chris could go anywhere with you."

Chris shook his head. "No, man. I couldn't. I don't mind headin' into Portland every now and then. Even had a good time in Europe. But I'm a bona fide redneck. Put me in a city full-time and I'd go nuts within weeks. I'd shrivel up and die, just like a nix out of water."

Dylan came closer. He was taller than Ery, and in the dark, with the flashlights throwing odd shadows, he was almost a little scary. His voice was soft, though. "I used to think that what I wanted most in the world was success in my career. I wanted to be a hotshot. But Ery, I'd be much happier as a nobody out in the sticks with Chris than I would be as Frank Gehry without him." He stood very close to Chris, and Ery swore he could almost see the energy that flowed between them, the pulsing and vital force of their love.

"I get it, guys. But I'm not you. And Karl…."

"Karl's not human," Dylan said.

Wincing, Ery said, "Yeah. And he's not-human 24/7. I'm…. Jeez. I'm not stupid or mean or wimpy or anything, but I don't know if I can handle that. I don't even know if I can handle a committed relationship with a homo sapiens!"

"You know my track record," Chris said. "Before Dylan, I didn't even have one-night stands. They were more like… fifteen-minute kneels. Most of the time."

"But by the time you found out what Dylan is, you already loved him."

"Yeah, but it just about ended us when I found out. It wasn't easy, Ery. Sometimes it *still* ain't easy." He gave a crooked grin. "I'm not the easiest guy to live with either. But we make it work."

"*You* make it work," Ery said.

Chris turned his head to look at Dylan. They communicated silently for a moment in that irritating way of theirs, until finally Dylan nodded once. "You sure, Dyl?" Chris asked.

"Yeah."

"Okay. Your call, I guess." Chris turned to Ery. "Stand back against that tree. Don't move suddenly."

As Ery frowned in puzzlement, Dylan added, "And whatever you do, *don't* do anything that could be interpreted as threatening to Chris. Not even as a joke." Then he unzipped his coat.

"Oh! Holy shit!" Ery scrambled backward until he bumped into the tree. A little shower of bark and needles fell on his head and shoulders. "But you said we couldn't do this. You said it was too dangerous."

"I can… control myself pretty well," said Dylan.

Chris nodded. "And Dyl thinks this is the only way to get the message into your stubborn goddamn head."

"Oh." Ery was nearly speechless with excitement and surprise. And his fluttering pulse certainly didn't slow down when Dylan pulled his shirts over his head and dropped them onto his coat. God, he was gorgeous. Yeah, he was taken, and Ery would never ever try to nail him, but that didn't mean Ery couldn't look.

Dylan shivered in the cold air and gave Ery a serious look. "I'll warn you—the change hurts. But it's not a bad pain."

For some reason, Chris snorted.

Then Dylan kicked off his shoes—he wasn't wearing socks—and pulled down his pants. He'd been going commando, which Ery wouldn't have expected of him. But then maybe he'd dressed knowing he'd just be stripping again soon. And if Dylan shirtless was beautiful, Dylan completely naked was enough to make Ery's mouth go dry.

He might have made a noise, because Chris shot him an unhappy look. "Get your jollies now, dude, 'cause this ain't gonna happen again."

Ery blushed. "I'm sorry. It's just…. He's…."

"I know." Chris winced and adjusted his jeans. "Jesus, I know."

Dylan seemed to be ignoring them entirely. His head was tilted up so he was staring at the sky, and even from the vantage point of the tree, Ery saw Dylan's jaw muscles working. Dylan's hands kept closing into fists and then splaying open.

Nearly whispering, Ery said, "But it's not a full moon."

Chris whispered back. "He can do it whenever, if he tries hard enough. He did when that pack attacked, remember?"

"Oh, yeah." Ery had forgotten that particular point. He needed to pay closer attention to the details of supernatural creatures' skills and features. Maybe he could buy a manual.

Dylan's skin twitched as if he had a really bad itch. He made a sound, a low noise somewhere between a groan and a growl that sounded more animal than human. His bones began to change shape, and that was awful, because Ery could hear the crunch of twisting muscle and tendon. The pain must be excruciating. But even as fur sprouted like grass on a lawn, and as claws and fangs grew, Dylan's cock filled until it looked red and achingly erect.

"Told you," Chris said very quietly. "He *likes* this kinda pain."

Ery could only nod dumbly. He glanced at Chris and saw that even he looked awestruck, despite having watched this transformation many times before. Not counting close encounters with a water spirit, it was the single most astonishing and spellbinding thing Ery had ever witnessed.

Dylan dropped to all fours. His face elongated into a muzzle and a tail unfurled from the base of his spine. He blinked a few times; when he finally opened his eyes fully, the irises were yellow. His ears migrated to the top of his head and became pointed and furry. His nose and lips darkened to black. As he threw back his head and howled, there was nothing human left of him at all.

"Holy fuck," Ery rasped.

"Yeah. Pretty much."

The wolf—Dylan—stretched the way a dog does after a good nap, with his front legs stuck out in front of him. Then he shook briskly. It was a little difficult to tell in this light, but his fur looked a little lighter on the sides than Dylan's hair. His back was tipped in darker fur and his belly was almost white. His legs were long, his body solid. Ery had no idea how Dylan's size compared to a normal wolf's, but he sure looked awfully big, standing there so close.

Then Dylan swung his head and looked straight at Ery.

Ery's heart stuttered in his chest. A keen intelligence showed in those eyes, and maybe just the tiniest hint of... something that reminded Ery of Dylan the man. A familiar energy, maybe. But they were a wolf's eyes, and the animal in front of him was the most dangerous creature he had ever seen.

"I need to paint him."

Chris shot him a surprised look. "Really?"

"God, yes." Ery already itched to pick up a brush, to try to capture that exquisite blend of wildness and astuteness, of confident calm and potential for ferocity.

Dylan trotted over. He went to Chris first and banged the side of his head so hard against Chris's hip that Chris staggered back a half step. But it was clearly a friendly gesture—a loving one, even—because Chris chuckled slightly and scratched behind Dylan's ears.

But then the wolf turned his attention to Ery. He stalked over, slightly stiff-legged, until he stood very close. Ery was terrified. He tried to remember how you were supposed to deal with potentially hostile dogs, and he hoped the same routine worked with wolves. He carefully avoided making eye contact. He held out a hand in a loose fist, palm down.

After sniffing Ery's hand for a moment—and, Ery was thankful to note, deciding not to eat it—Dylan apparently decided he needed a closer encounter. He thrust his pointed nose right into Ery's crotch.

"Uh...," Ery said.

Chris, watching with amusement in his eyes, shrugged. "Least he ain't tryin' to stick it up your ass."

That was a comfort, Ery supposed.

After a couple of healthy inhalations, Dylan moved back slightly and sneezed. Ery hoped that wasn't an insult. Then Dylan gave him another long, thoughtful look before trotting back to Chris.

Chris tugged gently at the fur of Dylan's ruff. "Yeah, Dyl. Have fun."

Dylan responded with a very short bark before leaping away into the darkness. Ery could hear the sound of the wolf's footsteps for a few seconds, and then he was gone.

With a whoosh of breath, Ery slumped back against the tree. "Jeez."

Chris walked over to Dylan's discarded clothes and began to gather them. "You wanna grab the flashlights?"

"But… Dylan."

"He can see just fine without 'em. Anyway, he's long gone. He can run like a sonofabitch, even in deep woods." He bent and picked up Dylan's shoes. "He'll show up at home later. After he's had a bite to eat."

Ery gathered the lights. He aimed the beams in front of them, illuminating their way back to the road. He watched as Chris tossed Dylan's clothing into the passenger side of the truck's cab. Then Ery handed him the lights, and they stood together between the truck and Bea.

"Do you see what we're tryin' to tell you?" Chris asked. "He's Dylan, right? He comparison shops for cheaper car insurance and last week he ordered a panini press online. But he's also that wolf. All the time, you know? Not just during full moons. He's got that inside him *all the time*." He shrugged. "And I still love him so goddamn much I couldn't live without him. You get it?"

After a moment Ery nodded. "I think I do."

"I know Karl ain't a werewolf. And you ain't Dylan or me. But shit, man. When you're lyin' there on your deathbed, what're you gonna regret more—lost career opportunities or lost love?" Chris sighed. "I'm gonna go home and wait for him. Night, Ery." He walked around to the driver's side of the Silverado, climbed inside, and drove away.

CHAPTER 18

THIS TIME Ery did not wear a boring suit, nor did he skulk. He did, however, agonize for ages before deciding on an outfit: his skinniest blue jeans, a tight white tank top with a V neck, his blue-and-black blazer, and a yellow cotton scarf with white polka dots. He'd had his hair done the day before, so he now sported an electric blue streak and a small fortune's worth of product. His hair was defying gravity. He looked pretty good, he thought. Which was a slight comfort, since he felt like he'd thrown his guts into a blender.

When Ery arrived at Stumptown Gallery, Julio and his partner, Ravi, were there to greet him with enthusiastic hugs, multiple cheek-kissings, and multilingual cooing. "I am so excited to share my discovery with the world!" Julio exclaimed, as if he'd unearthed Ery in some isolated cave.

Helena Kamski was at the gallery too, helping her staff set up. She offered Ery some blini and a few teeny-tiny elk kielbasa, but the mere thought of eating nearly sent him running for the bathroom. "I'm sure it's all wonderful, though," he said honestly.

He clutched a wineglass full of water and hovered near the storeroom door to watch as Julio, Ravi, and their employees did some last-minute fussing over the décor. He thought they'd done a fantastic job hanging his paintings. They'd arranged the lights in a manner that highlighted and flattered the works without being glaring or overwhelming. Ery also liked the way in which they'd ordered the paintings. If you walked the room in the proper direction, the exhibit felt almost like a story whose plot was just out of reach.

Julio straightened some lilies in a plain white vase, then approached Ery. "It's not your execution today, my friend. I assure you, I have shared your work with others, and you are already a success."

"Thanks. I just… I've been doing a lot of emotional bungee jumping lately."

"No more jumping for you. Now the world is your oyster." He patted Ery's shoulder and walked away. Ery wished Julio hadn't used an aquatic-themed metaphor.

Ery's grandmother was the first guest to arrive. He had offered to drive her, but she refused. "Edna can drive me, darling. You'll want to arrive early and stay late, and I imagine you'll be celebrating after. I'm not sure how long my energy will last." She looked very elegant in a dove gray suit with pink blouse and pearls, and she'd obviously had her hair freshly done—although hers was a more natural color than Ery's. Edna greeted Ery and then walked away, clearly wishing to give the other two a little private time together.

"Can I get you something to eat, Grandma? The food's great."

"Not yet, dear. I'd like to look around first."

"By yourself or with company?"

She smiled at him. "With the most handsome, talented grandson in the world at my side, of course."

As soon as she got close to the first painting—the one of Karl emerging from the pond—her hand flew to her throat. "Oh my!" She bent forward to peer closely, then took a step back for a wider view. After a long moment, she turned to Ery. "This is extraordinary work, dear. And I am not saying that as a doting relative. You know how good it is, don't you?"

"Yeah. I do."

She glanced around the room, her gaze catching briefly on the several other paintings that featured Karl. She smiled slightly over the one in the shower but lingered the longest on the big one with the shell. Then she looked gravely back at Ery. "Your nix, I take it?"

"He's not mine."

"He's beautiful."

"He is. But his... his *self*? His spirit? It's even more beautiful than the packaging."

She reached up to cup his cheek. "Oh, darling. You love him very much."

"I don't... I can't...."

"Don't deny it. Your love is clear in every brush stroke. And if he really looks at you like that"—she waved at a painting of Karl sitting on his cushions on the studio floor, strumming his guitar and looking up at the viewer—"then I believe he loves you too."

"Grandma...."

"It's the price of adulthood." She shook her head. "Sometimes even the best decisions come with difficult consequences." She tugged his head down so she could kiss his cheek. "Enough. You have more guests to greet. I'm going to tear Edna away from that painting of your nix in the shower before she has a stroke."

She was right about the guests. They came first in a slow trickle, then a steady stream. Ery hugged his friends and former coworkers and shook hands with people he'd never met before. He grinned when Drew and Travis walked in the door. Travis was pulling at the collar of his dress shirt. "He made me wear this," he grouched, jerking his thumb at his smirking partner. "Even though he knows I'm a blue-collar kinda guy." Travis had been the machinist at a futon factory for a while now.

"Well," Ery said, "you look great. You both do. And thanks for coming. I really appreciate it."

"Wouldn't miss it for the world. Besides, Drew tells me there's probably free food and booze." Travis smiled and adjusted the patch over his missing eye, while Drew shook his head in mock exasperation at his partner's lack of sophistication.

Ery pointed. "Over in the corner there. Jeez, I wish I'd thought to ask Julio to hire you, Drew. Some live music would be nice." Something or other was playing over the sound system, but Ery was too worked up to recognize it.

Drew waved his hand dismissively before gesturing around the room. "It's okay," Travis translated. "He'd rather just enjoy the show anyway. And holy crap, that model is hot!" He'd caught sight of the nearest Karl painting.

Drew somehow managed to agree with Travis's assessment while also looking slightly jealous, and Ery laughed. "Have a good time, guys."

He met a bunch of new people and fielded questions about his background, his inspiration, his influences. He tried to look simultaneously confident and humble and brilliant. The praise was wonderful—really, could people gushing over your work ever get old?—but he felt a little giddy and disconnected.

His former boss, Myra, was there with her much younger girlfriend and with no apparent hard feelings over his slightly dramatic exit from employment. Dylan's boss was there too, wearing a black blazer over his omnipresent black turtleneck and black jeans. He'd already viewed several of the paintings by the time he caught up with Ery. "Amazing work. Groundbreaking. I think there must be something magical about that farm—it seems to inspire great creativity."

Ery imagined that his answering smile probably looked slightly demented. "Yeah, it's a unique place, all right."

A few minutes later, as Ery was saying good-bye to an acquaintance from art school, someone tapped his shoulder. He turned around to discover Aleksy Kamski looking delicious and holding the hand of Dwayne, a cute guy Ery knew from his clubbing days. "I think I owe you thanks for several things," Aleksy said with a grin.

Dwayne clutched smugly at Aleksy even as he fluttered his eyelashes at Ery. He was the only person Ery had ever met who was a more eager flirt than Aleksy.

"So you guys hit it off?" Ery asked. He was pleased his matchmaking effort had been successful.

Aleksy's grin increased a notch or two. "Oh, we hit several things together."

Really, how could you not like a guy who spoke Double Entendre as his first language? "Glad to hear it. And I'm hearing a lot of happy noises over the catering tonight."

"Thank you for hiring us. It's our first catering job." He executed an elegant bow that didn't appear the least bit ironic. "It's an honor to be chosen for your event. You are a man of many talents, indeed."

Dwayne laughed, waggled his eyebrows, and whispered in Aleksy's ear. Ery didn't know what he said, but judging by the appraising look they both gave him, it might have had something to do with the couple of times Ery and Dwayne had briefly hooked up.

Ery actually blushed. "Hey! There's someone over there I need to catch real quick. If you'll excuse me?"

They did, but not without each kissing a cheek.

He wasn't lying about the someone. Actually, two someones. Rick and Kay, Dylan's brother and sister-in-law, had just walked in the door.

"Ery!" Kay gave him an enthusiastic hug.

"You guys made it."

"It's our very first date night since Fiona was born."

"Wow! Well, I'm honored to be your first, then." He was not going to ask why Dylan and Chris hadn't turned up yet. No way. "So there's food over there." He pointed.

"And wine?" Kay asked hopefully. "I just recently finished breastfeeding, and God, I want some alcohol."

Ignoring Rick's eye roll, Ery laughed. "Plenty of wine. And thanks for coming."

"Are you kidding? We wouldn't miss it. Dyl and Chris have been going on and on about how great your paintings are."

Nope. Not gonna ask. "Thanks." Ery shrugged. "I guess I'm pretty proud of these paintings."

Kay patted his arm. "I'm so psyched to know a soon-to-be-famous artist! Remind me to get your autograph later."

She and Rick began to walk away, but then Rick stopped in his tracks. "I forgot to tell you, Ery. Dyldo texted a little while ago. I guess he figured you'd be too preoccupied to be reading texts. Said he and Chris are running kinda late but they'll be here. It's probably taking him a while to force Chris into a suit again."

"Or maybe they got distracted and he's been getting Chris *out* of the suit," Ery countered.

Kay giggled, but Rick made a face. "Ew. Thanks, Ery. 'Cause every guy loves to get reminded of his baby brother's sex life." He waved and walked determinedly away, a laughing Kay at his side.

For his part, Ery sighed with relief. He hadn't spoken with Dylan and Chris since that night in the woods, and he'd been afraid they were royally pissed off at him. After he'd pushed Karl away, it would kill him if he lost his best friends too.

He was still feeling relieved when a woman cornered him with a lecture on why she thought paintings gave a more accurate representation of the world than did photography, and a skinny tattooed kid with an art-school haircut asked about some of his techniques. A middle-aged couple wanted to know whether he'd be willing to paint a portrait on commission, and although the price they named was fairly jaw-dropping, he politely declined.

Ery caught sight of his grandmother in the far corner, deep in discussion with a woman who was jotting things in a notebook. Jeez, was that a reporter? And if so, what adorable and embarrassing stories from Ery's childhood was Grandma sharing? He set himself on an interception course.

But before he got there, Julio grabbed his arm. "Ery, I'd like you to meet someone."

The someone turned out to be a silver-haired man with a much younger companion. Ery didn't catch their names during the introductions—he'd been introduced to too many people tonight already—but he realized he recognized them. They'd critiqued his work at the charity show in October.

Attempting a friendly smile, Ery shook hands. "Thanks for coming," he said, because that seemed like a safe and polite sort of comment.

The older man nodded briskly. "Julio tells me that despite the ridiculously high prices he's set on your work, they've all sold already."

Ery snapped his attention to Julio. "Seriously?"

Clearly seeing dancing dollar signs, Julio smiled. "Some time ago, in fact. Nothing is left except the one you asked me to withhold from sale." That was the one of Karl stepping out of the pond. It wasn't necessarily the best piece, but it was the first he'd painted after his muse decided she loved him again. And although he'd made the painting before he knew what Karl was, Ery had realized weeks ago that at some level he'd *always* known. The handsome man with the green eyes was ethereal.

"I knew the first time I saw your work that you were something special," the older man said. Ery didn't contradict him because what was the point? The man continued, "I'd like to make you an offer for that painting, Mr. Phillips."

"I appreciate your interest, but it's not for sale." Ery planned to keep that one for himself.

"I'll give you forty thousand dollars."

Ery almost fainted. Thanks to the check from his grandmother, he was far from hard up for cash. But it was one thing to be gifted a bunch of money from a loving relative and quite another to earn it, and from a single painting at that. But then Ery imagined Karl's picture hanging in this guy's no doubt pretentious mansion or ugly penthouse, and he just couldn't do it. Besides, that painting was *his*.

"I'm sorry," Ery said, "that one's not available. But I bet if you talk to Julio, he'd be willing to give you first dibs on whatever I have for sale next."

Julio nodded eagerly. "Of course! I'm sure we can work something out."

The man appeared slightly mollified, and Ery mumbled an excuse to escape. He was suddenly really drained. Conversation buzzed loudly in the gallery, bouncing off the hard floor and high ceilings, making his head ache. And the lights that had seemed so perfect a couple of hours ago were now too bright. Maybe he should see if there was any food left. Maybe he should duck into the storeroom for a short break.

As he started across the room to implement one of these plans, movement at the front door caught his attention. He smiled broadly when he saw who had entered—Dylan and Chris. Chris looked very sharp in dress pants and a silky maroon shirt, and Dylan had gone whole hog with a suit and tie. Ery changed course to meet them.

191

But before he got there, his friends moved slightly apart, and Ery saw that a shorter man stood behind them. He wore red boots, tight black slacks, and a silk shirt the color of a calm sea in the late afternoon. It brought out the vivid green of his eyes. His long white hair hung in a silky curtain. He caught Ery's eyes at once and gave a tentative smile.

Ery couldn't move. No, really. Due to the vision before him, he had been magically transformed into a statue. Pretty soon someone would offer Julio a couple thousand bucks for him, haul him away, and stick him in their living room.

As if the entire thing were carefully choreographed, the three men approached. Dylan and Chris moved to the side and Karl stood just out of arm's reach, directly facing Ery.

"You're wearing clothes!" Ery blurted.

Karl smiled shyly and looked down at himself. "Do you like them?"

"I…. Yes…." Ery looked frantically at Dylan and Chris for help.

Chris only shrugged, but Dylan cracked a tiny smile. "It took three days of online surfing for him to pick out this outfit and the better part of the evening to get him into it. He says he's only had experience in taking clothing *off* people."

"You look amazing," Ery said truthfully. But then, Karl also looked amazing naked. He'd look amazing in baggy shorts, a Hooters tee, and a backward baseball cap. "But… water…."

Grinning broadly, Karl dug in the messenger bag hanging from his shoulder. Ery hadn't even noticed the bag until then. With a small flourish, Karl brought out an enormous Nalgene bottle three-quarters full of water. "And Dylan says there's probably a bathroom here with a sink, if I need it."

"There is." Ery gestured vaguely.

"Good. Also, the river's only a short distance away. I can feel it now. That helps."

"I…." Ery could use some of that water himself right now. His mouth was the Sahara.

192

Karl's smile faded. "Are you angry that I came? Dylan and Chris said it wasn't a good idea, but I wanted to see everyone enjoying your paintings." He looked around briefly. "I think everyone loves them."

What Ery intended to say in response was *Yes, everyone loves them*. What came out instead, clear as a bell, was "I love you."

Oh, there was that smile again, brighter than ever. "I know," Karl said. "And I know you have to go away. But it makes me happy to see you again. Maybe you'll take just a little bit of me with you in your heart when you leave."

Not just a little bit. Ery's heart was full of Karl—*flooded* with him. One of Ery's science teachers once told him the human body was 60 percent water. But Ery's body was 90 percent Karl. Maybe more. And as words of advice from Dylan and Chris and Grandma echoed through Ery's brain, he knew something suddenly and with absolute certainty: if he went away from Karl, Ery would dry into dust and blow away.

Miraculously, Ery's legs turned human again. He flew to Karl and startled him with a tight, tight embrace. "I love you," Ery whispered into his ear. "I've never been in love with anyone, but I love you so much."

Karl regained his footing enough to hug Ery back. "I'll miss you," he said, also quietly.

"No. No, you won't."

"But… you know I love you, Ery."

Ery pulled away just a little. He was dimly aware that a lot of people were gathered around them, attracted either to the spectacle or to seeing Ery's model in the flesh. Ery didn't care. The entire goddamn state could be watching, or nobody at all, and it wouldn't make a lick of difference. Only Karl mattered at the moment.

"Karl, would you still want me if it meant you could never play a note of music again in your life?"

"Of course," Karl answered at once. "But—"

"And swimming. What if the most water you ever touched was in a shower?"

This response came just as fast. "I'd choose you. I'd always choose you, Ery. But I know you can't—"

"Bullshit. I *can*. I may not be as old as you, Karl, but I think I'm finally a grown-up. I've finally learned that pie-in-the-sky dreams, and fame, and impressing the world with my talent aren't what's most important."

Karl's eyes were enormous. Ery could drown in them. "What *is* most important, Ery?"

"Being happy with the people I love." He straightened his back and held his head high. "You won't miss me because I'm not leaving. I'm not going anywhere. We'll find a way to make it work. We're pretty creative guys. Will you keep me for good, Karl?"

In the entire history of the world, nobody had ever smiled that brightly. "For good and forever, my Ery."

They were hugging again, and crying, and the entire room thundered with applause, and Ery knew that if Karl weren't holding him, Ery would simply float away with joy. But even as the clapping faded, a new noise began—a drumming on the roof. Someone near the front windows exclaimed, "Look at that! I've never seen it rain like that."

Some of the people ran to the windows to see. But not Ery and Karl—they were still wrapped in each other's arms. Could stay that way forever.

Someone cleared his throat loudly enough to be heard over the din of the downpour. Reluctantly, Ery and Karl unwound. Ery kissed Karl's cheek and looked around them. Dylan and Chris were close by, Dylan's arm around Chris's shoulders and Chris holding Dylan's waist. They were smiling. So was... almost everyone else Ery knew. He smiled back and turned to Karl again. "Baby, there's some people I'd like you to meet. Let's start with Grandma."

CHAPTER 19

ERY HAULED himself onto the dock and lay on his stomach, breathing hard, the river water trickling off his back. His legs were still dangling over the edge, and he yelped and jerked away when someone tickled the soles of his feet. "Fiend!" he said, flopping onto his back. A light drizzle—really more like a mist—settled on his already wet face, making him blink.

"Not fiend. Stroemkarlen." Karl threw himself down beside Ery, squished up really close. "That was a good swim today, Ery. You're getting really fast."

"Not nearly as fast as you."

"Well, you're missing the webbing on your feet. And gills." He gave Ery's neck a sloppy kiss.

"Yeah. There's that pesky having-to-breathe thing." Honestly, he was amazed at how quickly and how well he'd learned to swim. Of course, he was motivated to please his teacher—the rewards were always way better than gold stars.

After a few minutes passed, Karl apparently decided Ery had rested enough. He began to stroke and grope, muttering little growls of frustration over the intervening neoprene. "I wish you didn't have to wear this," he complained.

"No webbed feet, no gills, no imperviousness to cold, baby." And the Columbia River in early April was mighty chilly. Ery thought he looked pretty snazzy in the black-and-cobalt wetsuit—which had set him back over four hundred bucks. But Karl said he looked like a colorful seal.

Karl hopped up and bent to offer Ery a hand. "Come on. Let's get it off you. The sun will be setting soon."

"Slave driver," Ery said with a grin. He allowed Karl to haul him to his feet. Then he followed him inside the house, enjoying the view as he walked. He never got tired of ogling Karl's ass.

They reached their bedroom downstairs and squeezed into the bathroom. Karl tugged the lanyard on Ery's back to open the zipper, then helped peel the wetsuit off him. The downstairs shower was only big enough for one at a time, so they had to take turns. Karl went first. Ery was hoping there might be some way to expand this bathroom sometime soon; he was going to consult with Chris and Dylan.

And that reminded him. "I talked to Chris this morning," he said, slightly distracted by the water streaming down Karl's pale skin. "He's gonna come here to the island on Tuesday to see about tearing down that wall. We thought maybe Dylan could come with, and afterward we can all head into Southeast and go to the coffeehouse together."

Karl stepped out of the shower and gestured Ery in, managing a good squeeze to Ery's ass as he passed. "That will be nice." He chewed his lip briefly. "I hope people enjoy the music."

"Pfft. They'll love it. You guys sound amazing together."

Several weeks earlier, Ery had consulted Drew about a replacement guitar for Karl. Drew had pointed him to a real beauty made from Sitka spruce and myrtle. It cost more than Ery's first used car, but in Karl's hands it sounded wonderful. Drew had also invited Karl and Ery over for a little jam session—with Ery and Travis as the very appreciative audience. The two musicians had played very well together, with Drew providing the shape and texture of some traditional blues and rock tunes and Karl embroidering those tunes with his own inventive notes. Never had Ery seen two men manage to be so eloquent without ever uttering a word. By the end of the evening, with Travis translating, Drew invited Karl to join him at his next performance at P-Town. Karl had been so enthused about the idea that he triggered a rainstorm.

If Karl and Ery began to hang out more with Travis and Drew, they might have to mention that Karl was a water spirit. *That* would be an interesting conversation.

Ery turned off the shower and reached for a towel, but Karl grabbed it for him and gave him a rubdown. "Don't get dressed, Ery."

"It's cold."

"We can turn on the patio heater."

As always, Ery gave in without much of a fight. They walked upstairs and through the room that was meant to be a master bedroom but was now his studio. Although the room boasted little décor except for Ery's paintings in progress, a large shelf prominently displayed three items: a cloisonné seagull, a nautilus shell, and a red-and-black stone. Ery waited inside in the relative warmth while Karl darted outside to get the heater going. The room worked really well as a studio, with large windows facing north across the river and easy access to the deck when the weather was nice enough to paint outdoors. The bathroom up here boasted an enormous soaking tub with whirlpool jets. Sometimes Ery teased Karl, saying that Karl loved the tub more than he loved Ery. He certainly spent a lot of time in there. When Chris tore down the bathroom wall, Karl would be able to bathe while Ery painted and they wouldn't have to shout through plasterboard and wood.

Karl slid open the glass door. "It's warm enough for you, Your Majesty." He grabbed Ery's hand and tugged him outside, where Ery scurried in an undignified fashion into the little island of heat. He collapsed into the chair closest to the heater. Karl sat down right next to him and grabbed Ery's hand.

The mist had intensified to a shower. One of the wettest springs on record, the weather guys claimed. Half of Portland headed to Mt. Hood on weekends for some spectacular late-season skiing. Dylan said the pond remained at high levels, but the house and barn were well out of danger and the ducks seemed to appreciate their expanded world. So no problems there.

"Do you want to go to the farm this weekend?" Ery asked.

"I'd rather go to the coast. That was fun! Maybe I'll find some whales to swim with again."

"You don't miss your home?" Ery asked for probably the hundredth time.

Karl gave him a patient look. "This is my home now."

It was a fairly pricy floating house on a private stretch of waterfront with easy access off the island when Ery needed to take Bea to work or out for errands. Sometimes Ery found himself wondering if Skuld the unicorn minded the move, but he was a little too embarrassed to ask.

"And it's a nice home," Ery agreed. "But there's a big difference between the Columbia and your quiet little pond. And you'd been there so long."

With a firm squeeze of Ery's hand and a headshake, Karl looked fondly annoyed. "I'm like the nautilus, Ery. I bring my home with me. And you're my shell. Wherever you are, I'm home." Then maybe he found the moment too sappy, because he laughed, let go of Ery's hand, and leaped over to scramble into Ery's lap. He snuggled up close. "See? We fit together perfectly."

Karl was heavier than he was, but Ery didn't mind the solid weight on his lap. He leaned his head against Karl's shoulder and looked out across the river. One of the nice things about their house was that they could be naked on the deck, and unless a boat passed by or some people in Vancouver had powerful binoculars, nobody would see. Karl liked to sit here every evening to watch the sunset, even though it was usually too cloudy for much of a show. Even then, it was nice to watch the darkness creep gradually over the water.

"Are you hungry?" Karl asked after a while.

"Not yet. Too comfy."

"Mmm." Karl traced the edge of Ery's bird tattoo and combed his chest hair with his fingertips. "Me too." After a long silence, he added, "Will you paint tomorrow?"

"Yep. Tomorrow's Friday." Karl had a somewhat vague sense of time. Calendars weren't generally important to water spirits, and Ery often had to remind him what day it was. Thanks to the forgiving and kind Myra, he had a great work schedule, with Mondays and Fridays off. Part-time hours earned him enough to pay the bills, allowing him to invest the rest of his grandmother's money and the proceeds of his paintings. Besides, it turned out he kind of liked the commercial stuff when he didn't have to do it all the time.

"Are you going to do another wolf painting?"

"Nope. I think I'm gonna paint Grandma. I never have, and she has such an amazing face."

"You look a lot like her," Karl said, chucking Ery's chin.

Ery took that as a compliment. "I want to paint her kneeling in the flower garden in front of her old house, like she used to before her knees gave up on her. She always loved to show me the new green sprouts and the buds. And the bugs and spiders and stuff. Life, she said."

"I'm sure your painting will be beautiful."

Smiling, Ery kissed Karl's shoulder. "My muse hasn't been quite so frantic lately. I guess she enjoys our relaxed waterside life." He didn't mind that the work was going a little more slowly, and Julio said that a gradual output would spark interest, increase demand, and raise prices. Heck, maybe Ery could rock the persona of the brilliant, sort of secluded, not too prolific artist. Like a J. D. Salinger with paint and brushes.

As Ery and Karl lazily conversed, Karl kept his hands busy—one of them combing the back of Ery's head, the other wandering over Ery's torso. Now he ventured farther south, and Karl rearranged himself so he could access Ery's hardening cock. "Oh, that's nice," Ery said. It would be even nicer, he realized, if he reciprocated. Karl's cock was within easy reach, and already the foreskin had retracted a little to reveal the delectable pink tip.

Sitting on the upper deck of his own house, watching lights twinkle on the river, slowly jacking the sweetest, most beautiful and exotic man in the world.... Ery would rather be here than watching people line up to admire his paintings in the frigging Musee d'Orsay. Being a grown-up was a pretty good gig.

He loved the sounds of the rain pattering on the roof and on the water, the distant roar of traffic over the Interstate Bridge, the slight creak of wooden moorings. And Karl breathing against him, his exhalations becoming slightly ragged as their hands sped up and their cocks became slick with precome. The smells were heady too: rainwater, river water, the salt and musk of a water spirit.

Without warning, Karl slipped from Ery's lap and fell to his knees. Before Ery could utter a word—either in protest or support—Karl engulfed Ery's cock in his moist mouth and swallowed him whole.

"Åh min gud," moaned Ery, who had picked up a few choice Scandinavian phrases for just such an occasion. He splayed his legs and threaded his fingers in Karl's hair. Definitely. Better. Than. D'Orsay.

Over the past months, Karl had learned to play Ery's body even better than he played his guitar. He knew where to stroke, where to smooth, where to tug. He knew exactly when to nip just a tiny bit with his sharp teeth and when to soothe the spot with his tongue. With barely a break in his rhythm, he could pull his mouth off Ery's dick, moisten his own finger with spit and a little precome, dive back down, and simultaneously insert the finger into Ery's eager body, crooking it just right.

Ery groaned loudly as he came.

Licking his lips and smiling smugly, Karl rose gracefully to his feet. He'd splattered his own chest when he came, and the white droplets glistened like pearls. He held out his hand to Ery. "Shall we move this indoors?"

An hour or so later, they lay tangled in bed. Ery felt as boneless as an octopus, if slightly stickier. "It's too early to go to sleep," he said, then yawned. The clubbing, up-all-night, breakfast-at-the-Hotcake-House version of Ery would laugh at him now. No, that wasn't true. That old Ery would be rabidly jealous of the new, adult Ery. "So there," he mumbled sleepily.

Karl lifted his head to blink at him. "What?"

"Nothing."

Karl let his head fall back onto Ery's chest. "I love you, but sometimes you're really odd."

That comment sent Ery into such a fit of severe giggles that he ended up with the hiccups. Karl had never before witnessed that particular malady and was initially alarmed. But when Ery explained that hiccups were harmless, Karl grew fascinated. He moved his head to Ery's chest and laughed every time a spasm jostled him.

"Will you get up and swim with me again in a while?" Karl asked after the contractions subsided.

"In the dark?"

"I'll make sure you don't collide with anything."

Ery thought for a moment. "Okay. Could be fun." He rubbed absently at Karl's head. "It's kind of weird how good of a swimmer I've become. And so fast. Actually, it's really weird." He'd gone from an uncoordinated dog paddle to a damn impressive front crawl within a couple weeks. He frowned at Karl's head. "Really, really weird."

"I spoke to your grandmother about this," said Karl. He rolled onto his back so they could look at each other as they spoke.

That was news to Ery. "When?"

"A few days ago. Remember, the day you forgot your phone when you went to work?"

"Oh. Yeah." That was the downside of the new living arrangements—he lived too far away from work to run back home to fetch anything he forgot.

"She called and we talked for a while. I like her, Ery. She said she'll trade me reading lessons if I teach her a little basic Swedish."

"That sounds like a good deal all around." Ery's grandmother had spent years as a high school English teacher—the kind who was really tough but received thankful letters from her students for years afterward. As smart and adaptable as Karl was, she'd have him tearing through Shakespeare in no time.

"I told her about your swimming. And all the water you've been drinking, and your long baths. And my dreams. And... have you noticed, Ery? I've been able to spend much longer out of water."

Ery had noticed. Karl hadn't had to get up in the middle of the night to shower since they moved in together. Ery had vaguely assumed that was due to the fact that their house sat directly over a whole lot of water. But now he realized they'd gone on quite a few excursions into town, including the evening with Drew and Travis, and Karl hadn't had to do more than sip at his Nalgene bottle or wash his hands occasionally. Jeez. Ery really needed to pay closer attention sometimes.

"What did Grandma say, baby?"

"Energy. She thinks maybe we've exchanged just a little bit of it." Karl frowned. "That doesn't upset you, does it?"

"God, no! It's actually kind of… kind of cool."

A bright smile spread over Karl's face. "I think so too. I wouldn't mind being a little more human. As long as I don't have to wear clothes all the time. Especially shoes."

"If you turn completely human, we'll move to a nudist colony."

Karl laughed, but then his face became more serious. "If we trade enough energy, maybe I'll start to age."

"Jeez, Karl, I hadn't thought of that. Fuck. We can—"

"It's *good*, Ery. I hope to grow old with you. And maybe you'll age a little more slowly."

Ery thought about that for a minute. "That's a pretty appealing scenario."

With a jubilant laugh, Karl rolled on top of Ery, caging his body with his arms and legs, surrounding them both with his smooth curtain of hair. It was wonderful.

"I have a theory too," Karl said, pitching his voice to a low purr.

"Oh?"

"I think I know the best way to exchange energy with you." And then he bent his elbows, dropped his head, and began to kiss his way down Ery's torso.

So often now, Ery felt as if his heart was a bird, beating its wings swiftly and strong, lifting him high. Or maybe a silvery fish, darting happily through dappled waters. Soaring or floating—in the end, they came to the same thing. They both brought him joy. And with Karl at his side, Ery would always be in his element.

KIM FIELDING is very pleased every time someone calls her eclectic. She has migrated back and forth across the western two-thirds of the United States and currently lives in California, where she long ago ran out of bookshelf space. She's a university professor who dreams of being able to travel and write full time. She also dreams of having two perfectly behaved children, a husband who isn't obsessed with football, and a house that cleans itself. Some dreams are more easily obtained than others.

Kim can be found on her blogs:
http://kfieldingwrites.com/
http://www.goodreads.com/author/show/4105707.Kim_Fielding/blog

and on Facebook:
https://www.facebook.com/KFieldingWrites.

Her e-mail is kim@kfieldingwrites.com, and she can be found on Twitter at @KFieldingWrites.

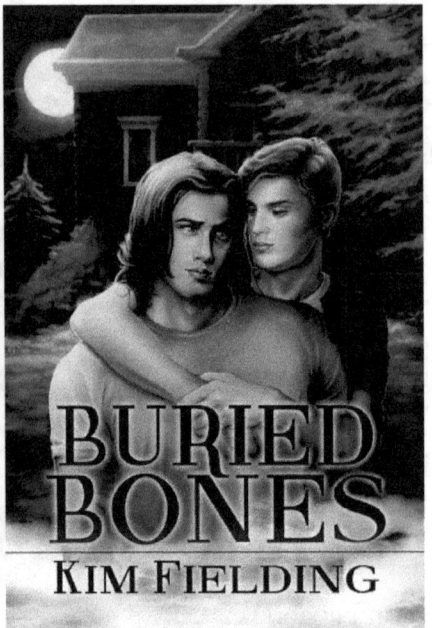

http://www.dreamspinnerpress.com

NIGHTSHIFT
Kim Fielding

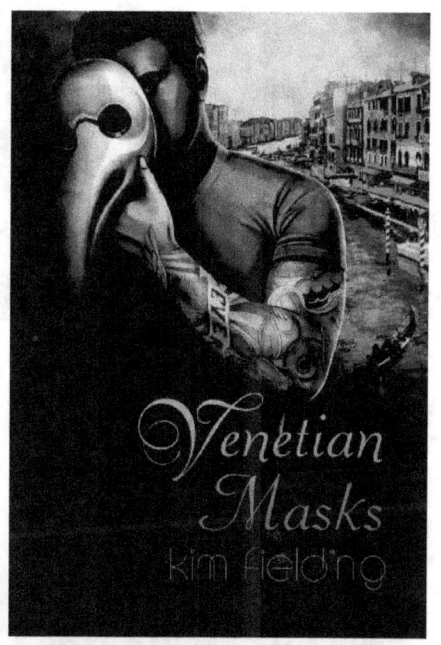

Venetian Masks
kim fielding

SPEECHLESS

KIM FIELDING

MOTEL.

POOL.

KIM FIELDING

http://www.dreamspinnerpress.com

KIM FIELDING

Pilgrimage

http://www.dreamspinnerpress.com

HOUSEKEEPING
Kim Fielding

KIM FIELDING

The
Tin
Box

THE PILLAR

KIM FIELDING

BRUTE
Kim Fielding

http://www.dreamspinnerpress.com

FOR **MORE** OF THE **BEST GAY ROMANCE**

Dreamspinner Press

DREAMSPINNERPRESS.COM